WHITE LION
CHRONICLES
RISE OF THE
DIBOR

To. Noah & Joshua!
May you grow to be
mighty Dibor for
the Most High!

BOOK
ONE

2011 :)

Other books by...

CHRISTOPHER HOPPER

The White Lion Chronicles (series)

The Lion Vrie – Book II

Athera's Dawn – Book III

CHRISTOPHER HOPPER
&
WAYNE THOMAS BATSON

The Berinfell Prophecies (series)

Curse of the Spider King – Book I

Venom and Song – Book II

THE
WHITE LION
CHRONICLES

RISE OF THE
DIBOR

CHRISTOPHER
HOPPER

SPEAR
HEAD

NEW YORK · BALTIMORE · SEATTLE

Cover design and layout by Christopher & Allan Miller for The Miller Brothers, and Christopher Hopper; The White Lion Chronicles logo by Jason J. Clement for jasonjclement.com
Interior layout and map illustration by Christopher Hopper; interior grunge background by Jason J. Clement for jasonjclement.com
Wax seal design by Hillary Hopper for hillaryhopper.com
Edited by Sue Kenney for kenneyediting.wordpress.com
Author Photos by Jennifer Hopper for jenniferhopperphoto.com

Published by christopherhopper.com in alliance with Spearhead Books
Visit spearheadbooks.com

Printed in the United States of America

First Edition: 2006
Second Edition: 2011

ISBN: 1463519664
ISBN-13: 978-1463519667

To my wife, Jennifer Lee.
And to my daughter, Evangeline Mae.
The beauties that I live to protect.

"For God was pleased to have all His fullness dwell in Him, and through Him to reconcile to Himself all things, whether things on earth or things in heaven, by making peace through His blood, shed on the cross."

~Colossians 1:19-20

THE WHITE LION CHRONICLES
BOOK I
RISE OF THE DIBOR

Dionian Essentials

Part One

Part Two

Part Three

Afterword

DIONIAN ESSENTIALS

LANGUAGE GUIDE

All written text of the following account has been scripted in English but was derived solely from the common Dionian tongue and usage of the people of Dionia. Names have been kept as original as possible except where deemed necessary by the author to make them more conducive and suitable for the reader.

Certain words and phrases have been left in the original tongue, scripted using the Latin alphabet for English readers and roughly translated accordingly, either because a direct translation into English was impossible due to the expansive vocabulary utilized by the native people and the subsequent inadequacy and lack of words existing in the English vocabulary, including expressions and words used in the common vernacular; or because an older dialect, such as First Dionian was used, making literal translation near impossible, as the only translation can be derived and implied from felt and/or experienced emotions.

The translation of all Dionian linguistics is based upon the spoken word, rather than the written word (though still used in documentation), making the sound, diction, emphasis and oral and guttural technique used to pronounce each word and phrase absolutely imperative in proper communication. For this reason, should this work be translated into any other language, all people and place names unknown in the written English and resulting translation into the desired language, as well as translation of unknown singular and plural nouns and phrasing, should retain the auditory qualities as properly pronounced in English using the pronunciation guide in parentheses directly following each footnote. If a consonant or vowel does not exist in the translated language, an author's note must appear to properly define and explain the desired sound.

Written:	Pronounced:	Meaning:
roua	*R'ROO-uh*	"ways"

NOTE: Here the "R'R" is pronounced as a rolled "r".

afe	*AYF-[eh]*	"one" or "one who"

NOTE: In this case, the sound of the "e" at the end of the word does exist commonly in English and must be spoken with a quiet, fleeting exhaled breath. This is also for all people and place names ending in "e." Not a true syllable.

Najrion	*NAH-sherEE-auhn*	character name

NOTE: The letter "j" followed by "r" in a name is pronounced with a soft "j" sound.

NAME PRONUNCIATION GUIDE

Here are a few common titles and names in The White Lion Chronicles that — with practice — will help the authenticity of your journey in Dionia.

Name:	Pronounced:	Name:	Pronounced:
Athera	*uh-THEER-uh*	Morgui	*MORE-guy*
Dionia	*dee-OH-nee-yah*	Dairne-Reih	*DAYern-[eh]-RYE*
Luik	*LOO-ick*	Ciana	*see-EN-uh*
Hadrian	*HAY-dree-in*	Rourke	*ROORck*
Li-Saide	*lee-SAYED-[eh]*	Naffe	*NAYHFF-[eh]*
Jrio	*sherEEoh*	Ligeon	*LIH-jee-on*

GLOSSARY GUIDE

The main spoken language of Dionia is appropriately named *Dionian,* or hereafter mentioned as *Modern Dionian. Modern Dionian* denotes the language utilized from the time period *after* the First Battle to the present. A reader will notice that in many definitions there is often one of two references made: *"First Dionian"* or *"an ancient Dionian word"* (hereafter mentioned as *Ancient Dionian*). *First Dionian,* or *The Old Tongue,* is traceable to the beginning of Creation, *before* the First Battle, and these words are most closely related to *Modern Dionian.* The syntax, emphasis, and pronunciation have remained relatively the same given its vast history, or with only minor discrepancies (enough to link it with a *First Dionian* reference). *Ancient Dionian,* however, is unique in its pronunciation *and* definition, as the root of each word is not necessarily tied to a modern equivalent or even *First Dionian* reference, meaning the origin of the word is simply unknown. Rather, such words have been adopted into *Modern Dionian,* though their history is in question.

Examples:

Boralee (*bohr-uh-LEE*): Ancient Dionian: *disciple;* unknown.

Frrene (*FREYN-[eh]*): Modern Dionian: *disciple;* First Dionian root.

GLOSSARY

Afe di empaxe li roua lonia ene froue napthixe bruna *(AYF-[eh] dee ehm-PACKS lee R'ROO-uh LON-ee-uh een froo nahp-THEECKS br'roona) First Dionian: literally translated, "One who holds the ways old and every spoken word," meant to mean, "A keeper of the old ways and all words spoken."*

Biea-Varos *(BEE-uh-var-OHCE): verb; forward command form of the ancient Dionian word most closely related to the modern word 'courage'; to be of great fortitude, resilience and persuasion; devoid of fear.*

Boralee *(bohr-uh-LEE): noun; ancient Dionian name meaning disciple, exact origin not known.*

Courbouilli *(coor-BOO-ih-lee): noun; armor made of leather hardened through boiling in oil; noted for its light weight while still maintaining great strength and resilience to blows.*

C'symia *(sye-MEE-uh): First Dionian: intimate and most respectful form of "thank you."*

Dairne-Reih *(DAYern-[eh]-RYE): noun; closest literal translation is "fallen kings" or "fallen angels"; the army war host of Morgui comprised of the fallen angels of Athera or heaven.*

Dairneag *(DAYern-ee-AHG): noun; a singular demon of the fallen angelic host; a member of the Dairne-Reih.*

Dibor *(DYE-bohr): noun; First Dionian: literally meaning "guardians", "centurions", or "a sacred protectorate"; singular Dibor or a Dibor meaning one of the members of the Dibor or brotherhood; also to address as a brother.*

Difouna *(dee-FOO-nuh): verb; slang of the command form of "difounale," Dionian word most closely related to the verb "to go."*

Dyra *(DIEruh): noun; a rare and little-known composite material made from forged elements; created by the Tribes of Ot in Grandath.*

Gita *(GIH-tuh): noun; plural, Gitas; 1. an ancient Dionian word meaning "basket"; 2. one round of Rokla played to five points.*

Gvindollion *(GIH-ven-DOLLY-on): noun; an ancient Dionian word literally translated, "The Circle of Seven"; council gathering of Dionia's Seven Kings.*

Iyne Dain *(EYEn-[eh] DANE): noun; literally meaning "Heart Quest."*

Jhestafe-Na *(jehs-TAIF-eh-nuh) First Dionian: literally translated "Gathering Day."*

Kafe *(KAY-feh): noun; 1. an ancient Dionian word meaning "loss"; 2. the red ball in Rokla.*

KiJinNard *(KYEY-shjih-nard): noun; closest literal translation is "dead hound"; refers to the dogs that have been "taken" and joined with the ranks of the Dairne-Reih.*

Lion Vrie *(l'eye-uhn - VR'EYE): First Dionian: noun; most closely related to the word used for a knight or a warrior of nobility.*

Lytthlaroua *(L'EYEth-lah-ROO-uh): noun; Ancient Dionian; literally translated "ways of the heavenly," this name for the angelic host, or angels of Athera; singular: lythla (L'EYEth-lah); plural: lythlae (L'EYEth-lay).*

Mosfar *(MAWS-fahr): First Dionian: name given to the tribe of Dwarves at the beginning of creation; meaning "Creation Keeper" or "protector"; singular a Mosfar meaning one of the members of The Mosfar or brotherhood.*

Narin Haus *(NAR-in HO): noun; literally meaning "Narin High," or the upper half of Narin overlooking the Bay of Cidell; Narin Bas, or "Narin Low" refers to the lower, seaside, stilted portion of the city.*

Peshe *(PESH-[eh]): noun; a deed or act, or by inaction or abdication of responsibility, an allowance, of engaging in behavior or receiving the nature of a spirit directly opposed to the will of The Most High, His Righteousness, Truth and Light; anything that separates a creature from the presence of His Spirit; a grievous mistake or error with detrimental consequences spiritually and naturally. 2. verb; to engage in the action of said deed, act, mistake, or error. Most closely related to the Middle English word "sin" or the verb, "to sin."*

Riddosseldore *(rih-DOSS-elle-DOHR-eh): noun; one of the largest Dionian mammals, noted for the enormous horn on the forehead and long trunk above the mouth; most closely associated with an elephant and a rhinoceros.*

Rokla *(ROCK-lah): noun; 1. an ancient Dionian word meaning "two stones"; 2. one of the main sporting events played by the people of Dionia.*

Sacre Fina *(SAH-cray FEE-nuh): noun; Ancient Dionian for Last Rights or Sacred Rights, the final wishes of a Dionian King before being called to the Great Throne Room.*

Sif Gate *(SIPH - gate): noun; a portal for the translation of Dairne-Reih from one realm or location to another.*

Stri *(STR-EE): noun; plural, Stri; 1. an ancient Dionian word meaning "gain"; 2. the blue ball in Rokla; 3. term used to indicate a point.*

Syler *(SIGH-ler): noun; plural, sylers; name of a seven-stringed instrument played with the fingers and hands, upon which both beaten rhythm and melody can be issued at the same time.*

Varos *(var-OHCE): noun; an ancient Dionian word most closely related to the modern word 'courage'; to be of great fortitude, resilience, and persuasion; devoid of fear.*

Vinfae *(vinn-FAY): noun; an ancient Dionian term used to designate the sword forged and used exclusively for the Dibor. Characteristics include its notable power when used in conjunction with the Tongues of the Dibor as well as its ability to differentiate between the Dairne-Reih and that of fallen man (or the taken).*

Xidaq *(KSYE-dack): verb; First Dionian; tense of the command form literally meaning to "attack showing [with] mercy."*

CHARACTER LIBRARY

Luik (meaning: *renowned warrior who gives light*): Dibor; Son of Lair, Prince of Bensotha; renowned for his mighty exploits among the Dibor; blond hair, grey-blue eyes.

Anorra (meaning: *one's good name and honor*): Daughter of Thorn, Princess of Ligeon. Skilled with the bow and on horseback, extremely cunning, agile, and a quick wit; long blonde hair, blue eyes.

Fane (meaning: *good-natured*): Mosfar; Son of Fadner, son of Dafe, son of Ad. Trained by Li-Saide in the ways of the Mosfar; red hair, freckled face, and of a thin stature.

Hadrian (meaning: *dark*): Son of Jadak, son of Jadain; went missing from his home in Bensotha; athletic with dark hair and deep, dark eyes.

Gorn (meaning: *faithful mountain*): Son of Jyne; origin unknown. Famed warrior of Dionia, teacher of the Dibor; deep black skin and piercing blue eyes, strong and muscular.

Li-Saide (meaning: *favored*): Mosfar; A dwarf of the Tribe of Li, aged counselor to the lineage of High Kings of Dionia, and Chief of the Tribes of Ot. Known for his large, baggy, multi-colored patchwork hat and quizzical bearded face.

Gyinan (meaning: *white hawk*): Highest centurion of Thorn's House and Anorra's teacher; slender, bald, with pointy features; narrow, pensive eyes; long jaw and tiny lips reminiscent of a bird.

Benigan (meaning: *kind, cheerful*): Dibor; Oldest son of King Purgos, Lord of Tontha; smaller than his twin brothers, though still a massive man; greater in speed and agility.

Boran (meaning: *victory*): Dibor; First of twin sons born to King Purgos, Lord of Tontha; black hair, like ebony; older twin of Brax, renowned for his immense strength, size, and climbing ability.

Brax (meaning: *exalted*): Dibor; Second of twin sons born to King Purgos, Lord of Tontha; dirty-blond hair; younger twin of Boran, renowned for his immense strength, size, and climbing ability.

Thad (meaning: *of good heart*): Dibor; Oldest son of King Thorn, Prince of Ligeon; looks the most like Anorra, long blonde hair, same blue eyes.

Thero (meaning: *son of thunder*): Dibor; Second son of Thorn, Prince of Ligeon; large-built, red hair, wide face, resembling his father.

Anondo (meaning: *ready and eager for battle*): Dibor; Third son of Thorn, Prince of Ligeon; strongly built; fair hair and skin; toughest of all his brothers.

Jrio (meaning: *cunning*): Dibor; Oldest son of King Naronel, Lord of Trennesol; known for his keen ability for sailing and mastering all vessels powered by wind; dark short-cut hair, narrow eyes and dark face; reminiscent of a ferret.

Najrion (meaning: *son of man*): Dibor; Second son of King Naronel, Lord of Trennesol; slender, tall, and dark.

Naron (meaning: *honor*): Dibor; Third son of King Naronel, Lord of Trennesol; similar in looks to Najrion.

Rab (meaning: *bright fame*): Dibor; Youngest son of King Naronel, Lord of Trennesol; of a dark complexion and smaller frame; known for his constantly saving, and being saved by, Luik.

Cage (meaning: *valiant spear*): Dibor; Oldest son of King Daunt, Lord of Jerovah; known for his ability on horseback; long dark hair.

Daquin (meaning: *soldier of attainment*): Dibor; Second son of King Daunt, Lord of Jerovah; known for his ability on horseback; a large brute.

Quoin (meaning: *swift*): Dibor; Youngest son of King Daunt, Lord of Jerovah; known for his ability on horseback; smallest of the three.

Kinfen (meaning: *heroic*): Dibor; Oldest son of King Nenrick, Lord of The Somahguard Islands; largest of his brothers; adept at all maritime skills; dark skin like all those of the Island people.

Naffe (meaning: *bright*): Dibor; Second son of King Nenrick, Lord of The Somahguard Islands; dark complexion, broad face.

Fallon (meaning: *sea wolf*): Dibor; Third son of King Nenrick, Lord of The Somahguard Islands; dark complexion.

Fyfler (meaning: *reigning elder*): Dibor; Youngest son of King Nenrick, Lord of The Somahguard Islands; dark complexion and closely cut hair; wise and a good leader.

Fedowah (meaning: *faithful, he who overcomes*): War horse of Tadellis found roaming Grandath; now belonging to Luik; a large dapple-gray with a pronounced head, muscular shoulders, and a speckled rear.

Cellese (meaning: *pleasant, in time of need*): Luik's dolphin at Kirstell.

Morgui (meaning: *beauty discarded*): A fallen lythla cast from the ranks of Athera; the enemy of Dionia and of the Most High.

Valdenil (meaning: *first among the fallen*): Son of the Dead; taken before the First Battle, made a prince under Morgui as he was the son of King Rill, son of King Ad; his first name was Velon; slain by Gorn in Bensotha during the Battle of Adriel.

Fonish (meaning: *noble and ready*): Adriel palace guard.

Pelidril (meaning: *origin, source of riches, wealth*): Team captain of Beneetha's Rokla team.

Analysia (meaning: *of high nobility, favor and grace*): Oldest daughter of Thorn, Anorra's older sister; noted for her refined manner much becoming of a queen; long blonde hair.

Lana (meaning: *fair and calm in still waters*): Youngest daughter of Thorn, Anorra's younger sister; curly blonde hair, sweet and jubilant personality; round face, always smiled, even when she cried.

Lair (meaning: *refuge*): King and Lord of Bensotha; father of Luik.

Pia (meaning: *faithful and duty-bound*): Lair's wife, Queen of Bensotha, mother of Luik; darker hair but a fair complexion.

Rourke (meaning: *storm of famous power*): Son of Lair, Luik's younger brother by fourteen summers; a squirrelly tuft of light brown hair, brown eyes, and a wide smile.

Ragnar (meaning: *strong counselor*): High King of Dionia, Lord of Casterness; dirty blond hair, wide cheekbones, deep-set green eyes beneath a firm brow.

Meera (meaning: *light*): Queen of Casterness, wife of Ragnar, mother of Ciana; fair skin, long blonde hair, delicate face.

Ciana (meaning: *The Most High has been gracious; has shown favor*): Daughter of Ragnar, Princess of Casterness. Born in Luik's fourteenth summer. Blonde hair, grey-blue eyes.

Thorn (meaning: *mighty hunter*): King of Ligeon, Lord of the Northerners; wavy reddish-blonde hair and a beard to match; neck was the size of an ox's and strong blue eyes set wide in his large face.

Purgos (meaning: *of great value*): King of Tontha, Lord of the Mountain People; hulking brute of a man; dark hair and eyes, broad shoulders, muscular; one of the longest-living elders of Dionia; fought in the First Battle.

Naronel (meaning: *mountain of the sea*): King of Trennesol, Lord of the North Sea; dark bearded chin, strong hands, black hair; an expert sailor and maritime explorer.

Daunt (meaning: *unwavering judge*): King of Jerovah, affectionately called "The Horse King"; master equestrian; black hair; tightly-knit body, long, sinewy, and strong.

Nenrick (meaning: *powerful ruler*): King of the Islands of Somahguard, Lord of the Islanders; a master of maritime navigation; dark skin, dark eyes.

CHARACTER QUICK REFERENCE GUIDE

The Eighteen Dibor

King Lair, Lord of Bensotha
Luik

King Thorn, Lord of Ligeon
Thad
Thero
Anondo
(Anorra)

King Purgos, Lord of Tontha
Benigan
Boran
Brax

King Naronel, Lord of Trennesol
Jrio
Najrion
Naron
Rab

King Daunt, Lord of Jerovah
Cage
Daquin
Quoin

King Nenrick, Lord of Somahguard
Kinfen
Naffe
Fallon
Fyfler

"Every man must come to his own end;
every man must die before he truly lives."

~Fane of the Mosfar

PART ONE

Chapter One

THE STRANGER

The forest air was unusually still. The dense canopy of leaves above allowed only a dim light to pass through, keeping the earthen floor mostly in shadow and the thick tree trunks looking like men wrapped in brown cloaks. The air was damp and cool, layered with moss and bark. A well-beaten path wandered through patches of ferns and grass like an aged man with time to spare.

The distant sound of horse hooves weaving their way through the woods brought a mild change to the air. It echoed aimlessly off the trees and betrayed no sense of direction. But to one side a glint of white whispered by and soon came into view. The apparition turned into a large dapple-gray horse with a pronounced head, muscular shoulders, and a speckled rear. He carried a powerful rider in a red tunic with a purple cloak slung around his shoulders. The man's face was well cut and handsome. Shoulder length dark hair adorned his dark eyes and full chin. The hand-and-a-half sword strapped on his thigh and the spear in his left hand looked natural and accustomed to his presence. A gold torc terminating in lions' heads wrapped his neck, and a thick band of gold his upper arm. His feet were bare and he rode without saddle, bridle, or reins.

Without command the horse stopped and perked his ears. The rider, aware of the strange hesitation, began searching the glades beyond with narrowed eyes. The smile that adorned his face just moments before had vanished. A bird flew between trees in the distance, but the stallion's countenance remained unchanged.

"What is it, Fedowah?" the rider inquired of the horse, but Fedowah did not move. The man's bare feet nudged Fedowah's sides gently causing him to instinctively respond in a few forward steps. But the horse remained fixed on something up ahead and came to rest once more.

"Come on, my timid one, let's press on." The rider tried once more to coax his stallion forward but this time the horse didn't budge. The rider finally swung down from Fedowah's back and landed softly on the ground, spear still in hand. He took a few steps out in front of Fedowah, glancing this way and that, looking for the unseen disturbance. His hand tightened on his spear shaft as he leveled it with his hip.

"Hey'a!" the rider said forcefully. "Come out quickly."

There was silence.

He took another pace forward. His horse did just the opposite and retreated a few steps. The rider turned back to his steed.

"Be brave with me, Fedowah. There is nothing to fear here." Fedowah pushed away the chill and shook his head in defiance of his emotions, giving a mild snort. He pressed his head low and walked slowly up to his master with a strengthened resolve. The handsome warrior patted him reassuringly on the side of his neck.

A small stick snapped from behind.

Fedowah spun on his heels, as did the warrior, both regarding a new stranger behind them. An eerie mood befell them both.

"What say you, stranger?" The warrior's voice was commanding and strong, despite him obviously being startled. Fedowah regained his own composure and stiffened with his master's demand. "Is this some folly that you would think to come up behind a man and his horse unaware? If this was not your intent, you will of course be forgiven."

The stranger stood covered in a dark cloak, face consumed by shadow. He gently opened his hands and the two ends of a broken stick fell to the ground. Fedowah watched them fall. The figure did not reply. It was clear now his action was purposeful.

"Speak! I pray thee, or else be removed from our way." There was silence. The warrior was becoming agitated but remained restrained. "Who are you, stranger? Please reveal yourself." The stranger said nothing. The warrior's eyes flared. His patience was quickly waning, something not common to his character. "I ask you again, who are you, good sir? Or, perhaps you are not good, as I would assume?" The stranger stood still. The warrior was tired of this insolence and moved a step toward the cloaked figure. But the stranger mirrored his move exactly, only backwards. The warrior's face squinted in wonder. This time he moved toward the stranger again but more quickly, hoping to apprehend the man. But again the stranger moved away in equal speed as if he knew ahead of time. The warrior could feel anger rising up quickly in his blood and tried to control it.

"Do you wish me to use my spear, dark stranger?" Without waiting for a response, the warrior swung the blunt end toward the bulk of the stranger's cloak, more to stir a reaction than to inflict injury. But the figure simply leaned out and away from the dangerous arc of the shaft. The warrior stood astonished. Now his heart was racing. He swung again, and then came straight down, but the stranger avoided both and simply stepped out of the way.

"Stranger, who are you and why do you act this way?" The warrior now felt ashamed of his behavior, but could sense his emotions running out of control. "Speak, or I will strike!" He pulled back his spear and aimed along its shaft, this time the point of his weapon poised to strike. His body had been clearly trained for such a stance of power, and there was no misunderstanding his intent or the desired effect.

"This is your last warning! Be removed from our way!" Small beads of perspiration were beginning to form on his face. Fear and anger were lacing tightly around his chest. He had been trained to resist these, as his being was never meant or designed to carry such things. But he had to act, to respond with strength to this insubordination. He did not like this stranger. He wanted him removed. He wanted him *dead*. The stranger finally spoke; slowly.

"I am not going your way, but it seems now that perhaps you are going *mine, Tadellis*," came a soft, sickening yet sweet voice. Fedowah grimaced.

The warrior froze, "*How*—how do you know my name, stranger?" He could feel his thoughts growing wild and his fortitude weakening. He unwittingly lowered his spear ever so slightly.

There came a subtle laugh from beneath the stranger's thick hood. "Don't you recognize me, Tadellis? Or has it been so long? Your weakness betrays you, Son of Trinade. I thought you were stronger."

The warrior lowered his weapon further but still held tight. "Do I know you? Remove your hood and let us end this mystery."

"So you finally *want* to know me?" The stranger started toward the warrior. "You *finally* want to look into my eyes?"

"Aye!" yelled the warrior, eyes ablaze and fury consuming him.

"So be it," said the hooded figure.

And with that the stranger strode within arm's reach of the warrior and removed his hood.

Chapter Two

PARADISE

Beyond the creativity of any artist, out of reach in its measure of beauty, and unsearchable in its scope of magnitude, nothing about Bensotha Valley was typical of the rest of the continent. Maybe this was the reason why the kings of the world had made this region their home for generations. Marvelous rolling hills covered in fern groves sloped down into wide stretches of grassy fields. There, any number of streams flowed like honey around boulders shaded above with massive oak trees that reached from the shore. Waterfalls could be found as often as there were glades soaked in mist and brilliant flowers of every color attempting to bloom before the majestic sunrise. Creation was at its height and the Sons of Man marveled at their Creator's depth and power. After all, it was created just for them. And His power inhabited every piece of His creation; each tree, rock, stream, animal, and even the very blades of grass resonated and sang for Him. From the very least to the greatest, the Great Creator's fingerprints touched all of life. It was paradise.

But what made this place even more beautiful was the unspeakable and marvelous fact that *His* presence was there, *the Most High*. For what is eternity without someone to share it with, and what is a lifetime without love to measure it by? As sure as the wind moved across the fields and brushed through the hair on the head; as much as the heat of the sun nestled into the skin and warmed the blood; as much as a kiss could coax a smile from any child; so too was the reality that all the people of Dionia were not alone.

Someone else was there among them, walking through the meadows and strolling along the streams, and they knew Him well. This invisible presence was not something they needed to be convinced of or persuaded to acknowledge. On the contrary, the company of their Creator was more visible than eyes could betray, more real than ears could hearken to, and more tangible than fingers could touch. They could sense the all-pervading power of the Mighty Father in every breath, every heartbeat, and every stride they took. They had not known a day without Him, and the mere thought of His absence had never even been a fleeting whisper in their minds.

His loving Spirit wooed them gently through life and its wonders, drawing them from one place to another, revealing a new element of His personality and creativity with the passing of every dawn and dusk. Just when they thought they might have seen it all, He showed them something all together new that dazzled and delighted them. The depth of His heart was boundless, and the breadth of His hands, unspeakable.

Being there in paradise for one minute would capture anyone forever. The desire to leave would dissipate as if it had never been known. Neither family, lands, nor possessions were as wonderful as He. Having any one of these, any man, woman, or child would give them all up in a heartbeat to be where the Father was if asked. Eternity is not so much about the place, but with whom you spend it. And while His hands designed all the relationships in the world, He knew that none could be as marvelous and all-encompassing as the ones with Him. He was a Jealous Creator. Having made what was in His heart, He desired only to share it, to have fellowship with those He created. Nothing in Creation's spirit longed for anything else more than it did for Him, not because He had forced them to, but because He was just so good.

Every person that walked Dionia's surface or sailed her waters knew the Master's voice. Communion with His Spirit was a continuous, unceasing event, a consciousness without termination. There was never a moment that passed without conversation being had, never a breath that was not savored for the response that it was sure to invoke. The Great

Spirit was everywhere at all times. And the thing that stood out most to everyone that touched the Most High's presence? His boundless love, void of condemnation and overwhelming in magnitude. Every being that moved under His gaze was smitten from the start, unable to comprehend how with every new day, the Most High's love grew more vast. It permeated the air such that waves of His compassion and all consuming desire would wash over and inundate a person with such delight that they could do nothing but sit and savor the unmerited favor of His heart.

And so it was, that countless ages passed there in paradise, each day a beautiful song ushered in and out by melodies of expectation and awe. No night was ever spent alone, but surrounded and wrapped in the embrace of a perfect, loving Father whose single ambition was for creation's good.

Today was one of Luik's favorite days. Though he had not lived long enough to make habits of much of anything, Jhestafe-Na[1] was what he looked forward to most each summer. Tribes from all over Bensotha would gather for seven days of festivities of the grandest sort. Even a few tribes from the other nearby realms of Ligeon and Tontha would journey down to participate. It was a celebration of life owing all to the Creator, and they knew no shame in their expressions of gratitude.

Tribes and families set up camps all along the great valley, laying out the spreads of their harvests in baskets and on blankets for all to take of freely. Fruits of every kind were heaped high, cascading clumsily from their respective places. All sorts of apples great and small, lemming bananas, and bushels of burgundy pods from the basher plants overflowed in cascades of color. Giant succulent peaches sat lumped tall in piles, ready to burst with their tangy juice. Mountains of mouth-watering juniper berries glowed yellow in the sun, as did great mounds of maize stripped of their husks. Baskets of nuts harvested from the outer glens of Grandath stood precariously stacked; until inevitably some group of children would run past and knock them over. Walnuts and dagnuts waited to be cracked, while the white pecans were scooped up by the handful. Children quickly picked up long stalks of cane, each sucking on them all day long and taking them wherever they went. Coconuts were cracked by the dozens, the milk drunk and the meat carved out. Succulent pineapples were chopped into bite-size pieces while others were ground into juice and poured into

---

[1] **Jhestafe-Na** (*jehs-TAIF-eh-nuh*) *First Dionian: literally translated "Gathering Day."*

goblets. Grapes were pressed into juice and aged wine was drawn from the storehouses. Barrels of mead flowed into mugs from dawn until dusk, and no person went hungry, no thirst went unquenched.

Luik sat in the shade of an alder tree and held an apple twice the size of his head in his hands, just staring at it, saliva building up in his mouth. He had been playing hard all morning, and his mother finally forced him to come have a bite to eat, in the manner only mothers can. But any reluctance he had at leaving his friends for a time quickly vanished when he drank some fresh orange juice she had prepared for him. She knew what he liked, and Luik liked that she knew. His father had been out all morning, surely mingling with the tribes and catching up with old friends.

"Hash Ta na been bash yeh?" Luik asked with a mouth full of apple.

"Peace, child," Pia said. "Take care of that bite before you speak." Her soft voice and pleasant appearance had a way of getting Luik to do anything, despite his strong will. He swallowed his apple and tried again.

"Has Ta na been back yet?"

"I have not seen him all morning. He is probably with King Thorn, I would think."

"King Thorn has come?" Luik asked with much excitement.

"Aye, he arrived last night."

"Last night? By himself?"

"No, my son," she smiled. "His daughters have come, too."

King Thorn, lord of Ligeon, was one of the most jovial kings Dionia had ever seen. As brute as an ox and powerful as a bear, he was also notoriously softhearted, won over with a glance of his three daughters or his beautiful bride, turning from roaring lion to songbird in an instant. Luik had always been fond of the princesses, but usually found them to be a distraction from more important things like adventures and wrestling. But something was changing in him, ever so subtly. He was right at the age where girls were turning from endured necessities to obvious points of interest, paling all others. Luik looked at his mother.

"Finish your apple first."

Suddenly the size of his apple was not as appealing as it was moments before.

"Can I put—"

"Finish."

"Aye, Na na." Luik realized his departure would have to wait. But it was only the first day of Jhestafe-Na. There would be much time to play and go see his friends later. Plus, he admitted he was feeling hungry, despite a strange new longing in his soul. He took another bite and sat back against the tree. He looked at his mother as she watched some children play in the distance. Her white linen sundress hung delicately from her shoulders, billowing tenderly over her pregnant belly and swaying in the breeze. A gold armband hugged her slender bicep and a gold ring adorned her finger. Her hair was tied back with a ribbon. Luik realized that she was the most beautiful woman he had ever known.

"Luik! Come on!" A boy shouted from an open area where some children played. Pia glanced over at Luik. He looked after his friend, Hadrian, and simply held up the giant apple he was working on. Hadrian squinted into the shadow of the tree. But when he saw the apple and Luik's mother standing right beside him, he understood fully.

"All right, when you're done!" Hadrian ran off. Pia waved to him and then sat down next to Luik.

Musicians of every tribe gathered to play with one another, sharing songs and stories through their ancient craft. The sounds of drums, flutes and sylers[2] sifted down through the valley, accompanied by the harmony of voices. The effect was soothing and thought-provoking, carrying the listener away to visions and memories of days gone by and those yet to come.

"What do you dream of, my son?" Pia asked, her voice accenting the faint music. Luik regarded her quizzically.

"*Dream of*, Na na?"

"Aye, what do you wish for in the future?"

"Well, I think I'd like to go back and play with Hadrian."

"Aye, I know that," Pia laughed sweetly. "But after you play with Hadrian, after Jhestafe-Na is over, even after next summer is through, what are you looking forward to?" It was a question he had never been presented with. His mouth hung open ready to bite his apple.

"I haven't really thought about that," Luik said with the first pensive wrinkle upon his young brow.

"Then perhaps now is the time to start."

There was a pause between them.

---

[2] **Syler** (*SIGH-ler*): *noun; plural, sylers; name of a seven-stringed instrument played with the fingers and hands, upon which both beaten rhythm and melody can be issued at the same time.*

"I suppose I would like to have a home someday, like ours in Beneetha, maybe," Luik suggested.

"That would be nice," Pia said, looking off into the valley with him.

"A horse or two and some land to work, a nice garden—"

"Lovely."

"And you will be there, Na na."

"Of course, Luik."

"And Ta na, too; he must be there."

"Always," Pia waited; "anyone else?"

"No, I can't think of anyone."

"I can."

Luik shot her a penetrating glare.

"Who?" but he knew the answer.

"Luik!" a voice broke from the meadow below. "Are you done yet?"

"No! I'll be right there!" he hollered back.

Pia was impressed that Luik was taking this seriously. Luik's face flushed red and he fought his adolescent shift from not caring to being embarrassed that someone might know his thoughts. He took another bite of his apple and resisted looking at his mother whose eyes burned the side of his face.

"I have seen the way you get when her name is mentioned. And you have always enjoyed her company for so many years. Do you think that is merely coincidence, my son?"

"What else would it be?"

"Destiny."

"What do you mean?"

"Perhaps she is the one you are supposed to be with, Luik. Perhaps she is the Creator's choice for you, His perfect design. Maybe she is your rib." Luik turned to look at his mother's soft eyes.

"Have you asked Him?" Luik asked.

"The question is, *have you?*" Pia replied.

"I will listen to His voice, Na na."

"I know you will," she said smiling, then leaned over and kissed him on the head. "Here, let me take that apple from you."

"But, I need—"

"You need to obey your mother when she tells you something! Now, off with you!" Luik grinned widely as she hit him on the back and sent him running down the hill. She sighed and brushed the hair out of her face. He was growing up so quickly, too quickly, she thought. No longer just a boy, but far from being a man; it was such an interesting stage of life for her to watch him grow through.

The sun loomed high into a crystal clear sky, warming everything beneath it just as it did every day of the summer. The children played unceasingly, reveling at having the company of so many friends around. There were streams to swim in and trees to climb. Some played games of hide and seek, while others hid items amongst the greenery of bushes or ferns only for others to try and find. The favorite game among the older boys and girls was rokla[3], and the rokla tournaments during Jhestafe-Na were the most exciting to watch. Though you had to be ten and six summers before you were allowed to play for your tribe, there was nothing to rule against small games of it played throughout every realm of Dionia by children great and small. And Bensotha was known for having the best tournament field in all the land. Likewise, the children of Bensotha worked hard to maintain the thought that they were the best rokla players in Dionia.

Luik desperately wanted to make his way over to the tents of Ligeon, but Hadrian stopped him, insisting that he play with them.

"What else are you going to do?" Hadrian asked as if nothing was more important than rokla. He placed his hands on his hips. He had a wide chin and pronounced brow for such a young age, just like his father's. His bare chest was tanned and his dark hair was a mess.

"I was going to see my father," Hadrian followed Luik's stare to a set of tents further up the valley, "he's visiting."

"The king of Ligeon?" Hadrian asked, thinking for a moment. "Aw, Luik, let them be! You can visit the princesses later when the sun sets, we need you!" He pulled on Luik's arm. Hadrian was hard to ignore. "Come on! We're making teams!" Luik finally conceded and ran down to the field with Hadrian.

"Just one!" Luik yelled back, making his intentions understood.

"Sure, sure!"

---

[3] **Rokla** (ROCK-lah): *noun; 1. an ancient Dionian word meaning "two stones"; 2. one of the main sporting events played by the people of Dionia.*

They made up four teams, seven people on each, as prescribed by the rules. Goals were marked out with two overturned baskets as side posts, each pair of baskets on one of the four corners of the giant square. Of course the real fields played by the adults were bigger and had huge walls that curved up from the field floor. This made running up them easy, as well as bouncing passes to teammates. But it would be a few more years before any of them would be old enough to run on a real field. Luik longed for that day.

The teams started back by their respective goals, toes pressed up to a starting line. The two balls lay in the middle of the field alone, the red kafe[4] ball and the blue stri[5] ball. When a player successfully threw the stri ball into any of the three opponent's goals, a point was added to his team; whenever the kafe ball was used to score with, a point was subtracted from the team whose goal was scored on, giving each team the chance to not only score points for themselves, but to also remove points from their opponents. Each round was called a gita[6], each point called a stri, and each gita ended when one team reached five stri or won by two points. The real tournaments were played over a few days made up of more than ten gitas, each lasting many hours, but the children settled for one at a time.

Children who were deemed too young to play, or those who simply wanted to sit this gita out, sat all along the field on blankets sucking on cane or eating fruit. They picked their sides and cheered widely whenever the opportunity presented itself.

The four teams stood hunched over, peering feverishly at the center of the field, ready to leap forward like cougars set on a prize. Suddenly someone from the sidelines yelled out.

"Difouna[7]!"

A tower of water bursting through a breaking dam couldn't have had more power than the twenty and eight young players that rushed toward the center. Their toes pressed off the line and their arms swung frantically, driving their young bodies forward. Luik pumped his legs as

---

[4] **Kafe** (*KAY-feh*): *noun; 1. an ancient Dionian word meaning "loss"; 2. the red ball in Rokla.*

[5] **Stri** (*STR-EE*): *noun; plural, Stri; 1. an ancient Dionian word meaning "gain"; 2. the blue ball in Rokla; 3. term used to indicate a point.*

[6] **Gita** (*GIH-tuh*): *noun; plural, Gitas; 1. an ancient Dionian word meaning "basket"; 2. one round of Rokla played to five points.*

[7] **Difouna** (*dee-FOO-nuh*): *verb; slang of the command form of "difounale," Dionian word most closely related to the verb "to go."*

hard as he could. He wasn't about to lose his reputation to another more quick than him, at least not without contention. The groups of seven ran hard, covering the ground rapidly, when one from each team stopped to hold a position halfway between their goal and the center. Another ten strides and two more broke off and ran parallel across the field to either side. And then a final pair slowed leaving just two teammates still beating for the center. The strategies of the adult players were studied carefully and new tactics were implemented all the time. But these were the most basic field positions for the beginners.

The four remaining pairs looked to be the fastest of each team. This was sometimes one of the most pivotal points of the gita, as it would often determine who would set the scoring pace for the rest of the match, especially if one team gained both balls, a rare feat indeed. The throng of other children around the field stood up and started cheering loudly, shouting out player's names with great effort, urging them on. Even a number of parents had stopped and gathered to watch, finding their son or daughter in the match.

Luik and Hadrian ran side-by-side, not looking at anyone else, just fixed on the kafe and stri. The eight players gained speed and converged on the two balls, heads low and intent on their targets. The cheering grew louder, but Luik could not hear it. He was so focused on his prize, everything else became secondary. Hadrian and Luik had been front strikers so many times; they knew what the others would do before they did it.

Luik took one last stride and then dove flat out toward the stri on the left. Hadrian did the same, aiming for the kafe on the right. They had beaten the other six players, by a step. Luik's right hand cupped the blue ball while his left hand palmed the grass. His shoulders absorbed all the impact, feet swinging up over his head in a handstand. As soon as his body swept past the upright position, he blocked his shoulders with a jerk and pressed away with his arms; body sailing feet first, his head trailing behind into an upright position. The effect was a front handspring that sent him sailing directly over the head of the player coming straight at him. He was still traveling at a full run when he landed and slowed to find Hadrian.

Hadrian dove after the kafe and then tucked into a ball, rolling through the legs of the boy in front of him. He stood gingerly and used his free hand to brush off his hair. The two sets of players coming in from their right and left had smacked together, butting heads and laughing, while the one Luik leapt over shoved them all into a disgruntled heap. The tangled mess of players smiled and leapt back up after Luik and Hadrian. The growing crowd shouted after the pair in a raucous cacophony of adoration.

Luik spun around looking for his teammates, but they were too far away. It never took long for his early possession to be challenged by the second strikers close by. If a ball carrier was knocked to the ground, the ball was relinquished haphazardly, resulting in a frenzied drive for possession by any nearby players. Strategy said that if pressing through certain defenders wouldn't be successful, passing the ball to a fellow player would more likely ensure a team's continued possession of the ball.

The two second strikers of the team directly ahead charged Luik and Hadrian head on, as did one each from each of the two other flanking teams; four on two.

"Behind me!" Hadrian yelled. Luik let him take one stride in front and then fell in step behind him. They had done this maneuver a few times before when outnumbered. Hadrian covered the kafe protectively and lowered his head for the impact, running full speed toward the four defenders. The crowd cheered wildly. Arms spread wide to grab Hadrian and pull him down. But just as they embraced him, Luik ran up Hadrian's lowering back and leapt from it high into the air. At the same moment, Hadrian tossed the kafe out in front of Luik where he caught it with his other free hand, landing safely on the other side of the trap. Hadrian let out a whoop as the bewildered defenders looked around for his teammate. But he was gone. Now only two more defenders remained standing near the goal.

The children were quite hysterical. It was rare that anyone ever carried both the stri and kafe at the same time, especially this close to scoring. They leapt into the air with hands waving, all shouting after Luik. Even Pia waddled down from the hill to watch and yell after her son.

"Biea-Varos[8]!" Pia yelled, hands waving. "Difouna! Difounale!" But the hundreds that gathered drowned her out.

Luik regarded his last two opponents with bemusement. *What to do?* He thought. He knew them both, Thero and Anondo, sons of king Thorn of Ligeon, at least two summers younger than he, and not nearly as

---

[8] **Biea-Varos** (*BEE-uh-var-OHCE*): *verb; forward command form of the ancient Dionian word most closely related to the modern word 'courage'; to be of great fortitude, resilience and persuasion; devoid of fear.*

agile. He started running to his right, and they angled to counter him. He appeared to lean harder into his steps, and then the defenders committed, running straight at him. It was a mistake. Just as they reached out to grab him, Luik faked further to his right and then suddenly spun around to his left, and a wide path presented the goal. The audience roared as he surged forward with not a person between him and his target. He dove forward into a roll and as he emerged from the tuck, righting once more, he used the resulting power to heave both balls through the air, skipping between the upturned baskets. It was a stri for his team and a loss for the other. Hadrian ran up, one arm embracing his forearm, the other around his back.

"Hey'a, Luik! Good job!"

"Hey'a! You, too!" Luik said through a wide, trademark smile. Other players met up and congratulated him, hitting his back and yelling. It had been a marvelous display of finesse and skill. The stri and the kafe were recovered by a group of young children and handed back over to the losing team to be thrown back into play. The game continued on for the better part of an hour, stri scored and taken to the sounds of cheering and encouragement. But at the end of the gita, Luik and Hadrian's team won, the final score five, three, one and minus two.

As dusk drew ever closer, fires were lit throughout the lower valley, as were torches indicating tribes and camps. Soon the sun vanished beneath the eastern horizon, and the sky glow diminished into the recesses of a blackening abyss. Luik returned to his family's camp and ate some berries and more fruit in the firelight.

"You were wonderful this afternoon, my son," Pia said gently.

"Thank you, Na na. I saw you near the field," Luik said between bites, careful not to talk with his mouth full. She smiled.

"I got there eventually. Takes me a little longer, you know."

Luik nodded his head.

"Whoa!" Pia said with a start. She laid a hand on her round stomach. "Come here, child!" Luik stood up and drew near to where she sat.

"It's the baby again?" he whispered.

"Aye, feel here." Luik placed his hand where she indicated. A little foot pressed up under his palm and rubbed quickly.

"Hey'a! It kicked, it kicked me!" They both laughed together.

Pia rubbed her belly. "Any day now," she said softly.

"I can't wait," Luik said. "It's going to be a wonderful day!"

"Indeed, my son, indeed." She adjusted herself to a more comfortable sitting position and then gave Luik a long glare. "Well?"

"Well, what, Na na?"

"Have you been to the tents of Ligeon?"

"No, not yet."

"But you could hardly wait to go earlier. Is everything all right?"

"O sure, sure." He brushed his arm with his hand. "I've just been thinking about what you said to me."

"O?"

"About *destiny* and all that." He looked up. "What if you are right? What if she is my rib?"

"Then the Most High will tell you so."

"But what do I say to her, Na na?"

"What you have always said to her, Luik."

He thought for a moment. "That she plays rokla like a bear?"

Pia laughed. "No, my son! Well, I suppose you still could say that, but what I mean is that you shouldn't treat her any differently than you already do now. When the time is right you'll know what to say. He will tell you. There is a time and a place for everything under the sun."

Luik swallowed hard. Pia worried it was too much for one day. But he had to know eventually and the time seemed right.

Soon he finished his meal and lay down on the soft grass looking through the leafy branches to the star scattered sky above. The two moons were brilliant tonight, he thought, much more so than any other. Every day was perfect in Dionia, and every night stunning. He enjoyed paradise and its pleasures. He couldn't imagine a more beautiful and tranquil place. Surely it was the jewel of Athera, spoken of in the realms beyond his own. No other world must be quite like his, he imagined. Luik breathed in its beauty and drank of its sustenance. It was all he had ever known and all he ever hoped to know.

"Where is your father?" Pia said eventually, interrupting his rest. Luik sat up. "He's been off all day!"

"Does that surprise you, Na na?"

"No," she smiled, "not a bit. Would you find him for me?"

"Me?"

"Aye. I can't go anywhere quickly like this," she said touching her pregnant belly. "Bring him back for me. I think you'll know right where to find him." She winked sweetly.

"All right!" And with that Luik was off and running down the hill from the glen and up the valley.

"He is like his father," she whispered under her breath. "If only…" But she cut her own thoughts short.

• • •

"My lords, you have a visitor." A head peeked through a crack in the tent.

"Show him in," Thorn said looking at the attendant. The man nodded and disappeared. Candles hung in the air all through Thorn's tent, with many more perched on stands of ornate wood carved with knots and intricate designs. The two kings sat on large pillows on the floor and sipped mead in large goblets. A moment later a young man slipped between the folds and walked into the candlelight.

"Who is this before me?" Thorn's voice bellowed in the stillness. He had wavy reddish-blond hair with a beard to match, strong blue eyes set wide in his large face, and his neck was the size of an ox's. He wore a dark linen shirt and long breecs that flowed down stocky legs and opened to bare feet. Arm bands adorned his bulging biceps and a king's torc gently embraced his neck. His majestic crown rested on a pedestal to one side.

"Luik, son of Lair," the young man said. Thorn looked across at Lair whose back still faced Luik.

"Is this your son, Lair?" The second king placed his goblet down and turned slowly to regard the stranger behind him. Lair, too, had blond hair and striking gray-blue eyes, but was not nearly as large a man as Thorn. He looked at the figure standing at the entrance and then turned back to Thorn.

"Nay, he makes to play games with us, King Thorn. Send him away." But for that remark he knew retribution would be swift, bracing himself for it. And swift it was as Luik plowed into him from behind, throwing his arms around his neck and falling into Lair's lap from above. Lair gave a grunt as air was knocked out of him, and then started to laugh, as did Luik and Thorn. Lair pummeled his son a bit before setting him upright and regaining a bit of his stately composure. Thorn grinned at the exchange.

"So is this truly Luik before me, son of the king of Bensotha?"

"Aye, my lord," Luik said confidently.

"My, how one summer turns a boy into a man!"

"Who clearly has not lost *all* of his boy!" Lair added with a hand to his neck. They all laughed again.

"Well, young man, you have certainly grown since last we met." Luik was pleased for the compliment. "And I hear you are quite the rokla player! Even besting two of my sons!"

"You won today?" Lair asked.

"Yep! Four stri and three kafe." Luik beamed.

"You know, Lair, Ligeon may have to consider making an exception to the age of tribal players," Thorn said in interest of snagging Luik.

"You think so?" Lair asked inquisitively. "Well, you don't need to lower the age if you want me to play for Ligeon, king. Just ask!" Lair grinned and grabbed Luik, rubbing his hair wildly with his fist.

"Very funny, Ta na!" Luik said squinting.

"Something to drink, son?" Thorn asked Luik.

"Aye. Thank you, my lord." The northern king poured a third goblet full of mead and passed it over. Luik took a deep drink and wiped his mouth with his arm. "It's very good!"

"Thank you. If you come to play for us in Ligeon, you can have all you like!"

"Now you stop that, old king!" Lair said and raised a finger to Thorn. They all laughed heartily.

"One must try!" Thorn replied with a shrug of his shoulders. He resettled himself and regarded Luik once more. "Tell me, what else have you been doing in Bensotha besides breaking tournament records?"

"Well, I work in the garden with my father and quite enjoy it. Everything has been plentiful this year. Of course playing with friends and exploring, and then there is helping my mother prepare meals."

"Aye, how is Pia doing?" Thorn turned to Lair.

"Any day now," he replied, grinning wide through his goatee.

"Hey'a!" Thorn grunted with excitement. "A new creation waits to breathe air for the first time! Blessings to your home!" And he made the sign of blessing over Lair and Luik.

"You are very kind, my old friend."

"Why must you keep calling me old, man?" He turned to Luik. "Do I look old, Luik?"

"Of course not, my king!"

"You see! He still would make a fine player for Ligeon, even if he can't quite see straight!" Thorn's shoulders heaved as he laughed.

"So, when are you coming to Ligeon next?" Thorn asked.

Luik turned to his father. Lair shrugged.

"When you wish," Luik replied.

"Very well then, I think I shall arrange something forthwith. And will your father be joining you?"

"I don't know. Ta na?" He looked back at Lair again.

"I don't see how I could let you go alone, what with him trying to steal you away and all!"

"Then it's done! Give me the days, Lair, and we will gladly receive you in our Great Hall."

"You are most gracious, King Thorn."

"Ta na," Luik lowered his voice, directing it to his father. "Na na sent me to bring you home. She said you have been gone all day."

"Ah, this is true," Lair conceded. "It seems one loses track of time when in the company of good friends." Thorn smiled back at him. "I will be along shortly, my son. Why don't you wait outside?"

"Have you seen my daughters as of late?" Thorn inquired. "I know they were asking after you."

"They were?" Luik was pleasantly stunned.

"Aye, seems they have always enjoyed your company. You may find them by our tribal fire or, perhaps, knowing them as I do, down at the rokla field waiting for tonight's gita to commence."

"Right!" Luik said with betraying enthusiasm.

"Off you go, my son," Lair raised a hand.

"But when will you be done?"

"Don't you be concerned, Luik. I have found my way home to your mother many a time without you." Luik grinned at his father's words. "I will manage. Now go!" Lair hit him in the thigh and pushed him out the tent. Then he resituated himself on his pillow and turned to Thorn.

"A wonderful lad," Thorn said affectionately after a moment.

"You speak kindly, king."

"I speak the truth, Lair! There is something about him, something of great significance."

"O?" Lair asked, surprised.

"He has been born for such days, for such a time as this." Thorn's voice softened from his traditional strong bellow.

"These days are as blessed as any, Thorn." Lair took a deep draft of his mead.

"Nay, there is something, I sense, that calls out for some, such as your Luik there. A great need, perhaps."

"A need? A need for what? Why do you speak in riddles?" Lair smiled hesitantly.

"Something stirs within me, my friend. Yet I cannot place it."

"Well, what of the Most High? What has He said of it to you?"

Thorn did not reply at first.

"Thorn?"

But Thorn was distant, intent on something within himself.

"Thorn!" Lair said abruptly.

"Aye. Just thinking." And then there was another long pause. Lair was perplexed.

"Thorn? Speak, man!"

"That's just it, my friend," Thorn whispered low. "I can't. The Most High has said nothing to me of this."

Lair lost whatever smile remained. "Truly?"

"Aye. In fact," Thorn spoke in a hushed tone, "He has spoken very little to me as of late."

"Of anything?" Lair asked, stunned.

"Aye, of anything."

Lair did not know what to say.

"I still feel his presence, but something veils His words to me." Thorn said.

"Well, why?"

"If I knew, at least that would be something to amend."

• • •

Luik made his way through the rows of tents drenched in shadow and the occasional flickering of torchlight. The emblazon of the white eagle stitched on every tent flap and adorning every peaked rise as flags, now dormant in the still air, put to rest any doubt that he was walking among the tribes of Ligeon. He could hear the nearby joyful melodies of praise, being given up as offerings to the Great God, meandering along the paths from up ahead. He walked in the direction of the ever-loudening music until finally coming into an open central square, crowded with people and bathed in the rich starlight from above. A devouring fire burned high in the middle and people danced in circles around the flames. The rhythmic beating of drums and cascading harmonies issued with flutes, sylers and voices stirred the evening air with indescribable color. Men leapt and women twirled to the music, all shouting and singing with all their hearts, songs of thanksgiving and praise.

"You, O Most High, are a Consuming Fire!"

Ribbons rippled through the night air like silken sheaves of water, guided from sticks in the hands of the dancing painters. They spun around figures and then shot high into the air as long arches or shimmering waves. Others carried tambourines and tossed them high, the spinning producing a wash of timed crescendos, only to be caught again in perfect time. They held them in their hands and beat them on their feet, knees, and hips as they danced, vaulting into the sky. The musicians sat all around, eyes wide and mouths singing, skillfully interpreting what was to be played at each given moment.

"A Consuming Fire, a Consuming Fire, we burn for You! We burn for You!"

Luik moved along the edges of the tents that looked across the square to an area where the majority of people were seated. He sat himself near some baskets of Juniper berries and took a handful, peering into the central circle. The vibrant colors and movement were breathtaking. He sat, eating berries, and watched as the rhythms sped up and the melodies grew in intensity. The dancers leapt higher and higher, so high Luik thought they may fly away if they had wanted to. Everyone clapped their hands and sang along.

"We give ourselves to You, O Consuming Fire! Consume us! Consume us!"

The seated drummers beat hard with their hands, so fast all Luik saw was a blur. Fingers danced over the sylers, and the flutists seemed to never take a breath. The pace continued to quicken and the melodies jumped about like gazelles bounding through an open field. Everything moved about so quickly, Luik hardly knew where to look. It was utterly captivating. Within moments the song had reached its fullest point and lingered at its peak in a flurry of life and longing as if the people were flames themselves. Then, all at once, as if guided by some unseen director, the entire organism leapt onto a final beat, a final note, and then completely ceased, each dancer falling to the ground in total silence, leaving only the massive fire to burn on in the center of it all.

And it was in that moment of stillness that Luik looked across the square, and there, bathed in the firelight, was a familiar face sitting among the attendees. Anorra. For a moment she did not see him. He took a deep breath and studied her face. Her delicate nose perched with deep blue eyes sat above soft lips and slender cheeks. Her long blonde hair framed the beautiful image half in shadow and half in firelight. Something had changed. It had been a whole summer since he had seen her last. And it wasn't so much that she was different, he thought, but that *he was*.

Suddenly he realized she was looking straight at him with a grand smile.

"Hey'a!" he mouthed silently and waved. She returned the gesture. For a moment he didn't know what to do next. He just sat there staring across at her, silence still filling the air. But a moment later the entire space erupted with shouting and clapping as all the people looked up into the night sky and began applauding and declaring the praises of the Great Spirit. A few started to stand up in front of him. He knew he'd lose sight of her.

"Over there!" he said aloud this time, gesturing with his head and pointed to a far corner of the square. She nodded and then was lost in the mass of people all on their feet. Luik pressed around the baskets and squeezed through a crowd of adults, struck by a few swinging hands and jumping bodies along the way. He finally resorted to exiting back among the tents for a clearer way to the corner. But she had beaten him, doing the same, and met him there in one of the rows.

"Luik!" The way she said his name struck him.

"Hey'a, Norra!" His voice cracked slightly.

They embraced and then stood back to look at one another. She wore a long light linen dress with flowered bracelets around her ankles and a ribbon in her hair.

"You got taller!" she said with a laugh. He looked down at his breecs and raised his toes up.

"You think?"

"Sure! It's nice."

"Thanks." Luik felt his face warm. *What was going on?*

"Hey'a, my sisters are at the rokla tournament right now. Wanna' go?"

"Rokla?" But Luik was lost. "O right!" he said clearing his head. "Aye, let's go!"

But for the first time rokla didn't interest him. He really just wanted to go somewhere and talk.

• • •

By the time they made their way to the sunken field, the game was well underway. People pressed hard along the rim shouting down into the giant square, while others sat all the way up the raised earthen berms above, enjoying the higher vantage point. Immense torches lining the sides of the court showered light into the playing area below. The field was dug out about half a tree length below ground level with steep walls that gradually curved flush with the bottom of the field. Unlike the children's version, the real tribal games had handmade nets that stretched between two posts making up their four goals.

Anorra pulled Luik through the crowd to where her sisters said they'd be. They sat far up the side of one of the grassy berms to the right, towering down over the onlookers and peering down into the field.

"Analysia!" Anorra cupped her hands and yelled to them as they hiked up the hill. Seeing Anorra and then Luik, the eldest hollered back and motioned for them to come up. They eventually reached the summit and Analysia embraced Luik first.

"It is so good to see you, Luik of Bensotha!" She yelled over the noise of the crowd.

"And you, Lysia!"

"I have missed you!"

"As have I!"

"Me, too!" came a smaller voice from behind. Lana pushed herself between them and threw her arms around Luik's torso. All three sisters looked alike, save for their size, with Analysia being the tallest and little Lana being the smallest.

"Whoa there, little one!" Luik said as if he were acting as a father. "And who's this?"

"You don't remember me? It's Lana!" she said indignantly.

"Aye! So it is! You have grown so much." He knelt a little lower and gave her a hug.

"Come, sit here with us," Lysia said. "Nearlyn is ahead with four stri, Lynatrel and Beneetha have three, and Newen, just one."

"Difounale!" Luik shouted. "Difouna Beneetha! Difounale! *Ben-ee-tha! Ben-ee-tha!*"

Two attackers in linen breecs closed on a player with dark hair and deep brown skin who lobbed the stri across to center field. A brown haired man jumped up off the shoulders of a teammate and caught the ball with one hand. He landed right next to a pair of second strikers and quickly tossed the stri to a pale skinny man with red hair. The red-haired man lunged in great strides toward an opposing goal, but two guardians closed from the sides.

"Biea Varos!" Luik hollered hysterically. "Your flanks!"

But of course the man could not hear him. He took a few more strides before pulling his arm back to throw the ball. Luik wasn't sure he would make it. The red haired man was struck from both sides, pressed between the guardians, but not before deftly loosing the ball on an open goal.

"Stri!" Luik yelled jumping to his feet. "That's four! Difouna! One more!" The sisters just laughed at his enthusiasm.

"I think your cheering is helping!" Anorra shouted.

"Aye!" Luik said, glued to the match.

"I like it."

"Aye!" Luik said, suddenly turning from the field. "What?" She just smiled back at him, eyes all aglow.

"Look!" Lana shouted. "The kafe!"

Sure enough, Newen had possession of the kafe and passed it gingerly from player to player as they advanced to the goal just to their left, a team that was preoccupied with their own advancement of the stri toward another goal.

"They're going to take Nearlyn's stri away!" she yelled again. Rokla was a fascinating game. The very team you wanted to lose suddenly became a team to cheer for as much as your own.

"Difouna Newen!" the four of them shouted together, all on their feet. "Biea Varos!"

One man carried the kafe behind a larger dark man who led the way. Four more teammates fanned out to the sides, leaving one behind to defend their own goal. But it was a risk they needed to take. One more stri made by Nearlyn and the gita was over. They needed to take away a stri helping themselves *and* the other losing teams also. It was just part of the game. Only two guardians protected Nearlyn's net, and neither of them was focused on the advancing team on their right flank. The ball carrier shouted to his man furthest left along the wall, a small agile little fellow, and told him to make a run. The core group charged the two guardians. The first guardian saw the rushers out of the corner of his eye and jumped out of the way, but the second one wasn't as fortunate. The huge dark man drove into him like a bull and caught him completely off guard, sending him flying through the air. The crowd roared. The first guardian, however, managed to squeeze between the attackers and slide at the feet of the ball carrier. He connected and tripped the man face first into the ground. The kafe popped up and into the dark man's hands. He had only a second to think. Nearlyn's attackers had heard the shouts of their guardians and turned to aid the outnumbered pair. It was then that the dark man saw his teammate running up the curved wall and around the corner behind the net. He heaved the tiny kafe and the runner leapt off the wall and caught it in mid air. Before his feet landed on the ground, the tiny man threw the ball out around the side post and curved it into the net.

"Kafe!" little Lana shouted, her hands waving frantically. The four of them jumped and yelled.

"Nearlyn has three!" Anorra jumped excitedly.

"Just one more for Beneetha!" Luik said.

"Difounale Beneetha!" Analysia yelled. The crowd was a churning sea of bouncing onlookers.

Beneetha had quenched the attack of Nearlyn's latest assault, as most of Nearlyn's players had retreated in the failed attempt to keep the kafe out of their own net. In doing so, Beneetha had intercepted the stri and paused to gather together in a full-out drive against Nearlyn, who now possessed the kafe. It was the two opposite teams on the field, Beneetha with the stri and hungry for one more point, and Nearlyn with the kafe and poised to take that point away. The other two teams would naturally prevent Beneetha from winning. But in a show of honor, Newen chose to even up the sides and advance with Beneetha.

"They're doubling up!" Luik said with surprise.

"And Lynatrel is joining Nearlyn" Anorra added. "What a great gita!"

The fourteen players on each side mounted toward one another in packs, leaving one man with their net. Beneetha surrounded their ball carrier as well as two other men in the middle of their advancing mass, while Nearlyn and Lynatrel spread wide, all the men with their arms behind their backs thus concealing their ball carrier.

"It's the one on the right!" Lana screamed from above with a clear view of Nearlyn's backsides.

The two teams converged moderately, only slowly gaining speed. As they reached half field, Nearlyn's carrier broke away from the line and revealed the kafe as he swung his arms. He ran quickly forward, leaving the rest of the team to charge in around Beneetha's huddled form. The opposing line wrapped in brutally hard and knocked down the sides of Beneetha's group, trying desperately to get at the three men inside. But they were not there, having bounded off the shoulders of the men in front of them landing clear in the open field, only a single guardian between them and their stri. Nearlyn was dismayed. They looked back to see if their carrier had scored, but Beneetha's guardian blocked the shot, deflecting the kafe up into the wall behind the net. If Beneetha scored now, the gita was over. And no one could possibly get to the last scene of the game in time to help the three-on-two situation.

The two flanking runners ran wide leaving the single guardian alone with the ball carrier. The guardian made a desperate attempt to intercept the pass, but failed. The striker on the right caught the stri, and in the same motion threw it sidearm at the open net. The crowd was hysterical! Luik leapt high and the girls danced, shouting all the while. The Beneethan players made a round of the field waving up to the cheering people above. A few onlookers even slipped down into the court and lifted a player or two up on their shoulders. Several more moments of revelry transpired before anyone noticed the remaining players huddled together near the middle of the arena.

Why aren't they celebrating? Luik thought. The crowd's antics slowly dissipated, everyone wondering at their behavior.

"What's going on?" Anorra said as a hush fell over the crowd.

The celebrating players calmed down and then returned to the group in the middle to see what was happening. They stood shoulder-to-shoulder all looking inward at something. Everyone above the field tried to get a look in, but the players were too close together. There was movement among them, and then the circle opened as three of the team members carried a man from out of their midst with the rest of the players following. The crowd gasped, and a foreign feeling surged through Luik's spirit.

"What happened?" Lana exclaimed.

"I—" Luik hesitated, "I don't know, Lana." He strained down at the odd image below. The man they carried looked pale and his eyes were closed. His right leg hung down in the strangest of ways, bent in a manner it was not intended to.

"What's happened to his leg, Luik?" she tugged on his breecs, pleading with him. "Why is he sleeping?"

"Peace, Lana," Analysia said placing a hand on her head. None of them had any idea what was going on. They were asking themselves the same questions Lana was. Why was that player's leg bent back like that? And why was he looking so abnormal?

Men slid the wallboards out of place that covered the dug-out stairs during the game. The single set of stairs along one side of the court served as the only real exit route of the high walled court. The players walked up out of the field through the corridor to ground level. A passive crowd slowly gathered to watch them walk past, all speaking to one another in hushed tones. Luik suddenly realized he wasn't the only one who didn't understand what was going on.

The four children descended from their lofty vantage point and followed the trailing mass of onlookers. They moved silently through the valley, a few of the throng carrying torches to help out the guiding starlight. They finally arrived at a grouping of tents and Luik assumed the players took the man inside one of them. For several more moments nothing happened. Eventually people began peeling away and walking back to their respective camps. Even Analysia and Lana became disinterested and said good night. But Luik stayed and Anorra wouldn't leave him. The crowd of people continued to dwindle down to a small few who spoke quietly with one of the remaining players outside the entrance of a tent. Luik and Anorra pressed closer trying to make out their conversation.

"No, really, good man, I'm sure everything is just fine. Peace be with you. Have a good night." The player placed a hand on a gentleman's shoulder in reassurance. "Our teammate is simply in need of rest. Be on your way, the night is getting late." Realizing his pleading wouldn't get him any further the man seemed to take the words to heart and turned to walk away. Then the player addressed the remaining few stragglers. "Please, my friends, I bid thee rest from this place. All is well and we will see you tomorrow."

Luik and Anorra moved behind a tree, peering around as everyone dispersed. The player remained at his post outside the tent making sure everyone left. Then Luik boldly strode out from the shadow of the tree and walked toward the tent.

"You there, be on your way," the player said, tiring of the repetition.

"What is the matter with your teammate, sir?" Luik asked, completely ignoring the command.

"It is no matter for you, young man," he replied softly, seeing it was only a boy.

"But he looked strange, and his leg—"

"Aye," the player interrupted, "his leg was oddly bent."

"Aye, what for?"

Luik neared and the player knelt low. "In truth, my friend, I do not know." He shook his head. "We have sent word to King Lair. He will be here momentarily, I'm sure."

"And he will know what has happened. He is my father." Luik pumped his chest out in boyish pride.

"Truly? Then you are Luik, I assume?"

"Aye! Luik, son of Lair."

"Hey'a! It is I, Pelidril of Beneetha."

"Right!" The two embraced.

"I did not recognize you in the evening light."

"That's all right," Luik said smiling, "I didn't know it was you either. You played very well tonight, Pelidril. I wasn't sure if we would win the gita, but your plays were marvelous!"

"Thank you, my friend. And I hear you are quite the rokla player as well. Maybe we will play together one day?"

"I would like that very much!" Luik said with great expectation. Pelidril was one of his favorite players.

"Ah, look there! Your father arrives," Pelidril pointed. Luik turned and saw his father bounding across a knoll and down into the glade of trees where most of Beneetha's tents lay scattered about. A few men came with him including King Thorn.

"Where is he?" Lair said flatly, addressing Pelidril.

"Inside," he replied.

"Hey'a, Ta na!" Luik said, immediately clinging to his father's side. But Lair looked down at him expressionless.

"Luik, stay here."

"But I—"

"Nay, wait out here, my son," he said sternly. It was a tone Luik had never heard him use before.

"Ta na!" Anorra said, bursting from behind the tree. She couldn't hold it in anymore.

"Norra!" Thorn turned to embrace his daughter but quickly set her back down. "Be on your way, child. Back to the tent with you."

"But I want to stay here with you."

"Nay, this is not your place."

"Children," Lair spoke up, "part with haste. You have no choice in this. We will come to you in the morning. Your mothers await and expect you promptly. Surely you do not want us to bear such a burden should you not return as ordered." Lair winked at them both with the only sign of ease. "Now leave!"

Luik took a step back and Lair walked past Pelidril and through the flap. Thorn followed right behind and the remaining men took up posts around the tent.

"What's going on?" Anorra whispered to him quietly. They took a few steps away from the tent, Luik still searching for the meaning behind his father's unusual manner.

"I don't know, but we should probably heed their request. I have never seen my father act like that before."

"Nor I," she added.

The kings returned the next morning as they promised, saying little of the evening's strange happenings. It turned out the player was fine, and by midday that afternoon, no one gave another thought to the incident. In fact, by the time that night's gita was underway, hardly a soul remembered what had taken place the night before. That is, everyone except two children from the western lands.

Chapter Three

ON TO ADRIEL

"Wait for me!" came a small voice, echoing off the water of a pond in a nearby wood. Three figures emerged from a distant glade and into the knee-high grass of Bensotha Valley, a fourth one following just behind. His red hair, freckled face and skinny stature put him at only ten and three summers old. He bounded over the thick green blades, his tiny legs reaching higher with every stride.

"I found an ogal stone!" said the redhead.

"That's great, Fane, but we're going to be late if we don't hurry," Luik shouted from up ahead, just a silhouette in the dim pre-dawn sky.

Realizing he had no place to carry his latest treasure, Fane tossed the prized stone carelessly over his shoulder, but glanced in its direction hoping to retrace his steps another day for rediscovery.

"The sun is going to rise over the western sea any moment!" Luik yelled from the front of the small stampede.

"We'll make it, Luik," Anorra replied with confidence.

They ran hard, beating down the long fingers of the field with every leap. Luik was relentless in his pursuit forward, and ran westward toward the coastal sea beyond. His youthful blond hair curled at the ends, fluffy atop a boyish grin and gray-blue eyes.

Fane caught up with the other three of his peers, happy they had stopped by to invite him. Anorra stretched out her hand to slap him on the back. "You'll find it again, Fane, I know you will." Her encouraging words splashed color into his heart, and he grinned wide as they continued to run.

"Thanks, Norra," Fane beamed, "and you can help me!" Anorra tilted her head back and laughed at the thought, knowing that she probably would, too. She was a courageous type. Her friends were always overjoyed when she journeyed south for a visit, and not nearly often enough, they thought. Though this Daughter of Eva was striking to look at with her long blonde hair, sapphire blue eyes and tanned skin, her feminine looks were deceiving. The truth be known, she could out-run, out-ride and out-swim almost any boy in the western lands, *and* look good doing it.

In fact, one of the only boys who could out-run her was Hadrian. His soft black hair lofted lightly in the air as he ran beside her, legs stretching out and back effortlessly. The tallest of the four friends, Hadrian was a quick thinker and always saw another side of things, pensive with his deep-set, dark brown eyes. And on any of their adventures it was always he who wanted to go first, hungry for the next escapade into the forest, sea or mountainscape.

The four children ran strong, never lessening the quick pace Luik set. Crossing stream after stream and jumping from rock to rock, they followed the valley's leading as it swung low toward the great Faladrial Ocean. By now they were well into Casterness, realm of the Great King Ragnar, lord of all Dionia. Suddenly Luik stopped, standing on the brink of a ridgeline with a grand waterfall just to one side. The waters rushed by his feet to the left and then dropped off five tree lengths, crashing below into a shimmering basin surrounded by a lush mossy floor.

"We're almost there," he said with his outstretched arm and finger designating a point in the distance. "Just a bit further. We don't have much time."

From their vantage point the lower valley floor spread out like a canvas of detailed imagery before them ending with the Faladrial Ocean set in the west. Weeping willow trees loomed like green clouds tied to the ground by massive trunks. Small white stone houses lay strewn about the meadows bordered by pools of water fed by a network of passing brooks. Seaside docks beyond corralled hundreds of boats and round-topped ocean dwellings with white stone paths. Intricate bridge-ways tied it together, all pointing to the most masterful piece of architecture in the entire known kingdoms of Dionia: Adriel Palace.

Adriel Palace was fashioned at the dawn of time as one of the first creations that Ad and the Great Creator Himself built, *together*. It was out of shared joy, knowledge, and delight that Ad and the Lord of Hosts constructed Adriel Palace, side-by-side. It was born out of relationship, not out of accomplishment. Nothing in the land could compare with her beauty.

Sitting high atop the rising rock cliffs of the Ison Peninsula, her white stone and marble walls gleamed brightly even without the morning sun. Her many slender towers and long archways soared into the sky, becoming the highest points of the horizon. The roofs were capped with pale slate. The wall and archway trim was etched and carved with scenes of fish, beasts, men, women, children, trees, and waterfalls, all laced with gold. Dark oak doors led to passageways, and suspended walkways hung from tower to tower. The scattering of blue, red, and yellow colored glass windows set in nearly every outside wall cast radiant beams of light dazzling through the air when the sun hit them just right during the day.

The great white stone palace wall, with its own carved relief of nature scenes, stood more than two tree lengths high and allowed only one entrance into the palace courtyards. The King's Gate was a giant set of hewn ironwood doors hinged and bound by straps of bronze, and it always remained open. The only entry more grand on the peninsula was that of the City Gate far below, which served as the main passageway through the city wall, standing nearly three tree lengths in height. Within the city wall were thousands of stout bleached homes with rounded roofs of purple tile and slate. Streets of white-washed stone crossed orderly over the hillside. They filled the space between the two walls and accented the wide marble pathways that led up from the City Gate to the King's Gate above.

Luik, Fane, Anorra, and Hadrian stopped above the waterfall only long enough to soak in but a taste of the beautiful feast before them. Then, as if hearing the same bell, they took off down the northern ridgeline, descending quickly as it swept west to the lower valley floor. They passed home after home, all interconnected with trails and bridges and spaced evenly with wide, freshly harvested fields.

After running for a while longer they met with a wide roadway that eventually became the main thoroughfare of the city. Fashioned out of white marble, the avenue gradually rose from among the numerous lowland homes and soared up the Ison Peninsula. The main road took them far enough out on the isle that they had passed the seaside dwellings along the coast; they were almost to the City Gate. Between gaps of the peninsula homes they could see water to their right and left far below.

Before long they had arrived, the towering city wall looming before them, stretching to the sides and fading around out of sight. They crossed under the staggeringly grand City Gate and entered into the city. But today the gate was not busy with horses and wagons coming in and out, nor were the streets pressed with their inhabitants. Rather, it was *empty*. Homes lay still and the streets were clean and abandoned. But the people had merely relocated in the twilight. Today it was not the city's entrance that was jammed with people, but it was the King's Gate that was.

And not just a few people. Thousands of people extended through the gateway and flooded the courtyards of the palace, right up to the inner square. And what a regal and royal people they were, all strong, pure, and reliant. The women mostly dressed in light colored sun dresses, their bare feet were adorned with toe rings and ankle bracelets, their hair long, laced with ribbons, shells, and flowers. The men stood agile and attentive, their waists wrapped in soft linens of blues, reds, and purples, their bare upper bodies molded, tanned, and strong. Some wore bands of gold around their arms and open-ended torcs of brass and bronze around their necks, while others wore only the rings of their family, their wife, and their region on their hands. The youngest children either slept in their mother's arms or sat at their feet, shaking off the slumber from an early morning. The older children held the hands of their mother and father, listening and waiting. All the people stood still engaging in whispered conversation, one eye on the person they were talking to and the other looking toward the palace beyond the wall. There was a hushed expectancy in the air.

"We made it," Hadrian beamed.

"But we can't see a thing!" Fane added. "We can't even see past the gate! What now?"

"I say we split up," came Anorra's sweet voice. Her blonde hair draped gently along a pink sleeveless silk shirt that extended past her waist and tied with a leather belt. "We'll be able to move easier alone instead of a group trying to squeeze through all these people."

Hadrian cast a quick glance toward the immense palace past the wall. "I agree."

"Then when it's all over, we'll meet back at the Sea Cave," Luik stated without room for argument. They each grabbed the person's right forearm to the left of them with their own right hand, forming a square of interlocked arms in a huddle. They nodded their heads and yelled out, "Varos[9]!" before splitting up and running each in their own direction.

Luik immediately went straight into the crowd, slipping between legs and scooting around people's waists avoiding their elbows and quick turns. As he made his way toward the gate he would inadvertently get stuck for a moment or two as people swayed into each other pinching off his escape between their backsides or hips. He eventually passed under the archway and into the courtyard, still packed full of citizens. He made a quick dash for one of the large fountains in the center and waded through its pool to make up some extra ground quickly. He paused for a moment, refreshed by the cool water around his legs, and glanced up over his right shoulder hearing a distinct whistle from above.

It was Anorra. Somehow she had climbed upon the roof of a house outside the palace wall, scaled the archway and then descended back onto the top of the palace stable in the courtyard. She crouched near an upper tile wall, waving down at him, her blue eyes twinkling. He grinned and waved back at her, never able to figure out exactly how she got away with that sort of thing.

Luik jumped from the pool and continued on through the mass of people. The main stone staircase leading to the front doors of the magnificent palace was bordered by a set of enormous gravel trees, one on each side. The contrast of their shimmering silver leaves against the black bark beneath was stunning. And their wide spreading branches made them perfect for climbing, which is just what he decided to do.

Seeing that a number of other youth already had the same idea, Luik was delighted to see some open space among many of the higher branches. He leaped easily to the first branch and pulled himself up. A few boys greeted him casually as he passed by, pushing himself higher from branch to branch. Others even assisted him with a boost here and there to

[9] **Varos** (var-OHCE): *noun; an ancient Dionian word most closely related to the modern word 'courage'; to be of great fortitude, resilience, and persuasion; devoid of fear.*

reach longer stretches of the loftier limbs. The silvery canopy above drew closer and closer until Luik's head popped through the top as he found a suitable limb for viewing the palace and made himself comfortable.

From here Luik could easily see the balcony of the main tower far above. What the people knew as the King's Balcony was now draped with purple and yellow banners and mounted with flags in honor of the morning's ceremony. Luik sat and wondered if the rest of his friends had fared as well as he in their pursuit of a prime vantage point. But his thoughts were cut short as he saw something flash out of the corner of his eye. He strained to look behind himself, back toward the stone animal barns in the courtyard. Far in the distance a figure on a large horse passed between gaps in the buildings, but too quickly for him to make it out in any detail. There it went again, but still it was impossible to tell. A thought passed through his mind and his heart raced. Could it be? He glanced ahead anticipating the next gap between buildings knowing he would certainly get a long look this time, but it never came, and his attention was again diverted.

As if prompted by an unseen gust of wind, three heralds burst out onto the portico above with brass trumpets raised to their mouths blowing the thunderous arrival of their king. Wasting no time at all, King Ragnar and his wife Queen Meera strode out between them robed in deep purple and bearing the crowns of Dionia in gold and gems. The king's flowing dirty blond hair framed a tremendous tanned face dawned with the courage and pride of a natural born leader. His wide cheekbones and deep-set green eyes beneath a firm brow commanded great authority. The queen was equally as stunning but with fair skin and long blonde hair pouring over her shoulders and delicate face.

As suddenly as he appeared, the throng of people below burst into a frenzy of cheering and thunderous applause. The women grew faint and the men raised fists high in honor of their hero in battle. The noise trailed off behind Luik out of the square, through the courtyards, and past the gate into the streets, echoing through the valley beyond. He imagined the sound could be heard even back at his small home in Beneetha where his mother and father awaited his return. They had stayed home on this joyous day as Pia felt she was not up for the last minute journey to Casterness. She always seemed to get overly excited whenever the family journeyed the short distance to Adriel, but this time it was clear that she missed not going. Either way, Luik thought it exciting that Ragnar's child and his own brother or sister could be born so close together, maybe even two royal children born on the same day. He couldn't wait to get back home and tell his parents all he had seen. Jhestafe-Na had been cut a day short as the news of the royal birth arrived in the evening of the sixth day. Everyone either packed up and went home or made the night's journey to Adriel for the festivities. Luik was excited that his parents let him go with Hadrian and Anorra. They stopped by Fane's tent on the way from Jhestafe-Na, his parents only more than willing to let him go with the lot. Everything else seemed to fade away with the news of the newborn's arrival, even the strange incident at the rokla tournament six days prior.

"People of Dionia, both near and far," proclaimed the king with a deep voice that traveled easily. The people's ravenous applause died quickly as he raised a hand. "I greet you in the Name of the King of kings and the Lord of lords! My heart is overwhelmed to know that so many of you would travel so far in such short time to share in my family's joy. Today the Creator of Life has found favor on me and my house by allowing the blessing of creating life to continue through my line."

King Ragnar turned slightly to receive a small bundle of cloth handed from behind him. He remained turned, examining the contents for a moment, and then swung back into view of the throng below. He closed his eyes briefly. Above his platform was a large round window in the tower with an exact copy on the backside, essentially creating a hole in the building that a person, at the right level, could peer directly through the tower to the ocean horizon beyond.

The king became intent and pensive, as if sensing the very world below him turning, aware of every mountain and every sea, every breath of every creature. What had been created was for his dominion and his rulership and for those of the Sons and Daughters of Men. The perfect, unblemished relationship between Creator and creation stirred with life and power, every being aware of its place and role, right down to the dust that embodied the roots of the smallest flower. In all and through all the Spirit of the Most High ebbed and flowed with pulse and passion, a rhythm born of divine desire and given over to Man to rule and subdue.

The king's voice suddenly roared with pride. "I present to you, Princess Ciana!"

As if knowing the moment of the dawning sun's arrival by heart, the king discarded the bundled cloth in his hands and hoisted a small baby high into the first golden rays of sunshine passing through the window above. The people below erupted into a thunder of praise delivered in excitement and euphoria. The king turned slightly from side to side acknowledging the full spectrum of those present before lowering the baby into his arms and calming the masses with an open hand once more. He raised his head toward the heavens and spoke to the Great God, beseeching a divine blessing on his newborn child, dedicating her into His hands and heart.

It was the first time that Luik had ever seen the presenting of a royal child born to the Great King of Dionia. The son or the daughter of a king was no different than any of the other peoples of the nation, and royal birth did not necessarily mandate a future position on the throne. Rather, it was more of a generational blessing that one would have the honor to be born to a king, placed there by the hands of the Most High Himself. The child certainly possessed the innate abilities and calling to rule over a kingdom, inheriting them from its parents, but they were an equal with all those of the land, still subject to the will and choosing of the Almighty for placement as king over a kingdom.

Royal children were many in Luik's knowledge, being one himself, but he was acquainted with only a few. He obviously knew Anorra and her sisters and brothers from Ligeon in the north. And also the son of King Naronel, lord of Trennesol to the east, though he could not remember his name, having only met him twice during rokla tournaments two summers earlier. Luik grew puzzled with his inability to remember the young man's name, as he had never forgotten *anything* before.

Luik also had heard rumors of a royal child, born to King Ragnar, who had left the palace early on as a babe with his nursemaids and settled on the other side of Dionia. But the stories were quickly proven false when the child turned out to be that of one of the court elders who had recently chosen to relocate to the Trennesol Council. Everyone was hungry for word of the next royal birth to the point of fabricating their own thoughts and wishes into reality.

Luik peered up at the small princess, amazed that she had caught the very first rays of sunlight on her first full day of life. Only royal children of Casterness were given that honor as the round window on the tower was the highest and farthest structure to the west, catching the rising sun's first beams.

King Ragnar raised his hand one last time, saying with commanding force through a broad smile, "Let the festivities begin!"

Luik watched as his majestic and noble king, chosen to rule by the Creator, waved farewell and turned back into his chamber to the sound of the trumpets.

From the courtyard below him to every house in the streets beyond, people scurried like mice busy with the affairs of the awaited activities. Doors along the palace's storehouse flew open as rolling tables slid onto the palace grounds full of food; Darrin apples and Maple apples, Wellem fruit from the north, Lemming bananas and every fruit of every type of tree in all the land; strawberries and peaches, plums and melons, grapes and oranges, mangoes and papayas; cheeses laid thick between loaves of fresh bread not ten minutes old; barrels of grape wine and mead rolled to stands next to each table, chosen from the king's own cellar. Musicians gathered like birds, strumming their lyres and tightening the heads on their drums. Tambourines shook and flutes piped. Singers immediately picked up the tunes being played and rejoiced in poem and rhyme as they went about their tasks. Within moments the entire peninsula was alive with color, song, and movement, celebrating the arrival of another child to the Kingdom of Dionia.

Luik sat for a moment leaning back on his perch high above the bustle of activity below and breathed deeply. What a wonderful thing to have witnessed, he thought. The breeze picked up with the rising sun, carrying the smell of the food below to his lofty tree-side throne. When Luik opened his eyes he noticed an object resting on the leaves just beyond his reach. Intrigued, he sat up and began to slide himself out on the limb to a place where he could grab what he now realized was a piece of fabric. Slipping his hand underneath the delicate cloth, he pulled it close and gently examined it, rubbing his fingers along embroidered letters on one corner reading *R.M.C.* It was the birth cloth of Princess Ciana, each letter standing for the name of her father, mother, and then her, *Ragnar-Meera-Ciana*.

Luik sat in wonder, realizing that the king had inadvertently discarded the garment a little too forcefully in his excited state, throwing it right off the balcony to the top of the tree below.

"Now what?" he muttered to himself, bemused.

He stared down at the large wooden doors atop the massive marble staircase leading into the palace. There was only one way to return the precious blanket that Ciana would one day give to her own daughter: *enter the palace.*

Luik tucked the fine gift under his tunic and swung easily down each limb, now empty of children who were busily eating and singing with their parents in the courtyards beyond. He walked briskly up the front steps, taking long strides to compensate for the depth of each tier. It wasn't until he reached the large gold bell at the doorstep that his heart began to race with excitement. He had never been in the royal palace.

He reached with trembling hand for the hammer on the wall and struck the heavy bell in the center. A series of beautiful notes reverberated out of the swaying motion, causing a number of people in the palace square to look on. Luik rested the hammer back in its place and turned to wait. Only moments passed, but they seemed like summers. Ever so slowly, the right side of the two grand doors inlaid with gold and ivory began to open outward. When it was big enough for him to squeeze through, Luik slipped sideways into the darkness, the door quickly closing behind him.

Chapter Four

KING RAGNAR

Luik looked around but saw nothing. No people, no chairs, no stairs. Not even a wall or a floor. He was in complete and utter darkness. Yet strangely he could still see his own body clear as day. *How peculiar*, he thought. He even tried to make shadows on his legs with his hands but none formed. He was totally alone with no idea what to do next. He thought to reach for the door but it, too, was not visible to his sight.

"Hey'a?" *Nothing*. He spoke loudly, but not even an echo returned to him, more like talking to a blanket. *The blanket!* he remembered. He pulled the object from his belt and kneeled to lay it on the floor, but held short. "I found this in the tree outside," hoping someone was listening. "I just wanted to make sure Princess Ciana got it back."

"Well, that is very thoughtful of you, Luik, son of Lair," said a small voice ahead.

Luik jerked up, a bit shocked at the sudden appearance of a tiny man with a quizzical bearded face and a large baggy hat that was made up of multi-colored patches of various and beautiful fabrics. He stood about ten paces ahead with his hands stuffed into the folds of his green hooded cloak. Apart from the blanket and his own body, this little man was the only other thing Luik could see in the entire room.

"How—how did you know my name?" Luik stuttered.

"The question is not *how*, but *why*, my young boralee[10]," he said with a smile. But before Luik could pose another question, the small muse of a man pointed to the cloth in his hand. "What have you there, boralee?" Luik glanced down at the cloth.

"It's Princess Ciana's birth cloth. I think it accidentally slipped off of the balcony into the tree I was sitting in."

"What some consider *accidents*, others have planned for generations." Luik could not respond. He simply extended his hand hoping the small man would take the blanket and show him out of the darkness. He did not feel uncomfortable; in fact, quite a peace seemed to fill the air about him. But rather he wished to return to more familiar grounds, ones that he could *see*.

Still holding the fabric outstretched, Luik asked, "Why can't I see anything in this room?"

The little man replied, "Because you are not *in* a room, boralee. You are in a space of time that reveals the nature of things and how they really appear. This is a place where nothing is hidden but all things are exposed for what they truly are. It also serves as a gate to any room in the entire palace, for those who know how to navigate it." Luik stood still wondering what he meant, feeling as if the man could see right through him.

"This needs to be given to Princess Ciana, sir," Luik bravely suggested, trying to avoid the complicated and stressing the simple.

"Then why don't you give it to her yourself, boralee?"

Suddenly the air about him shifted and he was surrounded by a sea of light standing on a polished marble floor. Around him stood rows of people dressed in dazzling garments of whites and purples, blues and yellows, long flowing gowns and layered tunics. Their faces shown like embers, bearing radiant smiles and glowing eyes, each more beautiful then the next. The walls behind them soared upward into the light beyond, devoid of ending. Straight ahead the people parted, revealing an aisle-way to a raised multi-tiered platform of carved stone surrounded by a stream of running water. Luik looked up to a set of thrones built of gold that sat at the highest point, glimmering in the light descending to their position. There sat the king of Dionia and his bride robed in splendor and majesty just as they appeared on the balcony moments before, now with the elders

---

[10] **Boralee** (*bohr-uh-LEE*): *noun; ancient Dionian name meaning disciple, exact origin not known.*

of the court attending them. Not a person moved, not a whisper was uttered.

"Come here my child," came the voice of the king, distant on his throne. Luik's heart raced like a puppy bounding after a butterfly. It seemed as though he had heard that phrase uttered a thousand times by the king. It was warm and inviting, familiar even. One foot after the other, Luik slowly walked down the aisle and approached the channel of water flowing around the elevated stage. He felt all the eyes in the room on him but he didn't care. He was in the presence of the King of Dionia.

"Why have you come, my son?" the king asked from his throne.

Luik, still holding the blanket, looked up with a grin. "I found Princess Ciana's birth cloth in the top of the tree in the palace square." He extended his arms slightly.

"And do you wish to return it to her?"

"I do, my king."

"Then come to me."

Luik seemed to shudder with the invitation. He took one step forward and then saw the crystal clear water flowing steadily in front of him. He glanced back up to the king.

"Come, my son," gestured the king with his hand and inviting green eyes. Luik stepped forward expecting the water of the shallow pool to wrap around his knees, but, to his amazement, found nothing of the sort. Instead his foot landed firmly on top of the water like walking on a glass window. Stunned for but an instant, he moved his trailing foot onto the miracle below and continued across until he reached the first step of the stone platform on the other side. Like a child he turned back to look at the strange water once more, amazed at its characteristics. *Fane isn't going to believe this*, he thought.

Ascending the stairs to the king's open hand, Luik knelt low as he cleared the final level, bowing his head in reverence. King Ragnar reached down with a hand under his chin.

"Creation bows only for a time until it is asked to stand as Sons," the king said softly, lifting Luik to his feet with just a finger. Luik gazed into the king's eyes. They were truly the most beautiful he had ever seen. Visibly trembling, Luik was not put at ease until King Ragnar placed his hand on his shoulder and pulled him in to the elbow of his arm. He turned Luik to look over at Queen Meera who was holding Ciana wrapped in blankets.

"Why don't you give her the blanket," suggested the king. "She's been waiting for you." Luik glanced at the king and then back at Meera. He slowly approached the baby, not wishing to startle her in any way. He peered past the layers of cotton wraps to a small face. Her eyes were sparkling blue and wide. Her lips were delicate and her cheeks were like red ivory flowers.

He gently laid the birth cloth over her and whispered softly, "I found your blanket Baby Princess. Take good care of it now."

"I know she appreciates it very much," uttered the queen, her beautiful brown eyes flashing beneath long eyelashes, "and so do we."

The king, standing from his throne, reached out for Luik. "We would like you to have this, Luik, as a token of our gratefulness to you." In his hand was a sheathed dagger with a white ivory handle and gold pommel and hilt. The black sheath was simple yet very refined terminating in a golden cap. Luik had never seen anything like it before. He picked it up tenderly and immediately noticed the dagger's weight and balanced feel. It was much more refined than those he used to trim branches and cut rope with in the garden back home.

"C'symia[11]," he said, wide-eyed.

Before Luik could even realize it, the king knelt down and swiftly picked him up into his arms in a full embrace. A flood of emotions surged through Luik's young body, causing him to feel as if he were going to pop like a bubble. Joy tears freely streamed down his cheeks and onto the king's robe. A sense of pure and total love coursed through his spirit as he embraced the king in like manner around his neck, squeezing with all his might. All the people of Dionia had an innate love for their king, as he was the embodiment of the Great Creator's manifest call for leadership among the peoples of the world. And in being so, he was also a perfect example of the Creator's love, servant-hood, and fatherhood, a model to which every other father in Dionia looked.

When the king eventually let go, he kissed Luik on the forehead and blessed him and his house in the name of the Most High. Luik's face glowed.

"Thank you," came the boy's humble whisper, tears drying into his skin.

---

[11] **C'symia** (*sye-MEE-uh*): *First Dionian: intimate and most respectful form of "thank you."*

"May you grow to be the Man of Valor the Great God has called you to be," stated the king. Running his fingers through Luik's hair, he then turned him toward the steps to where the small bearded man stood waiting on the other side of the stream. "From now on you will go with a king's blessing and not a mere man's blessing. Off with you!"

Luik leapt from the platform, bounding down the stairs, across the stream and nearly running full speed right into the dwarf in front of him.

"Ready to go, my young boralee?" questioned the dwarf.

Luik was puzzled. "Why do you call me that, good sir?"

But there was no time for a response. In the time it took to blink his eyes, Luik found himself standing back on the front step of the palace, the bell still fading in its musical ring beside him from when he first entered. It seemed as if no time had passed at all. He suddenly began to wonder if the thing that had taken place was but a dream. He looked around and ran his hands down his shirt. It was then that he felt the dagger tucked securely under his belt.

Chapter Five

THE SEA CAVE

The Sea Cave was a child's dream and the favorite meeting spot of the four friends. Whenever they could find an excuse to escape together for a day, the cave was their preferred hideaway. With Adriel Palace perched far above, steep cliffs descended from the westernmost point of the Ison Peninsula down into the ocean foam below. It was here, shrouded in an avalanche of boulders, that they had discovered a small opening to a room hidden beneath the landslide. Many summers earlier, Fane had dropped a small walking stick down into the hole by accident while walking along the ocean bank. It wasn't until Luik lowered Fane down with a rope that they had realized what a hidden treasure they had found.

Among other things, the asset the four valued most was the Sea Cave's privacy. As far as they knew, no one but them knew about it. And because no one had any reason to journey out along the rough terrain that ran around the base of the peninsula, there was no fear of their precious meeting spot being discovered.

"What took you so long?" yelled an inquisitive voice echoing against the damp rock surfaces far below.

"Hey'a, Norra," Luik shouted back. "I'll be right down!" He stood atop a large gray rock a little ways above the surf, his hair shifting in the

71

salty wind. Grasping a braided rope with both hands, he swung around the lower rocks and down into a gap below. Following a series of memorized hops from point to point, he let the smooth cord slip through his hands before dropping the final short distance to a sandy bottom. He turned and ran through a small corridor of tumbled rock that eventually turned into an arched hallway, cut not by the erosion of the elements, but by a skillful hand. All along the walls were strange markings that none of the children had ever been able to make out. The hallway eventually opened up into a giant room hewn out of the immense stone deposit with a tall domed ceiling.

In the center of the room lay a pool of water glowing with a soft green-blue hue that cast dim, wavering light against the walls, seemingly from the sunlight beyond. The children envisioned the hole opening up to the ocean without, but never took the time to dive and explore the world below the surface.

The small arched hallway was the only door into and out of the large space. There were no ledges cut into the rock walls, or pockmarks in the stone floor. Everything was smooth and untouched save more markings littered about the walls of the room, just as in the hallway. They imagined that at one time the hallway had led right to the ocean beach, but that a rockslide at some earlier time had sealed the entrance. The only time the children had ever found anything in the room was last summer when Anorra found a small leaf near the pool. They knew that something, at least a small animal, had journeyed into their lair, but that was the only time anything out of the ordinary presented itself.

Today three children lounged in the giant cave, attentively waiting for their fourth member to arrive. Hadrian leaned against the furthest wall. Anorra let her legs dangle in the cool water and Fane lay on his back with his legs up the wall to the left.

"So even the slowest animals do find their way home with all the rest after all," Hadrian sparred as Luik walked in the room.

"Aye, if the herd will be patient enough for them," countered Luik. They all smiled. Luik sat down along the pool and splashed some water into his hair.

"So, are you going to tell us what you were up to, Luik?" Anorra tilted her head as she talked. Everyone remained silent waiting for his response.

"I went to see the Great King," he replied slowly, letting his words carry their full weight. No one moved.

"You what?" Hadrian exclaimed finally. Fane's mouth opened wide from his upside-down position.

"Princess Ciana's birth cloth dropped down into the tree that I was watching the ceremony from, and I figured I had to return it to her. So, I went inside the palace to give it back to her."

"*Her?*" asked Anorra. "You met the Princess-child, too?"

"Yup," he chirped.

"Amazing." Hadrian scratched his head.

Fane still lay on his back with his head tilted to see everyone. "What was it like in the palace, Luik? Were there lots of people?"

"Aye," he replied. "All the elders of the court were there dressed in amazing clothes of scarlets, whites and purples draped from their shoulders and waists. There was beautiful light everywhere and music seemed to play without any musicians at all!"

"Did you talk with the King?" Fane said, continuing.

"He blessed me and then he gave me this." Luik reached behind his back and took out the knife, presenting it to his friends. Fane fell over, never taking his eyes from the object. Hadrian sat up slightly and Anorra just beamed, expecting nothing less. "He said it was a present to thank me for returning the Princess-child's blanket."

"Some present!" Fane shouted.

"I've never seen such a beautiful knife," Anorra chimed in. She reached out to touch its smooth white handle. "My father has one that he brings out for carving. He keeps it in a box in his room. We're never allowed to go in there, but—" Her words stopped. She blushed slightly.

Luik jumped in, trying to ease her underlying statement. "Hey'a, I don't know where you all were during the ceremony but did you see the Lion Vrie[12]?"

Fane sat up straight. "You saw a Lion Vrie? Impossible!"

"I saw it," Hadrian said smoothly.

"I didn't think they actually existed!" Anorra said, head tilted, "how can you be sure?"

---

[12] **Lion Vrie** (l'eye-uhn - *VR'EYE*): *First Dionian: noun; most closely related to the word used for a knight or a warrior of nobility.*

"I don't know." Luik tucked the knife back in his tunic. "But I can almost guarantee I saw one. He was riding between the stables in the palace courtyard. I could just barely make him out from my spot in one of the gravel trees."

"I was just behind one of the stables," Hadrian put in, "and I could see him, too."

"Why was he there, do you think?" Fane asked. "The stories say that they only came out during times of danger, like during the First Battle. Do you think there was something wrong?"

Luik waited a moment, thinking hard. "I'm not sure, but I bet my father will know."

The mystery of the appearance of the legend hung in the air like haze on a spring morning. More questions filled their heads: *where had he come from*, and *where did he vanish to? Had others seen him as well? Did the King know?* But the questions were soon long forgotten. Hadrian suddenly broke the silence with a shout that startled them all.

"Hadrian! What's the matter?" Anorra turned as he doubled over sideways on the rock floor. Luik jumped up and ran to his side, Fane also knelt near him. Hadrian squirmed with his arms wrapped around his body, his face contorted and creased. The three other children sat with new emotions, confusion and frustration, never having seen anything like this before. An emotion swept over them: helplessness; a need they could not express. An unseen force had penetrated right into the safety of their sanctuary and brought harm in its wings.

Hadrian stopped moving and then froze with his mouth open as if to yell but no voice came. Small beads of sweat formed on his face. His eyes were wide, fixed on the far wall, looking past his friends. Anorra was the only one who moved. She inched toward him with great courage and placed her hands on his side, concerned for her friend. Luik and Fane both knew that she truly was the daughter of a king. She looked up and began to talk to the Lord of lords.

"Great Father, please help my friend, Hadrian," she inquired with a soft voice. This was all she said, and that was all it took. Hadrian let out a breath so long they wondered how he ever got it in. His body relaxed, and he curled into a ball like a little child, tears streaming down his face. No one moved. And no one spoke. They didn't know what to say. There was a long silence as Hadrian whimpered softly beneath his hands.

"Hadrian," Luik prodded. "What happened?"

Chapter Six

THE AWAKENING

Luik ran down the beaten trail of the final hill that led to his family's cottage. Though many of the kings both ruled and lived in their Great Halls, Luik's father chose to live in a quaint setting a good distance from the Great Hall of Bensotha. Luik's home sat amongst a few alder trees in the middle of a large garden. A stream ran from one edge of the property to the other, over which a number of wooden footbridges had been erected. Flowers colored the edges of every stretch of path, and large boulders had been hewn by hand into sitting places and tables. Where the garden turned into a large planted harvest field that eventually touched the base of rising hills beyond is where Luik found his father.

Lair was bent over with a hoe, gently tilling up a patch of soil.

"Ta na!" Luik yelled as he ran around the last bend before entering the field.

His father stood up and turned toward his son. Luik bounded another ten paces and then leapt into his father's arms with a burst of joy.

"Ta na, it was amazing! Just amazing!" Luik could hardly get the words out of his mouth.

"Calm yourself, Luik," his father said. "Speak now, let's hear it." He released his son and knelt down to level with his bright eyes.

"I met him! I went in and met him! And he kissed my head and he, he—"

"Luik!" Lair exclaimed as he cupped his hand over his son's mouth and began to chuckle. "My son, your thoughts are much faster than your words. For my sake, do please let them catch up. Now, start over, but this time more slowly."

"The king! I met the Great King! And he gave me this." Luik reached into his tunic and pulled out the dagger. His father looked surprised and smiled widely. Luik recounted the whole story of finding the cloth in the tree and of the strangely dressed dwarf, all the way until he was back out in front of the palace again. Lair listened intently and smiled the whole time.

"What a marvelous time you have had, my son."

"I wish you had come, Ta na."

"As do I, but how could I have climbed so high in that gravel tree, Luik? I would have been in the back of the outer court and missed all of the adventure. Plus, I wouldn't have been able to see your baby brother brought into the world."

Luik needed only a moment to realize his father's implication.

"*I have a brother?*" Luik jumped hysterically and laughed. "When was he born? What's his name? Where—"

"Why don't I let your mother tell you all that? Run inside, young Luik." His father turned him and gave a nudge toward the house. Luik didn't need it, though. He was off and running like a cat. He rounded the pathway leading to the cottage and burst through the door.

"Na na!" he yelled.

"Hush, child!" Pia said directly. "Your brother is sleeping." She pointed to the small cradle in the corner of the room that had been his. In a complete contrast of behavior, Luik calmly tiptoed over to the wooden bed and peered in.

"What's his name?" Luik said without diverting his eyes.

"Rourke."

"Rourke," Luik said smoothly as he reached in to touch the little hand. "He is going to be strong."

Pia tilted her head. "Aye, aye, I believe he will be, Luik." She was pleased with his perceptive manner and encouraging way. He was all boy and yet so much a man. *Marvelous*, she thought.

"How do you feel, Na na?" He inquired, looking back at her.

"Just fine," she said, "The birth was easy and full of joy. Your father and I were singing as he was delivered, as we were with you. I will be fully rested by the morning. I suggest you go back out and see your father, Luik. He has been waiting for you all day."

"O but mother, I have so much to tell you!"

"Hush now; there will be time for that. But your father has missed you greatly. Go to him, Luik." She clucked her tongue and gestured toward the door.

Luik touched his new baby brother one more time and then turned. He was by his father's side in another instant.

Lair placed his hoe on the ground and picked his son up. "What more of your day do you have to tell?"

Luik was so enamored by his time with the king and the arrival of his new sibling that all else seemed to be irrelevant. Then, as the sun was setting in the east along the low-lying hills going into Grandath and the twilight sky was cooling, his mind turned to Hadrian and the strange event in the Sea Cave.

"Hadrian," Luik said under his breath.

"*What did you say?*" his father replied. Luik seemed suddenly distant and his demeanor changed drastically. "Luik! What did you just say? Where are your thoughts?"

A tear began to roll down Luik's cheek. His father caught it with a finger and held it up for Luik to see. Luik snapped back.

"Where did that come from, Ta na?" looking at his tear.

"From your heart, Luik."

Suddenly more tears began to flow and his heart was overwhelmed with a sensation he had never known before. He was sobbing and buried his head in his father's neck. Lair knelt down and held his son close.

"What's happening in me?" Luik wept. "Make it stop, Ta na! Please, make it stop!"

"I can't."

Luik pulled away to regard his father in wonder and then with compassion. His father was also crying. Luik suddenly broke open like an earthen vase shattered on the floor.

"We were in the Sea Cave below the palace talking. All of a sudden Hadrian fell over on his side. His mouth was wide open and his eyes were—were frozen on the wall. He was screaming, but—but there was no noise! Nothing! He couldn't move, and then—then Anorra asked the Creator to release him and Hadrian relaxed. I don't know what it was, Ta na! We didn't know what to do!"

Lair stroked his hair calmly and tried comforting him with gentle whispers. Luik sobbed for a few moments more and then, *peace*.

"I wished you would never have to see these days, Luik. But it has been ordained from the beginning, and I am a fool to think you might somehow be spared."

Luik listened then spoke. "Spared? Spared from what?"

Lair thought for a moment. "Hadrian's father, Jadak, was *taken* this morning."

"Taken? What do you mean, Ta na?" The word sent a shudder through his body. "Taken from *what?*"

"Taken from his existence as an immortal man."

"I—I don't understand, Ta na. Do you mean the Creator took him home to the Grand Throne Room?"

"No, Luik." His father paused, realizing that this needed further explanation. *It was time.* "Let's go for a walk, my son. Fetch my staff there against the cottage." Luik stood up and walked slowly to the house and retrieved his father's long oak staff. He smeared the remaining tears out of his swollen eyes and handed the shaft of wood to Lair. "Come," Lair said gently.

They set off across the open field toward the hills in the east. Upon reaching the first summit they walked down the backside and up another taller hill, but this one was wooded with old growth trees. They were quickly swallowed by the dense woods and continued hiking up the hill. Luik held his father's hand the whole way. They continued up higher and higher. Though he had explored most all of the land around his home, Luik did not remember this part of the forest.

When the trees couldn't seem to grow any denser, they suddenly emerged into a clearing, circular in shape with nothing but a grassy floor in the middle. By now the stars were stretching across the clear night sky and the light breeze had subsided. All was still and quiet as they walked closer to the center of the glen. Lair turned to face his son; his sandy-blond hair lay loose down to his shoulders. Like Luik, Lair's gray-blue eyes were piercing. But where Luik's face was already forming manly features that were strong and cut, Lair's was more rounded and easy. Lair stood tall looking down at his son.

"Luik, who made this glen and this wood?" He passed his hand before the trees around them.

Luik hesitated. The question was so simple.

"And who made the stars aloft?" Lair pointed his staff high above his head, yet still gazing at Luik.

"The Creator," Luik answered, as if there were no other answer.

"And who were they created for?"

"For us, Ta na." Luik was smiling now at the simple questions. *Give me another*, he thought.

"And why?"

Luik didn't even think twice before he answered, "For us to enjoy and take delight in the One who made them for us." This was getting fun.

"Aye, my son: for us to have relationship with the Lord Eternal in this *paradise*; to truly know Him intimately, to plunge into the depths of His joy and love and know them without end. A place where we could walk with Him and talk with Him face to face as a man speaks to his friend. To enjoy ages upon ages of this life with the Creator until He one day chooses to have us enter his Great Throne Room."

Luik was clearly enjoying this.

"But what if it were threatened?" Lair paused, letting the reality of his words sink in. "What if the very essence of *why* this world was created was put in jeopardy?"

"What do you mean?" Luik's countenance changed. "Why would such a thing ever happen? What would do such a thing?"

"Not *what*, my son," Lair stared straight into his eyes, "but *who*."

The mere thought of this was too difficult to understand for Luik. "You mean someone would *want* this place to be disturbed, to be changed, or—or—"

"Or *destroyed*?" Lair said, finishing Luik's sentence.

Luik stood in silence. His heart seemed to be pulling away from his body. Thoughts that had never entered his mind were now rushing in like a flood, and his spirit was becoming grieved.

"This is—is not possible, Ta na!" Luik said with defiance. "This could never happen!"

"O but it has already happened, my son."

"What? It has? Where? Not here! No, not here, has it, Ta na?"

"Well, aye, Luik, it has at least begun. But not as great as another world has felt it."

"What *other* world?" The questions were flying now. It seemed as if Luik could see into a whole other realm, but instead of making things out clearly, he could only peer into the vastness of its space and try to grasp for something tangible.

Lair took Luik by the arms and sat him down in the center of the grassy space. Sweeping his oaken staff through the night air far above his head, Lair began to paint a picture, a mystical vision of a brilliant blue and white swirling ball, suspended in midair and semi-translucent to the night sky above. Soon Luik could see it was a world much like their own, much like Dionia. As the world grew bigger in his vision, he could begin to make out details.

"Everything you see, the waters, the hills the forests and meadows, and all living creatures, it was all designed by the Master's voice and was set spinning just to please His will. And in this world you see, the Creator made a beautiful garden." Luik could see a majestic garden full of life and all sorts of living creatures. *That looks like Beneetha*, he thought to himself. His father continued, "And this world was once a part of the Great Kingdom, Athera, just as we are. But something happened. Something caused it to slip away, to slip *out of Athera*."

"What? What happened, Ta na?" Luik gazed into the beauty of the garden. Suddenly he saw two people walking together, a man and woman. They looked happy and content, working in the garden, talking with one another and with the Creator. Then his gaze moved to two large trees, one he clearly recognized. The other was foreign and the fruit looked strange, but more like an apple than anything else. And then there was a serpent sliding amongst them.

"Wait, what's that?" Luik demanded to know. "What's that little serpent in between those two trees?"

"That, my son, is *Morgui*."

"Morgui?" The name sent a chill through his body and his spirit was pricked. "How did he get there? What's he doing? Why don't they see him and tell him to leave?" He watched transfixed as the woman walked toward the serpent. She bent low. He thought for sure she would pick up the thing and throw it out of the garden. But instead she turned an ear to listen. The serpent was saying something. But Luik was more stunned to watch the man just hide behind a bush and watch on, doing nothing.

"Wait, what's happening, Ta na? Why isn't that man doing anything to stop her? Where is she going? Why is she talking to the serpent?" Luik felt a flood of emotions well up in his heart. Before long he could feel hot tears rolling down his cheeks. He watched on, feeling helpless that he could not speak to the woman and angry with the man who merely stood by and watched. The woman reached up to the foreign tree and picked off one of the strange looking fruits.

"No!" Luik cried and reached out his hands. But the woman could not hear him. She bit into the fruit. Luik covered his eyes, but the image was still there in his mind. Then the man came out from behind the tree, seeing that the woman looked no different, and he too ate of the fruit when she offered it to him. And there in the corner of the garden the serpent crawled quietly away. And so too did the image of the brilliant shining ball, as it was now a fading lackluster sphere, until once again Luik peered up into the stars and into the eyes of his father. Both of them had tears on their faces.

"I know that tree, Ta na. It looks like ours. But the other one I have never seen. Why did she eat of it? What happened next?"

"The Most High placed two trees in the middle of their world; one they could eat of freely, the other they could not. He gave the man and woman a command, but with it a choice to obey."

Luik felt a lump in his throat as the youth held back the tears. "And they disobeyed. They chose against His will."

"Aye, Luik, and this one act, this one audacious act of defiance, severed their connection with the Most High and hurtled their world out of His presence and out of the Great Kingdom of Athera."

"So, are they still alive? How did they survive?"

"O they lived, Luik. But their disobedience, by their own actions, brought a curse on every one of their children and even on creation itself, for *all generations*. The two people you saw became mortal beings, and soon after their bodies perished. That world lives on, but we know little more of its current state other than it exists under the curse that was brought on it by that one incident."

"So Morgui succeeded in drawing them away from the presence of the Creator?"

"Aye and what we do know is that they must now live by a set of strict rules and regulations that dictate where and when they may enter His presence. The Most High did not remove Himself from them, but they removed themselves from Him."

Luik sat in stunned silence, attentive now to the loud beating of his own heart within his chest. Lair sat down in front of his son on the grass.

"Son, how much do you know of the First Battle?" Lair said solemnly.

"I know that our world was attacked or threatened and that a group of warriors was formed by the king to defend our world."

"The Lion Vries," Lair said.

"So they are *real?*" Luik's face lit up.

"Well, they once were real. But it has been many ages since they were called upon. And do you know who it was that threatened our great paradise?"

"*Morgui,*" Luik said with defiance.

"Aye. The first of our kind was Ad and Eva. They, too, were charged by the Lord Eternal with the two trees. But unlike what you just saw, they did not believe the lies of the enemy and they drove Morgui out of the garden. Morgui did not concede defeat, as he was furious that his power and intention were thwarted. Instead of the cunning serpent you saw, he returned with a war host to combat the Sons of Man and strike them down in battle."

Luik sat with eyes wide, hanging on every word.

"The king of that age summoned together the most valiant men and charged them to defend our world's freedom. The battles that ensued were fierce and violent. The bodies of our warriors were only afflicted when they gave way to the emotional attacks that accompanied the enemy horde: *fear, anger, rage, pride, bitterness, and revenge.* It was then—and only then—that their bodies failed them and they fell in battle, many never to be seen again. Only a few ever came home who sank to such a state."

Luik tried his best to understand, though he found much of it difficult as his father was using many foreign words that he had never heard before: fear, pride… Luik understood the essence of what Lair was communicating more than anything else.

"What do you mean, *never seen again?*" Luik questioned. "They went to the Great Throne Room?"

"We don't know, Luik. They were not received by the Lord of Hosts that we know of. It was not a calling home at all. It was more of a *falling* into another state of being, devoid of the presence of the Creator." Lair struggled for the words. "It was *death*."

Luik held his breath. This was a word he had certainly never heard. He did not understand. How could they be separated from the presence of the Most High? His presence was everywhere, all the time! Or so he was raised to believe.

"How could they be," Luik hesitated, "removed from His presence?"

"Just like the first world you saw. They chose to believe the lies of Morgui, to think the way *he* wanted them to and not the way the Creator designed them to. So in choosing this way, they in fact grieved His Spirit and walked out from under the governing grace of the Almighty which sustained their immortal lives."

"But why didn't the rest of our kind and each passing generation become affected by these few men *falling*, like in the other world?"

"That is a good question, Luik." He seemed proud that his adolescent son was following him still, despite the massive amount of new information being given into such a young life. It was truly the right time. *And better from me*, he thought, *than from someone else, including...* Lair didn't let his thoughts go any further.

"*The first of creation decides for all of creation*. Ad and Eva chose Life and the result affected the rest of creation, setting a precedent for us all to follow, and so far we have. You are living in the Creator's blessing because they chose wisely and because His grace keeps us from harm. But that doesn't mean you can *stay* in His blessing. That is something every man and woman has to choose for themselves. And so far there has been little to distract us or lead us astray. We are a world devoid of *temptation*. In the other world, their poor decision cursed *all* life for the remaining generations, and they suffer for it. Their only hope is to resist the evil force of Morgui and choose *out* of it and back into the will of the Great Father. But that choice, I believe, is nearly impossible to make."

"So," Luik thought for a moment, "is that why Jadak was *taken* this morning? Did he believe a lie? Did he choose out of the will of the Great father?"

"Aye."

"But, then that means that Morgui has—has—"

"Returned," Lair's voice was soft and his eyes piercing.

"Is Hadrian's father *dead?*"

"That I do not know. I just received word that there is a meeting of the Gvindollion[13] to answer this very question."

"Why is there a question, Ta na? He was *taken*. He's gone, right?"

"Well, not exactly. There have been reports of this happening more recently. The strange thing is that these people have been *seen again*."

"Really? That's great!" Luik was hopeful.

"No, my son, it's not. For they barely resemble their former states, and they do not respond to anyone who has formerly known them. The rest of their appearance and behavior you do not need to be troubled with right now. I have given you enough."

"So, does this mean then that Jadak has been seen already? But he was only taken this morning!"

Lair paused and looked into Luik's pure eyes, knowing his life would never be the same. He wished this conversation had never happened. But he also knew that his son's very survival was at stake. Morgui was assailing their perfect world in a way more terrible and more grotesque than anyone of them could have ever imagined. Lair sensed the terror and the unknown.

"Luik, there are great mysteries that surround you, a tapestry of secrets woven around your life that you do not know and may never know, I hope. They serve to protect the innocence of the meek, the ignorance of the humble, and the life of the righteous. But I sense that you walk forthwith toward an impending destiny that causes the cords, which were bound to protect you, now to come undone.

"Aye, Luik, Jadak Son of Jadain has been seen this afternoon," Lair closed his eyes. "But he is not the man I once knew."

---

[13] **Gvindollion** (*GIH-ven-DOLLY-on*): *noun; an ancient Dionian word literally translated, "The Circle of Seven"; council gathering of Dionia's Seven Kings.*

PART TWO

Chapter Seven

GVINDOLLION

"And what news have we from the north?" said King Ragnar of Dionia. All eyes in the circle moved to look at King Thorn who bore the torc and crown of Ligeon. Today he wore a red linen shirt that nearly matched his fiery hair and loosely fitting woven breecs. He stood slowly to address the council. He seemed to be *more* than just a Dionian king.

"The people of Ligeon send greetings to the king of Dionia and enjoy a peaceful and rewarding existence as of late." Ragnar was pleased but apprehensive. "But the woes of the other kingdoms are not without company, for we too, in the lands of the north, are not beyond the reach of this growing plight." There seemed to be an unspoken groan within the air. The hope that maybe one of the seven kingdoms lay unscathed was quenched as King Thorn echoed the six who had gone before him.

"More and more of our animals have turned on man, fearful and resistant to our calls, some even becoming aggressive. A few children have been attacked and the assailing beasts destroyed. Our crops are producing less fruit than normal and there is a noticeable lack in the soil's life."

Ragnar felt disturbed as all of his kingdoms were experiencing the same trials. Only one question remained for the king of Ligeon.

"And of the *taken*," Ragnar said, "have any of your people been added to their ranks?"

King Thorn's face spoke long before his sorrowful words could be uttered, "Aye, your majesty, three in this summer and two in the one before, making our count five."

Ragnar was solemn. He was lost in thought when Thorn spoke again.

"But there *is* something worse." The whole of the audience could not imagine so. What was known as *The Gvindollion, or The Circle of Seven* was seated in marble carved thrones, each with the animal of their region carved on the head posts and the armrests. The circular room had a low domed ceiling with a window at the apex. Only two thick wooden doors on opposite sides of the room provided entry: one for the guests and one reserved only for King Ragnar and his attendants. Standing directly behind in the shadow of each throne were the sons of each king, summoned intentionally to be present at this meeting. They listened motionless, standing behind their fathers, stunned by the proceedings and the reports. Torches on the walls provided the only light besides the window above, and their gentle flicker was all that could be heard in the waiting silence of Thorn's ominous statement.

Luik stood behind his father with a perfect view of both King Ragnar and King Thorn between the seats. He had never seen Anorra's father without a smile and this alone caused great discomfort to him. Thorn, like most of the other kings, was dressed in the colors heralding his region as a flowing linen tunic brought close to his waist by a belt and left hanging past his knees. But despite all the despairing reports of the kings, Luik was confident being in the presence of King Ragnar, now for the *second* time.

"Do go on, dear Thorn," Ragnar prompted fatherly.

"My people have informed me of reports that many families have stopped feeling the presence of the Most High in their homes. It would appear His Spirit has left them." Initially no one could quite grasp the severity of the circumstance except Ragnar, but within moments it was becoming clear to all.

"Or perhaps *we* are leaving *Him*," Ragnar stated calmly. The torches continued to flicker. "There is even more that you don't know. Creation is much more sensitive than the Sons of Man to the moving of the supernatural as it is subject to us as superior beings. What we choose to do affects all life."

Suddenly the back door of the room opened and in stepped a small figure. Luik strained around his father's chair to get a better view. The door closed and as he walked into the middle of the circle, Luik could see that it was the dwarf from his first trip to the palace. He wore the same billowy patch-work hat and this time a creamy brown cloak. In his right hand he carried what Luik could most closely associate with a tree branch. The king spoke again.

"This is a fig tree branch taken from my personal garden yesterday morning."

The king let his words sit heavy upon each man's heart as they observed the branch in a state that they had never seen. The few remaining leaves were yellowed and dry, crinkled and turned inward. The whole of the wooden branch was twisted as if trying to turn back in on itself, but most notable was the fruit. Instead of plump, succulent figs, there were only two or three discolored, wrinkled sacs, one of which leaked a brown pus giving off a strong odor of rot and decay.

The dwarf placed the branch on the ground as all the kings regarded it with awe. He placed his hands over it and began to mumble beneath his breath. Luik could not hear what he was saying. Suddenly the branch began to move. The knotted kinks and twists slowly started to straighten and the places where leaves once held on were budding once again with new green wisps turning into leaves. The most amazing of all was the figs; their repulsive state was instantly transformed into the brilliant figs that all the kings were used to.

The dwarf picked up the branch and turned toward King Ragnar, to which the king gestured with his hand the sign of thanks. The little man passed by his throne, bowing slightly, and headed back toward the opening door. In stepped another hooded figure holding the door. Just before the dwarf exited, he glanced back looking directly at Luik. Luik was stunned. The dwarf smiled and then was lost through the passageway. The other hooded figure holding the door was not much taller than the dwarf. He, too, turned and regarded Luik, but this time Luik was even more at a loss. Under the cloak's hood was framed a face Luik knew all too well.

It was Fane. Luik's eyes went wide.

What are you doing here? He tried to mouth so as not to speak aloud. Fane shrugged his shoulders, with his trademark lippy grin and raised eyebrows, and in an instant he was gone behind the closing door. The world Luik knew had changed overnight and now it seemed, so too was that of his friend. *At least Norra and Hadrian are not here!* he thought.

"Noble Kings of Dionia," Ragnar brought back their roaming thoughts, "it is clear that our world is changing in a manner not congruent with the will of the Creator. Something, or rather *someone*, is pushing us away from the sustaining life force of the Most High. In reality, our great world is slowly being pulled further and further away from the Great Celestial Kingdom of Athera, and sliding from His influence. Its only cause, I believe, is the will of our race, *the will of Men*. Something is deceiving them to consciously choose outside of His governing power for their lives and to trust their own abilities and their own wisdom. They are being seduced, they are being deceived, and when they are convinced, they are being *taken*.

"I believe that this force could be none other than the working of Morgui," the king stated clearly. "It is he and he alone who would hold such contempt for the Sons of Man and for the God who removed him from his position."

"But his armies were defeated in the First Battle," said King Purgos, Lord of Tontha, the oldest of the seven, "I know; I was there."

King Purgos was known as one of the longest living elders of the world of Dionia, having never been taken by the Creator to the Great Throne Room and being allowed to live out his days as a king of the region of Tontha.

"Defeated, aye," Ragnar countered, "but not destroyed." All eyes were attentive to Ragnar's radiant face as he stood grandly and began to walk in the circle. "We fought valiantly with the strength of the Great King behind us, and we thought the will of Man was incorruptible, choosing to love and obey the Most High without thought to the contrary. I believe that Morgui realized the Sons of Man were resolute in their determination to walk in the ways of the Creator.

"Morgui saw his imminent defeat in the battle, but not in the *war*. His retreat, though an obvious victory for our world, merely signaled the eventual return of a foe now enraged by humiliation at his inability to accomplish with our race that which he has done to others."

"As with the race of the Descendants of Adam," spoke King Naronel, Lord of Trennesol.

"And with the Fallen Lythlae of Athera," spoke another of the kings, though Luik could not see who.

"Aye," King Ragnar confirmed. "Whereas those became fallen races, we still represent a goal to be conquered for him, not yet removed from our immortality in Athera. At the birth of our world Morgui's tempting failed, at least against those who set precedent for all generations to come, Ad and Eva. But Morgui is cunning and he has been at work against the Kingdom of Light for ages upon countless ages. His patience is surpassed by few. It is our own folly to think that he would not return before he has accomplished what is in his wicked heart: *to lead our world out of the manifest presence of the Most High and into eternal separation.*"

Ragnar's words went deep. Luik was trying his best to follow. He did not understand everything, but he did know one thing: *his world was in trouble.*

One of the kings, Lord of The Islands of Somahguard, spoke. "So with the *taken*, I have heard there are reports of them being seen *again*."

"Aye," King Lair said, "I have experienced this myself." Luik could not see his father's face, but he knew it was his voice.

"Do go on," King Ragnar gestured with his hand. Lair stood.

"Yesterday morning a messenger was sent to our home to inform me that Jadak, son of Jadain, had been *taken*. I was grieved at the news, hoping it was merely a rumor. But that hopeful thought was quickly denied me. A few hours later a stranger crossed my fields and attempted to enter our home without welcome. I engaged the stranger at the door after seeing him from a distance. He did not notice me until my hand was on him. He quickly spun on me and regarded me directly in the face."

"And it was Jadak?" inquired one of the kings.

"Aye, at least he was a *form* of Jadak. I didn't recognize him at first." Lair was clearly hesitant. Ragnar urged him on. "I was shocked at the being's appearance," he spoke slowly. "The face was contorted and gray. His countenance was sullen and dismal, as if there were no life at all in him. His eyes were dark, not in color, but in presence. The remaining clothes on him were torn and his body was bruised from some sort of beating or blows. His hair was patchy and a strong odor permeated the air about him. He was truly repulsive. In fact there was no resemblance to

Jadak's former state that would have led me to believe it was him, save the ring on his finger."

"The ring of Bensotha," Ragnar said.

"Aye, and etched on it, his family name. Suddenly his body began to shake. He let out a deafening cry, almost like two voices in his throat, and then he vanished. He simply was no more."

All at once the kings were aware of a gentle, low whimper. Someone was crying. King Ragnar sat up and walked to Lair's throne, peering softly around the back to the youth kneeling down. Luik's emotions had welled up once more at the thought of Hadrian's pain in the Sea Cave and of his lost father.

"Easy, my son," came the sweet, calming voice of King Ragnar. "Everything is all right." He knelt down and touched Luik on the shoulder. Instantly Luik's sadness left him, and he looked up into the eyes of the king, the tears stopping. "It is compassion like yours that will save us all," the king said; it seemed as if he knew all that had transpired. After a moment he got back up and was seated on his carved lion head throne.

"After much thought I have come to a course of action. You all know that I have summoned your unwed sons of age to this council meeting." Upon hearing this every son listened attentively with bated breath. The king continued. "I would ask that they would now step into the middle of our great council circle."

There was a moment's hesitation, but none of them were in the mind to question the king's orders. All of the sons present, numbering eighteen in all, stepped into the circle from behind their fathers. All of them were young as was Luik. They stood brave and pure, a strong innocence permeating their presence.

The king raised a hand and the door behind him swung open once more. *Who is watching for his hand? How can they see him?* Out walked the dwarf again and behind him, a huge brute of a man clad in a black tunic with black metal covers trimmed with gold over his forearms and a gold-scaled belt around his waist. A gold torc wrapped around his neck, terminating in lion's heads. A magnificent sword hung at his side, and he had some sort of strange clothing on his feet. His baldhead and deep black skin accented blue eyes and a strong jaw. Luik had never seen such a vibrant-looking figure and nearly missed what the king was saying next.

"Young men of Dionia, I thank you for coming to these proceedings. As you have heard, our world and its very existence within Athera are being threatened like never before. Because of your royal birth, you have been chosen to help defend our world and help hold together the fabric of our way of life as representatives of our leadership." Luik swallowed hard.

"On behalf of all our peoples and of the kings you know as fathers, I would ask of you to decide now whether or not you would serve us with your lives, to devote yourselves to this cause of freedom, to endure the hardships of sacrifice and whatever training that would be required of you. It is not an easy task that lay before you, and I regret that I cannot elucidate any further as to the details of your next steps. Your decision must be made, not out of your perceived ability of being able to *do* or *not do* a task, but rather out of your heart to serve, and this, *blindly*. For it is not your abilities that will preserve you, but rather your determined convictions and strength from the Most High." The king paused and regarded them thoughtfully. The Gvindollion merely watched on, each man observing his own son and waiting for his decision.

"If there are any of you standing here who does not wish to follow this path being offered you, I would ask that you please remove yourself from the circle and exit through that far door." The king pointed across the room to the door through which they had all first come.

No one moved.

The king waited a few moments longer.

Still, no one moved.

"Very well," the king's voice was raised and strong. "Your resolve speaks loudly, and I salute your bravery, young men of Dionia!"

At this all the kings rose to their feet and shouted, "Varos! Great is the name of the Most High God!" This was followed by many shouts and cheers as each king beat his chest or that of the many sons standing before them.

"Let us beseech the Great God for His guiding hand to be upon our sons," Ragnar said. The Gvindollion linked hands forming a large circle around the young men and then cried out in one loud voice, each praying heavenward to the Lord of lords, asking for His blessing. This went on for a long time, it seemed. As their voices grew, Luik could sense a sudden increase of the Spirit's presence in the room and in his own life.

He felt amazingly renewed and refreshed, not even considering himself to be spent in any way. His body was warm and peaceful. He liked this.

The strange dark man was still standing in the corner with the dwarf, both watching all. When the kings finally finished praying, King Ragnar clapped his hands and the man and the dwarf came to his side.

"This," Ragnar stated, "is Gorn. He is your teacher in all things from this moment on until he sees fit to release you." Gorn gave a simple nod.

"And this," Ragnar gestured toward the dwarf, "is Li-Saide of Grandath. He will be your secret guide and unseen ally." *Grandath*. Luik had never been there nor had he met anyone from there. The origin of this man only added to the mystery in his mind.

The door opened once more, and in came Fane carrying a large wooden box, obviously heavy as he walked leaning to counter its weight. Li-Saide opened the vessel and began passing torcs to Gorn one at a time. With each one he received, King Ragnar called out one of the boys' names, and Gorn placed the torc around the neck of each when he stepped forward. Luik could see each torc was handmade for the individual; and Li-Saide, Gorn, and King Ragnar seemed to know what boy belonged to which torc without even looking. The torcs were all of silver and terminated with the heads of different animals, birds, or sea creatures.

Luik heard his name called and walked forward without thinking. He looked at the king and then stared up into the face of Gorn, shocked at how large and wide he was now that he was just inches from him. The large man did not smile, but reached behind Luik's head and fed the open metal around his neck. It felt loose but he knew one day he'd fill it out nicely. Luik turned silently and resumed his place in the middle. When all of them had received their torcs, the king raised his hands and lifted his voice.

"I now present to you the Warrior Sons of the Dionian Kings!" The kings around them seemed to swirl as they raised their voices in shouts and clapped their hands, circling the boys.

In a rush of movement, the young men were quickly escorted out the door and back into the open terraced hallway that looked down onto one of the many palatial gardens. The door closed with their fathers still inside for the remainder of the meeting. Each young man began fondling the torc around his neck. Some took theirs off and examined the beautiful workmanship. They were all far too young to own such pieces as these in any normal circumstance, so they had much to delight over with their new gifts. Luik touched the ends beneath his chin and wondered what animal he had been given. He was about to take it off when his friend, Jrio, from the north in Trennesol, came and leaned by him on the railing. It had been a long time since he last saw Jrio. His dark hair and small eyes reminded him of the wood ferrets that lived in the alder trees beside his house. Luik cast him a smile but said nothing.

"Now what?" Jrio said returning Luik's grin.

Chapter Eight

THE WATERFALL

"We'll stop here for the day," Gorn said from up in front, his voice loud and confident. All eighteen boys found patches of grass to lie down on enjoying the few remaining hours of light. The road they had started upon nearly six days ago had taken them south out of Casterness, along the south coast of Bensotha and into the lower woods of Grandath. It was in these dense, old woods, dripping with history and ages of wisdom that they made their evening's camp. It was also the farthest Luik had ever been from home, as would every step of the days to come.

The Grandath forest was vast and expansive, taking up almost the entire center of Dionia. The section of path where they rested this night had a few lush patches of grass and intersected a wide stream of fast flowing water. A few rays of the remaining twilight found their passage through holes in the leaved canopy. The smell of moist bark and leaves hung softly in the air.

The boys sat in small groups, each speaking quietly. There were the three big brothers from Tontha who intermingled with the sons of King Thorn, the sons of Daunt from the Plains of Jerovah, and the four sons from the Somahguard Islands. Luik sat with Jrio, one of the four sons of King Naronel of Trennesol. And then there was Gorn who lay near a large oak tree by himself eating an apple. He still wore his black tunic and the metal on his arms as before. He didn't talk to anyone. Luik still wondered at this marvelous man who was now leading them on a quest they all knew nothing about.

"Where do you think he's from?" Jrio asked Luik.

"I have no idea," Luik answered. "I have never heard his name."

"Me neither." Jrio paused. "Where do you think he's taking us, Luik?"

"I have no idea."

Jrio listened to the murmur of the other boys. Then he leaned in close to Luik so as not to be overheard. "Do you think he's a *Lion Vrie*?" Luik tossed him a sideways glance with a slight grin.

"*I have no idea,*" he said with a slight laugh, repeating himself.

"Well, what *do* you have an idea about?" Jrio nudged him in the shoulder and they both laughed.

"I do have an idea that I'm hungry!" Luik grinned wide.

Suddenly, as if responding to Luik's comment, though he was sure Gorn couldn't have heard him so far away, the black man stood tall holding the core of his apple.

"My young boralees, do you see the single apple hanging from that tree over the stream at the top of the waterfall?" All eyes immediately darted to the foot bridge and the rushing waters, then up the current to a large waterfall and there, dangling from a wide-arching branch over the head waters was a lone red apple. "The first to fetch that apple will gain this gold arm band."

Hunger, incentive, and a challenge are all it takes to make any group of boys turn from a slouching pile of rocks into a torrent of young lions. A goal, a means, and a reward; this stirred something new in all of them. Luik felt the rush of his blood. He liked it.

"*Biea-Varos!*" Gorn said stepping out of the way. The boys tore into the soft earth beneath their feet and made fast for the stream, each vying for position. They all plunged into the deep waters, some by jumping from the rocks, others by diving from the high arching footbridge. Water splashed up high like a handful of pebbles thrown sporadically into a pond. Not one of them thought to remove their breecs or linen shirts.

The cool waters felt as refreshing to Luik as it did to all the other boys. But they savored it just momentarily. Luik opened his eyes underwater, seeing everything perfectly clear, including the countless bubbles swirling about him. The sunlight bounced off of brilliantly colored stones below, and fish were darting in all directions, startled from the violent intrusion into their peaceful world.

A flurry of arms and legs beat at the water, each boy swimming against the current and headed for the waterfall. Luik swam hard as well, kicking for all he was worth. He needed only a few breaths to cover the short distance, his body fit for the task. He sensed he was pulling ahead just a bit and took a glance underwater to his right. Jrio was parallel with him. And on his left, Quoin was just a stroke behind. No one was in front of him.

Within a few more moments they reached the waterfall with a second wave of boys right on their heels. Luik grabbed a wet ledge firmly and pulled himself out of the water. Jrio popped up next to him, as did Quoin. Jrio smiled as water poured onto his head. Quoin reached for another handhold, but it was too slippery, and he fell backwards. Luik threw his hand out and caught him by the wrist, Quoin halfway in the pool below.

"Hey'a! Thanks, Lu!" said Quoin pulling himself up with his free arm. Luik cast him a quick grin and then turned to the cascading, rippling wall before him. The small incident cost him the lead as Jrio took advantage of the fall and made it halfway to the top of the falls. Luik picked another ledge and then a place for his right foot, pressing hard against the weight of the pounding water, trying to not swallow volumes of it. He made quick work of the slippery outcroppings and caught up to Jrio a few moments later, tapping him on the heel with his hand. But Jrio didn't flinch. He pumped himself up over the headwaters and onto his belly in the shallow summit. Luik and then Quoin followed close behind.

The apple hung a small distance ahead, dangling from a low-lying tree branch above the stream. All three were running along the slate shelf now, water splashing high into the air. Jrio and Luik had always been equals in games of sport, so Luik was not about to let Jrio go uncontested. He dug in hard and reached for every stride. The apple was getting closer. Seeing that he could not keep up with Luik and Jrio, Quoin glanced behind himself only to see five or six more of his friends mount the shelf.

"That apple is mine!" Jrio yelled above the roar of the water, pumping his legs hard.

"Don't waste your breath!" Luik yelled back, ignoring his own words. They were both two strides away, Jrio even reaching for the apple with outstretched arm, when a small hand appeared from the leaves above and plucked the red fruit right from the branch. Both boys watched, bewildered, at the fruit being snatched right from in front of them. Luik stopped and regarded the upper branches as Jrio jumped up, grasping for the limb and shaking it in bitter defeat. But it was too late; the tree-climbing boy and his prize were already bounding back down the bank toward Gorn.

"No!" Jrio yelled. *"That was my apple!"*

Luik laughed, eventually plopping down in the water.

"Hey'a, that's not funny! He—he *stole* it from me!"

Luik just continued to laugh. "What a good race!"

The other boys, who had seen Fyfler, the smallest of their crew, snatch the apple up, all gathered where Luik was sitting and began to laugh as well. They splashed water at each other and wrestled for a time. Jrio just stood, hands on his hips. Then a loud, short whistle rang through the trees and bounced off the rocks. It was Gorn.

"Let's go!" they cried, and ran ashore and back down to the stand of trees and grass. Fyfler stood by Gorn, dwarfed by his imposing and massive physique. They all formed a circle as Gorn wordlessly handed the gold armband to Fyfler in exchange for the apple. Everyone applauded Fyfler with claps, whoops, and then laughs as the young boy realized his arm was far too small for the armband that slid right down to his fist.

"That's all right," Gorn said, leaning close, "one day your arm will make a fine dwelling for your prize. Until then, we must work on building that dwelling." Everyone cheered and then went off to their respective conversations as before.

Luik sat beneath a tree and Jrio followed, but this time a little ways off.

"Hey'a, what's over there with you?" Luik called. Jrio did not reply. *That's unusual*, Luik thought.

"Hey'a, boralees," came a strong voice. Gorn approached and sat between the two friends. It was the first time he had spoken to them personally. "What plagues you, young Jrio, son of Trionth?" Jrio turned. *Plagues?* He didn't recognize the word.

"What do you mean, Teacher?"

"What does your heart want to say that you feel you cannot express and your eyes betray so easily?" Gorn said soothingly.

Jrio hesitated. "He—he *stole* my apple. He stole *my* apple," Jrio's face took on a strange look. Luik winced as he listened. "*I was almost there. I had earned it. And he—he tricked—Fyfler tricked me!*"

"He did, did he?" Gorn said now hard in his tone.

"*Aye!*" Jrio said, making fists. "*And I'm so, so—*"

"Angry?"

"*Aye. Angry!*" Jrio stated loudly. He didn't even know what it meant. *Angry*. He felt a tight knot in his stomach and a lump in his throat. Blood was filing his face. "*But I don't want to feel this way. I don't like this at all!*" His brow was wrinkled. Suddenly, at Gorn's touch, a new emotion went through him. He felt ashamed, convicted. He repeated himself, over and over, "I don't want to feel like this. I don't want this feeling!" Tears began to stream down his bright red face. "*I don't want to feel like this. I don't want to feel like this!*" He pulled his legs up close to him, now sobbing.

Gorn spoke softly. Luik didn't think Jrio could possibly hear him. "*Pride* has emerged, *and pride must die.*" Gorn's face became stern, as if it wasn't stern enough already. "Do you want this to end, Jrio? Do you want *it* to leave?"

"*Aye!*" he cried out through his pain and tears. "*I want it to leave!*"

"It is not Fyfler who was wrong, is it?"

Jrio wept quietly now, considering. "No," he whimpered.

"Fyfler was just quicker and smarter. Instead of being pleased for your brother's success, you became *jealous and bitter.*" Gorn was right up in Jrio's hidden face. "*It is you who is wrong, isn't it?*"

There was a pause. With a heavy sigh, came the words, "*Aye. I am wrong.*"

With that the weight on Jrio lifted. Instantly he lifted his head, his face resolved. Jrio relaxed once more and Gorn pulled out the red apple, handing it to him. Peace reappeared and the air was clear once more.

"You see, young boralee, it was never about the apple," Gorn said. "And it was never about the armband. It was about *your character.*" Jrio examined the fruit and then looked into Gorn's eyes.

"I don't ever want to feel like that again."

"Ha!" Gorn beat his chest with his fist. "Jrio, son of Trionth, today you have learned two valuable lessons far in advance of your peers!"

"And what lessons are those, Teacher?"

"That there is more to a man that can die than just his body; that there is more that can kill a man than just his outward enemies."

Chapter Nine

THE WOODS OF GRANDATH

The lower stretches of the Grandath forest were rumored to be vast and seemingly unending, but Luik had no idea how grand they really were, until now. Three more days and nights they spent trekking through the unyielding shadows of enormous trees that reached right to the sky. And the sky was something you could see none of in this place. Only a dim, muted form of light was given entrance to this world of the trees. The trunks of each tree would have taken at least twenty men to hold hands around. The deeper they voyaged into the forest, the larger the trees grew; and not only the trees, but the leaves as well. Even with the boys being so far below the first sets of branches that soared above their heads, Luik could still see that individual leaves at *that* height looked the same in size and detail as leaves on branches of shorter trees that he could reach out and touch the branches of. They were massive, to say the least.

"Look what I found!" came the lofty voice of Fyfler. His skin was dark and his hair was a tightly knit tuft that hugged close to his scalp.

Everyone turned to see one of the giant leaves waving in his hand. Fyfler swung it over his head, nearly twice the size of his bare-chested torso. The boys all gathered to look at the monstrous foliage. Gorn also drew near, diverted for the first time of the day from his unrelenting pace through the woods.

"Where did you find that?" Gorn said, all the boys quieting.

"Over there," Fyfler pointed, "to the left of the path."

Gorn looked to the place Fyfler indicated, and then touched the edge of the giant leaf gingerly. The rim was dry and becoming brittle.

"Show me," Gorn said.

Fyfler turned and walked over to the place he had found the leaf. Gorn looked down but saw nothing, probing the grassy carpet with his foot. Gorn swung back, addressing the onlooking boys quickly.

"On we go!" he yelled.

The small pack of boralees turned as Gorn strode quickly by and resumed his pace once more. Fyfler held on to the leaf for a time and then eventually laid it back down to the side of the path. The boys spoke quietly to one another as they walked, the only activity they had time for since leaving Adriel, now ten days ago. But they found it enjoyable as they all grew more acquainted with one another, something of a necessity, as each knew of the others mostly in name and region, but not in person.

"What was that all about?" Quoin asked as he joined up with Jrio and Luik.

"I'm not sure," Jrio said, brushing his dark hair from his face.

"Somehow I don't think we'll find out right away either," Luik added with a smile and a nod in Gorn's direction.

"So how do you think our mothers took the news of us not coming back home with our fathers?" Quoin asked. They all smiled and laughed a little bit. Luik spread his arms and placed them on his friend's shoulders, offering a suggestion.

"Well, they probably know a little more about our journey than we do, I bet!" They laughed some more, all nodding. They had long ago exhausted the conversations about where they were headed, concluding that it had something to do with helping their fathers manage the strange occurrences that had taken place in the recent past and, as the king said, *defend* the kingdom of Dionia.

"So, any more thoughts about our teacher?" Jrio asked. They all looked ahead to Gorn, walking strongly. A strange bird, or so they thought, called in the distance. No one added anything more than what had already been said—nothing.

"Maybe the brothers from Tontha know something," Quoin tried helping.

Boran, Brax, and Benigan were the only sons of King Purgos, lord of Tontha to the north. Like Gorn, they were muscular and massive for such young ages, the oldest not more than ten and four summers old. They always stayed together and didn't talk to anyone else, tending to be much more reserved in their expression and dialog, similar to the vast mountain ranges that hallmarked their region. They each wore dark colored linen breecs and loose sleeveless shirts, their silver torcs the only other notable item. Jrio, the most flamboyant, ran ahead and spoke with them, Luik and Quoin unable to hear. A few moments later he slowed, allowing the three Tonthan brothers to move on and Luik and Quoin to catch up.

"Nothing," Jiro said.

"Nothing?" Quoin asked. "Well, what did they say?"

"*Nothing*," Jrio said again with a smile.

Luik found it amusing. "They sure are quiet, aren't they?"

"Aye, in a friendly, comforting sort of way," added Jrio.

"Maybe they don't *like* the woods," Quoin chuckled. "With all those mountains and sky in Tontha, they probably have never seen trees this big!" The others grinned, too.

"Well, I'll be happy when we're out of here, too, Quoin," Luik added, conceding a bit of the Tontha brothers' uneasiness.

They walked on for a few more moments in silence. Quoin spotted another enormous leaf on the ground to the right of the trail. The other two saw it as well. They wondered if Gorn had seen it. They walked on.

"Did you hear that?" Jrio popped his head up and looked to Luik.

"Hear what?" he replied. Luik had heard many strange noises since entering the woods of Grandath especially during the past few nights. There were bird and animal calls he couldn't place. He even saw movements out of the corner of his eye of strangely shaped creatures he couldn't identify. His father, as did all the kings, knew of every creature and living being in Dionia by name and type, build and function. It was a requirement of having dominion and stewardship of the world as Sons of Ad. And Luik knew he had much to learn.

"It was like a whisper in the trees," Jrio spoke while looking around above his head.

"No, I didn't hear anything, Jrio, but I know there's plenty to hear in these woods." They continued walking. "So what do your brothers think of Gorn?" Luik asked. Jrio's three brothers, Najrion, Naron, and Rab, walked together as a group near the back of the line. The Sons and Daughters of Trennesol were all known for their skill of handling and fashioning boats and vessels pulled through the water by sails and kites. The island of Sih-Nevin and the Sely Peninsula channeled easterly winds racing along Trennesol's sea coast into an almost continual breeze suitable for sailing the duration of each summer. Jrio and his brothers, all sons of Naronel, were among the greatest of their peers, and had never lost a race in five summers.

Jrio turned and regarded his brothers momentarily. "They think Gorn is from Somahguard, a descendant of King Felle. They say he looks much like the islanders in complexion, though he is much too large of a man to be related as close kin."

"And his clothes are different, too," Quoin put in.

"The four sons of Nenrick have never heard his name mentioned at their father's table at Ki-Dorne," Luik added. "I asked them last night." Just then Thero of Ligeon caught up with the three.

"Hey'a friends," Thero said. His blue eyes glimmered much like his younger sister's, Anorra. But his face was larger and much stronger. Thero and Luik enjoyed each other's company greatly whenever they had time for it. "What have you?" They walked on, passing another leaf on the side of the trail.

"Gorn," Jrio gestured. "We still can't figure out where he's from."

Thero thought for a moment. "He's not from anywhere around here," he said.

"What?" the rest said.

Thero went on. "My brothers and I think he's from somewhere else in Athera. We don't think he was born on Dionia. We think the Creator placed Him here from somewhere else."

Luik nodded with approval. "Interesting idea."

"Wow," Quoin let out with a long breath.

"Thad thinks he was sent here just for these times in order to help Dionia defeat Morgui. He *must* be a warrior! Why else would he have that sword on his belt and those metal guards on his arms?"

"I never thought about that," Quoin stated. "Do you think he's a *Lion Vrie?*"

"That's what I said!" Jrio exclaimed, suddenly aware that everyone else heard him and were looking on. He noted the surprise at his own outburst and hunched over, repeating himself much more quietly. "That's what I said, to Luik."

"Well, that would explain the sword, but those were just stories, buds," Thero said. "You know that." They all nodded in agreement.

"Well, I do know one thing," Luik summed it up, "we've been walking through these woods for a long time and these trees are getting bigger and bigger." They walked by a few more leaves on the ground. "And I haven't seen the sun in days!" The other three pounded their chests in agreement. Jrio passed a basher plant and pulled a pod of fruit from its stalk. He handed some of the red ripened clusters to Luik, Quoin, and Thero; all thanked him as they ate the sweet fruit.

"Did any of you notice that we've picked up the pace?" Quoin asked with some red juice on his chin. Quoin was the youngest of his family, but made friends easily with older boys, mostly due to his easygoing manner.

"Aye," Luik said hitting his chest, "we've been speeding up gradually, I think."

Jrio added, "It sure would be faster, wherever we're headed, if you had brought one of your horses, Quoin." The region of Jerovah was the breeding ground for all of the horses in Dionia. The plains were very conducive to keeping track of thousands of the beautiful animals, as they could be seen to the horizon. The descendants of King Daunt, as well as those before him, were the sole keepers of the breeding stallions for generations. Each Jerovian was an exceptional and skilled equestrian, Quoin not withstanding even at his youthful age; for all inhabitants train up their children in the ways of the horses from birth. Luik noticed a number of leaves scattered between trees to his left.

Suddenly, while they were deep in thought, each wishing they had a horse to ride, the entire troop stopped, holding short. It took only an instant to realize why. No one spoke; Jrio's mouth was suspended wide open, as were many others.

"Home!" Quoin exclaimed and ran ahead.

Gorn had stopped next to the last tree Luik could see ahead. Beyond that, just sky and a flat expanse of green he could have never imagined stretching on to the horizon, infinitely vast and wide.

"We have reached the Plains of Jerovah," Gorn turned and yelled back to the boralees. The long trek through Grandath was over. While Luik was glad to have seen the mysterious and marvelous trees of Grandath, he determined that he liked seeing the sun much better. Here, the sun was near to setting *on the horizon*, something Luik and the others from the west had never seen. Luik had always seen the sun fall below the hills to the east in Bensotha. Those in the north had only seen it disappear behind the mountains of Tontha and those that bordered Ligeon. But this was beautiful to see.

"We will rest here tonight," Gorn concluded. With that he chose a tree, and facing in toward the forest, sat down, and folded his arms. Everyone else ran out into the grassy expanse and found a place to sit near where Quoin and his two brothers had already laid down, not accustomed to the dense forest and happy to be where the sky took up its place once more. They all sat together in silence, all sitting closer than they ever had before, watching as the sun dipped lower and lower, shimmering different colors in the moist atmosphere, and its warmth dissipating slowly. They did not know it, but this band of strangers was already becoming one.

Their leader did not join them. In fact, no one thought about him as they watched the setting sun. Even when the sun had dropped below the edge of the horizon and the boys lay outstretched beneath the stars, sleeping and dreaming of what only boys can dream, Gorn's blue eyes saw deep into the woods of Grandath, watching and waiting for what no one else could have known.

Chapter Ten

JOURNEY TO THE ISLE OF KIRSTELL

The eighteen boys were up by dawn, now walking south with the Sea of Lens bordering them to the west and south. Gorn led them onward as usual but there was more liberty for them to fan out and take advantage of the wide-open space. Gorn never looked back or seemed to pay any attention to them; he just methodically pressed on. The intimate confines of the forest had prompted much conversing among the boys. But now talking receded with the increased mobility and desire to roam freely, all the while keeping Gorn in sight.

A fresh breeze off the nearby coast brought salty air through the grass. The green carpet swirled and waved in all directions, and the air felt refreshing and warm. The sun rose high into the sky, and a few of the boys began to play chase, running in all directions. A few others wrestled in the lushness of the field; but only just so long before they'd pick themselves up and run toward Gorn, only then to tackle each other again.

It was the eleventh day now and Luik found himself wishing to know the destination of their long trip. He was not alone; the question nagged at the mind of each boy. He knew his father would bring peace to his mother's unrest, but what about his friends? Were they thinking about him? Did they miss him? Did they even know he had left? Fane probably knew, as he had been there with the dwarf man in the council meeting. Did Fane know Gorn, too? And why was Fane in a cloak? How did he get in the palace? Did he get a chance to tell Hadrian and Norra what he had witnessed? But Luik didn't have time to think any further. He was struck in the back and thrown to the ground with two arms wrapped tightly around him. He let out a deep breath as he hit the grass.

"Got ya'!" Jrio exclaimed. Luik rolled from his friend's tight embrace and got to his hands and knees. Jrio was trying to reach for him a second time, but Luik dodged it and flanked him, picking him up by his belt and heaving him into a plush growth of ferns. Jrio let out a whoop and tumbled over, laughing. But that wasn't enough for Luik. He charged his bewildered friend and jumped into the air fully laid out. Luik came crashing down on top of Jrio's back and pinned him to the ground. Jrio flapped his legs and arms trying to shake Luik off.

"All right! All right! You got me!" he yelled with his last remaining breath. Luik rolled to the side and beamed.

"That's what you get for taking me unaware!"

"I'll remember that," Jrio said sitting up.

"And I thought you'd learned your lesson by now," Luik said, trying to rub it in a little. They both laughed.

"Guess I thought maybe *you* forgot," Jrio prodded.

"Ah! How'd he get so far ahead?" Luik said as he looked in Gorn's direction. Jrio looked on, too.

"O that's easy! You weren't content to stay down in the first place!" But Luik wasn't listening. He was up and running. "Hey, wait up, Luik!" Jrio was after him in a dash. They ran on and finally caught up to within a short distance of their teacher. They could faintly hear the sound of water crashing in the distance now and guessed that the southern shore of Jerovah was not far away. The sun marched on taking its own walk across the sky. Steadily the ocean sounds grew louder and clearer. Each boy could smell the salt in the air and had visions of playing in the surf.

Suddenly Gorn raised his hand high and stopped. The playing ceased and everyone gathered to him. He turned slowly to face them and lowered his arm. His dark black face was expressionless.

"From this moment on I want no single person to speak or utter a single sound from their mouths," he said first, staring into their eyes. "Understood? We are coming to the Isle of Kirstell, our destination."

There was a subtle stirring in the faces that looked on. *Finally! One answer out of the way!* Luik thought. "It is connected to the coast of Jerovah by a sand bar that is exposed by the low tide for just a brief time each day, allowing a man to walk the whole stretch from end to end without being caught again by the currents of the rising waters. Since we are late and the waters will be rising again soon, we will need to run." Everyone understood. "Boats cannot make the passage as the submerged coral reefs make the waters too shallow to permit one across without being damaged. Therefore we go on foot and we must make landfall today. Tomorrow will be too late." That all sounded just fine, Luik thought, impressed with Gorn's direct manner of speaking.

"Once you see the isle crest the horizon in the distance, you are all to run to it without hesitation. No one is to take their eyes off of the isle." He repeated himself. "No one is to take their eyes off the isle in front of them. Do you understand?" They all hit their chests once with a fist. "Make no noise and do not run until you see the isle. I will follow behind you and meet you at Kirstell."

Gorn turned and began walking. Though stern and direct with his words about the subject, everyone enjoyed the thought of another race since they were all in the mood for games; and this, *a race against creation.* The boys stayed even with Gorn now, not one daring to cross in front of him, but all eager to be the first to see the isle and set off running with as much of a head start as possible. Gorn was not diverted. He kept a quick but steady pace as always. Timing would be everything. Just a few more steps. The boys elbowed each other, trying to get any advantage they could. *Timing,* Gorn thought. *How much time will I have? Just a few more steps.* The shorter boys jumped, trying to look over the horizon. *Just a few more steps.*

Suddenly one boy took off running. It was Benigan from Tontha, followed by his two brothers. Luik figured as much as they were the tallest. Sure enough, there it was; the first speck of dark green poking above the swirling grass in the distance. Luik was off an instant later followed by Jrio, Quoin, and Thero who had been right beside him. They ran silently, legs pumping and arms swinging as hard as they could make them, covering ground like a stampede of horses. Between strides, they would all glance up and see the speck of green grow as the water's edge got closer and closer.

Gorn was pleased with the result of his stern and direct words, hoping to be as light as possible while still conveying the dire need to cross quickly. He found it difficult to balance a deadly situation on a spear point without allowing it to fall into a sea of fear. And fear was something he knew his students knew nothing about, but would momentarily, changing their lives forever.

Giving the boys a sizeable lead, Gorn began to jog, watching each youth dig hard and run toward the horizon. Then he did what he did not want any of them to see; he reached for his sword and drew it out in a single motion and brought it upright to his side. Anyone who had seen that swift action before knew this man was not a farmer or a fisherman, nor was he a herder or house maker, king or elder, but that this man was a *warrior*.

The boys were nearly running as a collective mass with a few slightly behind when they crested the grand sand dunes that led down to the water. The grass thinned giving way to white sand which was more difficult to run in, but all managed. They bounded over and down the final mound, most slipping and sliding. Quoin managed a summersault by accident and landed, surprisingly, on his feet. Fyfler floated down the dune at its steepest point effortlessly, as someone who has grown up in the Islands of Somahguard would be expected to do. Luik made it down well enough and heard Jrio's deep breaths coming smoothly just behind him.

Now all understood the sand bar. It was a narrow stretch of wet sand narrowing the further it went out to sea, terminating in a heap of enormous rocks that were the beginnings of the cliffs of Kirstell. The furthest reaches of the bar were already being swept over again by the high tide. By Luik's guess they would all make it most of the way on the sand but be swimming the last few lengths.

Kirstell looked, at first glance, like an emerald jewel ornately adorned with rubies, perched high on a tower of granite. The lush green foliage was like nothing Luik had ever seen, and from what he could tell, was speckled with a plethora of flowers streaming from every available tree and vine, though he was still very far away. Not to mention he was running as fast as he could.

About ten or twelve of the boys had already funneled onto the narrow stretch of sand and were well on their way out to Kirstell when Luik heard a loud cry from behind him. At first he was surprised that someone had broken Gorn's rule, but then realized that the sound was very unnatural. So he broke the other rule and turned back to look. But he couldn't believe his eyes. In a shower of sand and water, Luik stiffened his legs and dug into the bar, coming about in an instant. There was Rab, Jrio's youngest brother, pinned to the ground on his stomach. But what stood over him was something Luik could not explain, taking him many attempts to explain in the days that followed.

A large beast, about twice the size of a man, had one leg on Rab's back and another on the sand. Its flesh was a terrible shade of brown and black that was knotted and torn like tree bark, save for the reddish dripping fluid that emanated from it. The face of the beast was grotesque and the most unpleasant thing Luik had ever seen. The clawing arms flailed wildly in the air as it looked down at the victim under its foot. Rab was crying now.

Luik took off toward Rab, and the creature looked up, saliva drooling from between iron white teeth, eyes gleaming red. It seemed to give a series of clucks from its tongue as Luik ran faster, staring intently. Then there was the smell; Luik was stunned and missed a step as the putrid rank of the beast filled his head. He caught himself before tripping and held his breath. He had never seen such a creature nor did he know what to make of it, but one thing was certain: he was sure it intended to harm his friend and he must pull Rab away.

Luik did not know how to confront the creature, so he simply hunched low and ran with all his might intending to tackle the beast off his friend. But the beast was well ahead of him. A swinging arm came circling around and slammed into Luik's side. The blow sent Luik flying to the ground. He felt heat on his left arm and shoulder and winced from—from *pain*. It was then Luik also felt something else he had never felt before: *fear*. He was suddenly tempted to be *afraid* of the grotesque brute that gurgled and whined atop his yelping friend. For a fraction of time he didn't know what to do. He was overcome by a leading that crippled him and told him not to move, and if anything, to run away or cower. He was paralyzed. Then Rab cried out once more as the beast leaned with more weight into his back. Luik snapped at the sound of distress and pushed himself to his feet. He let out a yell of his own and ran as hard as he could at the monster.

A swinging arm went soaring high again, but Luik saw it and jumped sideways, throwing his good shoulder at its torso with all his might. The giant beast clucked, but did not move, and Luik had no choice but to take another breath of the foul air. He now had no idea what to do and stepped back, his assault utterly failing. The beast regarded him momentarily and then lofted its arm high, now revealing a dark horn at the end. Luik became even more afraid. Now the emotion was uncontrollable and he closed his eyes.

But the deathblow never came. He heard a loud word, not yelled out, but spoken forcefully with the fleeting air of a whisper. He opened his eyes and saw the monster falling to the ground and Gorn pulling his sword from its torso, dripping with the beast's fluid. It flopped, all the while whining and struggling to get up. In one sweeping movement Gorn lifted Rab to his shoulder and looked right at Luik.

"*Run!*" he yelled. Luik, overwhelmed by everything that had taken place, turned and began making strides back toward the isle. Within a short amount of time he was halfway down the sand bar with Gorn still carrying Rab just in front. His shoulder was aching and he noticed blood covering his left hand whenever he lifted his arm in a stride. He had never seen his own blood before, but he knew it was what kept him alive. Behind him Luik could hear beating on the sand and the strange clucking noise again, only multiplied. He ran hard but threw a fleeting glance over his shoulder to see a mass of various shaped and colored creatures pouring over the sand dunes behind him. All were running twice as fast as he, now converging onto the sand bar. Luik's heart quickened even more as did his pace. The strange fear had not left him still, and for the first time he began to feel a sensation much like when you fall asleep, only he was wide awake and not lying down. His legs were getting *weak* and he was beginning to have difficulty breathing. In fact, it seemed like there was fire in his chest from the air. Everything in him suddenly wanted to give up and just stop, just rest—just for a second or two.

"*Keep running!*" Gorn's voice broke through his thoughts like a cracked whip. Luik snapped to and picked up his stride once more, choosing to overcome his fatigue and pain with sheer will. The footsteps of the demon horde were much closer now, and so was the water swallowing up the sand bar. The ankle-deep sea splashed up in his face and sprayed his body, sending a refreshing wave into his senses. It was enough nearly to double his pace and catch up with Gorn. The water grew deeper with each step. Luik thought about when he should start swimming instead of wasting time with high stepping leaps. It happened sooner than he had thought. He dove forward; every amount of distance gained precious, and struck the water, arms extended. The water swallowed him and then released him to the surface. He kicked hard and reached for every stroke. But the sea seemed to slow his pace. Thoughts of resting filled his head instantly, but it was another sound that brought him back to reality this time: cheering.

Luik lifted his head out between strokes just enough to hear his friends yelling in the distance. He could see them all standing on various high-mounded rocks waving and pumping their arms frantically, some beating their chests, and all calling out with encouragement. His heart sang inside him. *Keep going. You're almost there. Don't stop now.* The tide was nearly high and waves began to close in from the surrounding seas with the hint of tidal currents taking effect. Luik was finding it difficult to keep the isle in front of him, but he barely managed. He wondered for an instant if the creatures were good swimmers.

Despite the worsening water conditions and the near paralyzing fatigue that swelled within him, Luik pressed on, each stroke bringing him closer to the isle. He saw Jrio, Quoin, and then the three sons of Purgos jump from their high rocks into the swelling sea. He thought it strange that they did and wondered why they just didn't stay where they were. He could see Brax and Benigan swimming toward him. But that's all Luik remembered.

Chapter Eleven

THE DWARF'S LAST APPRENTICE

After all the king's sons had departed for their trip to Kirstell and the Gvindollion session was adjourned, Fane carried the large box, formerly bearing the boy's torcs, and set it on a large wooden table in King Ragnar's sitting room. He had never seen the inside of the palace before and could hardly believe the events that had led up to this moment.

It was only a few days after the Birth Celebration of the princess, when Fane had journeyed back home to his family in Beneetha, that he received the strange letter. No one knew where it had come from; it was simply lying on his pillow next to his head when he rose early one morning. He pulled off the gold ribbon and uncurled the thick parchment that smelled of spice.

Fane, son of Fadner,

son of Dafe,

son of Ad,

Greetings in the name of the Most High, Creator of all things living and past.

You are hereby summoned to the court of Adriel for an audience with his majesty, King Ragnar, Lord of all Dionia. Your immediate presence is required and nothing should detain you or permit delay.

Prosperity and peace be upon those of your home and may they live to see their children's children.

Afe di empaxe li roua lonia ene froue napthixe bruna[14],

~Li-Saide of Ot

His mother and father were inspired for their son and delighted by the honor. It was the first time Fane had ever remembered his mother actually pushing him out the door rather than keeping him close to home. The mysterious letter gave few details and more questions than he would have liked, but he had never received a letter bearing such a request. His father walked him to the wooden bridge that crossed the stream and led into a grove of palm trees to the west of their home.

"I have only one thing to say," Fadner said to his son. "King Ragnar is the greatest of men and only acts as the Great God wishes him to." Anyone could see where Fane inherited his red hair and freckled face. Fadner knelt and leveled with him. "Whatever he asks of you, whatever he desires for you to do, listen to him and know it is if I were asking you to do it." He squeezed his shoulders gently. "No matter how long you are away, whether it be one day or one summer, know that the Creator is hearing your name with each sunrise and each sunset from me and your mother."

"Thank you, Ta na." Fane smiled at his father, moved by his words.

"Fane, there are dark days ahead of us." Fane's smile vanished. *What does that mean?* he thought. "I want you to be wise with every step you take and stay close with those whom the king appoints you to. Do you understand?" His father's expression had changed.

"Aye, Ta na, I will." Fane paused. "What do you mean by *dark days*? How can the sun be..."

---

[14] **Afe di empaxe li roua lonia ene froue napthixe bruna** *(AYF-eh dee ehm-PACKS lee R'ROO-uh LON-ee-uh een froo nahp-THEECKS br'roona) First Dionian: literally translated, "One who holds the ways old and every spoken word," meant to mean, "A keeper of the old ways and all words spoken."*

"Never mind that, son. I have not had time enough to tell you much of what I should have, for I did not realize how quickly things have advanced. No matter what happens, especially to your mother and me, you must serve the king. You must always do what he says and listen to his words."

"You and Na na? What's happening to you and Ta na?" Fane had never heard his father speak in such mysteries.

"I pray nothing will, my son, but we are not promised tomorrow. Soon we will only have the blessing of today, and that at its best, will be frail."

"Do you think for some reason I will never see—"

"You will always see me again, *always*."

They embraced there over the stream and Fane encountered an emotion he had never known before: *loss*. Though his father held him tight, right there, flesh to flesh, warmth to warmth, he felt as though he were not there anymore and unimaginably gone forever. He cried softly and squeezed his father's neck one more time.

• • •

Fane found the throne room to be exactly as Luik had described it, only this time there were no people there, just King Ragnar and the small dwarf. Fane, too, had entered into the black room, been met by the little man, and then was suddenly swept into the great hall of the king, walking up the tiered throne mount. He found the mysterious stream notably fascinating and thought that Luik would like it, hoping he would remember to tell him next time they were together.

The king addressed him after a fatherly embrace that he found quite comforting. He had never been this close to King Ragnar before, and then to have a private audience with him was peculiar, to say the least.

"I do hope that you were not too apprehensive about the vagueness of Li-Saide's summons, young Fane," the king questioned, dressed today in red linen breecs and gold trimmed black tunic. He gestured to Li-Saide standing below.

"No, my king, though I have been wondering why you sent for— *me*."

The king laughed. "For the same reason any king would summon you. There is a task needed to be done and you are the best for it."

"*Me?*" Fane's voice lifted.

"Aye, you, my son; as you may or may not know, strange times befall us, times of great concern and thoughtfulness. I know you are close with the young Son of Man named Hadrian. Do you know of his father as of late?"

Fane paused, acknowledging what the king implied, "Aye, my lord. Luik, son of Lair, told me about Hadrian's father, Jadak." He paused. "Though most of what he told me I did not understand."

"But you soon will," replied the king reassuringly. "You soon will." The king summoned Li-Saide with his hand and the little dwarf walked lightly up the steps to the summit. "You have met before, but allow me to introduce one of my elders and friends, Li-Saide of Ot." Li-Saide turned to face Fane, both about the same height, and extended his arm. Fane mutually grabbed the little man's forearm in the sign of greeting. Both said nothing but smiled. Fane could not believe this man was from the fabled city of Ot. It was just a story, or so he thought.

"Li-Saide is my most trusted aid and friend. He is knowledgeable of all things past and present pertaining to all life: the ways of beasts and of man, things that fly and things that swim, and all things that grow, both in nature and in the hearts of man, in this realm and in all of Athera." The king placed his hand on Li-Saide's little shoulder in recognition.

Ot really does exist? Fane thought. *Can he really be from there?*

"Aye," the dwarf whispered. "I am, and it does." Fane's eyes became enormous; his mouth opened wide but nothing came out. Before Fane could react further, the king continued with a smile.

"I invited you to come, young Fane, Son of Fadner, because I am asking you if you would entrust yourself into my care."

Fane didn't need time to think. He knew the answer was, "Aye, my king." He actually thought the question silly. "For if I am living at all," he went on, "it is because the Great Creator entrusted me to you the day I was born into Dionia. So, I am already yours, awaiting your wishes." Fane bent low. King Ragnar grinned wide with pleasure.

"You are wise, my son. Such things are truly only revealed to the meek in spirit by the Good God. Therefore, from this day forth, you will be a servant in my court. And I do hereby appoint Li-Saide as your teacher in all things great and small, and you, his apprentice. Listen to him as if it were I speaking to you. For all he says is good and just, straight and true. He will teach you to walk in Light and to guard and steward the gifts within you, and those around you."

"Aye, my king."

"If you have need of anything or wonder of more, it is he who will teach and guide you until he sees fit that he can teach you no more."

"I understand, my king."

"Li-Saide, I release Fane, Son of Fadner, to you and so charge you to impart and instruct all the rights to life and knowledge given you." The dwarf bowed quickly but reverently.

"My king," Fane implored, "I still don't know what my task is that you have summoned me for."

The king rose from his throne and stood towering about the skinny boy. "Why, my son, the world of Dionia shall never be like it once was, or is, ever again." His voice was louder now and Fane could not make out any smile. "There are those who would wish to see Life flourish, and then there are those who wish to see *death*." The word stung his ears. "Your task, young Fane?" The king bent low and then placed his hands on Fane's tiny shoulders. "*See to it that Life flourishes, and that, abundantly.*"

The king rose. "I will leave you two alone now," the king addressed Li-Saide. "I'm sure you will have much to discuss." Li-Saide nodded with a grin. Ragnar descended his throne mount to the rear and exited through a draped archway in the back of the room.

Li-Saide let the silence consume the room as Fane stood motionless. Dwarves had a knack for letting circumstances speak for themselves, and this was one of those times. The boy was barely managing to come to grips with the fact that he was actually *in* the Palace of Adriel, summoned by the king—*let alone* given a task by the king! He was nearly shaking with delight from inside out. It is a gift only of the young to trust while ignorant and to believe while blind.

Had he only known of the growing evil that was lurking, waiting to devour.

Chapter Twelve

BIRTH OF A WARRIOR

"My brothers went *where?"* Anorra tilted her head and stiffened her arms.

"My dear Princess Anorra," her father said, for in fact she *was* a princess, but she never permitted anyone to address her as such; that is, of course, except her father. Though she was still but a girl, the king noted that she was already taking on many of his wife's characteristics. "Peace be to you in the name of the Most High."

He lifted his hand and gestured for a chair to be brought. He helped her be seated in the great hall near the far open window. From high above they overlooked the majestic Bay of Cidell to the west, its beautiful waters speckled with diverse colored sailing boats like a willowing of butterflies dancing through a field in the afternoon sun. The Port of Narin, the capital city harbor that lay far below their window, was famous for its vast network of wooden walkways and homes built on raised platforms supported by stilts over the water. Though most all of the palace windows looked out over the bay and the port below, the palace itself was built facing east, with its western border stopping on the edge of a cliff.

"They have been summoned by order of King Ragnar for *training,"* Thorn consoled his daughter, trying to not give away too much but knowing that would be difficult to accomplish with her. He wore a white linen shirt open down the middle, tucked inside a wrap of brilliant blue. Two gold armbands clung to each bicep and a gold torc lay around his neck.

"What sort of *training*, Father? Where did he send them? Why didn't I get a chance to say goodbye? How long will they be gone?" Her hands were still fists beneath her pink wrap that was tightly tucked under her arms, her shoulders bare, and hair pulled into a horse tail. The king let her finish and then sat quietly, recovering from the onslaught and also letting her brood in her chair with his silence. "*Father?*"

"Anorra, my cherished one," the king said, now resolved in what course he should take. "You are one of my daughters, and a brave and industrious one at that. Imagine for a moment that a man owns an apple tree. All the apples on the tree are precious to him. If anyone came asking to have one and eat, that person must first ask the man who owns the tree. The apples hanging lowest are within anyone's reach and most accessible for someone to easily take, but the apples highest up are more special. Not just anyone can walk by and snatch those away. There must be great intentions before the owner would allow someone to climb the tree and take the most prized of his apples."

"Are you comparing me to *an apple*, Ta na? Are you saying I'm *round*? Do I look—"

"Peace, child!" he cut her off. Sometimes he secretly hoped she would grow quickly and marry even more so.

"All right. So you are saying I am prized because I am a daughter?" She spoke with an innocent tone laced with bite. She was good.

"Precisely."

"So then, as my father you'd grant me nearly any wish."

"Nearly anything." Hoping beyond hope this meant resolve.

"So I wish to know details about my brothers."

"Dah!" Thorn stood and walked to the window, exasperated. Anorra knew she was pushing him, but she was one child that couldn't stand not knowing something that everyone else knew. *She's too smart for her own good*, Thorn thought as he gazed out to the Faladrial, *and at just ten and four summers old.* He could feel things slipping away, getting out of his control. He knew by bringing his sons to the Gvindollion he was risking their lives. He knew that more than almost anyone, but he also knew many more lives would be lost if his didn't serve. They were strong and brave and would be of great value to the King of Dionia. That was hard enough; losing his daughter to the realities that awaited them all was unacceptable. How could he protect her? How could he place her out of harm's way?

He felt the presence of the Most High. He sensed the Great Spirit's leading deep within him. *Let me protect her, my son. Let me guard her.* Thorn felt a gentle breeze waft over his body. *Leave her to me.*

He wrestled things in his heart. *But she will never be the same*, he pleaded of the Spirit. Thorn knew how dangerous knowledge could be.

I never wanted her to stay the same, the Spirit replied. *I'm allowing you to be the one who changes her, not another. So teach her while there is yet time and while you are yet the one to teach at all.* Thorn didn't know where to start. *From the beginning.* He turned to face his daughter, still sitting. But even that was stolen as the great hall door far across the room swung open and a voice broke the silence.

"My king! My king! Come quickly!" It was Shyllin, a servant of the king's court. His face was pale and he waved his arm wildly, gesturing for him to come. The king regarded him plainly, yet surprised within.

"What is it, young Shyllin?" the king inquired. Anorra spun around in her chair to regard the shirtless boy, wearing just a pair of tanned breecs.

"It's Ciaphlie, Drannen's daughter! She's been attacked!"

King Thorn clapped his hands, and within him taking three strides toward the boy, two of his noblemen entered the great hall from a side door.

"Fetch me my sword, Kiln," he pointed to one, then the other. "Gyinan, come with me." Then he turned to Anorra. "And you," he hesitated resisting every fatherly instinct, *"come with me."*

Shyllin led Thorn, followed by Anorra, Gyinan, and a few strides behind, Kiln, who carried the king's majestic sword. They descended the long stairway down to the courtyard that lay to the east shaded in oak trees, then turned north out through the gate into a wide green meadow surrounded by homes on every side. Across the field by a cluster of homes, three men crouched behind a stone wall regarding something on the other side. A woman screamed just inside the doorway of an adjacent house watching them. Thorn, being led far enough, ran full speed past the boy. Anorra wouldn't be left behind or beat, so she quickened her pace, staying just shy of her father. Gyinan and Kiln flanked the king closing on the scene.

"What have you?" the king roared as he slowed. He heard a baby's voice crying in the distance but where he couldn't be sure. Two men remained kneeling behind the safety of the wall, eyes transfixed, while the third turned toward the king.

"My lord!" declared the one, "come quickly! But stay low!"

The king crouched down the last few steps, thinking it wisdom to listen when the men of the house of Jrillase gave caution, as they were all wise and noble men of valor and courage. The king's group finally met up with them and bent low behind the wall.

Lying on her back on the grass out in the pasture was Ciaphlie, just one summer and this one old. Her dress was torn and a red stain grew from her side. Her right arm was badly injured and torn. She screamed louder. One would have wondered why the three men remained by the wall. But it was in only another moment, when one of the beasts emerged from behind a small enclosure used for sheltering the sheep, that someone would see why.

"Look, there!" Gyinan pointed.

"It's only a dog," Kiln added.

"Aye," Jaiden, Son of Jrillase said, "one of *five*."

"Five?" the king asked with surprise.

"I have never seen this many," Gyinan added. The large dark hound walked dangerously close to the little girl, circled once methodically, and then withdrew to the rest of his pack. He had tasted blood. Thorn could see it in his eyes. The next pass would be fatal.

The king sighed quietly, "It's getting worse. So quickly, it's all growing worse." He brushed back his hair and took a deep breath. "Kiln, my sword." Kiln lofted it over to him. "We must make quick work. There is no time for redemption of the animals. They are too far gone. The girl will surely die if we lose one moment. Kiln, I want you to go to the left flank and stand on the wall drawing them to you any way you can. Shyllin, you on the right wall. Gyinan, you will follow me to cover and retrieve the child. Anorra, stay here and stay low. Biea-Varos!"

Kiln and Shyllin took off around the flanks, dodging homes until they found clearly visible spots on the wall to make their presence known. As soon as the king saw them, he bounded over the wall, Gyinan mimicking his vault, and they beat hard for the child in the middle. Three dogs emerged from the right enclosure and then two more from the left.

They had barely taken a step when Kiln and Shyllin began whooping and clapping from up above. The dogs spun in surprise and let out a thunder of barking and snarling, drool flying with every breath of defiance; but it was all that the king and Gyinan needed. They reached the child and Gyinan swooped her up into the bend of his arm and wrapped her close with the folds of his cloak. He immediately turned back toward the wall as the king covered their retreat facing the beasts. But by this point the hounds had lost interest in the diversion, and the blood craving was rekindled. When they saw their prize vanishing they took off for the king. Gyinan was almost to the wall when the first dog set upon Thorn.

But he was expecting it. He lofted his sword out to his side and easily brought the blade across the first dog's head and neck, sending it rolling. The second and third hounds, larger than the first, leapt high for Thorn's torso, mouths open and teeth poised. The first he caught by the throat with his massive left hand, while the other on his right he drove the blade directly between the two front legs and into the chest. The hound in his left hand fought hard, growling ferociously, until Thorn simply pulled the blade out of the other dog and struck it on the head with the pommel, breaking its skull. The fourth beast King Thorn struck in a full stride, lowering his sword hard from high atop his head and bringing it down on the dog's back. But the fifth he did no such thing to. It would not die at his hands. The final animal was for someone else to kill.

It ran toward him, drool flailing, and blood staining the fur around its mouth. This had been the one that attacked the child. The others, Thorn surmised, were just along for whatever was left. As the beast closed, Thorn swept the sword low with great speed, severing the two front legs completely off. The dog tumbled and came to a stop, unable to rise, yelping. Thorn breathed deeply and then turned back toward the wall. Gyinan and the child were safe, the babe's mother running from the adjacent house to receive her little girl. Kiln and Shyllin had come off the wall and were walking toward Thorn. And Anorra stood hugging the wall, eyes wide.

"Anorra! Come here," the king called sternly.

The youth was stunned, but she shook it off and at once climbed over the cobblestone wall and ran toward her father. Anorra slowed as she neared her father and surveyed the carnage strewn about her. Thick blood stained the blades of grass a deep red. Nerves still twitched in two of the dead dogs. And then there was the legless one, still wailing at the king's feet. She cuddled up behind Thorn, peering at the distorted face of what she was sure once was a very noble animal.

"No, no hiding for you today, Princess Anorra," said the king. He had never addressed her without a soft tone before. This was how he spoke to his sons, but never her. He backed away from her and held the blade in the palms of his hands, dripping with blood and a vile stench.

"Take the sword, my daughter. Hold it with both hands."

"I can't," she faltered. "It's too—"

"Take the sword, Princess!" Thorn's face was hard. She was clearly disturbed. Two shaking innocent hands reached out and wrapped tightly around the leather-wrapped handle. The king let go, and Anorra pulled hard to keep the weight of the sword upright. She watched the blood slide down the mirrored finish of the blade.

"You desire to know of your brothers. You ask where they are and what they are learning, and you want to know why. Well, my most cherished one," he pointed to the morbid beast before them both, "*this* is why. *This* is what they are learning. They are learning of what would drive a noble animal to turn on a mere child. They are learning how to protect the lives of the innocent and wage war against the Destroyer. So I give you the best answer I can, one that will satisfy your thirst, and all at once make you thirsty for a drink you never knew existed; *I want you to kill it*. Kill this beast, my Princess Daughter, my Warrior. Because the *evil* that rages within it, if given one chance, will destroy you, too."

Anorra was shaking. She never could have imagined the answers to the questions she asked, nor the events that had just transpired. It was all she could do to keep the sword straight and not collapse in tears. But something else drove her forward; there was an emotion she had never felt before welling up inside her veins and enabling her to act outside her means. She glared down at the lame dog still fighting with its hind legs. It struggled toward her and snapped its jaws, pitifully trying for anything. She could see blood around its nose. Then she made the connection: *Ciaphlie*. This animal had tried to *kill* a Daughter of Eva; it had tried to *murder*. New words, new emotions. Anorra's mind flew, trying to keep up with them. Suddenly she was faced with a choice. People of a more liberal mind would say it was between mercy and punishment, but in natural order and law, when a life is taken or attempted to be, another life is forfeited. No, Anorra's struggle was over something else. She had decided while watching her father back behind the wall and seeing the little girl brought to her mother, mangled and bleeding, that the creatures must be put to death. But she faced what seemed to be *two* emotions now, a choice between two courses of action, two very closely related results but with two very different motives: *justice* and *revenge*. She hardened her face and furrowed her brow, resolute in her course. Thorn took one step back. He watched with a bit of surprise, but half expecting, as his daughter effortlessly raised the sword above her head and with a shout, deftly lowered the weapon across the dog's neck. The dog didn't have time to yelp as the blade cracked through bone and tissue. It was over.

She stood over the corpse with the sword still pinned to the ground, just staring. Anorra took one long breath and then felt a hand reach in and remove the weapon from hers and then a whisper.

"So what was your motive, young princess? What did you chose to be led by?" came the king's soft and soothing voice. The meadow was silent. The warm breeze from the bay far below still blew gently over the cliffs and into the pasture. They stood alone together in the midst of the wreckage, the rest of their company by the wall. Anorra spoke faintly.

"At first I was upset that such a noble creature would strike Ciaphlie, just a baby. Part of me felt led to…" she paused, searching for the right word. But she couldn't find it, because she didn't know it.

"*Hate*," her father said. The word just seemed right to her.

"Aye, part of me felt led to *hate* it for its actions. But I could never hold such resentment for a creature that the Lord of Hosts breathed His own life into and set living by His own hand. So it could not be hate; it could not be *revenge*." Her father just listened. "So my motive was— was *righteousness*, I suppose. A law had been broken and a consequence is required. So justice must be swiftly executed." She turned and looked for the first time to her father and her king. "Is this wrong, Father?"

"No, my child," he said calmly, "this is not wrong at all." He knelt down and looked into her eyes. "Today you have proven and chosen your course. You have revealed your innate ability to discern between spirits that would influence you away from the Truth and to choose the more difficult way. You have shown a speed in passing sound judgment and delivering it swiftly. And you have shown courage, delegating fear to its proper place. I commend you, my daughter, for I am honored among fathers to have begotten you." The king took his blood-smeared hand and placed it on her head, the other on her left arm. His voice became much stronger, but not loud. "Today you are no longer merely my child or my Princess; but today you are a warrior and a judge, set apart by the Most High for His will to be exacted and for you to have dominion over the world He has placed you in. You will fight like no other, famous for the exploits you will engage in. You will protect in all your decisions, be renowned for your discretion, and honored in your wisdom. Today a new judge is established. This hour a warrior is born." He kissed her forehead and blessed her.

• • •

"And the child?" Thorn inquired of Gyinan. "She is well?"

Gyinan, Kiln, and Shyllin had remained by the wall with two of the other three men, watching all that Princess Anorra did. They stood motionless as she returned from the meadow with their king.

"Her injuries are healed and her smile has returned," the nobleman replied. "There was no sign of the wounds being related to peshe[15], as the age of accountability has obviously not been reached. The healing of her arm and side required no intercession or persuasion, as our established authority was sufficient over the afflictions." Gyinan always spoke with much more authority and knowledge than most, alluding to the fact that, as Anorra assumed, he had been around for a very long time and had seen a great deal. He pointed to the home next to them. "She lies resting in her mother's care."

The king requested entrance and then passed through the heavy veil that covered the small home's door. Anorra followed behind. There on a matted floor sat Drannen and next to him, his wife, Cimbia, holding the sleeping infant in the dimly lit central room. The parents both acknowledged the king, and Drannen stood to his feet. Earlier, he had been behind the wall with the other two men when the king first arrived.

"Thank you, my king, for rescuing our daughter." Drannen spoke reverently as he pressed one hand on the king's chest and the other against

---

[15] **Peshe** *(PESH-[eh])*: *noun; a deed or act, or by inaction or abdication of responsibility, an allowance, of engaging in behavior or receiving the nature of a spirit directly opposed to the will of The Most High, His Righteousness, Truth and Light; anything that separates a creature from the presence of His Spirit; a grievous mistake or error with detrimental consequences spiritually and naturally. 2. verb; to engage in the action of said deed, act, mistake, or error. Most closely related to the Middle English word "sin" or the verb, "to sin."*

his own chest and bowed. "I have seen the evil spirit rise in beasts before—as we *both* have seen, my lord," he corrected himself, remembering last summer. "But I never thought it would come to harm my own family. We are most grateful for your intervention." The king accepted the grateful gesture but waved off the praise as something that should be expected of all kings to do when their people are in jeopardy.

"And the child?" Thorn invoked the mother.

"She is fine, my lord. She sleeps," Cimbia said as she removed the blanket from the baby's face. Anorra moved out from behind her father and went in for a closer look. The little babe's eyes were closed and there was not a scratch on her face. She took the liberty of pulling the blanket a little farther away to see that her previously mangled arm was as perfect as the other, unscathed and unmarred. Fresh linen had been wrapped around her and there was no stain of blood that Anorra could see.

"Peace be on this home," the king said, turning toward the door. "And I pray you thank the Great God this night for His mercy and mighty power to save."

Anorra kissed the child gently on the forehead and rose to her feet once more. She smiled and then gave the sign of blessing, following her father out the door.

Chapter Thirteen

REPENTANCE

Luik opened his eyes feeling a warm shaft of sunlight settle upon his face. He looked up at a thatched roof and then turned sideways to regard the inside of the small single-roomed circular dwelling. The window across from him and the covered doorway were the only notable features of the plain cement wall. A large circular woven mat covered the floor, and a ceramic vase stood alone near his padded bed.

His head was thick and heavy and his spirit felt unusually strange. *Where am I?* he thought, but his mind gave him no mention of this place. All at once he was at odds with a fight to recall his own memory. He couldn't find it. *Why am I here?* Disturbed, he sat up, but never got all the way before falling back down, seized with agony. He let out a moan and pressed his eyes shut. *What is this?*

Hearing him stir, a head popped in through the door covering and looked him in the eyes. Luik blinked, trying to make out the face, but it was gone. He heard some voices from outside but was still in too much of a struggle with his thoughts to care about what they were saying. A moment later Gorn entered and knelt down next to him. The wrestling of thoughts was over; he remembered now.

Gorn was dressed in a different outfit. He wore a black sleeveless shirt with a V at the neck and a pair of thick brown breecs, clearly not woven or of cloth; they were made out of something else Luik had never seen.

"I see you are awake, boralee," he said with a low voice.

Luik coughed the first word then continued. "Aye, Teacher, but I feel strange. My body has never felt like this before, nor my head."

"And I wish they did not, boralee." Gorn reached down and raised the vase to Luik's lips, offering him a drink. Luik gratefully received the cool water from the vase, barely able to lift his head with the pain.

He continued, "However, I cannot promise that you will never encounter this again. In fact, all your friends will eventually, I believe. You and Rab are merely the first."

"Rab!" Luik said, nearly choking on his drink. "How is Rab?"

"He is doing well," Gorn replied. "Take a little more drink." He tilted the vase. Luik drank deeply.

"Thank you."

Gorn placed the vase back and crossed his legs. A few moments passed as Luik's memory recalled the events of the day, or was it yesterday?

"How long have I been asleep here?" Luik asked.

"Three days."

"Three days? I have never slept for three days!"

Gorn sat expressionless.

"What happened back at the sand bar, Teacher?"

"You were swimming toward Kirstell and then lost consciousness and slipped beneath the waves. Boran and Brax reached you first and pulled you up. Benigan, Jrio, and Quoin helped bring you ashore and situated you here. You owe them a great thanks." Luik just listened intently. After a moment, he asked another question.

"Those *things* I saw, did they make it to the isle?"

"No," Gorn said, offering no more.

The next question came with a bit of hesitation. "Teacher, what *was* that thing I saw over Rab?"

"It was a fallen lythlaic host, boralee." Gorn's eyes were intensely blue even with his back to the incoming light from the window behind. "Before Morgui was cast out from Athera and banished to the pit, he succeeded in convincing a third of the lythlaic servants of the Most High to join him. When they fell from their heavenly splendor they took on the true manifest appearance of evil, and that is how you see them now. While they fight for Morgui and his purposes, destroying life wherever Light may be found, not every created world in Athera, and those beyond, allows them to manifest like we see them here. In some worlds they are much worse."

"*Worse?*" Luik asked, stunned with surprise.

"Aye, boralee, they are *invisible*, not seen at all. They go about their evil work totally unnoticed by their victim, exacting whatever torture or destruction they are ordered to carry out without so much as a stirring wind." Luik remained still, digesting all that was being told him. Gorn continued.

"Morgui has amassed his followers into a war host, the *Dairne-Reih*[16], which he commands with deft precision. At various times he will unleash a band of his demon horde to accomplish any one of a number of tasks."

"His goals?" Luik nearly interrupted.

"Aye, Morgui has goals and they all center on one thing: to *kill, steal* and *destroy* the Sons of Man and to keep them from living eternally with the Great Father. He does not sleep and he does not eat until every last one that he can take—is *taken*. We are blessed to see the Dairne-Reih for what they are, boralee."

"Blessed? How so?"

"Because one of Morgui's greatest tricks on creation is to convince man that he does not exist. That he has no power. If they don't believe he is a threat, then they have no reason to resist him, and therefore allow the working of evil to go on unchecked and unhindered. But you have seen his threat *and* his intentions."

"You mean that demon wanted to take Rab, not just kill him?"

"Aye, boralee; we are all taken one day, but just *where* we are taken to is the greater question. A body may cease to exist outside of paradise, but a spirit and soul never do. It's *where* they continue to live that determines *what* they are. A spirit breathing and growing in the presence of the Almighty God? *Alive.* A spirit eternally separated from the life giving power and flow of the Great Father? *Dead.*" Gorn offered the water once more and Luik

---

[16] **Dairne-Reih** (*DAYern-[eh]-RYE*): *noun; closest literal translation is "fallen kings" or "fallen angels"; the army war host of Morgui comprised of the fallen angels of Athera or heaven.*

drank. Gorn set the vase back down and touched the white linen bandage around Luik's left shoulder. Luik winced in pain.

"I am going to remove this," Gorn said. Luik nodded, knowing it would hurt more. Gorn swiftly removed the bloodstained cloth wrapped around Luik's shoulder and bare chest, as well as the one on his bicep. The pain was excruciating for the young boy. He had never felt anything like this in all his life. He couldn't quite see the extent of the wound on his shoulder but the gash on his bicep was deep and swollen. Suddenly a familiar emotion returned: *fear*.

"This has not healed for a reason," Gorn said. "Everything has a cause."

"What do you mean?" Luik said feeling the fresh air burn on his flesh.

"You have, I'm quite sure, experienced injury before, have you not?"

Luik nodded.

"But you never felt what you feel now, did you? You never felt pain."

Luik nodded in agreement once more.

"And it always healed instantly, did it not?"

"Within moments," Luik said.

"As it is with all who abide in paradise. But this time you felt *pain*." Gorn suddenly became strong in his tone. "Pain is not from the Creator, boralee. He did not create it. It is, in fact, the absence of His presence. Pain does not enter unless something else leaves. So I ask you, what made you grieve His Spirit? What made you push His presence out in order to allow pain to enter you, now something that remains?"

Luik just looked at Gorn, but did not speak, resisting the emotion inside of him.

"What was it?" Gorn said, his voice rising.

Luik did not want to respond. He did not want to admit to it. Something was rising up inside of him, but he found it did not want him to give it voice. *Block it. Don't allow it.*

"What was it, boralee?" Gorn demanded, leaning in closer.

He could feel his face hot and filling with blood. Luik couldn't stand it anymore.

"Boralee! I ask you again; *what was it?*"

"*Fear!*" Luik yelled out, and instantly began to cry. The one word brought deep sobs along with it. "I was—*afraid*, Teacher!" He cried harder and began trembling. "I was so afraid." Tears filled his eyes and cheeks and then ran down to his pillow. "But why would fear bring me pain and keep my injury from being healed?" Gorn rested his hand on Luik's chest in compassion.

"Because, my young boralee, you did not trust the One who is with you always. You did not permit Him the right He always has had as your covering. You forgot Him in a moment and chose another covering. Instead of delegating your worry and fear to Him, placing it in His hands, you took it upon yourself, disbelieving in His power to save you and His power to protect you as He has always done.

"The pain of your wound suddenly manifested because His Spirit was not there to restrain it. The wound continues to fester and fight against your body's natural desire to heal itself because you have still not allowed the Most High the room in your spirit that has been taken up by your fear and lack of trust."

"So what must I do?" Luik said through his tears. "How can I have Him back? How can I replace the fear with His presence?"

"*Repent*," Gorn said solemnly. "Ask the Great God for mercy, that He might forgive you and have pity on you."

Luik wasted no time. It was normal for him to speak with the Creator. They walked and talked, conversing daily, but time had not allowed for him to notice the grieving of the Spirit's presence. *That must be why I felt so strange when I awoke*, he thought.

"Father God, hear me now. I am sorry for my fear." He smeared his tears away with his good hand. "I am sorry for allowing it to enter and take me away from You. Forgive me, please, for my lack of trust. I beg for Your mercy on me. Have mercy on me! Have me back; I can't live without your presence, Great Father!"

And then all was still. Luik breathed deeply and felt The One once more. His presence had returned, or rather, Luik had returned to Him. He felt the God-consciousness take up residence in his mind and the steady rhythm of Life beating in His veins again. The flow of the Great Spirit had resumed, and Luik heard the impression of His voice: *I am here;* and then the most gracious words Luik had ever heard from a King, *thank you.* Luik's tears flowed again, but this time they came from his heart. Gorn sat watching Luik journey back into the loving arms of His Father and marveled at the grace of the Lord. It was one of life's most beautiful events, all stemming from one of man's most morbid realities. A bird sang outside the window: a gentle breeze rustled the trees nearby and swept into the little room. A few more moments passed, and Luik opened his eyes, dried his tears and then broke the silence.

"I am home."

"I know," Gorn replied. "Your body is whole."

Luik immediately reached for his shoulder in surprise. His skin was as smooth as before—and no pain. He sat up propped by his arms, smiling wide. His back didn't hurt and his head was as clear as ever. He took another deep breath and then regarded Gorn.

"Thank you, Teacher."

"I merely showed you the way," Gorn said. "It is He that deserves the praise and you are commended for choosing the Way of Life."

"But Gorn," Luik added, "I have another question."

"Aye, boralee."

"If the presence of the Most High left me, why wasn't I *taken*?"

"Because you did not completely yield to Morgui's power. Somewhere deep within you, I do not know where, there remained a portion of the Great Spirit that held you from being consumed. Perhaps it is that you chose to flee and not to remain behind. I do not know. Not all who are tempted and fall are taken, boralee. In an instant, you were tempted to no longer trust the Creator for His protection, but to trust yourself. While you fell into the trap before your eyes, you did not fall into the fate opened for your spirit. Your body touched its possible mortality, but you ran from the possibility. Perhaps it is, too, in part to do with your courage to save your friend and to risk your own life. This is true love. Tell me, boralee, when the Dairneag[17] first knocked you to the ground, were you afraid then?"

Luik thought back for a moment. "No. No, I was faced with it, though. Part of me wanted to be afraid, but then I heard Rab cry out, and I knew I had to help him. I didn't have time to consider the fear then."

"So it was when you ran toward Kirstell then. It entered when you had time to consider the danger closing in upon you." Gorn wiped a hand over his bald black scalp and then rose. "You must never forget this day,

---

[17] **Dairneag** (*DAYern-ee-AHG*): *noun; a singular demon of the fallen angelic host; a member of the Dairne-Reih.*

boralee. It is a lesson that will serve you well in the dark days to come. Let its memory preserve you and its stain uphold you. Come, it is time to go. There is much to learn."

Luik stood quickly and followed Gorn out into the broad light of day.

Chapter Fourteen

THE DIBOR

Luik walked into the mass of his seventeen friends, welcomed by smiles and hits on the back. They shouted with joy to his health and courage in attempting to save Rab who was now, too, grasping his forearm with one hand and embracing him with the other.

"C'symia, my brother," Rab said softly in his ear.

The eighteen young men stood in a clearing directly in front of the main hall dressed in wraps and a few in breecs, all shirtless in the warm afternoon air. Lush trees lined the perimeter of the large courtyard and opened just enough to note the beginnings of paths that ran off in various directions from this central location. The sunlight filtered down through the leaved canopy arching high above, creating a wonderful green hue. Birds of every color and kind perched in the trees above, singing happily as if they also blessed the name of Luik, not wishing to be left out; flowers hung from tree limbs in bunches, cascading like small multi-colored waterfalls into midair. Their fragrant scent was mystifying and filled the head with euphoria. Colorful fruits of numerous kinds bent some branches low with their weight, while other glossy bunches stuck close to crevices in the limbed heights above. The grassy turf beneath was thick and full, but hardly long, as if cut evenly by a blade. The whole space was alive and breathing with life. Luik quickly decided it was the single most beautiful place he had ever been in all of Dionia, though he left room for future possibilities, as he hadn't seen the whole continent—*yet*.

Gorn mounted the steps of the main hall and stood on the outlying covered porch. The hall itself was made up of a grove of immense high-standing tree trunks that acted as a series of pillars to which hand-shaped lumber was attached in order to box out and fill its long rectangular shape. A densely thatched roof was all but swallowed by the foliage and flowers that draped down over it from above. Gorn raised his hand, and in obedience, all the birds went silent and each boy turned to face him.

"Young men of Dionia, I welcome you to the Isle of Kirstell, our destination but not our end. I bless you for choosing to honor your king and your homelands in embarking on a quest you know little about. Kirstell will be your home from this point on until the king or I grant you another. Here I will teach and you will learn. I will demonstrate and you will master.

"While here, you will not talk of the past nor the future, for both bring false hope and regret, faded memories and irrelevant wishes. You will only speak of the present and the now. You no longer come from Trennesol or from Bensotha, Tontha or Ligeon, but you herald from Kirstell of Dionia; this is your new home where you will be born again. This is where all you once knew will be merely a fading flower in comparison to what you will discover, both dangerously beautiful and beneficially grotesque. Your old self will be cut down to nothing, and who you are about to become will be hewn from the stone of reality and forged by the coals of experience.

"I have not addressed you until now for your number was not complete. But as you can now see, the sleeper has awoken and is made whole. From this moment onward you will do all things as a team; you will eat together, run together, train together, and rest together. To be separated is defeat and to stay together is victory. No one leaves without the others, no one stays behind alone. When one suffers, all suffer. When one is victorious, all have won. For the trials that await cannot be endured by one man alone, but must be faced by the valor and courage of many. Here there is no partiality. All are heirs to the Great God and serve Him.

"With the guidance and wisdom of the Mighty One I will teach you how to be warriors and masters of all things. You will be proficient in the ways of protection and guardianship, advancement and attack, salvation and redemption, planning and strategy, mercy and discretion, judgment and wrath. There will be nothing you cannot do or accomplish. However, time will also make you wise, if you allow her; for your greatest fear will not be of failure or defeat, but of succeeding at a task that does not matter. There will be many roads to choose from that await you. All do not lead to the same destination. You must become wise at choosing the right road.

"You must cherish each day as it is given you, for you are not promised the next. Circumstances beyond your control, at this moment at least, have been set in motion that threaten not only your lives, but those you have left behind. Tomorrow is no longer promised as it always has been before. There is a new season now added to your generation, one it has never known before. A time may come when there is only a handful remaining of those that stand here now and you can be sure that that will be a dark day indeed. For as protectors of Dionia, your survival and prospering will reflect her survival and prospering in turn. For you are no longer merely friends and kin, Sons of Ad; but today I charge you and address you as the Dibor[18], not *brothers* but a sacred *brotherhood* of those who guard the future of all Dionia.

"For, in fact, you were not proclaimed such just this day, but when last you were in King Ragnar's private hall. The mystery of the torcs you now wear around your necks signify the duty and office that you hold. You are bound to the land on which you tread just as it is bound to you. The terminus of each piece, different for each of you, designates your role, as you will soon learn.

"But I warn you; though the calling has been bestowed, none of you is able at this time to operate in your office. It is reserved for me, and me alone, to release you only when you have demonstrated mastery and understanding of all I have taught you. No one shall leave this isle without my knowing and blessing. For you exist now in a refuge of Dionia where no evil can penetrate and no harm may come to you. Not only does a natural sea separate us from the mainland, but also an unseen wall of protection. This is your sanctuary to learn and to fail, to test and to be tested. No fleeting word, no passing thought or intent shall go unnoted and untried. You must learn and fail here, for once you leave this place, errors will mean destruction and mistakes will mean certain death. The

---

[18] **Dibor** (*DYE-bohr*): noun; *First Dionian: literally meaning "guardians", "centurions", or "a sacred protectorate"; singular Dibor or a Dibor meaning one of the members of the Dibor or brotherhood; also to address as a brother.*

next time you journey beyond the shores of Kirstell, there will be no place for ignorance and no room for indecision. You must succeed.

"There is no length of time I can give you to allude to the duration of your stay here; but even if I could inform you of that, you must never allow the passage of time to dictate your state of contentment or dedication. This is your home now and I am your teacher. As to my origin, that is not for you to know.

"The isle on which you stand belongs to you: every rock, every tree, every bird of the air and animal that roams, and every fish that swims to its banks. When you are not bound within the confines of my commands, you are free to explore. Though I will warn you that you will see much less of such time sooner than later. For with obedience comes freedom, and with freedom comes power. Learn to govern yourself and you will be loosed to rule the world around you.

"This is the main hall," Gorn lifted both his hands, "and where you stand will be the center of your world from this point on. The hall itself will be where all decisions are made and is not to be entered without my authority. It is the one place you are not allowed to go on the isle. The courtyard here is your beginning and your end; the place at which you gather and the center from which you disperse.

"You will no longer sleep in the courtyard as you have been these past three nights, but I give you a new place to lay your heads. I will show you to your dwellings and then I will leave you to your own. You may eat and roam freely this last night for tomorrow we will begin. After tonight you will no longer eat as you please, but you will only eat *what* and *when* I tell you to. This statute must not be disobeyed for any reason. Here, all action has consequence, right or wrong.

"I am honored to be your teacher, but I am sobered with my task. What awaits you is difficult, far beyond the likes of which any of you has seen or dared dream of, but it is not impossible. The Great God is with you and will empower you all with every step you take; only put your trust in Him.

"As to the events that took place when we first arrived, know that you are safe now, as well as are the two brothers you nearly lost. If evil had a face, what you saw was its eye; it was looking for you and found you at the last moment. Now it knows where you are. The reason our journey was kept secret, as some things must be, was to protect you as well as our destination. All creation is listening and all creation speaks. Therefore we must be wise with what we say and when we choose to speak it.

"We will meet here at dawn, just before the sun rises." Gorn waited a moment, and then leapt in a single bound from the porch. "Follow me."

He strode directly through them to the opposite pathway leading out of the courtyard and up a steep hill. Thick trees teeming with leaves and flowers lined both sides of the clear-cut path that weaved mildly up the slope. The green hue still permeated the air around them, and the leafy ceiling became lower and lower until one could reach up and touch the closest branches and draping vines. Suddenly Luik and the others emerged from the tunnel-like passage into a giant leafy cavern held aloft by three giant old growth trees. Their trunks and limbs were enormous, twisted and knotty, wandering skyward. As Luik and the rest of the boys marveled at the expanse before them, they all noted a strange deviation in the tree's natural progression upward: *houses*. Thatched huts of various shapes and sizes were constructed around wide reaching limbs of the trees. Wooden footbridges stretched from hut to hut, suspended in midair by vines. Wooden steps that curled around trunks led to even smaller huts higher up, and then dangling ladders disappeared into the thick foliage above. It was a wonderful sight to the throng of boys standing far below, like a group of restless ants ready to investigate their new home.

"Welcome to the Tree House of Kirstell," Gorn said with the fleeting appearance of a smile. "I'll see you in the morning." Gorn turned and reentered the path back toward the main hall. Far-off footsteps beat up the suspended staircase to the first tier of dwellings behind him. He grinned, hearing shouts of glee and boyish delight echo through the woods. Gorn stopped, savoring the moment, for he knew it would be the last of its kind for a generation.

• • •

"There," Jrio pointed to a spot in the waves, "that's where you went under." Luik stood looking almost straight down into the water from their perched position on the upper cliffs.

After sorting out who would sleep where and settling into their respective huts in the tree house, Luik, Jrio, and Quoin decided to venture off and explore a bit of the isle together. Luik had wanted to see where the sand bar was and where he had been carried up, so the other two led him back along the first path on which they had come three days prior. It backtracked through the forest where the main hall was and then came out to an open field that made Luik realize the isle was much larger than he had originally thought. After following the well-beaten footpath through the tall locks of grass, they entered into a hedge of heavy vegetation that went on for a ways and then stopped abruptly at open space. Far out in the distance were the sand dunes on the coast. A salty wind swept up into their hair from the sheer rock surface below their feet.

"It's a long way down." Luik held onto a small tree. The other two agreed. "So you carried me all the way up from down there?"

"No," Quoin said, "not quite. Gorn told us there is no path. The only way to get up here is by that thing." He pointed to their right, following the cliff's edge. There, half hidden by brush was a wooden cage of sorts made of planks and bound with tightly knit wrapping at every joint and intersecting brace. It dangled from a small wheel by a cord and looked like it could hold about ten men.

"What is that?" Luik inquired curiously.

"I don't know its name, but it carried us up here." Quoin grinned. "We *rode* in it. We were the first to come since we escorted you and Rab with Gorn."

"We watched as more of those *things* chased after us all, but they stopped short of the waters as they rose." Jrio gestured to the beach.

"*Demons*," Luik corrected him.

"What did you say?" they asked.

"They are called demons, fallen lythlae from Athera; the Dairne-Reih."

"How do you know that?"

"Gorn told me. They are servants of Morgui."

"Morgui?" Jrio caught his breath.

"They wanted to kill us. They were stalking us the whole time since leaving Adriel."

The three boys stood still listening to the wind and watching long shadows stretch across the mainland.

"How many of them were there?" Luik asked.

No one responded at first. Luik was surprised. He asked again.

"My brothers, how many of them did you see from up here?"

Still there was no answer.

"Jrio," Luik turned and caught him by the shoulder, Jrio's eyes fixed on the beach beyond. "How many did you see?" Jrio breathed in deep, then spoke.

"The whole beach."

"The whole beach was what?" Luik demanded.

Quoin whispered quietly, but just enough for Luik to hear and Jrio to agree.

"It was covered with them, Luik."

Chapter Fifteen

CREATION SHIFT

King Ragnar's garden was surely a sight to behold. If Dionia was paradise, the King's Garden was its crowning jewel. Almost every blooming fragrant flower known among men could be found within its walls, each untouched and allowed to grow to the pinnacle of perfection. Obediently tamed trees, having no need for trimming, grew studiously from tiered marble soil beds and let their fruit unashamedly give witness to their own excellence. A channel of the water that flowed around the king's throne was diverted and sent out the back of the palace from a high spout in the stone wall, creating a waterfall that ended in a pool at one end of the garden. The simple brook from the pool fed the entire landscape with life before vanishing through a grate in the other end of the wall, which drained into the Faladrial Ocean a great distance below.

Fane walked beside his teacher as they strolled along a central path. He wore a simple brown cloak much like his mentor's but, of course, no multi-colored hat as his mentor wore. This was Fane's first time in the garden, though he had marveled at its beauty a few days earlier while looking from a window high above.

"And what do you think, my young apprentice?" Li-Saide asked without looking. "What is the first thing you think of here?" Fane had already learned to not think but to simply react with his first thoughts. There was no getting around his teacher's ability to hear his thoughts.

"The smell," he replied. "It is indescribable."

"Mmm, aye," the dwarf hummed. "The powerful force of the invisible, the diligent work of the unseen. There is something to be said for recognizing first that which you cannot see." He slowed to a stop, still not regarding Fane directly. "Tell me, apprentice," he continued in his aged little voice, "why the smell?"

"Because—," Fane was drawing out the word, struggling for an explanation. "Because I like it!" he said at last.

"So we are creatures that are moved by what we enjoy even if it be something we cannot see?"

"Aye, Teacher."

"Then can we also be disgusted by that which we cannot see?"

Fane furled his brow. "Disgusted? What could disgust me in this place? *It's beautiful!*"

"Come," said his teacher.

They walked on, weaving between different flowered bushes and low cresting trees. They crossed over a small wooden bridge as the stream bent in front of them and then came to a stone bench where Li-Saide instructed Fane to sit.

"Look there," he said, pointing across the round brick terrace in front of them to a strange looking tree beyond. Fane thought it looked naked, like a person with no clothes on. He got up and walked toward it. Only a few small clusters of leaves clung to its bare branches, and they did not look like any leaves Fane had ever seen before.

"Why are these leaves colored like this?" he asked without looking over his shoulder, mesmerized. He reached out and touched one of the red ones and it immediately let go of the branch and fell. Fane stepped back, startled.

"Why—why did it do that?" he asked in disbelief. He watched, following it down to the ground only to see a pile of the rest of the leaves that once adorned the tree; some yellow, some red, and others a dried and frail brown all curled up on themselves. He could hardly speak.

"What did this, Teacher?"

Li-Saide rose from the bench and walked over to him.

"So you think this unnatural?" he replied with his own question.

"Aye, Teacher. I have never seen a tree in such a state before. There is—there is no life in this tree."

"You are right on the first account, but wrong on the other. This tree is not dead, apprentice." Li-Saide removed a small dagger from the fold of his robe and walked up to the tree. He forcefully stabbed it once and then pried the wound open to reveal green and white living tissue beneath.

"However, it is sleeping."

"Sleeping?" Fane's voice rose. "How can it be sleeping?"

"All things you *see* represent something changing among the things you *cannot*. Remember that, young apprentice. The tree you see before you has been altered; its life cycle is changing. Just as the leaves are falling so, too, its life is falling, or rather *failing* for that matter. In order to conserve what life remains in its limbs, it begins to sleep as a defense against its foe."

"And what foe is that, Teacher?"

"*Death.*"

Li-Saide removed the knife from the tree and replaced it in the fold of his robe.

"So how is this tree different from the sickly branch you brought into the meeting of the Gvindollion? I saw you speak right to it and the branch instantly recovered and was made whole, fruit and all. Why not do the same here? Will this tree be all right?"

"I believe so. But I cannot speak to this tree as with the other, for its problem is not the same as the former. That fig branch you saw had been actually touched by evil, but not this one. It would seem that a new life cycle has begun here, a new season set on by—" the dwarf hesitated, "by a force so great it threatens to destroy all life. It is not just this tree that is being affected; all of creation feels it; it's the need to sleep and to conserve whatever remains so as not to have it stolen by the Thief. A force of evil has worked its way into our world silently and unbeknownst to all but a few. We can see creation fold under the weight of evil long before we do, for it is more fragile than we are. Creation is our telltale to see the shifting of the wind."

Fane thought for a moment. "So how do we fight the evil?" Li-Saide was secretly relieved that Fane did not inquire about what sort of evil had been allowed into the King's Garden and had actually touched that fig tree.

Fane continued, "How can we prevent this evil from harming creation that has not yet been personally touched by it?" He paused. "And how can we keep it from mankind?" He pondered his own question, and then burst out, "Jadak! Was Hadrian's father touched by this Thief? He was stolen by him, wasn't he? He was—*taken*." Fane grew solemn as he put the puzzle together in his mind; *Hadrian in the Sea Cave, Jadak, Luik and the other boys at the Gvindollion, the dead tree limb at the meeting, this sleeping tree—Morgui.*

"Morgui," Fane said under his breath. "I'm here to fight against Morgui." Li-Saide said nothing. "He has returned." Fane looked at Li-Saide. "The king has asked me to come because I am supposed to help defend life and you are here to teach me how. Luik and the others are with that large man; he must be their teacher." Fane took in a deep breath. All was becoming a little clearer.

"You are very perceptive for such a young man, apprentice. I do agree with the king in choosing you for this role."

"What role? How can I help? What am I supposed to do?"

"Do? No, no. The question should be who you *are*; then you will know what to do. You have been chosen to be a Mosfar[19], a Keeper of Creation, a Protector of Life. From the dawn of Dionia there has always been a mandate from the Great God to steward and have dominion over all creation. However, the Great Spirit set aside a tribe of men, the dwarves, to assume a select role in ensuring its procreation and perpetual security."

"The dwarves of Ot," Fane concluded. "So you are not just a fable."

"We are very real, apprentice, and perhaps one day you will see the secret city with your own eyes and read of its wealth."

"But why me? I am a Son of Ad and not from the tribe of dwarves."

"And thus you will never be sought after or suspected if you remain as wise as I think you are. Our tribe is in great danger for reasons that I cannot yet entrust you with. Right now it is my job to instruct you and impart to you all the ways of the Mosfar. It is for me to guard you above all else. Should I fail, I fear that Dionia may never know what has befallen her and may never remember what she once was."

---

[19] **Mosfar** (*MAWS-fahr*): *First Dionian: name given to the tribe of Dwarves at the beginning of creation; meaning "Creation Keeper" or "protector"; singular a Mosfar meaning one of the members of The Mosfar or brotherhood.*

"You mean I'm a secret?" Fane smiled in the midst of great despair, seeming to hear only the first part of what his teacher said. Li-Saide felt lightened by the simplicity of the comment.

"Aye," he chuckled, "you are *our secret*."

A few moments passed where the gravity of the situation waned thin, and child-like joy filled both of their hearts. It was Fane who spoke next.

"And what about this tree, Teacher? What can we do?"

"When men are taken, creation enters fall. A new season of life is upon us, young apprentice. There is not much we can do; for the tree before you is not directly being affected by peshe, but it is responding out of instinct to the change in atmosphere around it."

Fane became pensive for a moment and then spoke something softly.

"*Dark days.*"

"Aye, exactly," Li-Saide said with surprise. "Where did you first hear that phrase?"

"My father said it to me just before I left home. I didn't understand him, but I think I do now."

"Aye, apprentice, dark and *cold* days are soon upon us."

Cold? Fane had never heard this word before.

"It is the absence of the warmth you feel around you. It is a state you have never felt before, but you soon will."

"Hey'a! How do you do that? You heard my thoughts just then, didn't you? And back in the palace, too."

"It is a skill acquired by learning to trust the unseen more than what you can touch, just like your smell of the garden, apprentice. Now don't lose thought, focus; the tree."

"Aye," Fane said shaking his head, "so there is nothing we can do for it?"

"Maybe not for it, directly; it is responding to a cause that is, at this moment, far beyond our control. But the real question is *what can we do for the rest of its kind; for creation as a whole?* First you must learn how creation breathes and moves; you must know why the wind moves the way it does and what it's trying to say; you must understand the fields and the beasts that roam them; you must know of the trees and all the birds that eat of their fruit; and you must know of the waters and the creatures that swim in them. Lastly you must know of the greatest being that walks on Dionia: *man*. For mankind is the greatest mystery of all. I would think it the noblest of all tasks to figure and calculate the ways of man in all that he does, the achievement of a lifetime to explain his peculiar and unending intentions."

"So it is clear that I am to learn—"

"And to protect!"

"To protect creation," Fane added with a nod.

"No, no. To serve and protect its very life and those who will vanquish the Evil One!" Li-Saide became very animated, his little arms waving.

"Those who will vanquish the Evil One? You mean—"

"The Dibor!" Li-Saide cut him off.

"The Dibor, what's that?"

"Again, not *what* but *who*; they are to the preservation of all that is Good and True what the Mosfar have been to the sustaining of creation. They are the guardians of mankind and are set with the task of driving Morgui, once more, from our world."

"*Luik.*"

"Aye, Luik—and the others; they have all been chosen to endure the training ways of Gorn and The Dibor. They are of royal blood and, therefore, legally represent the inhabitants of Dionia. One day they, too, will train up a host of others to fight beside them, but for now they must be protected and invested into. Now they are where evil cannot touch them or bring them harm. Their task is more poignant than they know it to be; Morgui must not only be driven out, but he must be destroyed, if it is possible. For his power has increased since he first invaded our world and it has been growing ever since that day. What the Race of Men was able to do once, it must be willing to do again. But a third encounter, I am afraid, may not leave Adriel standing and the breath of men stirring. If Morgui is ever allowed to attempt again what he is now, his power will be too great and our world will not be able to stand."

"But what of the Great God, the Mighty One? Will He not save us?"

Li-Saide closed his eyes and sighed.

"Aye," he said, "it is written that the Bright and Morning Star, the Lamb and the Lion will save that which he calls His own. But we are no longer promised this next breath while an evil rages outside our door. The

Good God has placed in our own hands the ability to preserve ourselves and protect what He alone has entrusted to us. One day it is quite possible that this paradise may come to an end and we will be carried up to serve in His Great Throne Room. But against the wrath of such evil, many will fall; *many will be taken.* Morgui must not be allowed to act in such ways again. Something must be done, for we are in dire jeopardy by the Evil One of losing our immortality and our place in Athera. We must do everything in our power to resist him; *to defeat him forever.*"

Fane stood silent. The brook babbled beside him, but for once he did not parallel its behavior. His thoughts drifted toward his mother and father back home. He thought of the way life was and how beautiful he knew everything to be, of the joy of spending days with his friends, and the marvelous adventures they had taken together throughout Bensotha, and the thought that it could come to an end? It was too much to dwell on. He could feel something being stolen from him as he stood there. It was as if a part of him was being cut away. It was too deep to grieve over just now, but he would one day. Fane had no words to describe it, but he felt it. Li-Saide knew exactly what it was, *time, innocence, the simplicity of youth, and the faded memories of all-encompassing security.*

"Anything I can do to help Luik, I will. He is my greatest friend."

"*Luik?*" Li-Saide replied with near shock. "*Anything you can do to help the existence of your world is what you should say!* But alas, I perceive your heart, though I do not understand the ways of Man, I know you are driven by compassion and loyalty in ways dwarves are not. Wherever you derive your motivation from for now is fine, my young apprentice, but know that one day all this may pass and things that once moved you will seem unworthy and frail, trivial at best. Friends will pass, as will family and even causes. The only thing that will remain is the Word of the Most High. It will endure. It shall never cease. Let it be your guide and let His Great Spirit move you into all action. Then you will never be lost and your deeds never without justification or worth. Come, young apprentice, let us leave these things for now and speak of others, for I have had you linger here far too long. Let us enjoy the beauty of this place before there remains no beauty to be seen, only that which we once could see."

Li-Saide turned and began walking away from the tree in fall and returned to the pathway along the stream. Fane followed right behind. He tried as best he could to let everything told him rest, but his mind stirred incessantly. Li-Saide felt his unrest and tried bringing in a new topic of discussion, one a little more personal, for both their sakes.

"So, my young apprentice, as I'm sure you have been on many adventures, what is your most memorable? What trip do you frequent the most with your friends?"

They walked along together, and Fane felt relaxed by the question that began stirring fond memories. One adventure, or place, rather, came to mind more than any other he could possibly think of, for it was by far the most meaningful to him. He knew that their hideout was a secret and that they had made a pact never to tell a living soul about it, not daring that any should ever intrude on their private refuge. But how would Fane ever think to keep such a secret from a dwarf that could hear his thoughts? Plus, he reasoned, his secrets would be safe with Li-Saide, closest confidant and advisor to the king.

"Well, there is one place that we frequent more than any other," Fane said, now smiling, a flood of memories over running his mind.

"Aye? Do tell me, I should like to hear of it, I think." Li-Saide walked a little more loosely than before. The scent of flowers filled his little head hidden by the billowy patchwork hat.

"It's actually right nearby," Fane added for a little mystery.

"Interesting!" Li-Saide laughed, appreciating Fane's wit. "Do go on."

"It's our most favorite and secret place. In fact, I would guess that it's nearly right beneath our feet!"

Li-Saide was finding this quite amusing, wondering what in the world Fane could be talking about as he knew the grounds of Adriel better than anyone still living in Dionia! "Beneath our feet?" Li-Saide grinned wide, not being able to hear Fane's thoughts, as there were far too many of them now.

"Aye, but you must promise me that you will never tell the others. Luik, Hadrian and Anorra of Ligeon, that is. Promise? You have to promise!"

"Aye," the dwarf laughed out loud. "I promise."

Fane lowered his voice as if the trees might betray his trust.

"We call it the Sea Cave and it's—" but Fane was cut short and never did finish telling Li-Saide about it, at least not in the way he had hoped to. The little dwarf spun on his heels and grabbed Fane abruptly by the shoulders, shouting just inches from his face.

"*What? What do you know about the Sea Cave?*"

Chapter Sixteen

RUNAWAY

The boy in the field decided that working the garden beside his house had become much more difficult than ever before, for a number of reasons. Firstly, he noted, the ground was much harder to till than ever before, and secondly the fruit did not blossom as easily as it once had. Thus the amount of time required for both was increasing almost daily. Water from within the ground seemed insufficient so he had to dig new troughs from the main stream to channel water to the driest places. And for the first time that he had ever seen, the soil resisted him so much that at one point a tool broke while in mid-swing. Labor in the garden had always been a delight; but this was not labor anymore, it was becoming *toil*. And this was not even the worst of his troubles; for all these things would have been joys to endure if his father were still here to endure it with him.

"Hadrian! It's time to eat, my love!"

Hadrian put his basket down and stretched. *Food*: he always loved to eat and his mother always made sure his need was satisfied.

"Be right there, Na na!" Hadrian hollered back with a smile.

Nearly half the summer had passed since his father had been taken. To say that Hadrian missed him was a tragic understatement. He had experienced more longing and heartache than he knew possible. At first they were new emotions and left him weeping at night and saddened by morning. It was not like someone being called on to the Great Throne room at all. Sure, his father was gone but it felt like he would never see him again. It felt like he had ceased to exist; like he was *dead*. Hadrian tried to resist the overwhelming emotions as best he knew how, but instead of resisting them, he simply got used to them, sort of like old friends.

Plenty of people tried to console him and comfort him directly following the disappearance. They brought many beautiful baskets of flowers and bushels of fruit. Hadrian didn't understand the custom; was his father in the flowers? Was he tasted in the fruit? Probably the only person that helped settle him even remotely was the visit by his father's best friend, Luik's father, King Lair.

• • •

"Hey'a, Hadrian, Son of—" Lair stopped short, realizing where this was leading, *Son of Jadak*. Lair embraced the adolescent son of his dear friend. Hadrian wept bitterly. "Calm you, son. Easy now." Hadrian buried his tear stained face in Lair's neck, his chest heaving. He had been crying for two days straight.

"Where is my father?" he demanded sorrowfully. "I don't understand what they've told me. I want him back. I want him back right now."

• • •

"Hadrian!" his mother yelled again. He knew her tone; it would be the last chance to eat for the day if he did not go. He shook off the memory and ran back to the cottage across the field. Hadrian had been able to deal with the absence of his father by working the gardens twice as hard he ever had before. Somehow he knew he'd press through this, but the person he really worried about was his mother.

"Hey'a, Na na," Hadrian said giving her a kiss. The bright home resembled most of the others in Bensotha. Clean white walls curved and contoured from room to room, never bearing a hard angle. Circular holes of all different sizes were cut in the walls to serve as windows both to the outside and from one space to another within, and the floors were covered with brilliantly dyed mats. Shining candles hung from the ceiling, mounted in windows, and clung in special nooks along the walls. Even in the middle of day, their scent and light permeated the house. A few of the rooms were designated bedrooms for family or for guests, and small chairs accompanied each bed. In the central room, a large square table stood with four benches around the sides. Today, like all the others, it was topped with three heaping bowls of cut fruit mixed together in different varieties. A block of cheese sat with a knife in it, fresh bread still steaming, and a cup of squeezed juice. *Probably wellem nectar*, he thought, *my favorite.*

"C'symia," he said to his mother, squeezing her hand gently. He was truly grateful and he showed it by washing every dish when he was through.

He wasted no time in sitting down, thanking the Good God for his life, not just his food, and got lost in the bowls of delicious fruit his mother had prepared. She sat down, too, and they both partook. Somewhere between sipping his juice and the bread, he got lost again in his thoughts.

• • •

"He is gone, Hadrian," Lair said once the tears had settled a bit.

"But where? When is he coming back?"

"He's not, my son. It would take a very brave man to bring him back and your father would need twice as much bravery to return."

"What do you mean?" Hadrian pleaded. "I want my Ta na! Why did he leave me? Why did he leave me here alone?" Suddenly he became angry. "How could he leave me alone and just go without even saying goodbye?"

Lair's heart was grieved. He knew that the innate need for every man is to have his identity established. To a young boy, his father *is* his identity: the way he speaks, the way he walks and works; the way he plays and endures challenges; even the way he falls asleep at night tells the boy who he is supposed to be. The father imparts identity resulting in a boy's own sense of self-worth and meaning. But most of all, a father provides the model for how a boy is supposed to view the Heavenly Father one day when he is no longer just a young man, but an old man. There comes a time when all boys stop looking at their fathers and start looking past them. The goal of every father is to lead in such a way that when they step out of their son's path of vision that the young man is left staring directly in the eyes of the Great Father. Without all these things, a boy is utterly lost, searching for anything to cling to as a source of security and identity.

"Hadrian," the king's voice became a little harder in tone than he wanted, but he did not know how else to address his friend's son. "Your father has chosen to walk out of the Will of the Most High. He *chose* it, and not even I can understand why. All men are given a choice to follow something. Something, or someone, is leading us all, whether we choose to admit it or not. I cannot give you all the answers, but I will share with you everything I know for as long as it takes for you to understand it. The most important thing I can tell you is this; that you must make the right choices, Hadrian. Your father has chosen his path, but you must choose yours. You must not follow his ways. I charge you with this; no matter how hard things become or how difficult a path is, you *must* follow the ways of the Great God."

"But if I follow the ways of my father, won't I get to see him again?"

"No, my son, you won't. If you ever see the face of your father again, it will be in a form that you hardly recognize. He will be a shadow of the man you once knew." Lair quivered at his own words; at his own memory. "Even if you followed his path, the agony you would experience would be so unbearable that your thoughts would never even turn to finding your father. It would be the furthest thing from your mind. All you could think about would be how to quench the unending thirst in your mouth and ease the burning in your flesh. You would walk around day and night, never sleeping, never eating, completely at the control and mercy, if that's even what it can be called, of another much more fierce and evil than you could ever imagine. They are *the taken*. They walk around, from dusk to dawn and back again, doing the bidding of Morgui. They are not alive, nor are they yet fully dead, but once their physical bodies meet their mortality's end, they will be faced with judgment according to their deeds and separated from the presence of the Most High, *forever*. *That*, my son, is true death."

Hadrian nodded his head in understanding, trying to wade through the state of his heart and engage with the words being spoken to his mind. He was tired and felt as if every tear available in his body had been cried.

• • •

"Hadrian," his mother said, "where are you? Come back."

"Sorry, Na na. I was just thinking."

"Aye, and you also spilled your juice down your chest," she said with a slight giggle, pointing across the table. Hadrian looked down and wiped the nectar away frantically. She laughed some more. Suddenly he realized that this was the first time he had heard her laugh since his father was taken. Not wanting it to stop, he purposefully knocked the cup over with his elbow. At this her laughter filled the central room and echoed through the rest of the house. He laughed with her. It went on for a few more moments as Hadrian sopped up the rest of the spill with a towel.

"Well, Na na, that's the first I have heard you laugh since—" he went silent.

"Since your father was taken." She was good at finishing his sentences. He just nodded.

"You know, I really do miss him," she said fondly. "He was a good man and I guess I will never know what drove him away. Maybe—"

"Maybe it was my spills!" Hadrian held his cup high, still dripping with yellow juice. They laughed some more. It had been the first time since the incident that either of them could joke, even *about it*. The room got quiet again.

"He was my best friend, you know," she said. "He was made with just me in mind. I would be very lonely if I did not have the Great Spirit to keep me company and talk with me each night before going to sleep."

"Aye," Hadrian said, "I hear you speaking at night. He talks with me in the field, though sometimes I still have many questions, and often He does not answer like always."

"I understand. I experience the same thing," she said. "But, Hadrian, you must never let the answers, nor the lack thereof, ever harden your heart against the Most High. Always remember that He is not the enemy. Be careful never to confuse the two spirits. For there is only One Spirit; every other spirit is false and does not bear witness to Him. Never forget that. Never forget, now. Do you understand?"

"Aye, Na na."

"Morgui will try everything in his power to confuse you and burden you with thoughts that are not of the Maker. Morgui cannot read

THE WHITE LION CHRONICLES BOOK I | RISE OF THE DIBOR

your thoughts. He cannot see into your mind but he can attack your mind
and watch what happens. Depending on your reaction he will attack you
again and again more specifically until he pinpoints your weakness, either
betrayed by your own mouth, or by your careless actions. You must never
give him room; you must never allow him entrance. For once he has begun
his deceitful tricks you are never fully aware that you are subject to them.
The worst part about *being deceived* is that you never realize you *are deceived*.
It takes someone of great courage and fortitude to rescue you out of that
state; that is, of course, if you will listen to that person."

• • •

Hadrian was back in the field, finishing for the evening. It had
been a good day's work. There were few interruptions from visiting
neighbors today, and besides the evening meal, which was no interruption
at all, he was able to stay completely on task. Almost twenty bushels had
been harvested and twelve rows of new dew plants sown. He unhitched
the horse from the till and let him go free, thanking him gently for his
labor. Hadrian enjoyed the work, though he did miss his friends and all the
adventures they once used to go on together. Nothing had been the same
since Luik, Fane, and Anorra left Bensotha. He missed them terribly.

The sun was setting in the east while Hadrian was standing in the
middle of the western field, about to turn for home. He seemed to be
coping with his grief well enough. It was hardest to see his mother struggle
through the loss of her husband. With each passing day it seemed that all
people did was offer him advice, but none of it fixed the heartache inside,
or his mother's. He was getting tired, tired of sorrow, tired of empty words,
tired of fighting an unseen enemy, and tired of the pain. While the garden
entertained him and his mother's food nourished him, he was starving on
the inside. He wanted his father back. He wanted to be a boy again. He
wanted to play with his friends, go to the Sea Cave, play rokla, and swim
in the ocean. He felt old somehow, older than he should be, forced to an
age beyond his years.

"Why can't things be the same as they used to be?" he yelled out,
listening to his voice echo off the distant hills and fade into nothing.

"But they can," came a voice behind him. Hadrian spun around,
startled. A cloaked figure stood before him, face hidden in the shadow of

158

his hood. "Do not fear, Hadrian, there is no cause for alarm." The voice was tender and slow but Hadrian *was* alarmed. Everything in him told him to run. *Run away.*

"Who are you?" Hadrian said forcefully, attempting to conceal his obvious uneasiness. "How did you get in my garden?" He looked around for anyone else.

"I know where your father is," the smooth voice said. Something in Hadrian found it appealing.

"You—you do?" he replied. Hope was kindled. But then came all the words spoken by Lair, by his mother. "Aye, so do I, he's gone. He's *taken.*"

"Taken?" the voice said. "O no, Hadrian. He is still here. He did not leave; he simply did not want to be seen anymore. He's been asking for you, you know."

"Asking for me? Where is he then? Why can't I see him?"

"But you can! All you have to do is ask me!"

Hadrian felt sick to his stomach, but his loss and grief pained him much more.

"Where is he? Let me see him! I want to see my father!"

"Very well," the voice said, sweetening. "Look there, by the edge of your garden. Do you see that man standing by the grove of pine trees?"

Hadrian stepped sideways and gazed across the field. He studied the cluster of trees in the distance and there, surely as the voice told him, stood a dark figure.

"He's alive?" Hadrian's heart began to race. *It couldn't be, could it?*

"Run to him, Hadrian! Run!"

"*Ta na!*" Hadrian took off in an instant. He ran as hard as he could, energized by hope and powered by a love lost. The closer he got, the more excited he became. He ran with a smile across his face that could have been seen on the other side of Dionia. But what couldn't be seen was the other smile, the one on the stranger's face.

"Father!" he yelled now almost to the pines. He could see a man with his back toward him moving just inside the grove. "Father, wait! It's me! *It's your son!*" Hadrian was half crying and half laughing. Within another instant he was in the pines, but it didn't smell of pine; it was rancid and stank of decay.

"Ta na?"

Chapter Seventeen

SON OF THE DEAD

Upon waking from that first night spent in the Tree House, a whole new order of life was waiting just beyond the few remaining moments of twilight. Gorn walked beneath the shadow of the huge trees and roared the sleeping boys to life in the pre-dawn hours.

"The sun still sleeps, but you cannot!" Gorn bellowed from below. A few weary heads lifted from pillows only to shake away the fleeting sound and slump back to sleep.

"Arise, my boralees!" The voice echoed through the treetops once more, stirring the birds in their roosts, but no Dibor.

"The first to the courtyard receives a double portion," Gorn said in a milder tone, "while the last takes none." Then he gently recessed back through the leafy tunnel to the main courtyard, waiting on his words. At first nothing stirred in the forest, save for the songs of a few waking thrushes. But after a moment or two a soft patter of feet resonated through the woods; it started as little rhythms that beat along the suspended bridges and bounded down ladders; but soon it became a rapid hammering as all eighteen boys stormed down the trail to the courtyard, contending for position.

Jrio was first this time, still feeling the sting of Gorn's last challenge and not wishing to lose once more. He tore into the central square a good five lengths in front of the others, catching Gorn's acknowledging wink and then turning to watch the rest pile in. And pile they did, pressing one another so hard that they tripped and fell in a heap of flailing bodies, all sure they would be the first. To their disappointment, Jrio stood smiling in the muted darkness, waving a hand at them.

"Jrio!" Thero exclaimed. "How did you get here so fast?"

"He slept here," Quoin answered from beneath. The other boys laughed.

"No," Gorn corrected them, "he was listening to my voice." Everyone stopped laughing and composed themselves once more, rising from the sprawling mess. "And for this he will receive a double portion of fruit and water today." There was a genuine sense of feeling for Jrio's good fortune, though accompanied with a faint twinge of jealousy. But how much more it would be later that day after they had worked hard running and training, all the while hoarding within themselves an appetite and thirst unlike any they had ever known before.

"Who comes in last?" Gorn asked, looking back up the trail.

"Fyfler," someone said from among those standing together. Upon hearing that name, Jrio grinned slyly. The tables had turned.

"Learn well, boralees; one who is quick the first time may often slumber through the next time."

Fyfler lumbered into the dim square still rubbing the sleep from his eyes.

"What? What did you say?" he asked vaguely.

"I said, you will receive no fruit or water today," Gorn said sternly.

Fyfler was never late again, though the next day he would have been fortunate to be so, as Gorn woke them with the same words.

"The sun still sleeps, but you cannot! Arise, my boralees! The first to the courtyard receives a double portion while the last takes none."

But this time the boys were ready, anticipating the summons. They leapt from their beds, jumped from their ladders and ran down the track, having slept in their breecs all night. Upon arriving, the news was not what they had anticipated.

"Very good," Gorn said with a smile, standing with his hands on his hips in the dim light. He wore only a white tunic. "You were much quicker in obeying my orders, and for this I am well pleased. However, you assume too much of which you are not certain, and this may be cause for great error in the days to come. Simply because your experience leads you down one path does not always mean it is the *only* path. What was once a clear avenue may rapidly turn into a perilous route; hastening to your own end is not becoming of nobility. Yet being too quick and too slack both have their detriments; he that counts the cost while not losing pace will surely benefit greatly when the days grow dark.

"Cage, you were quick to be first. Well done. However, your double portion is that of extra training and not food. You will have extra lengths to run. And, Naron," Gorn turned to the last in line, though he was not tardy, just simply pushed to the back, "you will have the afternoon to swim at your leisure after the morning's exercises." Naron beamed. After yesterday's long workout, he was somewhat dreading another full day, one that the rest of the boys had to endure.

And so it went on like this, day after day, week after week, small rules being set up, only to change ever so slightly, viewed in a different light. The boys never knew quite what to expect. The moment they hoped too much in one thing, it was pulled out from under them and replaced by another, contrary to the first. Their boyish minds were slowly transformed into cunning, problem-solving devices, always looking for the hidden angle and unseen directive. They learned to be tough, growing more resilient to each unknown facet of every new dawn. There became more reason to cherish the smaller, seemingly less important elements of life than the grand ones they had become so comfortable with. The danger, of course, was pulling them too far away, and that too quickly, from the innocence of the child-like heart they arrived with. Gorn was ever aware of the gravity of such a task: to mold warriors that cherished life, not hardened mongrels that scorned it. For he knew there were plenty of those. So in all his teaching, Gorn made sure to always allow room for them to be boys, lest they forgot what they were so diligently working to protect: the innocence and youth of those after them. The rhythm was delicate, the balance critical.

Except for Gorn's random changes in schedule, each day was structured relatively the same. Every morning the boys were awakened just before dawn and brought into the square. A morning run took them out to a section of the island and then back. Sometimes it was through one of the many fields, or often through the woods, but always to return to the courtyard for a piece of fruit and water, that is, *if* it was in Gorn's mood. And, my, what fruit it was, so succulent and sweet! The boys dared guess they had never eaten such food in all their days, wondering why their homeland's never tasted so rich and juicy.

In the square they would each fulfill a required amount of exercises to build their strength, from push-ups and sit-ups to pulling their chins over a tree limb just by their hands. Then they would gather together and sit, listening to Gorn speak, sometimes for a few minutes, sometimes for the whole morning, imparting stories, words of wisdom, and great truths that he said would hold them in good standing during the trying days to come. When Gorn spoke they could feel their minds being nourished as much as their bodies were when eating Kirstell's fruit. The things they learned there in that secluded wood were more mysterious, more marvelous, and more terrifying than anything they could have ever imagined. They learned and tasted daily of the presence of the Most High, of His marvelous deeds and the secret places of His heart, finding basins of intimacy they never knew existed in Him; they learned of Dionia and the beginning of all creation; of the First Battle and of those who had gone before them both to *death* and also to the Great Throne Room; of wise sayings that, if dwelt upon, would root themselves deeply into the boy's spirits and never betray them; and of the art of war, against Morgui and the Dairne-Reih, strategies in battle and of tactics, and the leading of men. Gorn tested them day after day, asking them to recite what had been taught the day before, and then the week before, covering and recovering what he spoke until there was no doubt they could never forget it. The training of their minds and spirits was even more necessary than that of their bodies.

Following their lecture, Gorn would select a weapon for training: wooden swords, staves, bow and arrow, shields, wooden maces and flails, wooden axes and pikes, pole arms and blunted spears. At first the weapons reminded the boys of playing back in the gardens around their homes, that is, until Gorn demonstrated how each weapon could be used to *kill* an enemy in any number of ways. Each weapon and all of its respective functions were memorized and then placed within the realm of a simple number system the boys had memorized early on. Each number, shouted out by Gorn, indicated a space of placement, right flank or left, high or low. Depending on whether or not a trainee was parrying or attacking, the number meant a different placement and use for each weapon. Of course, they had to master every combination on every weapon.

Weapons' training was always extensive, lasting well into the afternoon, broken up only by a drink of water about halfway through. Once the tools were cleaned, cared for and stowed away, Gorn gave them a bite to eat and a moment's rest. But just when he sensed them enjoying their leave a little too much, he had them on their feet again and ready to give them the evening's Iyne Dain[20]. The Iyne Dain was a nightly task that varied as much in its means as it did in its subject. But one thing was certain, every Iyne Dain brought out something new in the group of boys, something they had never seen in each other or in themselves. It was a time of personal testing as much as it was corporately. After completing the evening's challenge, the boys would return to the square to have a meal and listen more to Gorn before trailing off to the Tree House.

Tonight was unusual, though, as they returned from the night's Iyne Dain to the square with a fire burning high in the center beneath the leafy canopy. Gray smoke permeated the air and seeped inefficiently up through the branches above, shrouding most of the sites of the courtyard in a thick haze. The boys hesitated as they entered from an eastern trail that led in from a nearby field. The smoke filled their lungs and burned their eyes, leaving each boy unsure of what to do next, retreat back into open air or press in further.

"Come!" a strong voice bellowed from somewhere within the smog. It was Gorn. Hearing their master's voice, the boys trudged into the square and held back tears. The orange glow of the fire saturated the atmosphere in a diffused wash as the outer reaches of the courtyard faded to black.

"Come, and sit by the fire," he summoned once more. The boys, still unsure of where Gorn's voice was coming from, circled the flames individually and then sat down on the ground in a ring around it. Coughs went up within their midst and each boy cupped his mouth with his hand in a futile effort to filter the caustic air. None of them had ever smelled such a foul and painful fume. It was like gravel in their eyes and thorns in their throats.

"What you have now is but a taste," Gorn said, still hiding in the vile fog. "*A taste of what?* you might ask." Suddenly they could see his form

---

[20] **Iyne Dain** (*EYEn-[eh] DANE*): *noun; literally meaning "Heart Quest."*

emerge from one side and stand behind their seated ring. "I tell you now it is a taste of Haides and the perpetual fires that prey on the flesh of those who reject the Most High." He turned and walked around the outside of their ring, continuing to talk.

"Though you may never see its gates or feel the agony of its flames, Haides is a very real place. Just because you cannot see something does not mean it fails to exist. To think such thoughts is proud and egocentric. There is one Truth, and it is by that standard that we hold all others to. Men may go on searching for it in error, but for those of us who were born with its light in our hearts, our greatest test will simply be to endure and proclaim that Truth until we meet our last breath.

"*Why does this fume hurt you so?* you may wonder. How can it prevail upon you with such discomfort? Because the flames of Haides were never meant for man or animal, but for the fallen hosts of Athera alone. The Most High created that place of torment for those who betrayed Him, but never intended it for his most precious creation—*us*. If he could, Morgui would take every last one of you. He is not content to suffer alone in such a barren and desolate cage, tormented through long ages that bring neither day nor night, only an incessant din of a reminder that haunts him of his error. Nay, he would smite you at the first opportunity, even now, were it possible. To kill, to steal, and to utterly destroy the creation and works of the Most High, that is his only ambition. Were he to gain such a foothold in our realm as he has in others that we know of, I fear our resistance to his temptation would be fruitless. But his power is gained only by those who enable him, only by those that give in."

Luik stared intently into the flames, sorting through each breath he inhaled with a focused intent on not coughing. He sat crossed legged with his elbows on his knees and his hands over his mouth and nose. The rest of the boys were in a similar state, wiping the tears from the corners of their eyes and trying desperately not to interrupt their teacher with their coughs.

"So where shall we journey from here, my boralees?" Gorn went on, lifting his arms in the haze. "To the beginning, I say; to the First Battle. Look into the flames and watch, look into the fire and perceive what few others remember."

Luik stared into the leaping tongues of fire and noticed that they seemed more dense than normal. Rather than slender shafts of light flickering through the air, they bunched tightly together appearing as a wall of fire. Luik noticed he could no longer make out the faces of his friends on the other side of the ring. There in the fire pit he began to see something, shapes emerging within the light, and not the form of the fire or burning embers, but angular and defined. He leaned in closer, forgetting about the intense heat and putrid smoke, and studied the image, trying earnestly to make it out. Suddenly a large face appeared and the eyes opened wide. Luik fell back in a startled jolt of surprise. He looked around, his heart racing. The other boys were equally taken aback; they had seen it, too.

"Take a good look, my boralees," Gorn instructed. "It is the face of a young man not four summers older than most of you." Luik studied the face in the flames. It was handsome and strong; a firm chin and broad forehead, his eyes glowing blue and beautiful. Luik's view pulled away until he could see the rest of the figure. The man was dressed only in a light blue wrap around the waist, his feet bare. His upper body was tanned and muscular. On each bicep he wore a golden arm-band and a golden torc around his neck. His long black hair draped over one shoulder and the gold ring on his finger signified royalty; he was a prince of Dionia.

"His name is Velon," Gorn said sternly, "Firstborn of King Rill, the firstborn of King Ad. His home was Adriel and the trees and streams of the Peninsula his childhood adventures. Velon was the first grandson to be born in Dionia, not more than a few years after her glorious dawn, while creation was fresh and new. In that time not a blade of grass lay out of place and not a leaf dangled in the air that didn't waver in obedience with the rest.

"It was also a time when the Spirit of the Most High was felt the strongest. His presence permeated everything and everyone. Velon walked and talked with the Most High, much as you have done growing up, my young boralees—but more so. His conversing with the Most High knew no limits. Every day he was free to ask a new question and explore the depths of His Maker's character with boundless searching. His delight of knowing the Most High knew no end, for He had made Himself available but only for the joy of watching His creation grow in fellowship with Himself.

"Velon breathed in the Spirit of the Most High from dawn until dusk and then lingered there in His presence all through the night as he slept. Nothing separated him; nothing diminished the sweetness of His

Maker's presence. For where could Velon go from His Spirit, or where could he escape from His gaze? Nor was Velon alone in this; for all of Dionia enjoyed such a relationship with the Creator, each as special to the individual as they were unique. For that is the majesty of the Most High, that He would know the intimate details of each man and woman He had created and share Himself freely with them. The dawn of Dionia was a beautiful and marvelous sight, untouched and unblemished in its divine purity.

"As it happened, Velon was taking a walk beneath the heat of the afternoon sun. Four of his friends also journeyed with him that day, making good company as they strolled under the alder trees and sucked sweetly on the green pime fruit they found along the path. Every day there was something new to savor and enjoy. Creation was continually unfolding from the Most High's hands, bringing delight to the Sons of Ad. When Ad first was formed he was commissioned with naming all of the plants, the animals of the fields, the birds of the air and the fish in the sea, and all the creatures that crawled about or buzzed by from flower to leaf. Velon was ten and eight summers old and his grandfather had yet to complete his task. Even with the aid of his wife Eva and their son, Velon's father, Rill, the Most High's extravagance and creativity were boundless and seemed to consume Dionia with unending surprise.

"As they walked through long grasses and beside the clear streams that meandered effortlessly around boulders and down cascading terraced ledges, the youth couldn't help but marvel at their Maker's genius. Every minute that passed presented a new brilliantly painted bug and bird, and the air was filled with a singsong of flitting creatures. Shadow monkeys swung from the trees above and hollered down to them in delight. Jenko lizards turned in their sunbathing to examine the beautiful humans that walked by. And swift four-legged animals that hadn't been named yet lifted their heads from chewing their grass to watch Velon and his friends pass through the trees beyond.

"Velon walked in paradise, and nothing, anywhere, could be more perfect than this. There was no toil, only a labor of love. There was no contention, only the delightful tension of expectation brought on by the wonder of a new day.

"The five friends enjoyed the rest of that afternoon, playing together and allowing themselves to be wooed away into the beauty around them. They walked on for hours, eventually mounting up a grand hillside and settling on the lofty summit in a small clearing of thick, soft grass bordered by a few trees. When night finally came, Velon stretched out on his back beneath the stars and placed his hands under his head. Crickets and cicadas stirred incessantly while songbirds roosting in their nests sang the stars to sleep. It wasn't long before Velon answered the same call and fell asleep with the stars.

"Some time later that night, a strange voice called out in the darkness. It started as a distant whisper but slowly grew nearer and clearer. 'Vel—on,' it said sweetly with the rise and fall of a song. 'Velon, arise and come.' At first he did not hear it, but soon it grew stronger and stirred him from his slumber. 'Velon, won't you come? Where are you?' He opened his eyes and looked around the starry sky thinking it was but a dream. Then he heard the voice again. But this time it sounded as if it were coming from over behind a tree on the edge of the clearing. 'Velon, please, *please* come!' He sat up quickly, now wide-awake, his heart beating harder. It spoke again and he glanced quickly to a small grove of trees standing tall over a steep rock ledge that descended to the valley floor far below. Velon rolled onto his side and pressed himself up. He shook the lingering effects of slumber away with a shudder and then took a step forward. The voice called again. 'Velon, is that you?' He looked around.

"'Aye,' he said ever so softly, not wishing to wake his friends.

"'O Velon, I've been looking for you!' The voice was sweet and pleading.

"'Who's there?' he asked, not able to tell if it was a man's voice or a woman's. 'What's your name?'

"'I need you, Velon. Why won't you come to me?' Velon was so curious that he walked toward the voice without having his questions answered. Had he known who it was he may have stopped, but then again, he may have walked on just the same. We will never know. Either way, each step he took brought him closer to a fate that would change Dionia for all time.

"'Aye, here I am. Now reveal yourself. Who are you?' Velon spoke a little louder as he stepped into the small grove of trees and passed behind a mighty oak tree, out of sight of his sleeping companions. Crouched against the tree trunk was a hooded figure, face hidden in shadow. 'Ah, Velon, it is good of you to come.'

"'Aye, and who are you, my friend? Where do I know you from that you would know my name and the place where I rest my head?'

"'Do not all the inhabitants of Dionia know her kings and their sons?' the figure replied. 'I am but one who admires you from a distance and merely seeks a midnight audience with you alone.' Velon was intrigued with the answer and knelt low in the shadows.

"'Then what is it you wish to discuss at this present hour, so early in the morn?' he asked the hooded figure.

"'What I wish to discuss? Nay, my prince. I am here for what you wish to discuss.'

"'What I wish to discuss?' Velon was surprised. 'I wish to discuss nothing at this hour unless it be with the dreams of my heart found while asleep!'

"'Aye, aye, prince Velon, the dreams of your heart,' replied the figure. 'Let us talk of your dreams together.' Velon bumbled through his thoughts, trying to find a rational response to this premise, but found none.

"'What is it you dream of?' asked the figure. 'What is it that your heart desires more than all else?' Though Velon found this encounter trivial and untimely he somehow felt compelled to answer the question. He didn't even know who this hooded being was, let alone want to betray an answer of such intimate origin to it. But any resistance from within his spirit was met with a strange desire to expose his deepest wishes. Only a small thread of reason attempted to guard his heart.

"'I desire to walk in the presence of the Most High,' Velon said.

"'Aye, aye, Prince Velon,' the figure said quickly, 'this I know to be true. But that is common among all Dionians. Tell me something *new*. Tell me something that you do not share in common with any other Dionian.' Velon made the mistake of dwelling on this suggestion further and following it down into parts of his soul that he was never meant to journey, into places of ambition, of *self*, of *pride*. 'Tell me, young prince, would you not wish to be lord over all Dionia?'

"'Lord over all Dionia?' Velon asked in shock. 'But my father is king of Dionia, and his father before him.'

"'Of course he is,' said the figure. 'But while he is king, he is not *lord*. He may govern over it, but he does not control it, he does not *rule* it.'

"'But that is meant for the Most High alone,' Velon said, a bit amazed, 'He created it and has entrusted its care to Man. Surely you know this, my friend. It is the way of things. The Most High Himself has spoken it among men.'

"'Of course, good prince, but what if it were not all true? What if you could have more? What if you could rule over it just as the Most High does? What if you could control all that happens under its sun and stars? What if all of its moving, its waking, its very being, could be willed by your every command? Think of it, young prince! You could have more power than your father and his father before him!'

"'This is not possible,' Velon glared into the shadow of the hood.

"'But it *is*,' replied the figure, rising slowly and pointing with a finger to the western horizon. At that moment the sun crested the farthest edge of the ocean, casting its first rays into the warming sky. Velon watched as the light set against Adriel far in the distance. Her magnificent walls lay as dark silhouettes trimmed with a radiant glow from the sun beyond. The valley exploded into a vibrant sea of green, and light danced on the distant swells of countless ocean waves. Velon caught his own breath at the sight of such beauty.

"'And I can give it all to you,' the figure concluded, suddenly casting its cloak aside, standing before Velon as a shimmering being of light. Velon squinted hard and raised the palm of his hand to shield the light from his eyes.

"'Who *are* you?' Velon pleaded, now in total amazement.

"'I am of the Lytthlaroua[21], the Lythlaic Host, born of Athera, who offers you supreme reign over Dionia,' the being said. 'Total lordship; it will all belong to you. That is what you want, is it not?'

"'Well, I—' Velon hesitated. He could feel his blood rushing through his veins, heart beating wildly. The invitation was playing to the secret desires of his heart, now flooding out of his soul and parching his emotions, begging for a drink to quench them.

"'It is not a hard thing I grant you, young prince. You are royalty after all. You deserve such a position of prestige. Why wait an age for a meager throne to be passed down to you when you can have a greater throne at your disposal *now*.'

"'And what must I do?' Velon asked.

---

[21] **Lytthlaroua** *(L'EYEth-lah-ROO-uh): noun; Ancient Dionian; literally translated "ways of the heavenly," this name for the angelic host, or angels of Athera; singular: lythla (L'EYEth-lah); plural: lythlae (L'EYEth-lay).*

"'Do? Why, nothing so simple but as to pledge yourself to me. I will make you *my prince*.'

"'Pledge myself to you? But I don't even know you!'

"'Look into my face,' the being said. Velon tried to look but the intensity was so bright he could not bear to look much more. 'I am *light*. I am *beauty*. I have been sent from Athera to grant you your heart's desire—the very thing you dream of at night.'

"'But how could you know this?'

"'Because I know *you*. And I desire to grant you this gift above all other Dionians.'

"'But why me?' Velon pleaded. His body was in a euphoric state, heart racing wildly out of control.

"'Because you are strong and seek greatness more than any other man among you. *You are the greatest among them all, Velon*.'

"'So in pledging my life to you, what is it that you require of me?' The offer seemed too good to be true.

"'Nothing, my prince, it is enough to know that you honor me above all others.'

"'Velon!' a voice shouted out behind him. It was Grinddr, his closest friend. Velon's discussion with the Being of Light had finally roused his friend from slumber. Velon peeked around a tree to see Grinddr walking into the small grove a short distance away, his short and stocky frame bumbling through the glen. Oddly, Grinddr was still in the darkness of the night, far from being warmed in the gentle bath of morning light from the horizon. The sun had not yet risen on him. *How strange*. Velon looked back toward the west to see if the dawn had indeed come on Adriel.

"'Prince,' the Lythla snapped, 'make a decision quickly or else I will ask the next greatest man among your kind.' Velon turned back to regard the being of light, taken aback by its sudden shift in manner. The voices of his friends seemed to fade behind him. He felt so many questions stirring in his heart. A strange confusion pulled incessantly on the gates of his spirit, signaling a disturbing lack of peace, a peace that he had always known. He was, for the first time, uncomfortable with himself. The cravings of his heart were strong and powerful, taking advantage of an unfulfilled desire that had been dormant his whole life and now sprang to life, given the opportunity. What had been conceived long ago in the secret recesses of his soul had finally grown and matured, ready to birth the putrid and illegitimate child of a nightmare, one which would hunt the Sons and Daughters of Dionia for all time.

"Grinddr shouted after Velon once more, trying to follow the sound of his friend's voice through the wood, but Velon did not respond. It was still very dark, and even more so in the wood. Finally Grinddr came upon the large oak tree. He could see someone standing in the shadows. He assumed it was his friend.

"'Velon? Who are you talking to?' Grinddr said. A sickening feeling lurched in his stomach. He rounded the large tree further and saw a dark figure standing with his back to him, shrouded in a hooded cloak. 'Velon? Is that you? What's going on?' he asked again.

"'*Velon?*' said a sickly sweet voice. The figure turned, face hidden under the hood. 'I do not know this one you name, *Velon.*'

"'Then who are you?' Grinddr demanded, his sturdy body tensing like a bull's. Something was not right here.

"'Me?' said the dark figure with fake surprise, placing a hand across his cloaked chest. 'Why, I am to be feared above all others, good Grinddr.'

"'*Feared?*' Grinddr was confused. There was something strangely familiar about this voice. 'Speak plainly, stranger. I do not know your speech. I ask you again, where is my friend Velon? What have you done with him?' The stranger let out a laugh that startled Grinddr and was sure to wake the others.

"'Your *friend* is no more, *fool!*' The hooded being took a step toward Grinddr, but the young man held his ground. 'I own him now, just as I shall own you, Son of Man! I am the Son of the Dead! I am the Destroyer, Prince of Morgui! *You will fear me!*' The figure raised his arm and swung an open hand at Grinddr's face. Razor edged nails cut into the young man's cheek, but still he did not move. Grinddr could not see the blood issue from his face and down onto his bare chest, but he could feel the hot sting consume his head. He neither yelled nor fought back. He was too innocent and naive to know better.

"'I will ask you again, dark stranger,' Grinddr said, now tasting his own blood in the corner of his mouth. 'Where is my friend Velon?' Disgusted at Grinddr's inability to retaliate in anger, and enraged that the young man would be so loyal, the stranger screamed out in the night.

"'*I am not your friend any longer, infidel!*'

"'My friend?' Grinddr took a step closer, trying to put the pieces of the puzzle together. 'Velon? *Is that you?*'

"'Nay, fool! You should not be asking such things! Be removed before I destroy you!'

"'Velon!' Grinddr could finally place the voice, but it was different somehow. 'I knew your voice sounded familiar, but what strange words you use! And why do you treat me this way?'

"'*I am not Velon, you worthless, pitiful worm!*'

"'No, I'm quite sure it is you, but what are you wearing, my friend?'

"'Stop it! Back away! I will kill you!' he hissed. Whatever small piece of Velon's heart remained deep inside, Grinddr was calling back to life, but the dark power Velon had given himself over to was stronger and within another moment had utterly consumed him. The figure raised a hand and swung again, this time delivering a hard blow to Grinddr's head. Grinddr stumbled sideways, the force nearly knocking him over, but he managed to stay on his feet.

"'What has happened to you, Son of Rill?' Grinddr asked, not giving a care to himself. 'Who has done this thing? Let me help you, Velon.' He reached out his hand in true compassion.

"'*Nooo!*' the dark being yelled in terror, lunging forward and drove his pointed fingers deep into Grinddr's chest. Grinddr let out a deep grunt and flew backward landing on the soft grass with the cloaked being on top of him. Grinddr's chest burned and his whole body felt warm. A nagging thought suddenly emerged in the recess of his mind. *Your life is over and there is no one to help you.* But somehow, with a courage and fortitude not his own, Grinddr resisted the lie and grabbed the dark figure by the shoulders. He could feel a bony form beneath the material, and shoved the being to the side, the fingers retracting from Grinddr's rib cage. But Grinddr's blood-soaked body was losing strength. He couldn't get up.

"'Velon,' Grinddr whispered, 'I know it's you. Don't go.' But the cloaked being had had enough. It shook violently with rage, casting Grinddr one last glare from beneath its blackened hood, and then scurried away over the cliff, shrieking as it went.

"When the three other remaining friends found him, Grinddr lay still, staring off into the west as a new dawn came on Adriel."

A few moments of total silence passed before Luik realized the blazing fire he had been staring at had all but disappeared, leaving only a heap of glowing coals. No one moved in the fire circle. The thick smoke had cleared out of the square, and a little time later, all the birds returned to their nests for roosting. Luik and the others breathed a heavy sigh, and to his surprise the smell of smoke was nowhere to be found. Luik was the first to break the silence.

"So the First Battle was not of armies of men and demon hordes," Luik said, still looking into the coals, "but a war of one man's pride and another man's compassion."

"That it was," Gorn replied. "Though it eventually did bring about the saga you mention, and Dionia was never the same for it."

"But how is it, Teacher," Luik continued, "that one who was so immersed in the perfect presence of the Most High, as was Velon, be lured away from His Goodness and follow after Morgui?" Gorn walked over and knelt by Luik, placing a hand on the boy's shoulder.

"That, my boralee, is the greatest question of our age. Perhaps it is the Most High's inability to guard us?"

"But you said He is our Protector, our Refuge, and our Strong Tower," Thero said with much surprise.

"So then maybe Morgui is stronger than the Most High?" Gorn asked.

"Nay," said Rab, "you also taught us that He is our Mighty Conqueror and strong in battle."

"And that the lythla in all their forms, even the Dairne-Reih, are subject to their Creator," added Quoin.

"So how is it then, boralees? Where is the fault?"

"It leaves only Velon," Jrio said with wonder. "But I don't understand. Why would he choose a course away from the Most High?"

"Because he has been given the right to choose in the first place," Gorn said, rising solemnly to his feet.

"I don't understand," Jrio said.

"Jrio, do you love your parents?" Gorn asked, nearing the place where the dark haired boy sat.

"Of course, Teacher."

"And did they *make* you love them? Did they *force* you into submission to love them?" Gorn knelt by the boy.

Jrio was bewildered by the question. "Of course not," he said.

"So then, if they don't make you by their doing, why do you love them?"

"Because I want to. They have always been my parents."

"Make it clearer, Jrio."

"How?"

"Because you have *chosen* to love them," Gorn said sternly. "The power of your love comes in that it was not forced or controlled, it was not exercised on you, but it originated from within you. It was your choice to love your parents. You may not think so, but you were given a choice to love them."

"You mean I did not have to love them? That seems absurd."

"Sure it does. That's because you never knew anything else but them. Your heart was attached from early on. Eventually you began choosing, even before you grew conscious of it. You are most fortunate because nothing ever came between you and the love for your parents, but consider if someone else vied for your love."

"Someone else?" Jrio asked inquisitively.

"Or rather, something else," Gorn added.

"I don't understand."

"Your love is powerful because it is a choice, not a requirement. Whatever you set your heart on feels the power of that choice, in this case, your parents. It was a joyous day when you began showing affection for them, but what if another person interrupted that beautiful relationship and started demanding your attention; drawing you away from your parents unto them? What if it was not even a person, but a desire of your own heart?"

"So you are saying that I could have just as easily chosen to love that new thing as much as my parents?" Jrio asked.

"As much, or more," Gorn replied. "You see, the Most High is the same way with you. If he *made* you to love Him, it would not be real love, but control. The very fact that you have *a choice* establishes the incredible value of your affections. In knowing this incredible wealth, along with his uttermost hate for the Most High, Morgui becomes that other being, that other element that interrupts the intimacy between you and the Most High."

"So Velon fell in love with Morgui?" Benigan asked from across the ring.

"Not quite," Gorn said.

"He fell in love with what he wanted," Luik concluded.

"That's right," Gorn said as he stood up again. "A seed had been planted in his heart, a seed of self-wanting and pride. Morgui was aware of this from the moment it entered."

"How?" Fyfler asked.

"Because he planted it there," said Jrio.

"Morgui took advantage of this free will we have," Gorn continued. "He knew that love is a choice, so he merely provided an alternate choice for Velon, as he does with all men." There was a short silence.

"So it *was* Velon."

"And the Lythla of Light," stated Jrio solemnly, "it was not a real lythla from the Most High."

"It was Morgui himself, parading around as an imitation of the being he once was," Gorn said.

"Then how can anyone know when it is a real lythla they meet?" asked Fyfler.

"A man sees that which he wants to see," said Gorn. "Velon was already *deceived* in his heart before he was ever *deceived* with his eyes. What Velon saw as light, his friend would have seen as purest evil. The presence of evil was the very thing that woke Grinddr up. Had Morgui stayed longer, Grinddr would not have perceived the being the same way that Velon did."

"Teacher," Cage asked from the other side of the fire circle, "what of Grinddr?" Gorn did not reply for some time, and when he did speak, it was not in answer to his question.

"That is all for tonight, boralees. To the Tree House." As disciplined students of Gorn's instruction, they all leapt up as one, turned from the fire circle, and ran to the far side of the square. They followed the path through the low-hanging limbs and then out into the vast expanse of their grand dwelling. Each boy mounted up a ladder or rope, climbing quickly to his respective section of the house. They skipped along bridges and swung to platforms, all without a single word being uttered. For that was their nightly order, to enter into sleep soundly and without speaking. Gorn had ways of knowing if his instruction had been kept, but high atop one tree limb where a small bungalow perched out in the leaves of the upper canopy, a faint whisper stirred.

"I don't think our teacher heard my question about Grinddr," Cage said under his breath as he lay on his mat.

"No, my friend," Luik said from the other side of the hut, "I think he did."

Chapter Eighteen

EYES OF THE EAGLE

Anorra had hardly been able to sleep the many nights following the incident with Ciaphlie and the enraged hounds. She was consumed with thoughts of her brothers, Thad, Thero, and Anondo, and also of Luik. She wondered how they fared and how their trip to Kirstell had been. Her mind was a blur of activity during the midnight hours. Despite the calming sea air that permeated her bedchamber each night, affording anyone else a sound slumber within moments, it was many hours later that she would finally drift off to sleep. Even then it was dreams of the Isle of Kirstell, to which she had never been, though her spirit seemed to know its every rock and field by heart. She could see them all, each boy training and growing in discipline. They ran in the mornings and learned under their great warrior-teacher in the afternoons. Then it was an exploit or adventure around the Isle in the evenings, each day different than the next. In the morning she would rise and once again be obsessed with thoughts of her kin and friend, not remembering a life before the knowledge she now possessed.

That knowledge in itself drove her near mad. Her perfect world, everything she had ever known, seemed to slowly unravel with each passing day. What had once been a serene and untouched life, a portrait of absolute purity, was now a blemished tapestry with a loose thread trailing away in the distance. Who was pulling that thread was hard to say. But this she did know: the stability and comfort found in each day's predictability had been violently shaken and disrupted to such a degree that each sunrise was guaranteed to be worse than all those before it. Anorra, she felt it more than most. Something deep within her, a connection she held with creation, a bond with the very folds of granite and moving walls of water, gripped her soul, pleading for answers. Maybe that was the thing that kept her awake each night, a whimper of the softest sort; a cry, like that of a small child hidden away behind a glade of trees. Creation was groaning, calling out to her under the starlight. It was in disarray, it was in chaos, and it slept as little as she did, urgently worried about the dawning of the next horizon.

"Anorra?" came a muffled voice, echoing off somewhere. Anorra slowly sat up in bed and looked around the bright room with squinted eyes. "Are you coming, ma' lady?" the voice said from down the hall again, this time much closer, and more urgent. It was Henna, her maidservant. *Is it morning already?* It seemed as if she had just laid her head down to rest but a few minutes ago. Suddenly Henna burst through the door, the silken window curtains fluttering from the abrupt motion. "Ma' lady, you are late again! He waits in the courtyard!"

"Shah!" Anorra blew the blonde hair out of her face in exasperation. "Not again!" She heaved the cover from her bed and leapt to her feet.

"It will be ten laps today, I fear, Princess," said Henna, grabbing Anorra's brown work breecs from the wardrobe in the corner.

"Aye, and another five trees to climb," Anorra added as she took the leggings and pulled them up, tying the drawstring firmly. She slid a black woven shirt over her head and didn't bother to tuck it in. Henna handed her a belt and knife, and with that Anorra was out the door and running.

"Wait, Princess!" Henna cried out after her, fetching another item and following her out of the room. "You forgot your sandals!"

• • •

"We are late again, are we, Princess?" said a smooth voice. A tall man stood out a good distance with his back turned toward her. He wore a long purple cape that swept the ground.

"I do apologize, Gyinan," Anorra murmured out of breath. She bounded down the stone steps and into the grassy courtyard to the place where the man stood in the middle. But no sooner had she made it within a few strides of him that he turned swiftly to catch her in mid-step with a strange and foreign instrument. She froze in bewilderment. Though she had never seen such a thing before, its presence, combined with its poised manner and direction of intent, gave her to instantly perceive the item as something of lethal potential. Out in front Gyinan held a long slender piece of wood that curved from his knees to well over his head. Tucked tightly into the fingers of his other hand, which was pulled back by his ear, he held a fine line that ran between the two ends of the wood causing it to flex strenuously. And resting laterally between both Gyinan's hands was a horizontal shaft, embellished on the far end with feathers, and terminating on the nearest with a small narrow head that looked to be razor sharp, and pointed directly at Anorra's face but a stride away.

Gyinan did not say a word, and neither did Anorra for that matter. It seemed like an eternity before she realized she wasn't breathing, but she dared not. Gyinan's thin eyes peered down the needle-like dowel aimed right at her head. Suddenly Gyinan shifted and spun to one side. He focused on something in the distance and then loosed the arrow with his right hand. Anorra lost sight of the missile as it vanished from his grip and suddenly she heard a percussive blow to the side of the courtyard Gyinan faced. Before she had time to look, Gyinan had summoned another arrow from somewhere on his person, slid it into the thin line now relaxed along the flattened piece of wood, and pulled back the bow. He looked quickly and released the shaft as before. This time Anorra watched for the projectile, but still had trouble following it. A second *crack* rang in the distance. She squinted her eyes toward a bench and some shrubs far beyond and figured that was where it had stopped. Gyinan drew back a third arrow and let it fly as before, and this time Anorra saw it from start to finish. The tall man lowered the weapon and relaxed his shoulders, drawing a deep breath. He turned his head to look at the astonished princess. She said the only words she could find.

"I promise to never be late again, Teacher."

Gyinan smiled, "Good." Then he turned back and walked to the targets he had fired at. Anorra followed directly behind. They walked about ten tree lengths before coming to a stone bench. There sat three green melons, each with the feathered end of an arrow protruding from it.

"Examine them, Princess," Gyinan said softly. Anorra looked closely at each fruit noting how the wooden shafts had penetrated the exact center of the round melons. And then, to her surprise, she noticed that the front of the arrows continued on out the other side and then into the back of the bench. She touched the entry point into the stone with her fingers.

"The pointy tips," she asked looking back to her teacher, "are they inside?"

"Nay," he answered.

"Then they have been broken off," she surmised.

"Nay," he said again with the same tone. "They are behind." Anorra was puzzled. She went around the side of the bench to see three tiny points protruding from the stone.

"But that's as thick as my hand is long, Teacher!" she said with much enthusiasm, pointing to the bench back.

"Aye, Princess, and it is granite at that."

"Then how can such a small—," she hesitated, "*small thing* do so much?"

"The same way such a small princess can do so much," he said with a pat on her shoulder, "by power, precision, will, and skill." Gyinan set down his bow and placed one foot on the front of the bench and grabbed the middle arrow by the shaft below the feathers and pulled with all his might. "There is no way I could ever retrieve this arrow by pulling it back out the way it entered."

"Arrow?" she asked, having never heard the word.

"Aye, it is the shaft fired from a bow."

"A bow? You mean the curved piece of wood there," she said indicating the wood and line on the ground.

"Aye."

"What keeps it from coming out then?"

"It is the shape of the head. Watch." Gyinan reversed his pressure and, instead of pulling on the arrow, he began to push it through the melon, and then the stone-backed bench. He gave a grunt and Anorra saw some stone crumble away on her side of the bench, the arrow coming nearly all the way out. "Pull it the rest of the way through, Princess. You can do it." Anorra knelt and grabbed the wood with both hands, pulling with all her might. Then it popped through and sprayed small crumbs of granite and dust all over.

"Well done," Gyinan encouraged her. "Look at it now." She turned the arrow around and looked at the blue-gray tip. It didn't even seem affected by the impact. From its point, the blade swung back on four sides, each a tiny blade, before making a sharp angle back up and under each blade, terminating at the wooden shaft, held on by thousands of tiny threads. She reached to touch the point with her finger. The head split her skin like water and a drop of blood came out. Anorra pulled her hand away and the wound healed instantly.

"My, that is sharp," she said with a smile.

"Aye, and stronger than granite," Gyinan said.

"What is it made of?"

"Dyra[22]," he replied.

"Dyra? I have never heard of that."

"Most people haven't, Princess. It was a gift from the dwarves, forged from deep within Grandath."

"And it is stronger than granite?"

"Nay, it is stronger than *steel*," he answered.

"Stronger than steel," Anorra said airily as she gazed at the strange material, twirling the arrow between her fingers. "So you will teach me how to use this weapon, Gyinan," she said more as an order than a question.

"As you wish, Princess." With that Gyinan reached under the bench and produced a long velvet bag of scarlet with a golden draw cord at the top.

"What is that? Where did you get that?" Anorra asked.

"It is your bow, your highness." Gyinan pulled open the cords and withdrew a new bow, but this one much smaller than the one he had used. Anorra dropped the arrow and held open her hands to receive the gift. It was stunningly beautiful. The bow was made of three different layers of wood, each one unique in property, function, and color tone, first dark, light, and then tan. Yet all were assembled in such a way that they curved and flowed as one. Small pictures of gazelles were etched along the front side with incredible detail as if they were dancing through fields. Flowering

---

[22] **Dyra** (*DIEruh*): *noun; a rare and little-known composite material made from forged elements; created by the Tribes of Ot in Grandath.*

vines edged up toward the terminus, and a smooth carved handle held fast in the middle.

"Put it in your hand," Gyinan said. Anorra brought the weapon upright. It was extremely light. She slid her hand into the grip. It wrapped around her hand, made exactly for her.

"It's amazing," she said with a smile. "It seems like it's a part of me."

"It will be, Princess, it will be; and look there," Gyinan said, pointing on the inside of the bow. Just above her hand she saw another small carving, but this one of an eagle with wings spread wide, caught on a lofty breeze.

"An eagle," she exclaimed. "I love them so!"

"Aye, and as such you will fight like one."

"Fight? Aye, fight," Anorra said coolly, remembering reality in the midst of her revelry. Gyinan reached back inside the scarlet bag and produced another item, this time a long leather quiver and strap. Five feathered ends protruded from the top.

"This is your quiver," Gyinan said. "It is the bow's lifeblood. Without its contents, your bow is just a pretty-looking tree limb." Anorra nodded her head in understanding. He handed it to her and she marveled at the embossing on its surface. She spun it slowly, looking at mountains that formed into a sleek waterfall and dipped into a sweeping valley that rose back up into mountains. There was her quiver, five arrows and her bow. What was missing?

"And what about the—"

"The string?" he asked right back.

"Aye," she said.

"That you have to make."

"Make?"

"Aye, *make*. The string is the smallest part, Princess, but the most important. You must learn that it is not always the loudest, the strongest, or the mightiest man or woman, that ties an army together, but often it is the smallest, quietest, meekest heart that advances the battle. This you must learn to be, so you will craft your own bow string." Once again Anorra blew the hair out of her face in an elegant defiance all her own, one that would eventually become her greatest asset in her struggle to survive.

And spin her first bowstring she did, and her second, and her third. Not only did she spin strings, but also fashioned bows and arrows as well; numerous ones, until she was so prolific at it that the trade was second nature to her. Gyinan not only taught her how to use the weapon, but also how to find the right woods, how to treat and prepare them, how to put curve in the wood, and heat it just right. He showed her how to find the right trees for making arrows, how to soak them and heat out the bends, and finally how to forge heads out of the precious supply of Dyra in the palace. He also taught her how to make them of steel, iron, and even stone should there come a day when none of the other elements could be found. Then he showed her how to make heads from coal-hardened wood.

And make them she did, tens and multiples of tens of them. She lost many in target practice and heaped them so high in her workshop by the forest that she had no room for any more. Weeks passed by end over end, long into the summer until the strange arrival of the cool breezes. Her father had said such winds of change would come. Her wise teacher and friend, Gyinan, made certain to answer every question she asked when it was within his ability to do so, or within his permission.

As the winds picked up, the colder skies brought clouds, and eventually strange happenings of water that fell from the skies, Gyinan took his teachings inside by the hearth. Anorra was used to fire, but never inside. Special compartments were built with stone in each room and then vented with long pipes through the ceilings and to the open air beyond. The logs burned brightly, well into every night, keeping the palace inhabitants warm and comfortable. At first the smell of smoke was hard to get used to, but eventually it summoned up memories of lessons Gyinan had imparted to her night after night. She would sit wrapped in a fur blanket as the flickering flames cast warm light on her teacher, who paced the room with arms flailing. He would relate story after story, principle after principle, truth after truth, until she fell asleep or couldn't handle anymore. He spoke of Creation and the Dawn of Time; of the Most High and Morgui; of the First Battle and Ad and Eva. He taught her new words she had never heard before, words like *pain* and *death*. Before too long the cold winds had parted and the coals of the hearths had died out. Summer had arrived once again and the flowers bloomed with delight and much scent, and her bow let loose a slew of arrows as before.

Ever since her father had first assigned Gyinan as her teacher Anorra saw him as a friend, and in many ways like a father. He truly spent more time with her now than anyone else, but Gyinan was always quick to maintain the King's relationship with the princess. It was important for Anorra to completely give herself to Gyinan's teachings, but equally as important to not lose her identity as a daughter of the King.

"You must never lose focus," Gyinan said from atop his horse. They had ridden all day northeast along the Hefkiln River toward the foothills of Tontha, and now stopped just before the border. Gyinan pointed to a single tree in one of the enormous meadows. "See there, that lone tree standing?"

"Aye," she replied, her bay mare gulping air beneath her, flanks dripping with sweat.

"Can you make out the bird nest in one of the upper branches?" he asked.

"Nest?" Anorra strained in her seat and leaned forward. The tree was a great deal away from their position but soon she managed to spy a small brown spot within the leaves. "Aye, there it is. I see it now," she said with confidence. "Teacher, you have good eyes."

He smiled. "Do you think you could pin an arrow on the limb on which that nest sits without bringing harm to those chicks?"

"Consider it done," she said, bringing up her bow and reaching to her back for an arrow. She knocked the shaft and drew the string swiftly. She didn't even take a breath before letting the arrow fly, shimmering across the meadow to find its mark along the branch about a hand's breadth from the nest. A female robin shot out of the tree like a startled cat.

"Not too much of a stretch for you?" he asked.

"Please," she rebutted.

"Good," Gyinan said through a smile. "Now I want you to split your arrow. Only this time ..." Gyinan paused and pulled out a wide ribbon of cloth from around his belt. He dismounted and walked over to Anorra, gesturing for her to lean down. He reached up and tied the ribbon around her head, securing the cloth directly over her eyes so that she could not see. She sat up straight and thought for a moment, getting her bearings.

"Can you still do it?" Gyinan asked.

Anorra didn't answer right away. She was still getting lined up in her mind's eye. "Aye," she finally said, "I can."

"Good," Gyinan replied, then reached for her horse's reins. He led the bay around in a few circles while Anorra balanced on top. Then Gyinan doubled back and led the horse around the other direction many more times. "Now," he said softly, "split your arrow."

Anorra let out a long sigh. The deed was near impossible, and she said so.

"Aye, impossible for you to do alone, that is," Gyinan answered right back.

"Well who is there to help me?" she pleaded, realizing her dire need for assistance.

"That is for you to find out, and me to enjoy watching you try." Gyinan walked back to his black horse and mounted, now watching quietly as Anorra gently held her bow and used her heels to guide her horse. At first she just made little commands turning left and then right. Gyinan could see her restless nature kicking in. She was overcome with another emotion besides just total frustration at not being able to accomplish a task: fear of hitting the bird's nest and killing the chicks. Soon she grew uneasy and spun her horse around in an arc concluding that the tree was behind her now. She stopped, and then a moment later she spun her horse again not satisfied that she was actually facing toward the tree. She raised her bow and pulled back the string to the corner of her mouth, held her breath and then loosed the arrow. If she killed those birds she'd never be able to forgive herself. She instantly lifted the blindfold from her eyes and squinted in the light toward the Hefkiln.

"Well, you missed the birds but you may have killed a fish or two," Gyinan said with a chuckle as her arrow splashed into the distant banks of the river.

"That's not funny!" she yelled out, turning from the river and casting her teacher a lethal glare, half relieved that she had missed the tree completely.

"You had no bearings or balance," Gyinan listed her faults on his fingers, "You failed to see the tree without your eyes, and you let the fear of your own inadequacy distract your focus, not only in trying to succeed but also in trying to protect those chicks. Come now, Princess, you didn't even make an effort."

"An effort? *An effort?* How could I? I was blindfolded and then spun around! I'd like to see you try it!" Anorra was quite exasperated.

"Gladly," he said with a wild smile. Anorra was shocked. Gyinan rode over and stripped the cloth from her hand, quickly wrapping it over his own eyes. He raised his bow and knocked an arrow. Then he pressed his horse into a wild spin, then back again.

"Satisfied?" he asked his student.

"No, spin more," she said indignantly, though finally starting to enjoy watching him whirl about.

"As you wish," he said, continuing in the action. Soon Anorra was half laughing.

"All right, that's fine, Gyinan. You may stop now."

"Thank you, Princess. I was getting quite dizzy there." Gyinan took a deep breath and tilted his head back toward the sky. He closed his mouth and then dropped his head, tilting his neck from side to side as if stretching. Then he smoothly nudged his horse to the left. Anorra smiled and then wished she hadn't, figuring he felt her pleasure at his misjudgment. He stopped. *But there was no way he could see her smiling.* Then he nudged the horse back to the right all the way through a quarter of a turn. Anorra didn't move. He sat completely still for a moment. He was facing directly at the tree. It couldn't be. Gyinan lifted his bow and drew the arrow back. Then, to Anorra's utter delight, her teacher spun the horse around completely facing the other way. *He didn't know where it was after all! He was guessing!* Surely hers would not be the only arrow in the river with the fish that day; and it probably would have been had Gyinan not arched over backwards and laid down on the back of his horse, arms outstretched above his head. He drew back the bowstring a second time and opened the fingers by his cheek. The arrow flew from his hand with a life of its own and Anorra watched in dismay as it whistled toward the tree and finished with a *crack*.

"I don't believe it," Anorra said.

"O believe it, Princess," Gyinan said sitting up and removing the blindfold gingerly. "I will rarely ask you to do something I have never done before, unless it is of course something that only you can do. Shall we?" He gestured toward the tree with an open hand.

"Varos!" Anorra exclaimed, kicking at her horse. Gyinan laughed and followed after her. A few moments later they were at the tree and Anorra slid off her horse before the mare had even stopped. She bounded over to the tree with a few strides and pulled herself up into the branches. Soon she reached the limb where the nest lay.

"Hey'a! You missed, Teacher! *You missed!*" Anorra shouted, betraying her over-eagerness to see him fail. "There is only one arrow here! Yours must be somewhere else in the tree."

Gyinan didn't flinch. "Look more closely at the arrow, Princess." Anorra, not one to disobey, pulled herself up close to the arrow and noticed bits of a splintered shaft impaled at the entry point. Then she noticed the three rings around the arrow near the feathers. Every arrow was made with a signature of its maker, and Gyinan's signature was three green rings, not the three red ones she used; it was his arrow after all.

"How can that be?" she whispered in wonder before thoughtfully descending back down to the ground. She walked over to Gyinan, still seated atop his horse, and said solemnly, "Teach me how to do that."

"With pleasure," he said with a smile.

They rode on even further that day, up into the mountains, crossing deep into Tontha along the steep single track trails until the valleys of her homeland had been swallowed up far behind. Their trek was mostly silent as Anorra absorbed the sights and sounds of a place she had never been before, albeit so close to her native home. The majesty of the peaks consumed her, stealing the breath from her mouth around every new bend of the path. The mountains loomed so high she thought a man could easily touch the sky above by simply reaching up an arm once standing upon a peak. Enormous rock walls surged upwards and Anorra strained her neck just to make out the summits. As the trail rose on the hips of the mountains, canyons opened their mouths in wide yawns below. Heaps of boulders lay like sleeping giants in the corners of the broad Hefkiln River that meandered through the mountain passes. As the trail edged along the steeps, Anorra was equally awed with the hollowed drop-offs as she was with the captivating heights. It was mesmerizing. The air had also changed. It felt cooler and smelled different, fresher somehow.

"This place is beautiful," she finally said, not knowing what else to say about such a breathtaking environment. "What do they call it?"

"The Domain of the Eagle," Gyinan said looking skyward. "See there?" He pointed with a finger straight up. Anorra followed his line high into the vast blue above, framed on every side by a mountain's summit. "The eagle," he continued. There it was, strong and bold, wings spread wide in an effortless task, floating as still as a lily in a shaded pool. "This is his home."

As they journeyed on, Anorra noticed more eagles, some soaring high above and others flying through the canyons with remarkable speed. Still others perched on precarious rock outcroppings, preening their feathers or stretching their wings in the sunlight. Occasionally she would notice a foreigner in their midst; a red tailed hawk, or often a spotted hawk. A few breeds of falcons also could be seen flying in the eagle ranks. She was more familiar with these creatures as their homes were traditionally found in Ligeon, the well-known birthplace of the hawk. It was also her people who were known as the keepers of these birds. But eagles she had never seen.

"There are many hawks here," she stated to Gyinan.

"Aye," he said as his horse walked along.

"Is it common that they would journey so far out of Ligeon to be in the mountains?"

"Only for a season."

"What season?"

"It has often been said that the eagles teach the hawks how to fly, and—" he waited a moment to see if her curiosity was truly pricked.

"And what else?" she said impatiently.

"And how to *see*," Gyinan finished, pleased with her interest. Anorra looked up and saw an eagle flying side by side with another bird, much smaller and more sleekly shaped. It was a blue hawk. They soared together into the prevailing wind with motionless wings outstretched, riding the crest of the breeze like a wave. The smaller and more agile hawk seemed to mimic the eagle's every move. Where it looked, the hawk would look. When it dove, the hawk dove. Suddenly the two birds dropped from the sky and plummeted downward at an unprecedented rate. Their wings folded back and their beaks pierced the air like knifes; *like arrows,* Anorra thought to herself. They leapt down out of the blue sky and into the scope of the mountains, the dark hulk of a landscape now their backdrop. They continued to race down with an unrelenting pace; if anything, they rushed on faster. Though the ground was surely rushing up toward them, it did not seem to bother the two creatures in the slightest. Soon they swooped below Anorra's height and into the canyon below. Here they began to mildly pull out of the steep angle of descent, but only enough to center in on an ambiguous point in the distance. With every breath Anorra noticed that they were getting closer and closer to the river. Her perspective was failing her; she could not tell now how close they were to the water. Just when she thought they would surely impale themselves on a boulder, the eagle pulled up and shot back skyward with a mighty flap of its wings; Anorra thought she could almost hear them beat the air. But when she searched for the hawk, she could not see him. Anorra gazed hard at the river. There he was, still flying on alone, now closer to the tumultuous, watery current than ever. *What was he doing?* Suddenly the hawk brought his wings out, slowing smoothly. At the same time his legs lowered and talons flared in a lethal motion. The claws brushed the surface in a spray of water before grabbing a small twig with a few berries clumped together on one end. He beat his wings and loomed up and away. The entire incident took only a few moments, but Anorra watched with such intensity it felt like a day.

"I have never seen that," Anorra said. She was not referring to the act of diving, but rather to the one bird showing the other bird how to perform a skill. "The eagle was *teaching him!*"

"So they say," Gyinan replied with a wide grin. And thus the term lived on. Anorra looked back up into the sky from where the unlikely pair first started their descent, and then followed the path again in her mind's eye. It was a huge distance they had traversed; surely it was impossible to see something so tiny, so far away.

"What did you say, Princess?" Gyinan asked. Anorra realized she had been murmuring her thoughts out loud.

"Surely it must be impossible to see something so tiny, so far away, Teacher," she said staring down into the canyon.

"Just as difficult as it is to see a tree limb blindfolded?" he asked. Anorra thought his reply was clever.

"But there is a difference," she said. "They are not blindfolded."

"But were they always able to do such feats? Perhaps when they were just learning to fly, could they do it?"

"Obviously not," Anorra surmised.

"Nor can you do such an amazing thing when you are so young. You must be taught, as you do not yet posses the skill, Princess. It is the same thing. You do not see it as possible simply because the skill needed surpasses your ability; just because a task is difficult does not mean that it cannot be done."

"Or impossible," she added.

"Aye, even the impossible task. Because you may be the one to make it possible. You must first believe that you can see; then you will see."

"Believe I can see," she restated softly.

"You have two sets of eyes, Daughter of Eva; one set natural, the other supernatural. They are the eyes of your spirit. Truly, they are more powerful than your natural eyes, and tenfold more reliable. But you must learn how to use them; first you must even realize that they are there."

"But how?" she pleaded with him. To this Gyinan produced the blindfold once more. "Agh, not that again!" Gyinan laughed.

"Come here, child," he motioned her to dismount as he did. They left the horses in the track and walked a short distance to where the edge of the trail met the rising of the mountain. He held out the blindfold to her. "Take this and put it on yourself. It must be you that ties this knot, and not me, as it can only be you that takes it off again. For you will be tempted many times to remove it and rely on your natural sight."

"What do you mean, Teacher?"

"Hush, I'm not finished. Only the Most High will be a witness against you if you remove it. I will never know, nor will I ever ask you. I will only ask if you were obedient."

"Then where are you going?" she asked uneasy.

"No, Princess, the question is where are *you* going?"

"Huh?" Anorra tilted her head.

"I am leaving you to walk up the mountain before us," Gyinan gestured to the steep slope that rose up beside them, "*blindfolded*. After reaching the summit you are to return to the tree we were at earlier in the day back in Ligeon. Only then will I ask you to remove the cloth from your eyes."

"But that's crazy! It's—"

"Impossible?" Gyinan posed.

"Aye!"

"So, it seems, is hitting a tree limb and spotting a sprig of berries from aloft. But it can be done."

"You have done this?" she asked holding up the blindfold.

"I'll tell you when you come to the tree. Thus far, you are at the peak of your training. I can teach you no more until this task is accomplished. When you return to the tree successfully, only then can we progress. Until that point I can take you no further."

"But what if I fall from a cliff or something? That is surely a great distance! Will my body mend?" Anorra was very concerned.

"That is quite a hard thing to say, Princess. Much fear enters a person when they have so long a time to fall. Is it in a measure beyond the body's ability to heal itself as He has designed to? We can only find out from experience according to each person's faith. The question is; where is your faith?"

"But how do I navigate? How will I know where I'm going?"

"So many questions, Princess! This is the point, dear child, that you finally have eyes to see and ears to hear, to hear the True Voice, the words of the Most High Himself."

"But I do! I hear just fine." Anorra was trying desperately to get herself out of this lesson, but her youth still clouded the relevance of the ordeal ahead.

"Aye, you do hear Him, Anorra," Gyinan said, "but in terms of His Love. Now you will hear His voice in terms of obedience and direction for action. They are two different things. Many people may love Him and be content there; but warriors who desire to advance must not only love Him but also obey Him. When His Light shines upon your path, you will know it more clearly than if you were walking in broad daylight with your own two eyes. Soon, you will come to revere your spiritual sight far above that of your natural vision."

Anorra just listened, taking in everything Gyinan said. Then she made to speak but fell short. "I am—," she couldn't find the words.

"You are *scared*, Princess," Gyinan helped. She had never heard the word before. "For the first time in your life you are uncertain of the future and of how to proceed. It is a path you have never been down before, nor can anyone impart this experience to you; you must forge it yourself. And you can, but you will need Him for every step."

"So I put this on," she referred to the cloth, "and then wait for Him to speak?"

"No, such is the mistake of many a man," he answered, "and they get nowhere. They spend all their days *waiting* for something to happen, but it never does. While they are waiting for the Most High, He is busy waiting for them."

"For them?"

"Aye, to make the first move; to give Him something to work with; to prove that they truly do have faith enough to move out of their security and trust Him."

"So what do I do if He hasn't spoken after the first step?"

"*Princess!* I'm leaving now," Gyinan turned and mounted his horse. "Put on the blindfold and I'll see you back at the tree. I will be there waiting no matter how long it takes."

"And if I die?"

"You won't die, Princess."

"How do you know? I thought *we can only find out from experience according to each person's faith?*" she said quoting his own words back.

"*Princess,*" Gyinan's tone was impervious. For the first time in her life Anorra was actually startled with his tone.

"Aye?" she said meekly.

"*Go!*" Gyinan said strenuously, pointing up the mountain. She watched as he paid her no more attention and turned his horse. He called after her horse, which cast her one last forlorn glance and trotted off, along with Gyinan and his mount, down the track and around the bend in the mountainside, eventually disappearing out of view. She sighed and held the cloth lightly in her hands. She looked around the beautiful space where she stood, turning in a circle to see the majestic eagles and other birds flying through the air; the mountains standing erect like noble kings of old and the gaping crevices that cradled the mighty river far beneath her feet. Part of her thought that she may never see these sights again. Many questions of doubt and of waning self-confidence raced through her head, thoughts which most people would never dream that a girl such as Anorra would ever struggle with, due probably to her defiant exterior demeanor. But at this moment she was very much fighting with her own abilities, or lack thereof: *can I truly hear the Most High when my life depends on it?*

Finally she had resolved it in her heart; she would never know unless she tried. She squared up to the enormous mountain before her and took a last deep breath. With her eyes closed, she lifted the blindfold to her face, tying it securely behind her head. Then she spread out the material from forehead to mouth, as wide as it would go in the hopes that it would prevent her from inadvertently peeking in case her eyes betrayed her will to not look.

"It's just you and me now, Father," Anorra said sweetly. "I give you my steps. Lead me as you may." With that she lifted her knee and placed it on a small ledge in front of her hips and began climbing.

Chapter Nineteen

DALLON'S SUMMIT

Two tens and five weeks had passed since the group of boys had set foot on Kirstell, though no one counted the days, and already they were quickly becoming young men, at the very least *man-like*. The joy of learning combined with the intimate discovery of friendship, teamwork, and resolute purpose forged a mindset unaware of the passage of time. The sun rose and set, glowing warmly on the boys as they pressed through each day, each one a new adventure that further nurtured the common bond they shared.

One new change they had all come to anticipate was the seventh day of every week; for that day belonged to them, the one time they had all to themselves and were free to rest. It was a relatively new freedom granted them by Gorn who said it was always important that they *play*, a concept none of them had any problems with, what with being boys and all. The rule was that they could do anything on the island they liked, spending their time in whatever way suited them, as long as they were not up before dawn and that they were to bed by dusk.

And play they did. When the sun rose on that seventh day even a riddosseldore[23] would have been foolish to stand in the path that led out from the Tree House. The boys beat down the trail as if they had just been loosed from a cage. Usually they would all decide what they would do the night before; most always choosing to stick together, proving just how strong their bond was becoming. This was something Gorn was greatly pleased with. Sometimes they would play games in the fields for hours, setting up goals for a rokla match and play all through the afternoon, breaking only for some fruit or a drink of water from the nearby waterfall. After one gita was won, they would make teams for the next round and keep at it until they had their fill. Other days they would go exploring with their wooden swords, imagining that they were on the hunt of a demon horde that had been eluding them for days, but were now on the verge of meeting in the death throes of battle. They would slay them on the rocks and on the hills, in the valleys and in the woods. There was no escape from the mighty Dibor.

Still other days found them splashing in the ocean among the sea rocks on the south side of the isle much like they were today. Wearing leather loin cloths, the boys took turns climbing up the giant boulders that piled high under a water-bordered cliff and leaping from the precarious heights into the ocean foam below. The sea was clear of reefs here, and shone a brilliant bluish green, clear as crystal, giving way to white sands beneath that stretched far out toward the horizon before finally vanishing into the great ocean chasm beyond, many fathoms deep.

The water itself was warm and pleasing. When not leaping in some twisted position or trying to out-do the splash made before the last, the boys would hold their breath and dive underwater. A myriad of shells were strewn along the sea floor, all different shapes, colors, and sizes, each as unique as the next. Many of the boys found large oysters and pried open their mouths to extract the beautiful pearls within. Fish of all kinds swarmed around the youth, curious as to their activities. Even a pod of dolphins stopped to inquire what playful business these humans had beneath the surface. The boys welcomed the dolphins with wide arms and bubbled laughs. A few youth even took rides by grabbing dorsal fins and jetting through the waves. The sea mammals loved to play even more than the boys it seemed.

[23] **Riddosseldore** (*rih-DOSS-elle-DOHR-eh*): *noun; one of the largest Dionian mammals, noted for the enormous horn on the forehead and long trunk above the mouth; most closely associated with an elephant and a rhinoceros.*

"Watch this!" Jrio yelled, floating on his belly. A dolphin swam up beneath him and Jrio straddled it, pushing himself upright with his hands on its head. The blue creature swam off with Jrio on his neck, Jrio's legs stretched out to the sides and arms flailing high. "Hey'a!" he shouted in glee.

"Wow!" Fyfler smiled with delight, treading water near some rocks. Suddenly another dolphin surprised Fyfler from beneath and picked him up in the same fashion as Jrio, although not nearly as planned or controlled. Everyone laughed to see Fyfler squirming and trying to keep his balance on the slippery thing. Then all at once the dolphin leapt from the water and Fyfler was shot high into the air, sprawling like a wind-tossed leaf, before splashing into the waves. He came up for breath to the cheers of his friends. While everyone was still yelling for Fyfler, Luik noticed something in the distance.

"Look, brothers," he yelled, breaking up the revelry. "I believe it's Gorn." Everyone stopped and looked westward just off the shore. There in the water Gorn held tightly to a large fin that carried him through the water at great speed. His right hand grasped a mighty dorsal fin while his left hand he used to stabilize his dragging body. All the boys stopped their playing and gathered in the shallows by the rocks. A few moments later Gorn pulled right up to them and let go of his ride, standing on the white sands with water to his waist.

"Hey'a, boralees," Gorn said with a wide smile.

"Hey'a Teacher," they replied in some manner or another. Gorn was wearing only a tight blue wrap around his loins today. His black chest was a formidable display of physique and toned muscle. None of them had ever seen him without a shirt or tunic on. There along his left pectoral, stretching diagonally to his stomach was a long, white ridge, the likes of which was foreign to them.

"Are you having fun?" he asked. Gorn had never posed such a question to them before and thus none of them answered right away. So he asked again. "No fun is being had here by anyone?"

"Aye!" Boran replied, his short black hair matted atop his head. "It is a rare occasion for a Son of Tontha to find such beautiful waters in which to play."

"'Tis true that no such place exists in the Northern Lands," said his twin, Brax. "While her shores are beautiful and clear, they fare not as warm nor accessible."

"Then I would expect you to be the most entertained of all, no?" Gorn asked.

"Aye!" the twins yelled, beating a fist on their wet chests.

"And the rest of you?" Gorn asked. The boys were not so accustomed to this playful side of their teacher.

"Aye!" they all shouted.

"Well, you still haven't convinced me," he said with a stern look. "So, a game!" With that Gorn turned seaward and brought his fingers to his mouth, whistling loudly. Suddenly the pod of dolphins surfaced and swam toward him. The largest of them came up underneath Gorn's palm as he laid it in the water. Its dorsal fin was the grandest of all, and obviously the one that he had ridden in. "Each one of you take a dolphin and hold tight. As *I* am the largest, I take Siahe, as *he* is the largest." Gorn smiled in spite of himself and then winked down at the dolphin beside him, who himself replied with some chatter and clicking. "Do you remember the apple over the waterfall?" Gorn asked. Everyone smiled and nodded, looking at Fyfler and Jrio, who did their best not to notice. "Well, I have placed a shell, a very beautiful and rare one of blue and silver, out on the peak of a mountain. The first to find it and return to shore will keep it as his prize."

"What mountain, Teacher, you mean Fadasha?" Cage asked.

"Nay, the mountain is not on Kirstell," Gorn replied. "It lies there, beneath the sea." He pointed out to the horizon.

"A mountain beneath the surface of water?" Luik asked.

"Aye," Kinfen spoke up. "I have seen them many times off the shores of Somahguard, as have my brothers." The four of them nodded in agreement. Their dark skin was used to the sun and air from the sea and had seen many a wonder in the ocean. "They rise up from the depths as if we were flying down on them from a watery sky, like an eagle that swims."

"Like a dolphin," his brother Fallon put in.

"Aye, as an eagle is with the summits of air, so a dolphin is with the peaks of the sea," Kinfen smiled, pleased with the comparison.

"And so there lies a summit beneath these waters of great magnitude," Gorn said. "Dallon's Summit is deeper than any of you have yet ventured, I surmise, even the brothers from the Islands," Gorn gestured to the four brothers. "It will be the bravest and most cunning of you all that locates the mountain and reaches the shell. I will warn you; the summit is far deeper than any mountain on land is high. Be cautious in your planning and wise in your execution."

"And what is the lesson here?" Jrio asked.

"No lesson, Son of Trennesol; only unless you perceive one." He winked at Jrio. Then Gorn turned and addressed the lot of them. "Are you ready?"

"Aye!" the boys yelled, beating on their chests.

"*Varos!*" Gorn yelled. Suddenly the shallows were a flurry of sea foam and splashing as the boys whistled and jostled to find a dolphin in the froth. Some grabbed the dorsal fin of the same dolphin, and the dolphin would have none of it, eluding both boys with a single flick of its tail. Others grabbed a hold of a dolphin only to find out how slippery they truly were and, upon giving a command to go, quickly slipped off and found themselves floating in the deep without a ride. Among the first to finally take off toward the horizon were Naffe and Kinfen, the oldest from Somahguard, both well-versed in the art of oceanic travel via dolphin and other sea faring mammals. Soon the younger two Somahguard brothers, Fyfler and Fallon, joined them as well as had Jrio and Rab, Jrio's younger brother. Luik finally managed to grab a dorsal fin with both hands. Having never swum with them before, he found it quite exhilarating albeit challenging to stay on. The creatures moved with tremendous speed and efficiency of movement, not to mention acceleration three times that of a horse. Eventually Luik looked around to see all the boys off and swimming with a dolphin, to some degree.

A few in the rear straggled along just managing to keep water out of their mouths. Benigan looked more like a bear trying to strangle his dolphin and wrestle it down. His arms were looped over the creature's head and Benigan spent more time submerged under its neck then in the air above. Even further behind was Gorn, simply watching as they all pushed on toward the open sea with no real direction in mind. Luik figured he just trusted his dolphin. But Gorn wore a strange grin on his face that gave Luik to think there was something more to this simple race. Soon the pleasant white sands below disappeared and the sea floor plummeted away into a vast and dark canyon.

After a long ride the boys in the lead slowed and then started plunging with their dolphins beneath the surface, obviously trying to look for the peak. They would dive down and then pop back up momentarily, still holding on to their water-savvy friends. No one spoke to the other as each boy was clearly on his own; and Jrio and Fyfler stayed far away from one another in an unspoken, though clearly friendly, second chance for victory. Luik took a deep breath and finally pushed on his dolphin's head signaling a dive. The creature shot straight down and Luik almost lost hold. He squeezed hard around the fleshy fin and then opened his eyes. He was much deeper down than he thought he'd be. The dolphins were even faster beneath the water with them onboard than when above, dragging a flailing body along the surface. Luik didn't see anything except schools of fish and an ominous blue expanse that stretched down into total darkness.

At first he felt as if he were going to fall down into the abyss below him; the water was so clear it was like being suspended above a valley of birds and looking down on them as they soared underneath. His imminent need for air and internal drive to return to the surface quickly prompted him to pull up on the dorsal fin between his hands, shooting back to the waves above. He sucked hard and filled his lungs with the fresh air. Normally he could hold his breath for quite some time—as long as he needed, as a matter of fact—but strangely, today required surfacing after what seemed to be an unusually short period. Little did he know that he was well beyond the protective covering of Kirstell and that the diminishing quality of life was even affecting the air he breathed; for in truth he was not down for more than a brief moment rather than the long spans of time he was used to.

After a second attempt, still seeing nothing, he noticed that those in the lead had decided, as he had, to move further out. Everyone was eager to be the first to make the big find. He prodded his dolphin on and after a few lengths, stopped in the water. This time instead of looking himself, Luik just waited above to see what the others had found upon surfacing; *still nothing*. A third and a fourth dive went on still with no results. Soon the anticipation and excitement of discovery had subsided and been replaced with a now long and tedious task of remembering where one had already looked and where they hadn't. Before long everyone climbed up on their dolphin and just sat as the creatures circled slowly in the water waiting for direction. No one spoke. And there was Gorn to one side just bobbing in the waves with his arms folded and a slight grin on his face.

"Did anybody see it?" Cage finally said, breaking the standoff silence. His long black hair was matted down his spine. He was certainly more used to riding horses, but he was starting to think favorably of these inquisitive and gentle sea creatures. No one answered right away; still worried someone may think the other was holding out. It was an awkward moment. "Come on, brothers!" Cage lifted his hands. "None of us are getting anywhere just sitting here keeping to ourselves."

"He's right, you know," Thad spoke up. Thad looked the most like Anorra to Luik. While he was the oldest of his brothers from Ligeon, and the strongest, he shared the same eyes and long blond hair as Anorra. "Why don't we try working together on this?"

"Together?" Quoin exclaimed. "Then who—"

"Gets the shell?" his older brother Cage asked, finishing his thought.

"Hey'a," Quoin replied.

Cage continued, "We all spread out and search for the shell. The ocean is far too large for us to search it without any sort of pattern or teamwork. When one of us locates the summit of the mountain, he'll signal the rest of us and we'll all gather on the surface. Then, at the same time, we'll all dive and whoever gets it wins it."

"Sounds like a good enough plan," Benigan said, happy just to be floating still in the water next to his ride. Everyone else seemed to agree, so they all devised a way to begin searching the waters in a rational way rather than the hurried and careless manner they had been employing. They all were glad to be doing something productive rather than just looking aimlessly with no plan. Soon the boys were off spread an equal distance apart and moving forward in the same direction. Then all at once they'd duck under the surface and take a peek. After about ten stops they turned around and slid over ten and eight positions so new territory would be covered. It was a great many passes like this until finally someone on the end yelled out.

"Hey'a!" Brax cried a loud with a booming voice. "Over here! I think I found something!" It took no time at all for all the boys to scurry over on their dolphins to where Brax sat waving his arms in the water.

"What is it?" Luik asked.

"See for yourself, but it's a hard to make out from here," Brax replied. All ten and eight of them stuck their heads under the water and looked straight down, eyes wide and searching. Large schools of fish swarmed to and fro while giant sea creatures lumbered along on slow paths. None of the boys had ever seen such animals before. There was so much movement that it was hard to focus on anything much beyond it all.

Though it was extremely difficult to see, after a moment of searching, a few of boys finally made out a glint of silver that remained motionless far below. It was fixed on a narrow point of rock that was visible for only a short distance and then vanished away, plummeting deep into the dark abyss beneath. Young Fyfler was the first to pop his head up.

"I see it!" he cried dubiously.

"As do I," Jrio stated calmly, just to make sure his opponent knew he hadn't forgotten the unspoken rematch.

"Well I sure don't," Rab said, rather frustrated with himself. Luik slid over and told him where to look. After popping up, Rab wiped the water from his eyes and shook his head in disbelief. "That's too deep! How will we ever get down that far?"

"So what now, Cage?" Fallon asked.

"We dive!" Cage yelled and then threw his dolphin into a wild dive.

"Hey'a!" the others hollered back and then followed fast after him. The waters were stirred into froth as all the boys commanded their dolphins to dive, water kicking up from the beating of feet and swooshing of tails. Beneath the surface it looked like three quivers of arrows were loosed downward as the boys and their dolphins shot down into the depths. They raced on, their mighty rides carrying them hard and fast through fleeting schools of fish and whizzing near enough the enormous giants that the boys could see the creatures' eyes to be as large as they were. Another moment later and the shell became clearer, though still very far off. The conical shape resolved and the silver and blue stripes around its form were unmistakable. A little more of the mountain it sat on was emerging, though still eagerly plunging into the darkness. The boys noticed they too, were entering that darkness and could feel the cooling waters squeeze the diminishing sunlight from around them. It was also about this time that they all realized the inevitable; *they were out of breath*. Some felt it come on slowly while others were shocked at the onset of a strange panic and burning in their lungs. While the shell seemed closer than ever, none of the boys were able to pursue it any longer; they all turned back. Though a few boys were so frightened at how far it was back to the surface that they let go of their rides and started kicking. Those few forgot to realize that their dolphins were as equally skilled at getting them back up as they were bringing them down. But the noble dolphins didn't take offense to the slight and quickly came up underneath the perishing few, racing them safely back to the surface with time to spare.

As fast as all the boys had plunged beneath the sea toward their prize, they returned just as quickly, and at that, empty handed. Each one of them breathed heavily, sucking gulps of air with heaving chests. A few patted their dolphin friends with much thanks for their swiftness.

"It's too deep," Kinfen stated. No one dared argue with him, as his word with regard to the ocean was final.

"Aye," said Naffe, agreeing with his brother, "that it is." Then they all turned to look at Gorn who still sat in the water a good distance away, moving slowly along with Siahe. Naffe addressed their teacher with his hands up. "You have given us a task that we cannot complete!" Gorn didn't seem to let the accusation bother him.

"Well, maybe *you* can't complete it," said Gorn with a certain air of mystery.

All the boys sat in the water, just floating. None of them had the breath to get so deep, even with as fast as their dolphins could swim.

"There has to be a way," Fyfler said.

"Not as easy as plucking an apple, is it, Fyf?" Jrio prodded with a smile.

"Well, not plucking it from you," Fyfler added. The other boys laughed at his wit.

"Right," Jrio said accepting being bested.

"There is a way," Luik said. All the boys turned to look at him. He was swimming with just his head out of the water. His dolphin was gone.

"Where is your ride?" Quoin asked. Luik smiled, raised a hand out of the water, and pointed down.

"No!" Jrio cried out, smacking his own forehead with his palm. Before anyone else had time to figure out was happening, Luik's dolphin surfaced beside him with a happy chatter and the shell in his mouth.

Luik patted the dolphin and removed the shell, speaking softly to her with words of appreciation. "I think I'll call you Cellese," he said. The rest of the boys just watched, still in shock, scolding themselves that they hadn't thought of such a plan sooner. "If Gorn used a dolphin to put the shell there, then I can certainly use one to get it back up here." With that Luik grabbed her dorsal fin and clicked with his mouth. Cellese circled around and then headed back for Kirstell. Gorn waved and tipped his head as Luik passed by, and then he waited for the rest of the boys who were still sitting in the middle of the sea, overcome with self-pity.

"Come now, boralees," Gorn boomed from across the water. They were obviously disappointed, but slowly coming to appreciate Luik's ingenuity. "It is not right that the Sons of Kings be of such lowly spirit. Come!" He motioned for them to make their way back to the shore. They made for it slowly at first. Then when they caught up with Gorn the pace quickened. "You will have your chance, boralees. Wait in anticipation for the next time." Gorn rode side by side with them as the sun started its late afternoon descent. He directed his dolphin over to where Jrio rode. "What think you, Son of Naronel?"

"I think he is a very cunning one, that Luik."

"Aye, that he is," Gorn spoke solemnly.

"He was not thinking of his own abilities, or their limits," Jrio went on. "He was looking at everything he had at his disposal. He was truly one step ahead of us all."

"Aye, but not by far. You would have settled upon the same course." Jrio appreciated Gorn's consolation but didn't take it to heart.

"Using the gifts found within creation is a valuable resource," Jrio surmised.

"And is this the principle you learned today?" Gorn asked, well pleased.

"Nay," Jrio said shaking his head. "Though that is a good one."

"O? Then speak of it."

Jrio looked up at his teacher with a toothy smile. "Make sure you grab a faster dolphin."

Chapter Twenty

THE TREE

Anorra climbed up the mountain's face on her hands and knees for more than half the day now late into the early evening. Her legs and arms were burning, a sensation she had never felt before. And her body was growing extremely tired and weak from the great exertion of energy it took to scale the hillside. The higher she climbed the more movements slowed, overcome with fatigue. The only relief she felt was from the strong winds that whipped up at her from below. She had no idea how high she was or even if she was climbing in the right direction. What was the most disconcerting was her not knowing if the path she was on was leading toward the summit or toward an impassable route such as a rock slide, a gorge, or a flat wall.

Not long after she first started climbing Anorra was quickly overwhelmed with concern not only for where she was headed, but also with where she had already been. More specifically, could she manage to get back down to where she was a few steps before in order to try a new route should the current one prove faulty? All in all it was an unnerving exploit that spent as much energy trying to cope mentally as it did physically.

Worst of all, she still had not heard the voice of the Most High. Nothing within her or without had confirmed any sort of direction. She felt neither leading nor any guidance from the Great Spirit. She began to find it irritating that she wasn't hearing His voice and that she simply couldn't lift her blindfold, summit the mountain, and then walk back to Gyinan. But she knew better. Summiting the mountain was not the point; *not dying was*, or so she thought.

Even though she had not heard the Most High's voice, she *did* feel His presence. It was always like a soft stirring in her, an underlying current, and a continual awareness of His presence; she was not alone. Even though she heard no words or felt no leading, she knew He was there. It was a sense, among her many, that would be one of her greatest assets. It is not always the loudest voices that steer us in the right course, but the subtlest undercurrents that do.

One foot after the other, one hand placed after the next, she pulled, heaved, and clambered her way upwards, now quite sure she must be nearing the top. The falcons and the eagles screamed out near her; she was as close to them as ever. The wind licked violently at her hair and threatened to tear the cloth from around her eyes. Though her soul would have loved to blame it on the wind, her spirit overruled it, and she reached back to tighten the knot behind her head. Still she pressed on and soon felt the ground leveling ever so slightly. It was rounding off. She must be getting close. Every movement was very deliberate, each hand being placed only on something that she first tried shaking loose and pulling away. Only when it seemed completely secure did she place her full weight on it. This manner of climbing was extremely laborious and obviously time- consuming. But she couldn't afford a mistake; a misstep here meant certain death. Shrouded in darkness she pressed on, relying completely on her own ability to discern the proper path and to test every handhold and footrest herself.

The leveling off of the ground became more apparent as the rocky terrain smoothed out, and she intercepted small plants and mosses over the ground. Soon she wasn't so much climbing as she was hunched over, pressing up and around large boulders when she had to. The wind had also shifted, coming straight at her face rather than from below her. She must be nearing the summit. Now she was not as worried about hand placement as she was about her steps. This was much different than climbing where all four limbs were used; rather, one misstep meant being thrown off balance, or worse, stepping clear off a cliff. At finally feeling flat ground, she started with just sliding her feet forward, scuffing the soles of her sandals along the gritty path she made. Her toes prodded for a drop-off or rock, though none presented themselves. She was growing impatient with herself. *You flower! Get yourself together and toughen up! You're not going to fall. Just walk straight.* So she took a deep breath and lifted her right leg, extending it out a good ways, and then completely leaning forward on it. When it touched safely ahead she sighed, pausing to do the same thing again, taking her time to extend her left leg out and then leaning out on it fully. It touched safely and she laughed out loud.

Well, at least I'm making up more ground, she thought. *I must look so strange to those birds. Wait, the birds, where are they?* She suddenly realized that she hadn't heard their cries over the last few moments. It was silent. Then she noticed the wind had stopped. It was quiet, too. *That's unusual,* she thought. In fact she heard *nothing.* There was no sound anymore. Everything was completely still in her little world of darkness as if it had all vanished away instantly. She decided to take another step. She lifted her leg high in the air and was about to step forward on it with all her weight.

"*Anorra, stop,*" came a voice from deep within her. She froze. It was so present and all consuming. *It was Him.* She didn't dare move. No wind, no birds, just her balancing on one leg and the voice of the Most High. Then she heard Him speak again.

"*Do you see where you are?*"

"No," she said out loud. "I see black."

"*Look with the eyes of your spirit, My daughter.*"

"But how, O Lord?" Anorra asked trembling. It was the clearest He had ever spoken to her.

"*Believe that you can see. Believe that I am here to guide you. Trust me. Do you trust me?*"

Anorra didn't even think. "Aye, O Lord! I trust You!"

Suddenly it was if she were looking through the blindfold in broad daylight, but with colors much more brilliant and dazzling than she had ever known. She looked down at her raised foot and saw that it hung out over a cliff so deep it dizzied her. She screamed but resisted the urge to step away. Oddly, there was no fear at the sight of such a great height nor at the thought that she had almost plunged headlong over the side.

"Is this truly where I am standing, O Lord?" she asked.

"*Do you not believe it with your spirit? Then see it with your flesh.*"

Anorra reached up and removed her blindfold. Just as she had seen, she was balancing on one foot with the other suspended out over a drop off that plummeted to the bottom of a massive gorge. But seeing it with her eyes brought on the deadly emotion of fear, something that took her off guard.

"I don't want to be afraid!" she yelled and started crying. Anorra was overwhelmed from her journey, from Him actually speaking to her, and from her precarious position.

"*You have nothing to fear if you trust Me,*" He said.

"Then I'm putting this back on!" Anorra pulled the cloth back over her eyes, suddenly realizing that for the first time she was more content to *not see* with the blindfold on than *to see* with it off. *I do trust Him*, she realized. Such a feeling of love washed over her that her tears were no longer of fear but of gratitude. For a whole moment all she could do was think of being wrapped in His arms, bound safely to his chest. She was secure there in the darkness, hidden in the secret place, nestled into the cleft of the mountain with her Maker.

"*And that is where you will always be when you trust in Me.*"

She felt His words surge through her own spirit and then, just as before, the vision in her spirit returned. The dazzling colors were back and everything was in brilliant detail, unlike anything she had ever seen. *I want to see like this forever,* she thought to herself. Her left leg was beginning to get tired.

"*Now go back to Gyinan. He will teach you more.*" Anorra did not argue. She pulled back and away from the cliff with the blindfold on, yet seeing more clearly than she ever had before.

Unlike her ascent, she bounded down the mountainside with the ease of a gazelle, leaping from boulder to boulder and running down the path. She had never felt so free in all her life, and yet she marveled at how such newfound release was discovered only in context of losing what was the most comforting to her, *her sight*. It was startling to realize how quickly the very blindfold she detested had suddenly become her door to true freedom. The route that she had formerly climbed up on her hands and knees she now raced down with giant steps from one ledge to the next, leaping over crevices and giant cracks. It was the most exhilarated she had ever felt. Before long she was back on the mountainside path that she had started on, what seemed like a week before. She stopped to look around the canyon with her newfound sight and then to the meandering river below. The passage lay mostly in shadow now, as the sun would soon be setting in the east. But to Anorra the world around her was sparkling and vivid; even the oncoming darkness couldn't prevent *these eyes* from seeing.

She turned down the path and ran as hard as she could, eager to tell her teacher that she had succeeded after all. Her heart was soaring. Her gait was long and she ran swiftly, taking each bend on the cliff-side track as if it were a raging river careening down a winding rock bed. Even on the tight turns she would run up the inside berms and then back down again. She felt that not even a horse could keep pace with her, though with the dim light and steep heights, one surely wouldn't even lope remotely. Her confidence was greater than it ever had been before. Her confidence was in *Him.*

Soon the mountains slowly faded away casting their long shadows across the valley toward Narin. Anorra was running along the gently rolling foothills like they were small mounds of dirt, wasting no time on getting to the tree. Not long after the sun vanished from the sky, Anorra arrived in the familiar field with the Hefkiln River to one side and the single tree to the other. And there, in about the same spot as they were before, stood Gyinan with the two horses. He regarded her passively and made no move toward her. She didn't stop but kept right on toward him until she slowed and stopped at his side. In the twilight he could see the blindfold wrapped tightly around her eyes, though he had seen it long before in the spirit.

"How is it, Princess?" he asked softly with the corner of his mouth rising ever so slightly to a smile. Anorra let her actions speak for her. She grabbed the mane of her horse and swung up onto his back. She reached for her bow and quiver, which Gyinan swiftly passed up. Nocking one arrow and discarding the quiver to the ground, she pressed her horse around in a violent spin in one direction and then the other. Then she leaned back over his hindquarters, drew back the string, and loosed the arrow. This time she could see it fly straight to its mark as if she were riding on the feathers on the shaft. Anorra sat up and regarded her teacher from beneath the blindfold.

"I believe the arrow remaining in the tree will have three red rings," she said with a new boldness that he had never heard, "not green."

"So you have learned to see with your spirit more surely than with your natural eyes," Gyinan said with a profound air about him.

"I have," Anorra said pensively. "*He* spoke to me up there, Teacher, more closely than you even speak to me now. I had to *trust* Him."

"Aye, and so you have." Gyinan was more pleased than he had been in quite some time. She was surely his greatest student, if also his most strong willed. Yet even such resilience had been broken in one day because of the subtle softness of her heart.

Anorra paused for a moment recalling the ordeal. "You said you'd tell me if you completed the training on the mountain," she reminded him promptly.

"Aye, I did, with only one difference."

"And what's that?" she asked inquisitively.

"I had to do it *twice*."

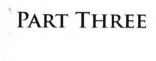

PART THREE

Chapter Twenty-one

GIFT OF THE VINFAE

It had been four summers since Luik had last touched the mainland with his own two feet, since he had seen his mother or embraced his father. But then again it was four summers of memories and growth that he would not trade for anything. For there was absolutely nothing about the Isle of Kirstell that made him want to leave and nothing about his time here that made him regret stepping forward in the Circle of The Kings.

Kirstell had truly become his home in every way, just as Gorn had said it would be. He had memorized every part of its character: every field and every slope, every palisade and every forest waterfall; every cliff and pool, every beast and the song of every bird that clung to the branches that he now called his own. He knew the isle as if it were a person. It sang him to sleep at night and called him to wake at dawn. Every day was a delight. *I could stay here forever*, he told himself every evening, but he knew he could not. Maybe that's why he savored every day he had on Kirstell so much. He knew they were numbered. By now he was well aware of his calling and the purpose of his training: to defend Dionia and her people and to defeat Morgui at all costs, even his own immortal life.

Every day was scheduled and disciplined, but he loved it. Every meal, every exercise, every conversation was ordered and allowed no room for error. The boys, now strong young men, had learned to take advantage of these moments and cherish them as a fine gift. Through trips to the seaside for a swim and hikes up to Fadasha Peak, the group of boralees became tightly knit like best friends. And through the rigors of training and the strict demands of required excellence, they were grafted together as brothers, as Dibor.

"One!" *Crack!* Nine sets of staves struck each other in a loud clatter of noise finding their numbered position in space.

"Four!" *Crack!* Again, the sound was penetrating, this time preceded by the swish of wood swung quickly through the air.

"Two!" Another whooshing swirl of wind and then *crack!* The numbers kept coming and the staves kept swinging, each connecting with their target. An attack became a parry and a parry became an attack. The Dibor stood in two lines facing one another in the courtyard. They sparred beneath the green canopy, hands calloused from years spent spinning the wood.

"One!" The percussions sounded again. Now the commands came furiously, issued at lightning speed with no time to think between them.

"Four! One! Two! Four! Three!" And each number brought the blows of wood in cunning rhythm, aimed at the head, waist and legs. The Dibor flowed with the commands as easily as a brook meandering down a hillside trough. They didn't even give thought to what was ordered; it was simply a natural reaction to instruction.

"Excellent!" their teacher cried out. "Form the ring!"

Gorn stood in the center as the group of Dibor left their line of sparring partners and circled around him facing outward, shoulder-to-shoulder.

"Three!" Gorn yelled. This time staves were swung, but just the air moved out of the way in front of them. "One!" *Swish;* more numbers were called. "Lock staves! Advance North!" Suddenly a clatter arose as the staves swung and lay horizontally, each Dibor holding the center of his own staff and the ends of the two others on each side. As if they were one breathing mass of flesh and wood, the Dibor all stepped in unison toward the north, advancing quickly, the ring never loosing shape.

"Halt!" Gorn yelled. "Turn in."

The ring members stopped, unlocked their staves and turned inward at the same time, each individual toward his left shoulder until he faced looking at Gorn in the center.

"Luik! Cage! Center!"

The two men stepped forward swiftly and raised their staves to ready position, feet spread wide. The rest of the group took a step back to open up the circle slightly.

"*Xidaq*[24]!" Gorn roared.

Cage swung first, bringing his staff from right to left in a lateral arch. Luik took the blow in the center of his weapon between his gripped hands, staff vertical at his left side. Cage countered with the opposite side of his staff and aimed for Luik's exposed ribs, but Luik pivoted and used the still upright staff to block again. His opponent spun in the direction of the failed swing and curled around behind Luik. He bent low and swung a third time at the shins, but Luik drove his staff into the ground by his heels, not having enough time to turn and address his attacker. The blow glanced off of Luik's defense but returned, again, on the other side. Luik, still with his back to Cage, stepped cleverly around his planted staff so that it now blocked his right side. Cage grunted with annoyance. Luik jumped high into the air and skillfully turned to face his opponent, sensing another onslaught. Sure enough, Cage was wielding another wave, this time lowering his weapon down from above with both hands at the base. Luik braced his staff above his head and deflected the incoming strike, this time pushing the blow away and knocking Cage off balance. Luik saw it and took advantage of his first opportunity to attack. Cage, fumbling backwards, did not even have time to react as Luik lunged to the right, jabbed his staff behind his calves, and pulled hard. The force took Cage right off his feet and he went sailing to the ground. Luik pumped him once in the side and then spun Cage's staff free from his hands before straddling the fallen Dibor with his weapon to the neck. The match was over.

"Excellent!" Gorn said loudly. The rest of the Dibor cheered from their ring, standing in the courtyard in front of the main hall. This tree-covered place had become their center, their focus. Every day started and ended here and most of their lectures and weapons training were learned

---

[24] **Xidaq** (*KSYE-dack*): *verb; First Dionian; tense of the command form literally meaning to "attack showing [with] mercy."*

and honed at this very spot. Luik got off his victim and offered his hand. Cage smiled and accepted the offer, jumping up.

"That's the last time you pull that trick on me, Luik, son of Lair!"

"Hey, if it didn't work every time, Cage, Son of Daunt, I wouldn't keep using it on you!" They both laughed and rejoined the ring.

Gorn was pleased and he had every reason to be. In all his days as a warrior and a teacher, he had never seen such a dedicated group of Dibor. Many had come and gone, but none like this. Four summers of training, four summers of reward. Every skill he had given them was mastered, every technique learned and applied without question. They played hard and worked even harder, meeting the challenges of each new day with a bold drive and eagerness to succeed. They would soon be ready to enter the service of King Ragnar. Gorn studied their faces silently. Each boy he had brought to the island had become a man, passing many tests that justified that name. Their bodies were shaped and cut, muscles tight and strong. Their skin was tanned and their eyes sharp and resilient. Endurance had been brought to its peak and Gorn figured that surely there was not a more cunning and deadly team of warriors in all Dionia. The only thing keeping them back—none of them had actually killed anything yet.

Killing was never the goal; victory was. But until a man killed something, certain emotions that couldn't be communicated any other way would never be understood. It was something they were trained for, to execute swift and deliberate justice in order to starve the ranks of the enemy and keep the free dwelling in liberty. Surely some of these young men were destined to be heroes, their names sung for generations; that is *if* those generations had the chance to be born, something that Gorn felt the responsibility to ensure at all costs. Thus came the decision to take on the task of training up what could be the final Dibor. Never before had their fate rested so much in the hands of so few. There was no time to train more or even select them for that matter. What *could be* done was *being* done and it *had* to be enough.

"Quoin, summon the horses," Gorn said. "Tonight we ride to the south."

Quoin stepped from the ring and gave a sharp but melodic whistle with his fingers in his mouth. Then he returned and took up his place. The Dibor had learned never to question their teacher unless it was absolutely necessary as most of their questions were eventually answered in the course of due time. This was one such occasion. No one spoke. They just waited for the horses to arrive.

It was a low, far-off rumble at first, but soon became a shaking as a stampede of horses burst into the privacy of the Dibor's gathering and flooded the central courtyard. The men did not move but stood their ground watching Gorn calmly, their backs to the beasts. The horses filed in around the ring and stood, each individually behind one specific man, breathing heavy and fast. Manes shook and nostrils exhaled, skin fluttering. A few whinnied and stomped their feet, ready for a run.

"Thank you for coming, majestic Horses of the Maker, the finest creature to be fashioned that runs the land on four legs and carries the Sons of Ad. Tonight we will ride south at my command and no other." Gorn leveled his gaze back to the Dibor. "Let us ride swiftly, making camp by dusk."

He clapped his hands and suddenly the ring broke, each man turning to face his steed and blowing softly in its nose. Necks were stroked and shoulders patted. Then all the men pressed themselves up onto the horse's backs and swung their legs over. A last horse entered the ring to pick up Gorn, and with a final shout he led the way out of the courtyard and along a fleeting path.

The group of Dibor rode fast and hard; each having already mastered the fine art of riding bareback and without the use of reins or rope. All commands were given with the feet, legs, and the voice, to allow the rider to use his hands for battle. These techniques required diligent practice and balance as well as patience from the horses. For all generations the Sons of Ad had ruled over the beasts and birds of the air with a kind hand. Creation had no reason to fear or disobey mankind and therefore their relationship was one of mutual trust and co-labor. Man and beast had learned to care for each other in the kindest of ways, both doing for the former what the later could not.

All the men loved riding, but especially Luik. Fast and hard was how he liked it. Anything less seemed too slow and nearly worth getting off and running himself. As long as the horse under him was willing to run, he was willing to ride. Even the three brothers from Jerovah marveled at Luik's natural skill and aptitude for riding. They, of course, helped Gorn with teaching the others at times, as they were born on horseback, in some cases, literally.

They bounded east, headlong across a field of tall wheat and then followed a hedgerow of trees as it bent south toward the coast. Long, green-rolling hills overlapped and meandered further south, descending lower and lower. They drove fast, passing within inches of large boulders and rock-mounds along the way. They enjoyed it, but the horses surely loved it more. The sun dropped lower and lower into the eastern sky before finally kissing the horizon that hid the Islands of Somahguard far beyond. Luik loved this. He wished every day could be this pleasant and vivid. The smells, the sounds, the colors, everything was accentuated here on Kirstell. It was enough to make a man cry at the beauty of it all.

Soon Gorn slowed, signaling the end of their trip for the day. *At least there's a trip back*, Luik always figured. Gorn pulled up short of the Southern Cliffs and got his horse as close as possible before peering over the side to the rocks and pummeling waves below.

"Dismount and make camp. Fire here," he pointed with a stout hand to the grassy flat in the middle near the drop off, "sleep there," pointing to a boulder more inland. "Release the horses and thank them. Bid them return in the morning at dawn."

The group of Dibor quickly did as they were instructed. The horses were let go first and strictly told not to eat anything before cooling off. Then half the Dibor sought out timber and built a sturdy fire while the others removed unwanted stones from around the giant boulder making their sleeping area more comfortable for later on. When all was finished, dusk had given way to night and the Dibor returned to sit around the fire with their teacher. Gorn sat with his back to the cliff and a star-filled sky behind him. A few of the Dibor noticed a large heap of long objects each wrapped in different colored fabrics directly behind him. He must have fetched them while they were busy working, they figured. Gorn had not carried anything on his horse, so the presence of the items was quite an intriguing mystery.

"You all came to this isle as boys," Gorn addressed them looking through the flames. "You arrived ignorant and frail to the ever-increasing power of evil. But every task I gave you, you met with courage and diligence. Every challenge was met with bravery, no matter how difficult it appeared. All the ways of Life have been imparted to you; at least they have taken root in good soil and will continue to grow so long as you allow them. You have learned how to command the natural and discern the supernatural.

Your hands have been trained for battle to make war on those that oppose Life and seek to destroy the freedom we have taken for granted.

"You have arrived as boys, and until now I have always addressed you as boralees, rarely calling you by name. This was so that you might lose your identity and your self-pride. You have all felt the effects of peshe in some way or another during your time here on Kirstell." They all nodded silently in remembrance, each recalling different memories. "You have walked through, now strengthened to endure what lies ahead.

"But in order for you to contest the evil that lurks beyond these shores, you must have more than what you have had so far, the first of which being your title. I no longer call you boralee, but true Dibor, for you have truly shown yourselves to be students of my word to the point of action and conviction. And never again will you address me as teacher, for that title is now passed on to another far more deserving of it than I. From now on you will call me Gorn and address me by name, for I am a fellow brother in battle with you. Your lessons are over; not that you will ever cease to learn, for learning will never cease as long as you are a creation of the Most High who alone is infinite in knowledge and power. But you are no longer students in my care, but now my brothers.

"And know that your time of testing and training has granted you passage into a state far greater than a title or rank, but into manhood itself; let no one ever summon you as a boy. For you have left childish ways behind you and have matured in spirit, body, and mind. Tonight I address you as men."

Gorn paused for a moment, letting the weight of his words sit upon the ears that listened. Then he stood and lifted his hands high.

"Great God, Maker of all Creation, seated on the Throne of the Heavens, I ask You for Your Spirit to indwell these men and forever guide them into all Truth and Life. It is only Your Spirit that sustains us, O Most High, as You are our Light in the midst of utter darkness.

"You have trained their hands for war, and You have given them eyes to discern both things above and things beneath. May You ride with them from this day onward and may it be known in all the Kingdoms of Athera that here stand the greatest among men. May they be swift like horses and war like lions. May they live to see their children's children, and may Peace and Prosperity be established through their exploits. A blessing be upon them for all generations."

The air was still and nothing stirred.

"Luik, son of Lair, rise."

Luik was so lost in the presence of the Most High he almost didn't hear his name called. He was surprised to be summoned and quickly stood having no idea why. Gorn reached down and lifted the first long, shrouded object from the heap. He reverently unwrapped it to reveal an exquisite and marvelous sword unlike any Luik had ever seen. He let the piece lay in the garment still draping from his widespread hands.

"Luik, tonight you are called forth as a Man, a Son of Ad, a Prince of the Great King and an Heir to His Kingdom. I charge you this hour to fulfill your calling and make your election sure. If you will honor all men, love the brotherhood, fear God, and honor the kings, endeavoring to always defend that which is Holy and True even in the face of certain destruction to yourself and those that serve you, say, 'I do.'"

"I do."

"In so accepting the call of the Dibor and all aspects inherent with its office, I hereby proclaim you, in the audience of your brothers, Luik of The Dibor, son of Lair, Man of Dionia.

"Because you have earned and displayed the rite of passage and so acknowledged your commitment to Life, I bestow upon you the gift which no other can wield and no one else has right to own except the Chosen; *the Vinfae*[25], *sword of The Dibor*."

Gorn gave the sword over to Luik and he grasped it by the handle. A strange energy flowed through his hand, up his arm and filled his chest. He had never felt anything like it and could only describe it as a fire in his veins, but altogether tolerable. The sword seemed to carry some sort of life force within its short blade that came alive in his hand, and no other. The blade was wide, moving up from the cross guard, tapering slightly inward at the middle, then flaring out again at the top just before coming to a point. The grip itself cradled each individual finger and the metal pommel was a large rounded sphere of detailed carvings. Endless knots and weaving vines graced the pommel and cross guard ornately. Similar vines were masterfully etched along the length of the blade itself. The superbly balanced weapon felt light and agile, though Luik had not even

---

[25] **Vinfae** (*vinn-FAY*): noun; an ancient Dionian term used to designate the sword forged and used exclusively for the Dibor. Characteristics include its notable power when used in conjunction with the Tongues of the Dibor as well as its ability to differentiate between the Dairne-Reih and that of fallen man (or the taken).

the chance to wield it yet. Gorn also handed him the colored fabric wrap, and beneath it Luik felt the leather scabbard and belt, a material they had learned was hardened hide taken from slaughtered animals. It was also useful for very tough garments including breecs, shirts and certain types of armor. Luik returned to his place, now empowered like never before. His spirit soared. It felt as though he could touch the stars in the sky above with ease.

"Thad, son of Thorn, rise." Gorn summoned the next to his feet. He repeated the same process saying the same words and giving away another of the Vinfae, each sword as unique as the first.

"Thero, son of Thorn; Anondo, son of Thorn; Boran, son of Purgos; Brax, son of Purgos; Benigan, Son of Purgos; Jrio, son of Naronel; Najrion, son of Naronel; Naron, son of Naronel; Rab, son of Naronel; Daquin, son of Daunt; Cage, son of Daunt; Quoin, son of Daunt; Fallon, son of Nenrick; Naffe, son of Nenrick; Kinfen, son of Nenrick; Fyfler, son of Nenrick."

When the ceremony was finally finished and each man had taken his turn, the fire was a heap of burning embers. The waves still beat hard upon the rocks below and echoed up the cliffs as a dull rhythmic roar. Gorn sat back down, the pile of swords depleted.

"Tomorrow I will give to you the Tongues of the Dibor. It will not be a lesson, but an impartation of power through the laying on of my hands that will allow you to deftly wield the Vinfae as the mightiest weapon Dionia has ever seen. It will combine your skill as Warriors with your knowledge as Sons to clear a path for you in the midst of darkest evil to Morgui himself.

"But for tonight, we rest and drink deeply of the sweet smell of Kirstell, for tomorrow will be your final day on the isle. Tomorrow you are returning to the mainland."

Chapter Twenty-two

STIRRINGS

Fane sat on top of a giant boulder perched high in the Border Mountains, a chain of peaks that separated Bensotha from Ligeon, running from the Faladrial Ocean to Grandath. Rays of sunlight streamed down through heavy clouds, a phenomenon very new to Fane and the rest of Dionia, but one he found strangely beautiful. The new season of fall had become more pronounced with the passage of time, and after each summer it grew what Li-Saide had termed *colder*. But just as his teacher had assured him, the next summer would herald a new start, a new beginning, an assurance that things would warm once more. New leaves would unfurl and new flowers would bloom. The dwarf had said it was creation's way of foretelling a great resurrection and rebirth. High on the ridge overlooking Bensotha Valley, Fane sat marveling at the horror and yet the brilliance of the dying leaves, exploding in a smattering of color. His nostrils were filled with a brisk air soaked in woody smells and earthen tastes. He closed his eyes and listened. After a few moments, he leaned over to a feathered quill and began to write in a parchment book beside him.

Fane had been roaming the mountainsides for weeks ever since Li-Saide left him in order to make his annual journey to Grandath. The absence of his teacher for a few days always came with strict orders, including points of study and assignments covering any number of subjects. But this year when Li-Saide left, it was different than all the others before. It had changed the course of Fane's life *forever*.

• • •

"Wake up, Fane. I need to speak with you," the tiny voice whispered, a hand jarring Fane's shoulder abruptly. Though the room was dark he knew it was Li-Saide. He shook off the slumber and rolled over in his bed, not even realizing his teacher had just called him by his first name; the dwarf never had before.

"Aye, Teacher, what is it?"

"I am leaving for Grandath."

"Now?" Fane sat up, wide-awake.

"Aye, *now*; it is essential that I make haste and lose no time." Li-Saide's voice was urgent.

"Is something wrong, Teacher?"

"Of course, apprentice. There has been for some time. Don't ask questions that yield no new information."

"Of course," Fane said as he recalled his training. "Then what are my instructions during your absence?"

Li-Saide paused. "Come with me, apprentice."

Fane got out of bed and walked from his room in the palace through a hallway and then up a spiraled staircase. Fane was much taller now and shadowed high over his teacher. He followed Li-Saide higher up the stairs until they emerged through the floor of one of the many grand towers that lofted high above Adriel. This turret had no roof, just the circular outer wall. It was so high that Fane thought he could touch the stars, but knew it was technically impossible. The sky bowl loomed brilliantly overhead reaching from the ocean horizon in the west to the eastern hills of Bensotha in the east. All was still. It was many hours till dawn. Li-Saide spoke quietly as if not wishing to wake the sun.

"There are many lessons for you to learn yet, Fane, Son of Fadner."

This time Fane heard his name.

"The principles required in order to perceive the lesson have been set in place, I do believe. A lesson without context is wasted. What remains to be learned I cannot teach through example; you must learn it through experience. Thus, when I part you tonight, I do not leave you with an assignment. I ask you a favor."

"You need something from me?" Fane asked bewildered.

"I need your help. Dionia needs your help."

"My help?"

"Do you not remember why the King summoned you? He said that you were needed for a task and are the best for it. *Tonight the task begins.*"

Fane swallowed hard.

"The Mosfar of Grandath, the Tribes of Ot, have called me and I must go quickly. There is a great shaking at this time and the strength of Morgui is growing. We are sliding farther into the shadow lands and the immortality of Man is fading.

"While you have never seen the secret city of Ot and there exists no council here to bestow a title upon you in the Old Ways, I suppose it is ordained to be this way in order to keep your existence unknown from the enemy. But I *am* of the Tribes of Ot and my blood runs from the first created; I *am* a Mosfar, bound to its ways and entitled to its knowledge and Life-giving power; including the right to ordain as I see fit.

"It would seem that all things in your life have come upon you before your time, but then it is not for us to judge the timing of the Most High, nor the rank He sees fit to bestow. Time does not attend our wishes and does not beckon to our call. It marches forward, gaining pace rather than losing it. There is much I would still like to share with you, but it must wait for another day, and then it will not be as teacher, but as brother.

"The Most High is our witness and our Judge tonight. Beneath these starry hosts He watches and writes all that transpires. Nothing is hidden from His gaze and wherever two or three are gathered, He acknowledges what is done, for He is present. Tonight atop this tower, He is our Counselor, He is our Tribe."

Li-Saide held up his hand and opened it. Caught by the starlight and the two moons in the southern sky, a green emerald set in a gold ring dazzled radiantly in his tiny palm.

"I bestow upon you the Ring of The Mosfar. You have demonstrated excellence in the Ways of Understanding and I have never had a pupil so eager to learn what no other from the Sons of Ad has dared to investigate. From this moment on you will go with the title of the Mosfar, though it must never be spoken except in my presence or that of the Tribe, for

Morgui cannot kill what he does not know exists. Be wise with the use of your power and knowledge, and let not your right hand know what your left hand does. Know that you are always safe in the presence of the Mosfar and that when you need them, they will find you. Go when they send for you. You will know them by their fruit and the ring they bear on their finger, this ring. Tonight you join their ranks. Tonight you are a Mosfar."

Li-Saide took Fane's middle finger on his right hand and slipped the ring over the knuckle. Then he asked him to kneel and placed his little hand on his forehead.

"On this one, O Heavenly Father, I impart all wisdom and knowledge that You have given me, that he might walk in the ways You have laid for him and do all that You have commanded him among men. Be his Strong Tower this night, I ask. Let the Way of Life be spoken from his mouth forever and let all darkness be put to flight by the Light present in him. Let Your Spirit guide him from this moment onward. Protect him in what I bestow upon him this night. So be it."

The place where Li-Saide's hand touched Fane's forehead suddenly became hot and opened up yielding to a stream of fire burning down through his head and chest to every limb of his body. Fane yelled out but couldn't hear his own voice. His tongue spoke but it was words he didn't know and couldn't hear. The ring on his finger burned and became so heavy he fought to hold it up. Weight started to press down on his shoulders and bear down on his head. It was heavy but not crushing. He was reeling and felt as though he may tumble over the side of the tower.

"Fane," Li-Saide spoke and it all stopped.

Fane opened his eyes and he was kneeling in the same spot. He breathed deep. All was calm and normal as before.

"So, you felt it." Li-Saide stated more than inquired.

Fane stared at him, speechless for a moment, and then asked, "What *was* that?"

"It was the weight of Responsibility and Authority. And did you hear what you were speaking?"

"No," he replied thinking Li-Saide must find him a fool, almost embarrassed. "I cried out from the fire inside, but I could not hear what I was saying."

"You were speaking in the Tongues of The Mosfar."

"*I was?*" Fane was astonished. "But I don't know that—them—, uh, it."

"Aye, you do now. It will return when you return to it, and next time you will hear what you are uttering, though you may not understand at first. With time you will learn and eventually know each word and see their power. I wish I had more time to teach you, but the gift itself is a greater teacher than I. Do not quench it within you, and yield to His Spirit's leading just as you have done tonight.

"Arise and look there to the north."

Fane stood and found his strength renewed. He looked north along the coast that disappeared in the twilight and then saw the glimmering peaks of the Border Mountains in the moonlight.

"You see there? I want you to go to those mountains."

"What shall I do there, *tea*—"

"No, from now on I am no more your teacher. I am Li-Saide of Ot, your brother and your friend."

Fane was overwhelmed.

"What shall I do there, Li-Saide?"

"*Listen.*"

"Listen for what?"

"Listen to the rise and fall of the waves in the west; listen for the rustling of each leaf and the blowing of every reed; listen to a bird that sings in Trennesol and a gazelle that leaps in Jerovah; listen to the rhythm of the waterfalls and babbling of every stream; listen to the groaning of the deep hollows and the stirrings of the fathoms below; for they are all speaking, they are all calling and crying out. They are telling us of secrets that are yet to be discovered, mysteries that are waiting to be revealed. You have ears to hear what others will not, and you have a mouth to speak what others dare not say. What was rejected from the lips of those before you will be received when you breathe it to life. There is a gift in you that no other has ever dreamed carry. Listen to the Great Voice of the Most High and of His Spirit. He will speak to your heart and tell you what you need to hear.

"I will return to you there in those mountains when I am finished and I will ask you what you have heard. You must do what I am not able to. You must hear the things that I cannot, for I am a dwarf, but you are a Son of Ad. Never before has there been one who is of the race of Man that has been charged with keeping the Old Ways and guarding them, for dominion was given to Ad, but guardianship was placed in the hands of dwarfs. You are the first of your kind, and I dare not think the last, as there may come a day when my kind is no more. Tonight a mantle is passed.

"Remember what you hear whispered in your ear. And be certain and faithful to do this: *write down everything you hear*. For a day has come where the memories of man will fail and what was known may cease to be known anymore. You will find a book, a quill, and an inkbottle beneath your bed. Take them, your cloak, and ring with you as the only items for your trip, along with the sandals I have fashioned for you."

"Sandals?"

"Aye, for your feet; a day is here where the ground will bite at your feet and a snake at your heel. What was once sufficient is no longer."

"When should I leave?"

"Now, and quickly, for already things are being spoken which cannot be missed."

"How long should I plan to wait for you there?"

"There is no more planning. Plans of kings are failing, how much more ours. Stay until I come, or until I send for you. Now, go, Fane of the Mosfar! Go with my blessing and that of the Great God and His speed! Look not behind you or to the right or the left, but run straight and run true! *Listen* to what is spoken and write the words that are uttered in secret. We must know them all."

Li-Saide gave the sign of blessing and then turned back down the staircase. Fane watched him part for only a moment and followed quickly behind, bounding down the steps after him. He descended quickly hoping to follow Li-Saide into the courtyard and see him off to his horse. But as quickly as he emerged from the tower door and into the hallway the dwarf was gone, *vanished*. Fane whispered the dwarf's name trying not to disturb anyone sleeping nearby. It simply echoed off the marble walls and returned to him unanswered. Fane walked through another door to a portico that overlooked the main courtyard. He at least wanted to see his master off safely as he had made a habit of doing every time he left.

Fane looked down from the porch but saw no horse and no stable hand. It was empty. What Fane *did* see shocked him far worse than the absence of any means to take Li-Saide out of Adriel on the long journey to Grandath. It was something he had never witnessed with his own eyes and, more than that, had never heard of being done before: *The King's Gate was closed.*

Chapter Twenty-three

SIEGE OF JAHDAN

It had been eleven days since the Dibor had left the Isle of
Kirstell. It had also been eleven days since they last enjoyed the blossoming
sights and smells of flowers and green trees. For in the Plains of Jerovah
there were very few trees and mostly endless stretches of long grass, and
that not even green but faded and growing stiff with yellow. Luik surmised
that Kirstell, in its seclusion from the mainland, was kept from the change
of seasons that Jerovah was clearly experiencing now. Some of the days
were cloudy while others bright and strong. One thing was for sure; it was
getting colder. And the long road to Jahdan, Capital of Jerovah, was full of
winds that stirred up dust and innumerable shreds of brittle foliage.

The Dibor marched on, all wearing leather breecs and dark long-
sleeved mantles. Their torcs glimmered in any stray beams of sunlight,
and their mighty swords hung easily at their sides. Sandals were buckled
around their feet, and a few of the men carried sacks with skins of fresh
water and fruit inside. The water was necessary during the fall, Gorn had
taught them, as all of the streams and rivers got low or dried up. What little
surface water there was in Jerovah would have nearly vanished.

Gorn had marched them northeast across the middle of the Great
Plains, land of the horses, telling them that King Daunt had requested their

immediate presence. Luik found the journey a bit tedious, as every day seemed as though they were traveling down the same road they had the day before; it all looked the same. Quoin, Daquin, and Cage beamed, notably enjoying the walk and at ease under the great expanse of sky overhead and the monotonous landscape. It was home for them. Luik did note, however, a small concern when they spoke to each other about the dying grasses and the lack of water; but even more so, the lack of horses.

"Mind if I join you, Dibor?" Luik said easily as he slowed, allowing the three brothers to catch up with him.

"Nay! Come, friend!" said Daquin, biggest of the three, slapping Luik heartily on the back. "You are most welcome among us." Luik picked up their stride.

"I heard you make mention these past few days of the lack of horses." Luik gestured to the horizon. The rest all shook their heads.

"Aye, this is true," Cage said. "Normally we all would have been greeted by a great many of them, and every day I might add, seeing as how there are three sons of the King here." He smiled and puts his arms around his brothers.

"So where do you think they have all gone?" Luik asked.

"The same place we are going," Quoin put in, "Jahdan."

"Whenever they are in need of care or protection, as in times past, Jahdan has been their haven and home as all the inhabitants are knowledgeable of the horse and its ways."

"Can Jahdan care for so many beasts?"

"Ah, so you have never been to our home, Luik, son of Lair?" Daquin smiled wide with pride at the thought of telling of its many virtues.

"No, I must confess."

Daquin beat his chest once and let out a deep grunt. "It is a refuge, a jewel of protection circled by many a strong tower, each stretching high into the sky." He spoke with an unusually poetic air for his grand size.

"They must be tall," Quoin interrupted, "in order to watch for the horses and keep track of those that are closest to the city."

"Right," Daquin said while eying his brother, clearly annoyed by the interruption. "And tall they are; each with its own attendant and flame keeper."

"That is how the horses and people wandering in the plains know which direction to walk at night if they lose their way. The bright fires illuminate the evening sky," Quoin again chimed in.

Daquin cast his little brother a stern glance and then continued.

"Aye, so there are many bright towers that surround the city." He paused and regarded Quoin in anticipation. Quoin made to speak but caught the menacing glare and decided to keep quiet. Daquin grinned, pleased.

"Along every street is a place for the horses to drink, made up of a network of waterways and pipes that supply water from deep within the ground. It was our father's own design. Man and beast roam freely. Our love for the great horses can be seen in the etchings and carvings found on every street and home. There is no greater amount of carvings anywhere in Dionia. The homes are made of brick and stone, colored white and a pale brown. Stables and shops exist to make the finest riding dress for both man and horse. I am sure you have heard of our garments?"

"Aye," Luik responded. "My father has two saddles and a number of your blankets."

"Ah!" Daquin pounded his chest again. "You see? Our fame spreads even to the halls of the kings!" He continued on in his explanation, smiling ever bigger now.

"The city lies west of the Nollen Sea and is only a two-day walk from the southern border of Trennesol. Out of its four gates you can swiftly run in any direction to your destination." He paused and took in a deep breath. "I long to see it once again."

They walked on speaking of the beauty of the city and sharing stories from their youth. The Dibor stopped only once to drink the rest of what little water remained. They were getting close. The winds continued to stir up clouds of dust that nipped at their eyes. After one such gust, Cage strained his eyes into the distance and saw what appeared to be a giant, high-rising billow of dust on the horizon.

"Look there!" he yelled.

The Dibor rubbed their eyes and looked to where he pointed.

"Aye, I see it," Gorn replied.

"I see it, too," Quoin added. "It is the horses. They have all gathered at Jahdan and are stirring up the ground. Nothing else could send up that large of a dust cloud."

Gorn studied the movement of the haze far beyond.

"I wouldn't be so sure," he said.

"What do you mean?" Quoin caught up with Gorn.

"Watch the cloud where it starts at the horizon. See the violent shifting in the density?" Quoin peered hard.

"Aye," he replied slowly. "So maybe they are—"

"Running?" Gorn finished.

"But they never run in the city. Why would they be—" Quoin cut himself off and answered his own question. "*The Dairne-Reih.*"

"Quick men! We must get to Jahdan!" Gorn roared.

The entire group dropped anything not worth carrying and lurched forward as one man in a full-out run. Legs beat quickly, and chests angled ahead leading each stride. Arms swung, and each man never looked away from the slowly growing haze. Luik wondered at the condition of the city. Was everyone all right? Who was hurt? And how many of the demons were there? He was eager to face them again. Last time they had taken advantage of children and nearly killed Rab. But this time the evil beasts would meet warriors extensively trained to cut them down and inflict swift judgment. Every stride brought him closer to the reunion, every breath nearer to wrath. It seemed like hours before any progress was apparent, but it wasn't long before someone yelled out the emerging of the towers above the skyline.

"Press in, men! Make haste with God's speed! The Towers of Jahdan present themselves!"

A new burst of energy came over the warriors and the pace quickened as if it had not been previously fast enough. Luik was running all-out getting every piece of ground he could from his efforts. Suddenly Cage spoke loud next to him.

"Luik, this is not good!"

"What?"

"The towers, I count only five. There should be eight!"

"Are you sure?" Luik was breathing heavily.

"Absolutely," Cage yelled back between gasps. "There are two on either side of every gate in the city." He sucked down more air. "It looks like the two on the west gate are gone and one at the north gate."

"Well, at least we know where they got in," Luik yelled back. "Gorn, did you hear that?"

"Aye, Luik!" Gorn hollered back over his shoulder to them, trying to overcome the sound of their small stampede. Within another few moments the hazy city walls appeared above the horizon surrounded by a throng of moving bodies. Gorn raised his clenched fist and brought the Dibor to a dead stop. They all stood looking at the city in a swirl of dust and wind.

"The horses!" Quoin burst out. "Look!"

The bodies running around the perimeter of the southern city wall were not of man or that of the Dairne-Reih, but of the noble horses of Jerovah. And that, *tens upon hundreds upon thousands of them*, all running and rearing in a sea of turmoil and confusion, the air thick with debris.

"Circle in!" Gorn yelled with a gesture. The Dibor came in and stood shoulder-to-shoulder looking at their leader, all breathless. It was harder to breathe than ever before, for as long as Luik could remember. It had never been like this for the last four years on Kirstell and never like this growing up.

"It would seem the Dairne-Reih have indeed attacked Jahdan." Gorn brought out his sword and drew a circle on the ground. "Entry has been made here at the west gate and here at the north. I would only assume that they are headed here toward the king's hall in the center and are taking out whatever stands in their way.

"The horses have retreated to the south and east along the outside walls, too frightened to leave the only refuge they know. But we will use them to our advantage. Cage, Daquin, Quoin; I want you to gain control of the horses as best you know how and send them through the southern and eastern gates." The three brothers nodded. "I'm counting on their numbers and sheer mass to flush the Dairne-Reih back out the way they came. Follow the horses and take out any of the enemy's number that remains behind.

"The rest of you, come with me, half to the west gate, and the other half with Luik to the north." Luik did not let his deep surprise show. "And be ready! When the horses come they will be fast and deadly! I am assuming that the inhabitants of the city have either fled or remain inside their homes. *Biea-Varos!*"

"*Biea-Varos!*" the Dibor shouted back in trained voice.

Luik ran toward the west end of the city with Gorn on his flank just a short distance away. The Dibor filled in evenly behind him and Gorn, each deciding whom to follow. To his right he could see the three sons of Daunt pull away and head toward the churning mass of hooves and manes. He made the sign of blessing toward them and wished them well.

Before long the western gate, or what remained of it, became visible around the long curve of the city wall. The two towers had collapsed in a giant heap of rubble and carnage, smoke rising from the two now demolished signal fires. Enormous boulders and chunks of wall lay strewn about like pebbles carelessly tossed by a child. As the Dibor ran closer, the horror of the scene became more evident as shreds of clothing lay pinned beneath piles of large stones. Luik held back tears, resisting the urge to run toward a motionless hand that extended from a heap of ruined wall. Then it hit him: this was not training anymore; *this was real.*

"Follow me!" Gorn cried out, peeling away with his group and running headlong through the smoldering entrance into the city. Luik ran on, passing by the mouth of the gate on his right. He looked momentarily to see what awaited Gorn and then thought otherwise. But it was too late; through the smoke and ruins his fleeting glance had fallen upon a street filled with the demonic war host, lunging and ebbing like a turbulent stream. He suddenly remembered Rab on the beach and his first encounter with a Dairneag. The red eyes and the mangled flesh were memories that he wished not to remember, but the scene before him left him no choice. Only now there were countless numbers of the demons, each flailing clawed hands and dripping with their own fluid. They stood nearly a man and a half high, twice the size of a Son of Ad. It was just as he remembered but there was one difference; this time they would not be fighting a boy. They would be fighting a Dibor.

Luik's pace quickened and even above the distant sounds of battle clash he could hear the years of training now echoing in his head.

Trust in the Lord in the fullness of all you are and ever will become.

Luik ran hard, embracing everything that had become a part of him.

Do not rely on your own knowledge and ways of life.

The city wall was rounding toward the north.

In all your ways acknowledge the Most High, placing your utmost trust and confidence in Him alone and no other.

He could hear a raucous noise up ahead, a medley of screams and blows lined with a strange clucking noise. He drew his sword and heard seven more answer behind him.

And the Great God will direct you in all the ways He leads, making them straight and true.

The distant gurgling and clicking grew louder as Luik's battle party rounded the last distance of wall, the gate now in full view. He saw seven of the Dairne-Reih, or was it ten? Their dark-colored bodies thrashed at the entrance, pressing through as two more climbed up the outside of the last remaining tower of the north gate. Luik and the others ran silently, gently swinging their swords with every stride. He made a signal and the Dibor fanned out now eight abreast. Their attack would catch the demons by surprise. That is, until one of the beasts near the back of the pack turned to its right and saw the men; but it was too late.

Luik drove hard into the center of the pack. His sword swung through the midsections of two Dairneag doubling them to their knees with a deafening scream. A third he gored through the neck. Writhing in pain, it shook and then dropped in a desperate attempt to scream through the hole in its throat. He stopped the swinging blow of a fourth Dairneag with his forearm and then thrust his blade deep into its abdomen. The demon looked down at the sword and then regarded Luik, narrowing its red eyes. Luik attempted to pull his sword out, but muscles inside the beast clenched it tight. Its other arm rose high into the air ready to strike. Taking advantage of the beast's height, Luik released his sword and rolled between its legs standing quickly behind it.

"Jrio, your sword!" he yelled to his friend nearby.

A blade lofted through the air. In one motion Luik caught the handle and spun with its momentum terminating with a heavy blow that severed the demon's leg. It fell to the ground and Luik dealt the deathblow to its head.

"C'symia, Dibor," Luik hollered to Jrio as he passed back the Vinfae and then retrieved his own. Luik paused to look around. His war band had made quick work of almost two-tens of Dairne-Reih. A few of his brothers pressed through the gate, including Rab, who was repaying the enemy in a violent reunion. The three massive brothers from Tontha stood by him.

"Brax, Boran, you're the strongest and best at climbing. I need you to take them out." Luik pointed to the small group of Dairneags that assailed the top of the tower. "We must preserve the north tower. Should the city fall, *which it won't*, it's our fastest way to summon more help. Benigan, come with me, we hasten into the city." The four of them beat their chests and dispersed.

Brax and Boran began climbing the remaining tower in pursuit of the summit-bound demons above. All three brothers were strong and well versed in navigating the mountain peaks of their homeland; their robust and hardened bodies bore witness to it. Luik had always been impressed with the size of their arms and strength in their backs, even as boys. To them there was no greater joy than spending a whole day climbing a sheer cliff just to spend a few moments atop a majestic mountaintop.

Luik and Benigan joined the rest of their war band just inside the north gate. They stepped through a swath of bodies that lay strewn about on the main road. Rab, Jrio and their two other brothers, Najrion and Naron, hacked away at the Dairne-Reih that continued to advance south into the city, unaware of the Dibor cutting away at their rear. Luik and Benigan quickly killed any enemies that slipped between the swords of the four brothers from Trennesol. The smell was horrendous as deep gouges in the demon carcasses spilled bile and fluid onto the stone road. Luik noticed that while the Dairne-Reih all looked similar, small differences denoted distinct uniqueness and personality, if there could be such a thing. Some of the beasts had horns protruding from the head while others had a series down their backs and even a few from their legs. Hands and feet of various sizes and digits bore either sharp claws or giant horns, both used for slashing, he assumed. Mangled locks of hair lay matted against flesh and bone. Some of the beasts even varied in size and frame ranging from those hunched over and burly to those tall and upright. In fact, Luik could now see that there were many mutations all from a similar design. He advanced several more paces and cut down ten more before a sharp whistle from the tower above caught his attention.

"The horses, they come quickly!" Brax yelled down, hand pointing out one of the four windows toward the south. *The brothers from Jerovah must have met the horses with success and done well*, he thought. Just then Boran heaved a demon corpse out the west window and smiled as it sailed through the air and broke on the ground far below.

"Brothers of Trennesol, return to the gate!" Luik hollered loudly. He could feel a subtle rumble of the ground beneath him. "We must seek refuge against the outside of the city wall!"

Rab slew one more beast for good measure before following after his brothers. Luik and the others ran beyond the entrance and abruptly turned to kneel against the outer wall on each flank. The ground was now shaking noticeably and a shaking filled their ears. The horses were advancing swiftly.

"Once they pass," Luik gave orders across the way, "we re-enter the city and search out any Dairne-Reih that have survived! Wait for my command!" Then he noticed it; someone was missing. The ground shook. *Rab!*

"Where is Rab?" he yelled. The others stood sharing his surprise. Rab hadn't come through the gate. He was still inside the city.

Luik rounded the entrance once more, and his eyes immediately began scouring the field of bodies. Up ahead there was a great commotion among the war host, and they had stopped advancing. A thick haze of dust and debris advanced northward.

"Rab! Rab! Where are you?"

He saw movement to one side of the road against a dwelling. Rab struggled to press a large demon off him, pinned beneath its weight.

"Hey'a!" Luik ran quickly to his friend. He grabbed hold of the corpse and pulled it sideways freeing Rab.

"He set upon me from the roof." Rab rose to his feet covered in the creature's excretions.

"Must I always save you, Dibor?"

"I am grateful, but this time I was ready." He brandished a small dagger in his hand, covered up to his elbow with the Dairneag's blood-like fluid.

"Marvelous! Next time you're on your own," Luik smiled, amused. "Let's go!"

They both turned and began to run, but the frightened rank upon rank of enemy had begun running for the gate, too. The demons' stride was twice that of a man. Luik and Rab halved the distance to the wall but it wouldn't be enough. They dared not look behind them, but the crazed Dairneags were set to obliviously trample over them. Luik searched for another refuge and then he saw it; a small space between two buildings big enough for a man, too small for a Dairneag. But it was too far for them both to get there in time.

"*Rab, in there!*" Rab looked to where Luik pointed. With that Luik shoved the smaller man across the lane, causing him to trip and fall headlong into the gap. Rab picked up his head, shaken by the jolt, and pulled himself further back as a violent gush of horses and demons swept by the opening. A thunder of hooves and crushed bodies washed by and filled the small refuge with debris and a horrid stench. Rab tried to yell for Luik above the roar but he couldn't even hear his own voice.

Chapter Twenty-four

THE REPORT

What once seemed mute and without utterance, suddenly was now with voice and jostled for a position to be heard among the throng. Every tree, every valley, every beast that walked the ground and bird that hung aloft, even the very rocks all cried out, vying for an audience with him. It was as if he had been given new ears; ones that were able to hear into a realm he never knew existed, and what he heard was a cacophony that few others ever had.

It was a few weeks before he was able to order the voices in his head enough to make out anything intelligible. All creation was speaking, groaning beneath the weight of something more intense than he had realized.

Has creation always spoken this prolifically? Fane thought to himself. *If it has, we were too loud to hear it, too ignorant to entertain it.*

At first all he could do was listen in astonishment to what each report bore but soon after, he would remember the words of Li-Saide; *write it down.* And write he did. Every feeling, every thought he listed and logged. Every shifting of the wind, every step that broke stride with the masses, and every bird that fell when it should be flying was pressed with his quill to the page, but more importantly, pressed into his heart.

There was a grief in the air that he somehow surmised had not always been present. *Creation could not have possibly been this downcast before now,* he wrote. *For misery and foreboding does not reflect the character and unchanging nature of the Creator. For Him to instill such a dire mood is not possible. Can God break His own Word? No. Something has changed. Something is frightening the land, and I fear it is growing.*

He still sat high above in the Border Mountains looking down across Bensotha Valley. In fact, once the voices had become ordered, he could not pull himself away from the rock on which he sat, writing furiously by day and into the night. He broke hardly enough to sleep and never to eat or drink, fasting from both. It had been seven weeks since the dwarf had left him in the palace and in that time Fane had faithfully filled the parchment book and nearly emptied the ink reservoir. The day that he finished the last page and closed the back cover was the day he heard his friend's voice again.

"They told me you were coming." Fane didn't turn around, he remained fixed on the sky beyond. Li-Saide sat next to him on the giant boulder, both of them somber.

"Then you are learning quickly and advancing well, Fane of the Mosfar. I am pleased."

"You speak as if there were another option, friend; for when one has a masterful teacher combined with an impending and dire future, one *must* excel no matter how poor a student he is."

"Well said," Li-Saide noted with pleasure. "So who was it that betrayed my coming, the birds of the air?"

"No, my friend. You hid from them well. It was the wind."

"The wind?" the dwarf turned to face Fane in surprise, quite shocked.

"It smelled you long before it saw you," Fane said holding his nose and grimacing. They both burst out laughing, echoing down the cliff face. The dwarf punched him in the arm.

"Then I shall remember that for next time," Li-Saide spoke through his grin as he turned to embrace Fane.

"You have been gone for a long time, friend," Fane stated.

"Aye, 'tis true. There was much to do, and much more still left undone."

"Then why have you come here? Why not wait till the task is finished?"

"Because, I am told that you know what the rest of us do not," Fane tilted slightly but said nothing, "a secret that no one else knows; and maybe then one or two more perhaps."

"I have heard many things, Li-Saide." Fane's demeanor was solemn. He waited for his next sentence to form and considered his words, looking pensively into the sky. "The birds sing it as a song, the beasts hum it as a chant, and even more, the ground groans and gives utterance that I cannot discern. I have heard many things and many more wait to be uttered." He reached down and handed Li-Saide the parchment book. "But what I do know thus far can be told in these writings." The dwarf was surprised and looked pleased.

"Aye, Fane, I trust what you have written but there is something more that you have not written. You dare not think it, let alone speak it, for fear of being wrong and the great calamity that will befall those who hear it, but I pray you speak, my friend. What is the stirring of your heart? What is the report that your own spirit bears that no other living creature will tell?"

"But I think I cannot speak it."

"Aye, I know, friend, but you must."

"But I have no words for the compelling voice inside of me! I don't know how to utter what it desires to say!"

"Then you must let *it* do the talking."

"I'm not sure I yet know how, Li-Saide. What needs to be said I'm not sure can come from my mouth. You see, what I have heard up here in these weeks has been spoken by countless numbers of bird and beast. Even the ground cries out, straining under an evil weight, groaning in unrelenting agony, waiting for a deliverer, waiting for relief. Countless voices have rung in my ears and saturated my spirit. There have been so many now that I could not possibly sum up the total, so I simply am at a loss as to how to speak for them all in one voice."

"But you don't need to speak for *them*, my friend. You need to speak for *Him*."

There was a long silence.

"I need to speak for the King of kings, you mean." Fane looked down at his feet.

"Aye. I, too, have heard the groaning of creation waiting patiently for one to bring justice in his hand, but there are other things I cannot hear, plans I do not know, and schemes I cannot unravel. It is at this point that creation is unable to tell me all I need to hear. There must be more, and only One knows of it.

"So I beseech you, Fane of the Mosfar, speak now! Speak for the Most High! Yield your spirit fully to Him and give yourself over!"

Fane sat motionless and looked off in the distance. It was several moments before he said anything more. Li-Saide could feel the enormous weight now manifesting.

"I sense there is a great evil mounting to make war against those who are still living. The beasts and birds have told me of the battle in the east and of the fall of the towers of Jahdan but it is simply a beginning, *and* a distraction."

"A distraction from what?"

Fane pointed south. His eyes narrowed, and he murmured to himself. His body started to shake, and he eventually closed his eyes and pulled his knees in close. *I must yield all*, he thought to himself. Fane jerked suddenly and rocked back and forth on the rock, giving way to the Spirit inside of him, and then spoke as if far away and distant. The dwarf knew this tone of voice all too well; it was that of those who prophesy and foretell what is known only by the Most High Himself. *It was the voice of a Prophet.*

"See and behold, a great shaking is soon here, violently snatching the Sons of Ad and all of creation!

A dragon builds strength to the south where Grandath and Bensotha meet the Sea of Lens.

It drinks of the water and eats of flesh, growing stronger with every moment. Its mouth will devour your sons, and its eyes will seize your daughters.

See, a mighty arm administers destruction, one that will be written about for ages to come. It turns white marble to coal and the strength of stone to ash.

Rain will fall on young and old alike.

Kings will fall standing side by side and riding to their end.

Dying leaves will scatter to the secret places, blown about by the wind.

Every man's heart will be made known for what it truly is.

All the land will be covered by a blanket and sleep for a season.

The dead will be seen walking, and the living will call unto the lost.

Every man must come to his own end; every man must die before he can truly live."

When the Great Spirit stopped speaking through him, Fane collapsed and lay across the boulder. The weeks of no food and little sleep suddenly caught up with him, rendering him completely exhausted and limp. Li-Saide rose quickly and pulled a water skin from his belt. He realized the only thing sustaining Fane had been the Great Spirit Himself. The dwarf poured some of the liquid into Fane's mouth urging him to drink but most of it spilled out.

"You need rest, my friend. We must get you to Narin, and quickly. And we must get word to the King." Li-Saide looked down over the valley that stretched on to Casterness in the fading light. "A great army builds to the south."

• • •

"Someone knows," came a low whisper from beneath a hooded cloak. "Bring me the KiJinNard[26]. They must not reach the Great Hall of Narin."

• • •

A child played in the field nearby her family's home just a two-day walk from Beneetha. The cooling air had not dissuaded this little girl from going outside. She adapted quite well to her changing environment and rather enjoyed the fluffy new garments her mother had fashioned for her. Just five summers old, she loved to climb in the trees and race around the brook, splashing rocks into the water. Today she was collecting clover blossoms in an adjacent field and bounced from patch to patch, stuffing the small clusters in her pockets.

But she was too young to give any concern to a strange rumble in the distance. Far-off beatings sounded like muted drums thumping over the hills. Still she went on, gently singing a flitting melody as she grasped for handfuls of clovers. The beating grew louder, and soon the ground shook ever so slightly.

---

[26] **KiJinNard** (*KYEY-shjih-nard*): *noun; closest literal translation is "dead hound"; refers to the dogs that have been "taken" and joined with the ranks of the Dairne-Reih.*

"Hieralee?" her mother emerged from their home and shouted in her direction. The little girl played on, completely oblivious. The mother looked around for the strange noise and then called out her daughter's name again. "Hieralee, come here! Hieralee!" But the little girl still did not hear her.

Rising above the southern hill appeared five mammoth four-legged beasts. They ran furiously and ate up the ground under their feet with unrelenting speed. They wore chains around their necks and snarled, dripping with mucus from disfigured fangs and noses. The mutilated creatures vaguely resembled a Great Hound in form; a pronounced head and long in its hindquarters. Any sense of nobility and virtue was nonexistent. The skin was raked and mangled with fur, limbs were bloated and discolored, and the breath was fowl and rank. Saliva dripped from their mouths as they bit at the air. Their eyes were wild, possessed in a frenzied excitement searching for something to devour; *and they were heading straight for Hieralee.*

Hieralee played on but then suddenly heard the sound of her mother screaming in the distance. She looked up to see her running through the grassy field, waving her arms hysterically. Hieralee smiled and screamed back with a delighted giggle following and waved her arms, too. She liked playing games with her Ta na and Na na. Suddenly realizing this was probably a game of chase, she turned and started to run away. She never did see the horrible creatures that closed in on her.

Her mother let out a gut-wrenching yell as the five KiJinNard hounds reached her daughter. She had not been fast enough to rescue her child, but even if she had been, what could she have possibly done? The monster's shoulders were as tall as a man and their physical power far greater than hers.

It was the lead hound that saw the child first. Its eyes narrowed and it lunged for the babe, mouth gaping. Hieralee's mother watched in horror and sank to her knees sobbing, giving no thought to her own safety. Just as quickly as the nightmare had appeared, the hounds vanished over a northern rise and the beatings of their paws faded just as quickly. Everything was silent save for a wounded mother who grieved for her baby. It had all happened so fast; too fast, in fact, for her to see what really happened.

Through her own sobbing she heard a very distinct and clear sound, one that turns the head and gains the full attention of any mother: her baby's cry. She ran forward, regaining her feet as she stumbled and yelled out for her child. She headed toward the little girl that lay tumbled in the long grass. Tears streamed down Hieralee's face, and she was notably shaken.

"There, there, your Na na is here! Everything is all right, Hieralee. I'm here! It's all right! Peace be on you!" She held the little girl tightly and kissed her face, both of them crying. Then she turned Hieralee around and examined her, but she found no injuries. She had merely been tossed. Somehow the giant hound had missed her. Maybe they were running too quickly or maybe they just had something else on their minds. In any case, her daughter had been spared. She picked the child up and ran for home as fast as she could. She feared greatly for whoever encountered those creatures next.

Chapter Twenty-five

BLIND RESCUE

Rab thought the stampede would never cease. An endless blur of horse legs and dust soon became the only visible thing seen from his lair of safety. Hooves clacked along the lane and beat out through the gate beyond. The signs of any fleeing Dairne-Reih vanished long ago, and the whole time all Rab could do was think about Luik.

When the horse charge finally began to thin and the last of the noble creatures passed by, Rab emerged from the gap between the two buildings and surveyed the road. The fallen Dairne-Reih had been beaten to a pulp, and the street cradled a thick soup of putrid flesh and maimed carcasses. Rab covered his nose and mouth, having never smelled such a putrid air in all his life. The lane was deathly still, and out through the gate in the plains beyond he could see the diminishing stampede. Suddenly an emotion of great loss filled his heart and tears filled his eyes; somewhere among the dross of wasted life lay his friend.

"Luik!" he cried out. "*Luik!*"

The only response came from his brothers and the rest of those outside the wall who came around the corner when they heard his voice. Their faces were forlorn and distraught.

"Did you see him come through the gate?" Rab frantically yelled to the Dibor now walking toward him. They shook their heads.

Hope kindled in his heart as his older brother, Jrio, took command of the Dibor. "Search the side streets there and there! I'll look over here!" They all split up only to return a few moments later into the main road: *nothing*. Brax and Boran came down through the spiraled staircase within the tower and emerged onto the street.

"We watched the whole stampede pass," they said.

"Did you see Luik?" Rab yelled over.

"No," Brax said slowly. "I fear he is gone."

The feelings were uncontrollable. The entire group sensed the deep agony that mounted with every heartbeat.

"I have something over here," Benigan said, kneeling in the muck. They all gathered around him. He pulled up a half circle and wiped the gore away, revealing a gleaming silver torc.

"His torc," Rab whispered. The piece of metal jewelry sustained not even a nick from the forces that ran it over. *If only his body could have been as indestructible*, Rab thought.

"There is nothing left of him, brother," Jrio said with a hand on his younger brother's shoulder. "He is gone." Tears ran down Jrio's hardened face. He reached for Luik's torc and handed it to Rab. "Here, brother, I think you should keep this. He gave his own life to save yours." Rab took it and hugged his older brother.

"There will be time for mourning later," Jrio told the others. "We should all make for the center of the city and meet up with the rest of the Dibor. There will surely be a few remaining enemies in the side streets who escaped the stampede. Keep your guard up."

The men pulled themselves together and began the trek into the city's center, trying to shake the grip of heartache with every step. The four main roads that ran from the gates inward were nearly straight with only minor deviations in course along the way. The whole city was eerily quiet and still. Nothing moved. Jrio still sensed uneasiness in the fact that none of the city's inhabitants had yet emerged from their homes. They marched on, feet caked in the foul rank of death. The scene should have been a triumph for the Dibor, but it was not. There seemed to be a mutual, unspoken sense that this was not what they all had in mind; vanquishing the enemy, saving their people, uplifting the horn of the Most High, surely;

but not losing a friend. The weight of the mire that clung to their feet seemed to pull their spirits down even further. The corpses of the slain attacked even when dead. Wickedness, taking advantage of the mourning, began to weave a noose around each man's neck, cinching tighter with every stride until they all would step far enough over the edge that the rope would fulfill its intent.

A voice called out down the lane. Far away Jrio could see it was Fyfler. They were nearly at the center of the city.

"Hey'a!" Jrio called back. Fyfler began to run, yelling and waving his hand as he did. "Hey everyone, look! It's Fyfler! The others must be close by." Their spirits rose and they yelled back in elation. Suddenly Jrio realized exactly what Fyfler was saying. *Hiding*, Jrio whispered the words to himself, *they're hiding*.

"Circle, Dibor!" Jrio let out a deafening cry. The war band responded more out of training than consciousness and wondered at the command. "The enemy ambushes us in hiding!"

"Where?" Brax questioned facing out from the war circle. "I don't see them?"

Just then a giant Dairneag leapt from the roof of the closest dwelling and landed in the center of the Dibor, flailing wildly. All were caught unprepared by the insurgent who took advantage of his position and knocked one side of the group to the ground, and then swung at the rest. Benigan managed to spin away from the menacing creature, drawing its attention from the other Dibor on the ground. Jrio rolled, resisting the onset of fear and any resulting pain from the blow by pressing his spirit into the presence of the All Mighty. It was a technique that he had mastered quickly after first learning of his own frailty and failings at the waterfall almost five summers before. Any damage from the impact of the demon's arm was instantly healed and Jrio stood whole and resilient. His arms tightened and he lowered his head gazing directly at the beast. *What a despicable being*, he thought with great indignation at having been preyed upon without warning. Jrio took two steps and leapt high into the air. The Dairneag turned but too late to do anything about it. Jrio sailed over its left shoulder and then plunged his sword point deep into the upper chest through the soft part of its neck from above. He landed with a soft step on the opposite side, and the demon crashed into the street, dead.

The Dibor cheered momentarily, all regaining their feet, but the victory was short-lived. Just as Fyfler neared, a large host of Dairne-Reih emerged and beset them from the side streets and rooftops from every direction, now even more enraged from nearly being trampled in the massacre. The Dibor were caught in the middle of the crush and Fyfler lost sight of them. This time the element of surprise had swung fully to the demons' favor, and the Dibor were on their own, having lost their battle form.

Boran and Brax managed to work together, as came naturally, and swung hard at each foe, defending one another's flanks, ducking and swinging in conjunction with the other. They were amazing to watch, truly knit from the same design. Had they not been twins from birth, one would have wondered at the uncanny sense of dualism. Their bodies and features were nearly identical, save for the hair; Brax as blond as wheat, Boran as black as a raven. They cut a wide hole about them, and one by one each Dibor found his way into the circle, expanding the size. But the onslaught grew with more Dairneags adding to the fray every second. They slid in from the rooftops and poured from in between the dwellings and tall buildings. Whereas before they were simply attacking an unsuspecting city in the kingdom of Jerovah, now they were pitted against a worthy opponent that had stirred their blood, or whatever coursed through their veins. They fought with purpose and a drive that was not present before. All the Dibor felt it, their circle getting tighter in the battle crush.

"We cannot hold them here much longer!" Jrio yelled to Benigan who responded with a grunt. Even Fyfler felt helpless for his friends. He stood on the outside hacking away at a few of the fringe demons but they were so engulfed with fury that they passed him off, rather engaging with the small pocket of Dibor in their middle. Fyfler wished the rest of the warriors to the south would come, but after Gorn sent him to seek out Luik's band, he now feared they too were besieged in the same manner. His heart was torn for both groups; only the fate of one could he see.

Jrio and the others were now pressed tightly together, and the pressure was beginning to hinder their ability to swing their swords. His heart resisted the onset of fear once more, something that he was told would try to attack him in every battle, as it did all Sons of Ad. The temptation to pull his mind from the skill of battle and think more about his own survival than that of his brothers was strong. His spirit was weakening but he held to what Presence remained, knowing it was all that sustained him, all which kept him alive should he be struck down.

"We must—" he sucked in a breath of air as he swung and severed a demon's arm, "find a way out of here!"

"I see no quarter being given, my friend!" Benigan hollered above the battle clash.

They were just moments from disaster. Jrio's mind raced, searching for remedies and cunning solutions, but none presented themselves. *Great God*, he whispered in his heart, *please deliver us*. That was all he could think to say. But that's all that needed to be said. He suddenly felt the ground surge and rumble violently beneath his feet.

"The horses! They are returning!" Jrio cried out as he leveled his sword on another victim, hacking away at its torso. "Get out of the street! We must move as one—over there!" Jrio signaled to a lane that branched off abruptly from the main road. They began taking large steps in its direction, resisted every step of the way by the demon host. They would sooner survive the Dairne-Reih than the wrath of a wild pack of horses, and made for the side street as such. The twins punched a hole to the street while Benigan, Jrio, and Rab parried the retreating rear, and Naron and Najrion guarded the flanks. The ground shaking was fierce. The horses were here. The group tumbled into the street while Fyfler dove for another lane nearby. The returning stampede flung a few of the demons into the tangent streets but the majority was run over, never even sensing the danger due to their uncontrollable blood lust.

Jrio had the quick idea to mount a nearby brick and clay staircase in order to survey the scene from atop a high building. When he reached the summit he could see the entire city, thick and dense with dwellings connected by a maze of streets. Just below him the stampede galloped, pounding every breathing thing into the ground like a death drum. What surprised him the most was a figure riding bareback on one of the lead horses.

Luik!

Jrio turned and yelled down to his brothers, some of whom were already mounting the stairs.

"*Luik!*" He could hardly contain himself, his voice breaking up. "*He's alive! And he's leading the horses!*" Jrio's heart beat fast, and elation quickly turned into a sweet humor as Rab stood next to him.

"Who does he think he is? Always coming to save me, huh." Rab held his fist high and then burst into laughter.

Thank You, O Most High. Jrio felt a tear run down his cheek. He let out a sigh of relief.

"Praise be to the Most High God! May His Name be forever famous among the Tribes of Men!" Benigan yelled loudly from one corner of the roof and then let out a whoop to which they all answered and cheered aloud. Above the din of the horses Luik heard cheering and turned in his seat. Back over his shoulder he could see his fellow Dibor huddled on the roof all waving their hands and yelling loudly. A wide grin spanned his face. *Praise be to the Creator, they rest easy.*

Around the central ring that bordered the king's hall and then off to the west, Luik flew by Gorn and the others who had finished off the remaining Dairne-Reih and stood high above him on the rooftops. The horses ran swiftly, still upset from the siege of their homeland. It had been all Luik could do to prompt them to return to the city gates earlier. But now they, too, sensed their safety and the defeat of the enemy. They ran on, approaching the western gate, and Luik raised his hand and let out a whoop, victory ringing in his voice. The large dapple-gray horse that he rode sensed Luik's elation and let out a whinny in chorus. His speckled face and hind quarters were brilliant and Luik felt an immediate bond with the animal. That and the fact that it had saved him from certain death sealed an immediate and surely lasting connection.

Luik rode on and patted the horse's neck with one hand, clenching his thick mane with the other. But just then, as they swept under the arch of the western gate, negotiating ruins of the crumbled towers, Luik heard a devilish scream that whistled through the air toward him. He turned and out of the corner of his eye caught the blur of a dark figure hurtling at him. The red eyes and gleaming teeth were unmistakable. The Dairneag had leapt from the city wall and struck Luik with such force it ripped him off his horse and sword, fortunately throwing him clear of the adjacent rush of horses. Luik tucked into a ball and rolled, trying to absorb the violent fall as best he could. He felt his back scrape across the hard ground and tear into his flesh. His head struck on a fallen tower stone and the impact of the enemy had knocked the wind right out of him. His body felt hot and ached all over. He tasted blood in his mouth. *The presence of the*

Most High, he felt his spirit rise up within him. *The presence of the Great Spirit be with me.* But he didn't have time to say anything else.

He spun around hoping to confront his aggressor, but the demon beat him to it. A claw flew down and tore at Luik's chest, sending him back to the ground. *Get up,* he told himself. Blood poured from his stomach. *Get up, Luik!* This demon was clearly enraged beyond control, spiteful at the loss in the siege. Luik got to his hands and knees but the enemy was still behind him. He started to crawl and heard one footstep follow him but no blow came. *Why doesn't he strike?* Then Luik realized how vile the heart of these creatures really was. *It's playing with me.* Luik saw his sword stuck in the ground just a few paces in front of him, but the beast saw it too. Opting to toy with his prey before devouring, the demon leapt over its victim and knelt by the weapon. Luik's strength was weakening as blood left his body. Why weren't his wounds healing? *Faster,* he thought, *I need my strength back more quickly!* He continued to crawl toward his sword but it seemed like a false hope. The demon now faced him, the sword between them. Luik thought he could see an evil grin cross over the demonic lips. *It surely has a soul,* he insisted.

It seemed to be beckoning Luik to reach for his weapon. It silently taunted, its foul smell weaving the throes of death. But Luik's strength gave out and his shoulder bit hard into the ground. The demon became impatient and sought to end the prolonging of his vengeance, and what better way than with the man's own weapon. The Dairneag clucked and reached for the upturned handle, raising the Vinfae high above its head. Luik had not even the strength to roll or turn away. All he could do was look up at his enemy. It clucked again but this time it started to scream and its arms trembled. Why did it linger? Why didn't it persist at dealing the deathblow? Was it truly that wicked? Soon the shaking became violent. Something was wrong. Luik suddenly remembered the words spoken to him the night he received the sword. *I bestow upon you the gift which no other can wield and no one else has right to own except the Chosen.*

The sword! It only knows my hand or that of another Dibor! The astonishment kindled hope within him and Luik pressed himself up just a little. He regarded the Dairneag with defiance now, but still felt helpless to do much about it. The beast's whole body began to tremble, still holding the sword over its head. All at once smoke rose from the handle and the demon's hands burst into flames. It held on, flesh bubbling, till its pain threshold was surpassed, and it had no choice but to throw down the weapon. But it was still too far away for Luik to reach it. He looked back up at the demon that now walked directly toward him. Luik tried to regain his feet, but the pool of blood that he sat in gave reason to believe that would not be possible. Both hands of the monster rose into the air and its claws spread wide, dripping with its own burnt flesh. Luik took a deep breath.

Thwap! A noise came from the assailant's body. The demon arched its back and let out a scream. *Thwap!* It came again, and then again like the whisper of a whip through the air slapping a wall. Five, six times it came. *Thwap!* With every successive strike the demon twisted and beat at the air blindly. *What was it?* Then Luik saw thin sticks protruding from the body, each terminating in feathers. *Arrows!* Luik looked around but saw no one. Two more struck in succession. Finally the Dairneag tripped and gave way to the relentless bloodletting. It wallowed, writhing on the ground and clucking in the back of its throat all the while. Finally it drew a last breath and then seized in the dust, never breathing out. *It was over.*

Luik rolled onto his back hoping to see his rescuer, but the plains to his left were barren, save for the horses, and the city wall and rubble at the gate were still. He held his torn gut and waited for his body to heal itself; or for the Creator to take him home. There was nothing more he could do. This time he gave no office to fear or doubt. No evil assailed him. It was simply that his body had been severely damaged and quite possibly beyond its own ability to mend itself as it had been designed. A few moments passed and he could feel his heart beat lessen, gaps between pulses growing longer in duration. His vision began to diminish and he gently closed his eyes and rested his head for a moment. Perhaps his condition was too far-gone. Perhaps it was truly his time to be called home into the Great Throne Room of Athera.

If there was evidence enough before to cause his friends to think him dead, there would surely be enough this time to lay any suspicions to rest. What doubt could possibly be left unanswered with a corpse?

His vision dimmed and then dwindled to black, but he could hear a group of footsteps coming toward him. He felt cold and completely removed from his body but sensed a great commotion stirring without. Voices shouted out, then faded off as echoes in a deep chasm, diminishing into the depths. A moment passed, and then whispers filled the space, a group of people all speaking under their breath at once. *What are you saying?*

Luik tried to speak but he couldn't. He grabbed at each voice in the cold blackness, hoping to make out the words, but the lines slipped through his fingers and he drifted further away into oblivion. *Wait! Come back! I want to hear what you are saying!* He wrestled in the throes of death, not content to let things end like this. *He wanted to know what they were saying!*

Suddenly a gust of wind swept underneath him and hoisted him high into the air. It swirled about him with a dizzying effect like a hawk caught in an updraft. It was warm and comforting and drew him back toward his body. The crowd of whispers grew louder, and a dim glow of light grew in the distance. *Speak more slowly!* He demanded. But the whispers continued on in their fury, only growing louder by the second.

Then, as if being underwater for far too long, he emerged with a splash and gasped for air, eyes wide open.

"*He's alive!*" they all shouted. The Dibor, now complete once more, all knelt around Luik laying their hands on his body. Luik lay in surprise with all his brothers surrounding him from above.

"Who's alive?" he asked them.

"Why, *you are*," Fyfler said softly.

Everyone stood as a few helped Luik sit up. He looked down at his shirt, torn and caked with his own blood. But beneath the garment he felt no wound. He was whole once more. Nothing in him ached, no pain remained, and all was as before.

"What were you all doing?" he asked, still quite surprised.

"We found you nearly dead," Gorn spoke. "Your body was beyond repair and your faith was waning thin."

"So we used our own faith to bring you back," Jrio added.

"When one cannot believe for himself, others must carry the burden of faith," Gorn continued. "You could not ask for a miracle of healing as your body was too far failing. Even our own design is becoming subject to a mortality that is unwarranted by the Creator, but cursed by Morgui. The evil mounts within our own borders. As Dionia slips from the everlasting promises and statutes of Athera so, too, do our surroundings and even our own bodies."

"Did anyone notice how it was much harder to breathe than before?" Jrio asked aloud. They all nodded. Benigan and Brax helped Luik to his feet.

"That's because the air you breathe no longer has the life it once did," Gorn answered. "Until our unwelcome visitors are banished, it will be a condition you must get used to and endure."

"Well, we're all glad you didn't decide to leave us," Rab said to Luik.

"Hey'a, so how did you manage to escape the stampede, anyway?" Jrio asked.

"And then ride back in on the horses?" Cage added.

"You saw that, too?" Rab asked with much surprise.

"We all saw it," said Gorn. He put a hand on Luik's shoulder. "Any Dairne-Reih that managed to hide from the first stampede never saw your second charge coming. We owe you, Luik." The Dibor all beat their chests once and then made the sign of blessing. Luik was humbled by their honor.

"Well, just as the stampede was upon us I threw Rab into a small divide between two buildings, knowing that neither of us would have enough time to get there on our own. Then I turned to face the retreating Dairne-Reih and vaulted over them like we used to as boys." He winked at Jrio. "The demons obviously weren't concerned with me in the least and ignored my passing by overhead. I was able to jump off one demon's head and land on the first horse I saw. I assume he knew I was a Son of Ad, and then I simply gripped him with my legs, letting him know I was more than able to ride. I was saved from the trampling, and then rode the stampede out into the plain. Knowing there were probably still many Dairneags that had avoided the rush, I coaxed my steed back to the city for a second pass. It wasn't too hard. Once they got far enough away, their instinct, when confronted with fear, told them to retreat back to their home."

"So you swept through again and then killed that last giant Dairneag out here by yourself," Jrio stated.

"Well, made a good target for him is more like it." Luik tugged at his torn shirt with a smile. "But it's to all of you that I owe my gratitude."

"How so?" They were puzzled.

"Well, it was you who killed him."

There was a slight pause. Each man looked to the next a bit amused.

"I didn't kill him," Jrio said.

"Nor I," said Cage shaking his head.

"Nor I," said each of the rest, including Gorn.

Luik was quite confused.

"Well then, who did?"

They all shrugged their shoulders. The issue lay unanswered.

"Let's return to the city," Gorn said. "There may be many injured or in need. We must secure the city and attend to the wounded."

They all turned toward the west gate and filed through the wreckage of the two towers. Luik was the last to go but stopped just before pacing through the entrance. He heard hooves beating the ground behind him. He turned quickly to see a horse closing the distance between them. When it got closer he realized it was the horse that had rescued him and carried him through the stampede. It slowed and then came to a halt right in front of him, breathing heavily.

"Hey'a my friend," Luik said and patted his neck. "C'symia, noble creature. I am grateful for your help." The horse whinnied and blew hard through its nostrils. "And I wonder what your name is?"

"Fedowah," Cage said from behind him. Luik turned, surprised that his friend had lingered close by. He dare not argue with this Dibor, as the sons of Jerovah knew every horse by name.

"Why, that's a strong name, I say." Luik stroked his face then turned back to Cage. "Where is he from?"

"We found him many summers ago roaming the Central Forest alone."

"*Grandath*," Luik whispered under his breath.

"His breed and confirmation look as though he may be from the stallions entrusted to King Purgos in the north, but without a record we are unsure. He is definitely not from the plains here. He is far too massive and muscular, more suited to the woodlands and mountains than the long stretching valleys."

"Well, he is a mighty horse." Luik turned to him once more and blew gently in his nose. "Until we meet again, Fedowah, *one who roams alone*."

Luik turned to follow Cage back into the city, but Fedowah stuck close behind. As soon as Luik noticed the animal was following him he looked back, as did Cage.

"It seems you have a companion now," Cage said with a grin.

"A companion? How's that?"

"All creatures were made for the joy of the Creator. But horses were one of the few creatures made for the service and friendship of Man. It is a part of who they are. And once they decide upon a particular man, they are hard-pressed to ever leave him. It would appear that Fedowah has chosen you."

"Me?" Luik raised his voice looking at the horse.

Fedowah stomped his hoof.

"And if I want him to leave me alone?" Luik asked.

"The only thing that will break his faithfulness to you is death: yours or his. You will be his from this point on, and he will serve your needs until his body fails him, or yours does."

Luik admired the nobility of Cage's words and marveled at the horse, *his horse*. *What a truly amazing creature*, he thought. He had never heard of a horse *choosing* a master. Normally it was the other way around.

"Then may I ask him to wait right here until we are done inside the city?"

"You may ask him anything you wish, and to the best of his ability he will perform it so long as it doesn't bring harm to you."

Luik looked at Fedowah in admiration.

"I need you to wait for me right here," Luik said quietly. "I will be back later."

Fedowah just looked at him.

"No really, wait here. Do you understand?"

The horse reluctantly beat the ground again and Luik was satisfied. Luik and Cage then turned and walked back to join with the others inside.

"He sure has a personality," Luik said softly to Cage.

"My brother, you have no idea."

• • •

A hawk sat astute in the top of an old pine tree, his neck feathers being sifted by the strong westerly winds. He had heard an unnatural noise for the better part of an hour, steadily growing louder. Watching down the mountain in the distance, he saw flocks of smaller birds spring from their hidden roosts and take to the air in sporadic behavior, obviously startled. Something was beneath the tree line and it was moving up the mountain.

The hawk gazed on with its piercing eyes. A loud growl sounded up the cliff face and then a series of barks and snarling. This was very unusual indeed. The hawk grew restless and spread its wings, picked up from the tree by a strong gust. He circled from a great height and watched as strange shadows passed quickly through the woods disturbing all wood life below. Then where the trees cease to grow and the granite walls begin, the hawk saw five great beasts break from the cover and begin to climb up the mountain. Their claws smashed through rock and dug deep into the stone face. They tore up the cliffs and the crags, chasing a scent that nothing would deny them of following.

Though they had only just entered the southernmost portions of the Border Mountains, it would not be long before they were through and clear into Ligeon. The hawk had nothing better to do than to follow.

Chapter Twenty-six

HOMECOMING

The air continued to grow colder with each passing day. The leaves of the trees had long since fallen away and the sky spent more time filled with gray clouds than with sunlight. Still, the Bay of Cidell was beautiful beyond description. From where Fane sat in the Port of Narin, housed somewhere within the stilted network of raised platforms and homes, he drank of the fresh sea air and the beauty of the water. His head and back were propped up with mounds of pillows in a giant chair. Heaps of blankets warmed him thoroughly as he looked out of a seaside window and watched the waves roll underneath the stilted dwelling.

Three nights before, Li-Saide had carried him down out of the Border Mountains and requested the use of a cart and horse from one of the villages in the northern foothills. The people of the town were only too happy to help when they saw the condition of his companion. Fane was unconscious for the entire trip but awoke to hot tea and fruit in a bowl by his bed. Li-Saide had left him alone since the morning and gone to look for King Thorn, Lord of Ligeon.

The dwarf had done everything in his power to keep their unexpected arrival a secret, from entering on the far north side of the city when the southern one was much more convenient, to holding off their arrival until dusk. Going straight to the great hall would have surely sent word around the city that King Ragnar's Councilor had arrived, and that with a strange guest. Instead Li-Saide opted to find transient lodging and requested that his guest be left alone while he left on errands. The owner was only too happy to be of assistance to a dwarf and provided him with the most spacious dwelling in his possession, one that looked westward, right down on the water on the edge of the platform city.

That evening, when the light began to fade and a cold breeze swept in from the north, Li-Saide returned to fetch Fane and advised the owner that need of the lodging services was no longer required. He thanked the owner, gave him a small gift, and bade him farewell. Both cloaked with hoods pulled over, Fane and the dwarf walked quietly through the maze that made up the Harbor. A number of large central standing platforms served as the foundation of the city while other smaller and more numerous platforms branched off, all connected to one another with catwalks and bridges. Each wooden platform hovered nearly a tree's height over the waves below, and on top sat any number of homes, shops, and gathering halls all constructed from timber. Narrow roped suspension bridges connected longer stretches while wide, solid timber roads spanned shorter ones. As night fell, wall-mounted torches were lit all across the city, which made navigation much easier in the fading light. Li-Saide also grew concerned for who may be watching in the firelight. It was of utmost importance that their presence be completely covert and unknown.

They passed by numerous dwellings, evening music and songs emanating from the larger gathering halls. Stories were sung and told to children who listened with great attention beside the fire. That was another thing: the colder days had caused the people to search for new means to stay warm besides just wearing more clothing, most of which needed to be amended for colder temperatures. King Thorn had given permission for the people to construct wood-burning fireplaces out of stone in their homes. Although burning wood was not strange in the least, it was a fairly new practice to heat a dwelling with it. Along with their clothing, amendments were made to their homes in order to keep the cold wind from blowing through, keeping the heat trapped inside. Animal skins and tightly woven linens were used to seal up windows and entranceways. Some families even made wooden doors that swung like those in the Palaces and Great Halls.

Li-Saide and Fane continued walking and eventually converged onto the main artery that connected to the mainland. With the advent of internal fireplaces and the increased need to keep warm, heating foods and drinks as a comfort had become a more popular practice. The fragrances that wafted through the air combined with the lingering sounds of singing and sylers created an effect that wooed them both to want to stay but there was no time for such pleasures now. *Maybe someday*, Fane thought, *but not now*. Then his mind began to wander, and he wondered if there would ever be a day for him to enjoy life again.

They crossed the main bridge, making their way down the stone road along the beach, and then mounted up the hillside headed toward the upper city. Fane turned back occasionally to see a stilted mass of flickering lights that sent up a mixture of melodies and smells, swirling into the dark night air. Cresting the summit into Narin Huas[27], the roadway was swallowed into a dense swarm of homes once more. Up ahead a figure emerged from a small dwelling and stood in the street. Li-Saide quickly pulled Fane close to a hut covered in shadow. The man looked around, stretched his arms and back, and then returned back inside. They had not been seen. Fane let out a sigh as did Li-Saide.

They continued on without any disturbance and walked briskly through the winding city. Soon the road opened up into a large grassy meadow with buildings bordering every side. There to one end was the Great Hall of Ligeon, home of King Thorn. Torches protruded on each side of the main door as well as on the ramparts and crenellations above. A wide marble road ran straight down the meadow to the Great Hall, passing first through the large gate in the outer wall. But Li-Saide and Fane remained close to one side of the meadow as they walked, shrouded in darkness. Just before reaching the wall, Li-Saide froze and grasped Fane's arm tightly.

"What is it, Li-Saide?" Fane whispered.

"Listen, far in the distance, do you hear it?" the dwarf pointed a finger to the sky.

"The music?"

"No—further."

Fane closed his eyes.

"A hawk; it's the cry of a distant hawk." Fane finally said.

"Aye."

---

[27] **Narin Haus** (*NAR-in HO*): *noun; literally meaning "Narin High," or the upper half of Narin overlooking the Bay of Cidell; Narin Bas, or "Narin Low" refers to the lower, seaside, stilted portion of the city.*

"And?"

"And when was the last time you heard a hawk cry out *like that* in the middle of the night?"

Fane thought briefly before replying.

"Never; something's wrong."

"Aye, Fane of the Mosfar, something is definitely wrong." Li-Saide looked up into the sky. "Listen, he is speaking again."

Fane looked up as well and tried to make out the voice.

"Something is coming," Fane said. "It's a word of warning. He has been tracking it for a great distance since dawn."

"Something that is unnatural and seeks to take life."

"Dairne-Reih?" Fane asked.

"No, it must be moving much too quickly to be Dairne-Reih."

"Then what else?"

"I don't know, but we dare not linger here to find out. We must warn Thorn of this new threat to his kingdom. Come, to the Great Hall."

Li-Saide turned to continue along the outer wall toward the gate, but there was something else that entered the meadow. He looked to the far edge behind them, and where the marble road entered back into the dense city stood three giant hounds with two more pressing through from behind. They sucked air violently, their chests heaving.

"Fane, don't move," Li-Saide said thinking quickly. "When I tell you to, run through the gate and through the doors of the Great Hall beyond."

"What?" Fane whispered in astonishment.

"Do not question me!" Li-Saide's hushed tone was commanding. "They are after you. Morgui must know that you are aware of his plot. They have come to keep you from delivering any report to the Kings of Dionia; but, for them, that is too late."

"Too late? Seems they still have a chance if you ask me."

"True, they could take us both very easily."

Fane was not encouraged.

"Then how is it too late?"

"I already delivered your message to the King."

"You what?" Fane was astonished. "What message? What plot? I don't know about any plot! I just know about the siege in the east and a disturbance in the south."

"That *disturbance*, my friend, is an army of unimaginable size."

"An army?"

"Aye. Do you think it's possible to continue our little conversation over a bowl of fruit later this evening? Right, then, you make for the hall, I'll distract them."

"Alone? If you already delivered my message then I have no greater responsibility than to protect my friends! I'm not going anywhere!"

Unfortunately for them, Fane spoke a little too loudly and all five beasts centered in on their position in the shadows. The first hound led the rest as they charged, headed directly for Li-Saide and Fane.

"Let's use the wall here," Li-Saide said. "They still can't see us."

The monsters shredded the ground beneath them, advancing at great speed. Fane's heartbeat raced, all his senses telling him to *get out of the way*, but he just stood there next to Li-Saide completely motionless. The hounds neared, now snarling, as they could smell the flesh of their prey. *Just a few more moments*, Fane thought. The ground shook beneath their feet. The beasts were enormous! They had crossed the entire length of the meadow in nearly half the time it would have taken a horse at full speed!

"Go!" Li-Saide yelled out, completely giving away any secrecy of their position. They both lunged in opposite directions parallel to the wall and then rolled to gain more distance. The first three hounds smashed hard into the granite wall, crushing their skulls deep into the stone and tumbling onto one another in a heap. The impact blew out a whole section of the barrier that tumbled into the courtyard on the other side. The noise immediately drew the attention of the guards, two of which came rushing out of the front doors of the Great Hall and another six on the roof above. Still another pair who had been walking the grounds of the courtyard rushed over to survey the damage, completely startled by the barrage. They began yelling to each other, as only those on the roof had a clear view of the meadow. But the combination of the darkness and the horrific sight of the KiJinNard made their response slow in coming.

The first three hounds lay dazed and provided an elementary cushion for the following two that further pummeled their predecessors into the wall. For an instant the five beasts lay as a mangled heap of limbs and bodies, but the two monsters least affected by the collision sprang up and quickly regained their feet. They spun around in a frenzied attempt to locate their meal. Fane had lunged away from the gate toward one side of the meadow's edge while Li-Saide, after rolling, picked himself up and sneaked around the inside of the gate.

"Archers on the roof!" Li-Saide cried out, adding a second cause for the guards to be startled. They peered down in wonder at the little dwarf, as did those in the courtyard. "Archers, light your arrows and illuminate the meadow! The rest of you, mount the ramparts on the wall and target the five beasts. They must be killed!"

The guards above quickly lit their nocked arrows three at a time with the torches and sent a shower of them plummeting into the grass far below. Fane was surprised to see the falling shoots of fire but ran hard for the meadow's edge. *I need a plan!* he thought to himself. His mind was racing. He turned around to see two of the hounds pick him out in the firelight and set off after him. The nearest leapt with its mouth gaping wide. It snapped closed at Fane's back and tore through his cloak. But that's all it got. Fane could feel the hot breath blow around his neck as the monster picked him up off his feet by his garment. He swung from the creature's mouth but the other creature became insanely jealous and jolted the first with a growl for a chance at the victim. Fane's cloak ripped and spilled him out like a sack of fruit off a horse cart. The two hounds fought momentarily, giving Fane just enough time to regain his feet and make a dash for the meadow's edge once more.

This time the beasts did not follow; all five were too busy repelling an onslaught of arrows. Fane turned to see both the archers above and those on the wall driving a steady assault into the monsters. The hounds swung helplessly at the air in a vain attempt to thwart the invisible terror. As each archer sowed three sets of ten each, the creatures' progress was retarded, and the blood flow became great. Whatever life sustained them was drained and brought them to their knees. The arrows continued to fly into the piles of flesh until all were sure that the assailants had no chance of reviving. Fane walked a wide arch around the mess, still giving the guards plenty of room. Soon the last of the weapons was fired, and all was still again.

The entire incident only took a brief time from start to finish. The collision with the wall and the loud shout from Li-Saide managed to draw but a small handful of onlookers, mostly fathers looking out their windows from homes bordering the meadow. It had happened so quickly no one else from the Great Hall even bothered to come out. The guards in the courtyard rushed to the heap of corpses and quickly began devising a way to remove and dispose of them. Li-Saide also walked out and embraced Fane.

"You fared well, my friend?"

"Aye, Li-Saide; though one of them seemed to think my cloak was not only attractive but tasteful." Fane turned to bare his back. The entire section had been torn completely away and a foul drool saturated the edges.

"Better the cloak than you, I trust," Li-Saide chuckled as he checked Fane's skin and then spun him back around.

"Shall we help these men with their duty?"

"No," the dwarf quickly contended. "We must get inside. We have made enough of a scene. Who knows what else might be lurking or watching in the shadows?"

They weaved back through the maze of smoldering arrows and examined the dead hounds. Fane leaned over to Li-Saide as they walked briskly.

"What are they?"

"They are the KiJinNard, Hounds of the Dead."

"Dairne-Reih?"

"No, Dairne-Reih are fallen lythlae, which these are not. Remember that Morgui does not have the power to create, to inspire new design. He can only pervert what was once created. The power of creation is only a trait of the Most High, that He alone reserves the right to, and grants only to the Sons of Ad. These beasts were once immortal. Don't you see the likeness?"

"You mean to tell me those are *hounds, our dogs?*"

"Aye, our hounds made mortal."

"Then they were *taken.*"

"Precisely."

Fane took a deep breath, and they walked beneath the gate. The steps climbed up to present two massive doors; and Li-Saide, not bothering to knock, simply walked in with Fane behind.

The entry room was a long, dimly lit hallway with rows of candle stands lining the walls. Two men stood permanently on either side bearing long swords and dressed in courbouilli[28]. They said nothing and spoke nothing, obviously unmoved by the events outside. Their duty was to

---

[28] **Courbouilli** (*coor-BOO-ih-lee*): *noun; armor made of leather hardened through boiling in oil; noted for its light weight while still maintaining great strength and resilience to blows.*

prevent anyone or anything from entering at all costs, the Great Hall's last defense. Nothing could pull them away from their post.

An enormous rug of burgundy and blue lay on the floor, something Fane had rarely seen done. As they walked across it he noticed how deeply his feet sank into it and how soft it was. They passed a series of doors on both sides of the hall, eventually stopping at one near the far end of the hallway. Li-Saide knocked twice and listened for a muffled reply.

"Come," someone said on the other side.

He pushed open the door, and they emerged into a dark, large room with a stone fireplace dancing with flames at one end. Closed windows made of a clear, solid material looked down onto the sleeping port city below. Fane marveled at their design and found their hard yet transparent qualities remarkable. He assumed that they kept heated air trapped inside while still allowing light in and a clear view of things outside for the onlooker. Wooden high-backed chairs were arranged near the fire and Fane could see the detail of the knot work carved into the stone mantel. The lines weaved through one another like ribbon, endless from start to finish. The chairs were also carved with delicate designs of circular knots and animals. It all reminded him of Adriel Palace, but with its own very unique sense of expression and personality.

"Greetings, King Thorn," Li-Saide said softly.

"Greetings, Li-Saide of Ot. Please come, sit by the fire with me."

The couple strode to the chairs, and each took up one. Fane bowed his head and Thorn returned it with a pleasant smile and a nod. The king sat clothed in long garments and wrapped in a fur mantle bound around his shoulders with a gold brooch. The fire was warm and chewed away at the wood with bites and pops.

"I trust you are well and refreshed from your rest, Fane, Son of Fadner?" King Thorn said as he reached for two mugs of hot herbed drink and handed them to his guests.

"Indeed, my King," Fane replied with a smile. He took the mug and smelled the warm spices. "I have always heard that the sea air of Narin restores the senses and delights the spirit." Thorn was overtly pleased at his words.

"Is that what they say? Well then, I shall have to try it myself sometime," Thorn said with a laugh. Fane chuckled. "I welcome you into my kingdom and into my home, Fane. You may stay as long as you like and eat and drink your fill. I have a room prepared for you."

"I am grateful, my lord."

"It is a pity you could have not been with us these past evenings three, but I understand Li-Saide's reason for caution as he expressed it to me earlier this day. Upon hearing of your arrival, I had wished to bring you up with armed escort at once, but the wishes of your friend beckoned for subtlety and stealth. Know that you are safe within these walls so long as I am King of Ligeon and the Most High sets His guards upon my gateposts."

"I am truly grateful," Fane inclined his head once more. "And to your guards and their protection I am already in debt."

"Already? Then something has assailed you?" Thorn asked with great surprise.

"Assailed both of us."

The king stood from his chair.

"Please, my king," Li-Saide said calmly raising a small hand. "Everything is well and at peace."

"Is it then? I was not informed!"

"You had no need to be. Your men were of invaluable assistance in a timely fashion. My friend here only requires a new cloak."

Fane shot Li-Saide a glance. The King of Ligeon need not know such trivial matters.

"A new cloak?" the King asked, regarding Fane.

"Fortunately for me, it seems our attackers liked wool better than flesh, your majesty." Fane stood lightly and turned.

"Aye, I see. I will have one fetched for you at once."

"My King, that is—"

"Gyinan!" the king called. A slender man immediately entered through a side door. "Fetch me a cloak!"

Fane inclined his head once more and sat back down. "I am grateful, your highness."

"You are my guest, for which you will be treated as family. So, who were your attackers?" the King inquired of Li-Saide.

"KiJinNard, your majesty."

"The Hounds of the Dead," whispered the king under his breath. "So they betray us once more."

266

"As in the first battle," Li-Saide added.

"Aye, as in the beginning," he paused in thought. "How many?"

"Five, my lord."

"Then they ran with a great purpose, its completion imperative."

"And they nearly got it," Fane smiled, rubbing his back.

"But it was too late for them," Li-Saide said, "even if our brother here was destroyed." Fane was learning Li-Saide's way of jesting.

"Aye, I see," said the King. "You should both know that I have sent a messenger to Casterness with a dictation of the prophetic word spoken by Fane."

Fane turned to Li-Saide with surprise. Li-Saide simply nodded and looked back at the king. *What prophetic word?* He did not remember his utterance. The king continued.

"It should have arrived by now."

"Then no man was your messenger," Li-Saide stated.

"Correct. It would take far too long and risk too much danger to utilize our normal means of communication. It was our servant, a hawk, whom I did call upon." Li-Saide liked this king and his ingenuity. "I sent five more to the other kingdoms. I assume the tribes of Ot are already aware?" Li-Saide nodded.

Thorn addressed Fane.

"I must say that we are very grateful to you. I fear that without your sensitivity to the realm of Athera and the voice of the Great Spirit, we would be blinded and unaware of the enemy that grows in the south." Fane was speechless, and clueless. He simply smiled and acknowledged the King's kind words.

"So no one else knows you are here?" the King continued.

"Well, it would seem that Morgui knew we would be coming here," said Li-Saide. "But his initial means to destroy us have been thwarted, as we sit here safe with you. Our path to the palace was clear and our backs were free save for our brief encounter in the meadow."

"Then no one else knows you are here."

"I trust it is so, though the darkness sustains many unknown eyes."

"Ah, very good then. I am pleased."

Just then the side door opened and Gyinan presented the king with a fresh cloak of blue dressed with gold.

"Ah, Fane, your new cloak."

Fane took the garment with much care and awe. It was a dense knit lined with a soft black interior. The edges were embroidered with gold thread in weaving lines and circles of intricate knot work. Even the hood was rimmed with endless knots.

"C'symia, my king," Fane said reverently. The king nodded with a smile and waited for Fane to put it on. Fane was so in awe of the work he held it for a bit longer before realizing the king was waiting for him. He jumped up and stripped off his old one, which Gyinan quickly took away, and then placed the new mantle over his head. A swell of pride overtook him and the new smell of the garment filled his head. It was much heavier than his first one. He reseated himself and felt twice the man he once was.

"It suits you well, Fane, Son of Fadner."

"Truly," added the dwarf.

"Now you bear a mantle from the King of Ligeon. Go with my blessing from here on. I speak for all the Kings of Dionia when I say that we are blessed by your life. May your ability to serve Dionia and the Most High only increase from this day forward."

Fane bowed in his chair and thanked the king once more.

"May I ask what your intention is, King Thorn?" Li-Saide prodded.

"My intention? Why, by your word, I plan on gathering all my fighting men, leaving only a few to guard our great city, and journeying south to Casterness. If Adriel is in need, then I am the king to give aid." King Thorn pumped up his chest and beat it once.

"When do you leave?"

"Tomorrow at dawn."

"Then may we accompany you?" asked the dwarf.

"Ha!" The king beat his chest again, standing fully. "By the Great Spirit, it will truly be a war band of the greatest acclaim! All the heroes of Dionia, together! What a journey indeed!"

"We are hardly heroes, your majesty," Fane put in.

"And we make up just two," Li-Saide added.

"Aye, but kinsmen await you here," the king said, "and that of the noblest kind!"

"What kinsmen?" Fane asked.

"Come, into my Great Hall we go!"

With that they all stood and left the warmth of the fire. They followed the king across the room to the first door and then further down the hallway to a pair of great oak doors at the end. He pressed them open and entered into an enormous room with arched ceilings towering above. Torches burned on every pillar and a great circular hearth danced with flames in the center of the hall. Tables and benches lay orderly throughout the space and on the far side, a throne and accompanying high backed chairs perched atop a marble pedestal. Every wooden beam, every stone pillar, every marble slab was carved and etched with endless knots and ribbon-like designs. It was a delight for the eyes.

But what delighted Fane's eyes even more was the sight of a face he had known long ago as a boy. A crowd of men sat around the hearth all drinking mead and eating from platters of food. And there, leaning against a far pillar, was his dear friend Luik. When the king entered, the men hushed and all stood to their feet.

"I present to you Li-Saide of Ot and Fane, Son of Fadner!" The king roared with a deep voice. The men returned the king's enthusiasm with shouts and beat their chests with a fist, lifting their mugs high in salute.

"They will join us on our journey south at dawn. They are my guests with you tonight. Eat well and drink your fill!"

The men acknowledged the king's words with a shout and then circled around Fane and Li-Saide greeting each other and exchanging names, but Luik's joy exceeded that of his brothers.

"Fane!" Luik yelled. Fane glanced quickly toward the familiar voice.

"Luik?" Fane gasped. "Is it truly you, my brother?"

"Aye, it is," Luik said with a wide grin. He pushed his Dibor aside and strode across the room to embrace his childhood friend. "How long has it been, my friend?"

"Five years," Fane said smiling wide in the throng, "five long years." Luik thought the new term strange; *years*. But he knew what Fane meant.

"You wear a king's robe, I see?" Luik touched the garment.

"Aye, and you, the clothes of a warrior."

"Such is what the times demand," Luik said with a smirk.

"'Tis true," Fane nodded.

"I see the sun has failed to whisk away your freckles but succeeded at making your hair as red as a peach!"

"Now really, did you expect something else?" Fane chuckled in spite of himself.

"No, you are wise. And I suppose my complexion has not changed much," Luik said brushing back his thick blond hair.

"Well, not much for the better, but that may come one day," Fane grinned widely. Luik punched his arm with a loud laugh in reply. "But your arms have definitely gotten stronger!" Fane said rubbing beneath his shoulder.

"And you," Luik turned to address the dwarf. "I remember you from the palace, is it not the same?"

"Aye, Luik, son of Lair. Greetings in the Name of the Great God, peace be with you."

"And with you." Luik made the sign of blessing. He turned back to Fane. "I am surprised to find you here! What brings you?"

Fane laughed. "Surely we have much to talk about."

"Indeed! And what the years have established I hope will not take as long to explain or this will be a long night!" All three of them laughed. "Come let us sit by the fire." Fane agreed.

"I will pass on your invitation," said Li-Saide, "though I trust you will honor it again during our voyage south?"

"Very well, Li-Saide of Ot," Luik bowed slightly. "Health to your enemy's enemies, and may your night pass quickly to awaken a beautiful dawn."

Li-Saide made the sign of blessing and made his good nights, eventually turning from the Great Hall and exiting out through the main doors. Fane and Luik crossed the hall and sat on a bench near the hearth. Luik poured his friend a fresh mug of mead and honey and asked for the fruit board to be passed. He introduced him to all his brother warriors. The sons of Thorn, Thad, Thero, and Anondo, bade him special greeting as this was their home.

"So, my brother," Luik asked finally, "what of your life and things past? What of things gone by? Quickly now, so that we may talk of brilliant things to come!"

They spoke well into the night, first Fane telling of his audience with King Ragnar and then his many years spent by the side of the dwarf. He retold stories of what he had learned, stories of humor, and then stories of great loss and grief. He omitted his passage into the Mosfar but did tell of the evening's attack outside in the meadow.

"Had we known, we would have come to your rescue!" Luik spoke boldly.

"Ah, but it was for others to rescue us, my brother," said Fane. "And they did so with great ease, I might add. Had things been worse I doubt you would have been forgotten."

"Very well," Luik seemed pleased enough with the response. "Well, I might say that those hounds would have had a great debt to pay had they harmed you further and not died as they did."

"C'symia, Luik. Though I would ask you to remember that had they not torn my old cloak, I would not have such occasion for this new one!" Fane brushed his shoulder lightly in reference to the blue mantle he now sat comfortably in. Luik smiled.

"Friend, I am sure that you would have received such a gift anyway. From what I understand, Dionia owes you a great debt."

"I confess I am not entirely aware of the honor, or the need for it."

"Need?" Luik said exasperated. "How else would the warrior tribes of Dionia be called to arms against an army they formerly knew nothing of? As I see it, you have a great gift, my friend, one that should be recognized for what it is; *hearing the heartbeat of the Father and listening to the voices of a creation that speaks of His ways!*"

Fane was deeply moved by Luik's words. He lowered his face and closed his eyes briefly, not knowing how to receive such a compliment.

"Words of honor become insults to the speaker if they are not received by the one who hears them," Luik exhorted.

Fane looked up. "C'symia," he said softly.

"It is clear to me that you have learned a great deal, Fane. But I expected as much. You do remember the last time we saw each other?"

"The Gvindollion," Fane said.

"Aye, and when I saw you there I knew that you had been chosen for a very special purpose, one that no other could handle."

"And I knew the same of you, Luik, son of Lair."

"Aye, but I was chosen along with ten and seven others; you were singled out, my friend."

"And so you will be, one day."

"You have been given knowledge that no other man has yet touched, maybe not even Ad himself!" Luik said shrugging off the comment.

"You make grand assumptions you know little about, and if you so acknowledge me in *hearing* the voice of things to come, I warn you against passing off my statements as myth. I mean what I say; you will be singled out. The Lord Most High exalts those whom He wishes to exalt and brings low those whom He wishes to bring low. He will give strength to His kings and exalt the horn of His anointed."

Luik was stunned. He did not know his sparring would facilitate such a strong rebuttal. A smile crossed his face.

"Then I receive your words, Fane. Forgive my foolhardy neglect of your wisdom. You truly are what they say. It shall never happen again."

"May I hold you to that?"

Luik thought for but a moment. "Aye, so I have spoken, so I am bound."

"Very good," Fane smiled. They took a deep draft of their mead and wiped their mouths. It was a good night, and both men were grateful for the reunion. Memories flooded their thoughts, sweet whispers of the fond days of their youth. They couldn't help but remember the other two people that filled the missing shadows.

"What do you know of Anorra?" Fane asked with a pleasant smile. Luik blushed slightly but Fane didn't notice.

"Not too sure, my friend," Luik replied. "Though we sleep here in her homeland I have yet to inquire of her whereabouts. I assume she must be near."

"I would very much like to see her," Fane said.

"As would I," Luik said, looking off beyond Fane. A slight moment passed until Fane spoke up again.

"And Hadrian?"

Luik snapped back to Fane. "That I do not know," Luik said. Fane sensed a solemn tone in his voice.

"Do not know?"

"Know where he is, I should say," Luik clarified. "You?"

"No," Fane shook his head, "though I have felt something in my spirit."

"Go on," Luik prompted.

"I fear for his soul." Fane's face was dour. Luik said nothing. "Last summer when traveling through Bensotha while Li-Saide had taken a certain trip, I ventured to Hadrian's home. His mother greeted me warmly and offered me food and drink. When I asked about Hadrian she said he had gone on errands." Fane paused.

"And?" Luik asked.

"And nothing. The conversation moved on to other things. It's just that when I mentioned his name I felt a great sense of grief in her. I dared not pry more for the grief she had already endured with her husband."

"So you have not seen him at all in these past summers?"

"Nay, not once."

"Those are some long errands," Luik tried to make light of the situation. "Do you know of anyone who has seen him?"

"Sure, I have heard his name mentioned throughout the countryside. People talk of him stopping at one place or another, or farming his mother's property. In fact, many times I arrived somewhere having just missed him moments before, unable to track him afterwards." Fane thought for a moment and lowered his voice. "It's almost as if he's—"

"What?" Luik leaned forward.

"He's avoiding me."

"You think he's hiding something?"

"I don't know, my friend," Fane looked at him, "but something is not well." Luik sensed Fane's malcontent and couldn't think of anything to say. He deferred to Fane to choose the next thought and waited patiently until the mood lifted.

"Enough of this," Fane spoke up, slamming his mug on the table. "It's a night for joy. Now, tell me of this war band you travel with! I must know more!"

While the night grew late, all the Dibor had remained in long conversation and enjoyment of the blessings of Narin. That is, all but Gorn who had retired for the evening much earlier. So Luik stood on his bench and made each warrior introduce himself to Fane, first by name, family, kingdom, and then Luik would finish with a slight jest about each. They, of course, had their own recourse to give, usually about how they either beat Luik in a game or, in a few instances, how they saved him from danger. Much laughter filled the hall, and they were all glad. With every story there seemed to be a further kinship and bond that deepened beyond the realm of sight or touch among them. Someone standing in the room watching would have been overwhelmed by an underlining sense of destiny and greatness, one which future generations would hear spoken to them at night before they closed their eyes to sleep as children, and retold to them as examples to imitate when they grew up as adults.

Luik joined with the others in sharing stories of their training, camaraderie, and eventually to their most recent battle at Jahdan and of his narrow escape from certain death. Only this time no one boasted of saving him.

"No, really," Fane laughed, "who was it? Who saved you this time, my friend?" He hit Luik in the arm, half returning the earlier blow as if children once again. But no one spoke up and they regarded one another plainly.

"No one knows," Cage said from the far end of the table.

"And believe me," Rab said, "if it were one of us, we wouldn't let him forget about it!" The mood changed and the air was filled with laughter once more.

"Well it is late, Dibor. My bed calls for me and I dare not leave it in distress!" Luik leapt from his chair and made for the double doors. "Shall we retire?" They all agreed and pushed back from the table, finishing their drafts and licking up the last bits of food.

"I think we'll sleep well tonight, what with a warm stomach and all," the dark-haired man they called Jrio, said to Fane. "I haven't eaten this much in quite a while!"

"Hey'a! I agree, friend!"

But not everyone in the king's house would sleep that night. On a south-facing exterior portico that looked out toward the Border Mountains stood two figures in the shadows, as diametrically opposed in appearance as two could be: one tall, dark, and muscular, the other small, pale, and husky in form. Even their clothes were different, one wearing leather armor and maille, the other a clumsy cloak and floppy hat. They made unlikely acquaintances and even more remote friends to the eyes of a passerby. But the fact was they were friends of the oldest kind, weathering the greatest trials and tests two brothers in arms would ever be asked to bear up to that time. It had made them hard in some ways and softer in others. But years of history gives you intuitive knowledge about someone and about life that you can't learn any other way. As they looked off into the night sky together, they knew what awaited them to the south. They had seen it before, and they had defeated it before, too, in their own strength with their own hands. They had seen death and pinned its head beneath their heel. They had held its neck in their hands and choked the life from it.

But something was different this time. Something told them this battle would not be the same. Not because their enemy had changed, but, perhaps the fact that their enemy had *returned*; they hadn't actually *destroyed* the evil that had assailed them the first time. While they had driven it from their realm, they had not completely destroyed their foe. It had indeed been successful in *returning*. So therefore, their first efforts had not, in fact, been enough. This greatly troubled their hearts. They remembered the bloodshed. They remembered the fear and the angst of battle. They knew what it meant to come face to face with pure evil and the thought of slipping into an existence eternally separated from the Most High and His goodness; to truly know and see *death*. To their tribute, they had succeeded; but in winning the battle and apparently not the war.

What worried them the most, though, was themselves. *They* had not changed. *They* had not gained any new skills or strength. They would be the same coming against a foe that was very much *not* the same; in reality their enemy had grown stronger and more fluent in tactics and stealth while they were the same men that faced those generations ago. Li-Saide and Gorn were not alone in this; the Kings of Dionia recognized it, too, and they had no answers. All anyone could do was hope that the Dibor would be stronger, that the heroes of old would answer the call to once more lend their arms in battle, and that those who survived would share their secrets with the generations to come.

Mankind had resisted but they had not destroyed; they had driven out but they had not stopped.

"And what do you think, my small friend?" Gorn asked the dwarf.

"My heart speaks louder than my head, so I cannot tell you what I think, but what I feel."

"And that is?"

"That is, that what awaits us will consume us."

"Meaning, we are not able to stop it."

"Correct." Li-Saide thought for a moment and then continued. "Unless, we have help; unless there is someone else who can stop it for us."

"A Champion?" Gorn asked.

"A Savior," Li-Saide answered. "It has long been foretold that one would come. What I heard spoken through a prophet these few days past has caused me to think deeply on this."

"What did he say?"

"Every man must come to his own end; every man must die before he can truly live."

There was a long silence.

"What do you make of it?" Gorn asked.

"We are going to greatly fail, my friend. We must before we can somehow survive."

"But failure means death, dwarf. You are aware?"

"Quite."

"It doesn't make sense. Then there must be one to resurrect us, this *Deliverer*. One of us must survive to save the rest, and by his virtue redeem the fallen and the taken!"

"But what if no one does survive."

"Someone must!" Gorn paused. "And I think I know who."

"As do I."

Chapter Twenty-seven

CONVERGING ON CASTERNESS

The next morning came very quickly for Fane, Luik, and the other Dibor. The sensation of fatigue and sleepiness was a new and ever-increasing sensation for them. But they did not feel it half as badly as those who had already begun the trek to the capital region of Dionia, now two days before them. After receiving the messenger hawk, King Naronel of Trennesol immediately made preparations to join King Daunt of Jerovah and King Nenrick of Somahguard on the eastern border of Grandath. Trennesol's three thousand fighting men, combined with Somahguard's one thousand and Jerovah's six thousand, would make up the greatest contingent of Dionia's strength. But whatever strength they had was already being tested, and the battle had not yet begun, or so they thought.

The urgent message King Thorn had written spurred the other kings to make haste in their journey to Adriel. Each countryman quickly left his family and home and joined the outbound army. Rather than walking, the kings pushed their armies to run. Although running was as common as breathing, something was awkward about it now, something that none of the fighting men were prepared for. Not only was the air they inhaled poor and cold, but the sleep they had relied on to nourish their bodies over the past two nights was unfulfilling. It was a fight even to simply wake up at dawn. A strange oppression over the land seemed to call them back to sleep each morning. Many men needed to be roused by others, prodding them relentlessly in the ribs and speaking to them. By the time the three armies met up on the central edge of the Great Forest, the fatigue and weariness was visibly notable in all the men.

"Any suggestions?" Nenrick asked the other two kings, his black complexion and dark eyes quite captivating. They sat together around a fire in the middle of a large tent. The tent had been erected as a central meeting point for the kings and could be raised and torn down quite easily, and quickly if need be. The accompanying armies made camp stemming outward from the King's Tent like spokes on a wheel, intermingling freely, losing no time in rekindling old acquaintances and family ties.

"My pride says to move on quickly as the need is great, but—" Naronel paused, grasping his dark bearded chin.

"But what?" Nenrick pressed.

"But I fear the men may collapse in the Central Forest if we push them without a day's rest."

"A day's rest?" Daunt the *Horse King,* as he had been affectionately dubbed, spat. His body was long and sinewy, yet strong. He wore his black metal armor as if the fight were today. His dark breastplate over-exaggerated the muscles of his stomach and upper chest and was embossed with a horse and rider. Smooth matching vambraces encircled his forearms and a purple tunic dressed him down to his thighs. A gold torc grasped his neck, and dark leather riding boots came up to his knees. "And while we delay, the enemy war host could be invading our capital city! How can we rest?" He stood in exasperation at the thought.

"Because, I fear," Nenrick spoke up, raising a calming hand toward Daunt, reaffirming Naronel's point, "if we don't, our men won't make it through the Central Forest with enough strength to fight off the invasion. Then our entire trip will be a vain attempt, only furthering to satisfy the enemy's blood lust with more easily-taken victims."

Daunt pondered their words and finally conceded. Turning back to Naronel he relented.

"Ah, you are right, Naronel. Forgive this man's driving spirit." Daunt sat back in his chair.

"Think nothing of it, my brother," Naronel said. "I, of all men, understand your heart's passion for Dionia, and I, too, wish we were there *now*. But we must make choices here that will have great effect there. Ideally we all would have wished to hear this news sooner, no?" They all nodded. "But it was not possible, and what's done is done. If it were not for this Fane, Son of Fadner, whom I have not met, we would have no suspicion of a planned attack. So we must rejoice that we even have any knowledge at all!"

"Here, here!" the other two cried, all coming to reason. Naronel continued, running a strong hand through his black hair as he thought.

"So let us be comforted and wise with what we have been granted in knowledge by the Most High; King Lair is surely already at Adriel and has sent scouts to the south to confirm the prophetic word and take an account of the activity there; Purgos and Thorn are heading south at great speed, and if they have not met up already, they surely will quite soon. Perhaps they are already crossing beneath the King's Gate as we speak, making safe and sure the white walls of Adriel!"

"Let us hope so!" Nenrick exclaimed.

"So what are you suggesting, King Naronel?"

"I'm suggesting that we allow our men to rest for a day, and if our arrival into Bensotha comes late in the fight because of it, we will flank the enemy, taking them by surprise. It is better to have men ready to fight a day late than a slaughter easily given a day early. Ours will be a welcomed second wave of retribution to any lingering attack of the enemy."

"Then you place great faith in the western Kings to repel the Dairne-Reih war horde?" Daunt questioned pointedly.

"Aye, Daunt, I have to."

"Why must you, lord Naronel?" Nenrick leaned across the table.

"Because if I don't, then I admit there may not be a city or a people left to save when we get there."

• • •

Two days after they set out, King Thorn and his fighting men, along with the elite Dibor accompanied by Li-Saide and Fane near the front ranks, drew close to the end of their hike through the Border Mountains. As they reached the summit of one of the final peaks before descending to the southern foothills, Thorn lifted a hand to signal a rest. The command rippled back through the long line of men that slowly came to a halt.

Fane looked off to his right and looked out across the Faladrial Ocean. Although he had stood at this very point just weeks ago, penning every detail his spirit illuminated, it strangely seemed like an infinitely longer time had passed; the sky was much dimmer, the air was much colder, and an unseen blanket lay over all the land, heavy and almost suffocating. Fane saw that the men were notably tired, even from walking up one side of a mountain.

"If Morgui cannot destroy you face to face, he will destroy that which sustains you," came a familiar voice from behind him, and beneath.

"It seems he is a wise and cunning enemy after all," Fane said, acknowledging the dwarf's words without turning from the beautiful ocean beyond. "He is truly a worthy adversary, I might add. Yet the beauty of the sea still sustains my burdened heart. Despite all that has happened, it has not changed."

"O but it has my friend, it has, and you should know that of all people."

"Aye," Fane conceded. "But at least it looks the same from up here," he said with a show of melancholy.

"True, the waves do roll on, and the majestic expanse still looms to the horizon."

"But I am encouraged, Li-Saide."

"How so?"

Fane turned and sat on a nearby boulder.

"I feel as if we are not the only ones fighting for life here." Li-Saide said nothing, waiting for Fane to go on. "I sense that creation is reluctant to give up life, to succumb to this ever-increasing resident evil. It's as if I can feel it fighting back the onslaught with every moment that passes. It is grieved, but more, it is calling out, crying for…" he reached for the words.

"For help?"

"More; for men to take their place and rule with a power beyond their own strength, for true greatness to be revealed. Creation is groaning. It is holding out, waiting for us to weed out this enemy once and for all. But I sense it is growing weak under the strain. I am not sure how much longer it can hold up, how much more it can take."

"Have faith, my friend," Li-Saide said, patting Fane's shoulder. "The darkest circumstances are sure to forge the bravest remedies."

Just then Luik strode to where the Mosfar quietly conferred.

"Hey'a, my brethren!" he said with a bold tone. "How do you both fare this day?"

"Well, my friend," Fane said as he stood to embrace with their forearms clenched together. Li-Saide nodded in like kind.

"I trust you are not too tired from the hike or the strange air we breathe?"

"Nay, we endure," Fane replied.

"As do I, as do I," Luik smiled and bade them to sit back down on the boulder. He knelt on the ground.

"Li-Saide, I wonder, in all your travels have you happen to come upon either of our other two childhood kinsmen?" Luik asked, pointing to Fane.

"By that I trust you mean Anorra and Hadrian?" the dwarf implied.

"Aye, just the two." The names both brought about an unmistakable joy in Fane and Luik, something only those who have forged friendships out of the wealth of childhood would know about. Fane eagerly anticipated Li-Saide's response.

"Your friend Hadrian I have not seen, at least not lately." Li-Saide paused and said nothing more. Luik dared not insist he explain, knowing that the wise old dwarf only ever said what needed to be said. "And Anorra, well, you know as well as I that Narin is her home and Ligeon her land, so I could only direct you toward her father." Li-Saide raised a hand and pointed to the king at the head of the line. King Thorn stood holding the lead to his horse, surveying the land below. He wore a dark leather breastplate with leather vambraces on his arms, all of which were embossed with gold in the same patterns as were found throughout his Great Hall. His black maille surcoat beneath ended at his hips and leather pants were tucked inside hardened boots. Flag bearers stood beside him with the blue emblazon of an eagle, wings outreached, and the rich fabric flapping stiffly in the wind.

Luik thanked Fane and Li-Saide, noting he would see them again shortly. Then he stood and moved toward the king. Luik was suddenly aware of the awkwardness of his impending question; he was no longer a mere boy asking the whereabouts of a king's daughter; he was a man and by now she was a young woman. Poor phrasing could give the wrong intention, and his face flushed slightly.

"Hail, King Thorn," Luik called out. Thorn turned from his study of the distant valley.

"Luik of the Dibor," he replied with a shallow smile. "It is good to see you this day. I trust your ride has been smooth."

"Aye, my king. My men have been well fed and my horse is content for the time being." Luik gestured behind him.

"Two things we should never take for granted."

"Aye," Luik said with a chuckle.

"Aye," the king nodded.

"Aye," Luik said again suddenly realizing his repetition. The king's smile dissipated in the awkwardness. There was a pause as he waited for Luik to continue. "Right then," Luik said as he cleared his throat. "My king, I wish to ask the whereabouts of your daughter, Princess Anorra." The king brightened and made to reply. But Luik's slightly flustered condition worsened and rather than letting the simple question await an answer, he stumbled on into an unneeded explanation.

"As you may know, I had three friends when I was young. Well, I had more than that, but my three favorite ones were your daughter." He shook his head. "I mean, she wasn't my favorite at all, rather, she was a girl. Aye, well, she was the girl within the three of my favorite friends I had as a child that I spent the most time with, alone." Luik was clearly bumbling and the king regarded him blankly now. "Your majesty, your daughter, Anorra, was a good friend of mine growing up. I am not implying that I wished to see her, because I do not wish to. Aye—rather, should she be available, to see, I mean, I would have liked to see her at the Great Hall but I—"

The king cut him off with a hand to his shoulder, putting an end to his embarrassment.

"Luik, son of Lair," the king smiled. "I am pleased that you remember the Princess and I think nothing but good will that you ask after her." Luik sighed. "If I knew of her whereabouts I would surely disclose them to you. However, I have not seen her in four weeks. She requested permission to tend to what she termed a *desperate situation*."

"So she left Narin?"

"I believe she left Ligeon."

"With a sentry?"

"No."

"No?"

"She is alone."

"Begging your pardon, my lord, but *you allowed her to leave Ligeon—alone?*"

"Pardon given, Dibor; knowing the Princess, as I'm sure you do, it was a request I could not easily deny. She would have none of it. With such a mind as hers made up, my declining her would simply render her disobedient. Rather than bring such an extreme, I would just as soon keep her free of ill conscience and bid her leave freely, which I did."

"In such days a Princess roams freely in Dionia." Luik was astonished. The king waited a moment.

"Dibor," Thorn spoke up. "Clearly you have changed much since the last I saw you at the Gvindollion. You have been shaped and molded in almost every way, something we knew would happen. In the same manner, I would tell you this day that the friend you once knew is not as she once was. She has chosen a path far different from her other sisters."

"She has been released?"

"Nay, she has been *mentored.*"

"Mentored? Mentored in what?"

"Well now, that would be a question best answered by her teacher." Thorn gestured to one of his assistants nearby. "Gyinan."

Luik was surprised. "Your house servant?"

"My sentinel," corrected the king. "Gyinan is an old and trusted friend of my house, proving himself faithful for generations. There is no other like him."

"Where is he from, my king?"

"The more you speak, the more I think you should move elsewhere with your conversation." Luik nodded wisely and thanked the king for his time.

"I look forward to speaking with you again, Luik. It is an honor to be graced by the presence of the Dibor."

Luik turned and breathed deeply, grateful that a potentially grievous situation was amended, and that, quickly. He admired the king for his humility and grace in dealing with such folly as himself. He gathered himself up again in preparation for another encounter with a member of the king's house. Gyinan stood erect and slender, his bald head and pointy features unmistakable. Narrow slits for eyes made it seem as though he was continually in thought. A long jaw bone and tiny lips reminded Luik of a bird and with his long flowing blue mantel and silver chain maille surcoat, it seemed like he could mount up and fly away at any time.

"Greetings Gyinan of Ligeon," Luik spoke boldly as he neared. Gyinan spun around deftly, almost stepping on Luik's words with his action.

"And what makes you think I indeed hail from Ligeon, Dibor?"

This was clearly not the reception Luik was hoping for.

"I simply assumed that since you serve at Narin—"

"That I am from Ligeon?" The question hung in the air like a stinging challenge. Luik wished to play but it was too early to find leverage. He would concede and wait for an asset to present itself.

"Aye, that I assumed."

"Then clearly the master warrior still has much to learn." Luik felt slightly outmatched, and slightly belittled. But in both the games of strength and wits he had learned to use momentum and an opponent's strength in his own favor.

"Then educate me, Teacher. I am hungry for knowledge."

Gyinan was surprised at his easy rollover.

"Truly?" Gyinan paused and perceived the man before him. Luik felt as though he were looking straight into his soul. "What is it you wish to learn?"

"A mystery not even a king can answer."

Now he had him. Gyinan was hooked, and Luik had clearly earned it.

"Excuse me, my friends," Gyinan said, turning to the other servants of Thorn's house, and they bade him leave. "Come, Dibor, let us speak of this mystery." They walked a short way down the path to a clearing of rubble that overlooked a steep cliff. The wind puffed cold and hard, and Luik wrapped himself among the folds of his wool cloak. He suddenly noticed small white specks fluttering around him in the air, and then they disappeared quickly. Gyinan regarded him pensively and paid no attention to the strange anomaly around them. Clearly Gyinan controlled the situation without words. But Luik knew Gyinan was not the only one with control.

"A White Falcon, the most prized of the land, the envy of all, sits caged on a table." Luik spoke, allowing his hand to pass in front of him for effect. Gyinan was not moved. "It has never flown in the sky but it has felt the wind on its face; it has never journeyed to the horizon but it has watched the sun vanish there ten times ten. One day it is released from the cage, able to finally roam free. So, tell me, Gyinan the Wise, where does the White Falcon go?"

"Do you mock with your flattery or just manipulate, Dibor?" Gyinan's narrow eyes never blinked. It was a harsh word. Luik tried desperately not to betray his embarrassment. "Wherever its heart leads him," Gyinan answered. "Wherever seems best for him to go."

"But freedom must have direction," Luik pressed.

"And direction he will find. It suddenly appears to me the question is not where the bird is going, but why a man would want to know where it is going? There is only one reason a man would seek such an answer."

"And why is that?"

"It is clear in your face, Dibor; *you care for her.*"

Luik was taken aback.

"There are many kinds of love, Dibor, but the only one that surpasses a father's is surely that of a lover, of a husband. A father must eventually *release*, but a lover is *bound*; he must answer the unanswered questions that a father is content to forfeit. So this is the mystery that even a king does not know; or rather a mystery that a king needs not chase after?"

"Do you know where she is, Gyinan?" Luik said flatly, unable to wrestle against Gyinan's intellect.

"How many summers has it been since you saw her last? Five? Six? And what did you feel then? Alas, I antagonize you shamelessly. Forgive me, Dibor. It is not my place to criticize loyalty or love." Luik was surprised by Gyinan's sudden confession and waved his hand. Clearly there was more to this stoic man than could be seen. "The answer is *no*. No, I do not know where she is; yet I do know why she left."

"Why?"

"You wish to end our sport so quickly?"

"But she may be in danger!"

"Humph!" Gyinan spat. "Have you so quickly underestimated my teaching? Clearly the king told you of my role or else you would not have picked me out of the rest back there. She is no more in danger than you are of winning a battle of wits against me! If you refer to her as a fabled White Falcon, then a White Falcon she is; quiet, quick and little seen, a survivalist and an aggressor, a predator, one not easily pinned down. She wields the sharpest of blades and the most cunning of bows. Her feet are as swift as the gazelles and the enemy no more knows of her coming and going as it does the wind; it neither sees where she comes from nor where she goes, but it feels her and the swift fury she invokes."

Luik was astonished. "So she is a warrior?"

"Aye, and a fierce one at that."

Luik turned to look out at the horizon. So they had embarked on similar paths after all, he pondered, yet in two different spheres and under two different teachers. Though it did not surprise him much, as she had always been a force to be reckoned with as a child, besting even some of the strongest boys at games of speed and cunning, him included. It was more wondering what she looked like now that caused him to dream as only young men do.

"Then perhaps she left to face the enemy, but why alone? The Dairne-Reih is not to be trifled with. That is a fool's errand!"

"Maybe it was not to face an enemy at all; we both know she is not a fool."

"Then why did she leave?"

"For the same reason the bird did."

Luik pondered the response. "Our game continues?"

"Aye, it does that."

• • •

As they descended out of the Border Mountains, the white specks in the air fell much more steadily. Not to mention they increased in size, too. Soon a fine layer had collected all over the rocky ground. Luik overheard talk from different parts of the advancing line until the term *snow* had been associated with it. He tracked this back to Li-Saide who said they were tiny bits of water that had *frozen* in the clouds above and now fell to the earth. It took a while to explain clouds, but soon Luik understood that water was being released up into the sky and formed into clouds. It was all a part of the transformation and self-cleansing that creation was going through due to the presence of Morgui. Fane seemed unaffected by the conversation, *as he had probably already learned all this*, Luik thought. Li-Saide said the snow was a lot like *rain* but Luik had never heard this word, either. He soon would never forget it.

The lower elevations brought a milder temperature which would have been welcomed had it not meant that the snow turned to rain, and a cold rain at that. He was startled at first, as were most of the men who had never seen it before. The sense was like being drenched by a river, *upside down*. It wasn't long before Luik's clothes were soaked completely through and his skin was damp and growing cold. Both he and Fedowah marveled at the strange thought of water coming down from the sky rather than up from the ground, but after a while the infatuation waned thin and the discomfort was nagging. At first Fedowah winced at the onslaught and tried to avoid being struck, twisting his head from side to side. It was a strange sensation to have water running down his head, and he innately did not appreciate it. But soon he conceded to the rain and permitted himself a good shake every few minutes, something that almost threw Luik off his horse the first time. Fedowah's body shuddered violently and he let out a whinny.

"Whoa!" Luik yelled, grabbing at his mane frantically. When it had ended he let out a loud laugh. "Feel better now?"

"Better than we do," commented a man nearby. Luik looked down to see some men walking on foot fully drenched in dirty water and matted horsehair. A few others behind laughed, too.

"Fedowah, now hear me. I think it wise that you best stop shaking this water off; you know more will come and you only succeed in making those around ungrateful." Everyone smiled at his comment. Fedowah shrugged it off.

The unrelenting rain continued all through the second and third days. Despite the numbing cold and dampness, the pace for Adriel was a steady run most of the way. They advanced more quickly than Luik had thought they would. The long entourage of some two thousand men-at-arms and on horse stretched across Bensotha Valley for a great distance. Luik changed frequently from riding to running on foot in order to warm his body up.

"If he can't kill us by the sword, he'll kill us with the cold," Fane yelled from under the hood of his cloak during a rest; though it was not really meant to rest. Everyone felt fine, but the rain was so heavy that no one could see. The horizon had been grayed out an hour ago and now it was difficult to see but a few lengths ahead. Luik estimated it was late morning but the sky was so dark he couldn't be sure anymore. He was losing track of time.

"Or by drowning us!" Luik yelled back. They both laughed.

"But it's true, you know. We were never meant to live in such conditions. He makes to thin our lines before we even arrive."

Luik could feel the subtle attack delivering its blow. Even in the past two summers when conditions worsened, the most he'd gone without seeing the sun was but a day, if that, but a whole week—plus the rain? It was enough to make even the bravest and resilient of men completely distraught. He found humor and laughter a suitable remedy until the real answer could be exacted: *defeat Morgui*. It was all he thought of before he fell asleep each night. It consumed his thinking whenever he was not singing to the Most High or speaking with his friends. *Defeat Morgui;* with every rain drop that set upon his face he was pushed forward with the task. He had never seen the lythla, only his handiwork, but he was sure there would be no mistaking him.

"What did you say?" Fane asked through the downpour.

"Huh?" Luik snapped out of his thoughts.

"You said something—about seeing Morgui."

"I must have been talking to myself."

"I'd say. You know they say he is beautiful."

"What?" Luik shouted over the noise of the rain.

"He's beautiful!" Fane yelled back.

"Morgui?"

"Aye, the one. They say he masquerades as a *lythla of light* and that his beauty is renowned throughout Athera."

"Truly? But how can someone so wicked have such glorious attributes?"

"Because he was fashioned by the hand of the Great God Himself. Surely you must know that."

"Aye, Fane, I do. But one forgets, as it is hard to equate any sort of beauty with such evil."

"True, but know that he never lost his beauty, yet he did gain a repulsive spirit, one that merited his banishment from Athera. The trick is that now he uses that glory as a temptation, as a mask. He is captivating, mesmerizing even, and can only be denied by the strongest. If you were to confront him he would reveal his form but never his spirit. In the time it took you to marvel at his face he would prey upon you to utter destruction. Only those that resist the urge to stand in awe see what truly lies beneath. He is a cunning foe, Luik, a worthy adversary. He knows the hearts and ways of man better than we do ourselves. He studies us every day of his cursed and wretched existence. There is no thinking that we can outwit him. Our only hope is to exude a power greater than his. He seeks only to spite the God that cursed him and destroy as much of His creation as possible."

"And that would be us."

"Aye."

The rain beat hard, attempting to mute even the words of their conversation. They stood there huddled close to one another, their feet lost in a deluge of mud and pooling water.

"How far down the coast do you think we are?" Luik asked Fane.

"I'd say we're almost to the coastal town of Nearlyn."

"Then if we run hard we should be to Casterness by nightfall tomorrow."

"Not if this weather persists."

"You think it will?"

"Perhaps. I guess it depends on what other methods Morgui may try to employ in order to slow us."

"I'd say this one is working fine."

They both chuckled slightly.

"Hey, it's letting up a bit."

"So it is," Fane said lifting a drenched hand palm up.

"On your feet! To your horses!" came a call from the front of the line, presumably Gyinan or one of his own attendants. The message rippled back through the line with stunning speed. From one rank to the next each man prepared for the march and then, eventually, the controlled run that had brought them this far in such little time.

"Have you ridden in a while?" Luik asked his friend.

"Nay, but—"

"Then take Fedowah." The horse turned his head at the sound of his name.

"You are most gracious, Luik of the Dibor."

"Think nothing of it. I need the warmth of a good run."

Within another few moments the whole line was moving again, slowly at first and then the lead rank broke into a steady, long stride. Seconds passed between following ranks as each took its lead from the former and picked up the pace in kind. Soon the entire army, on foot and horse alike, was running in unison. It was an impressive display of organization and intuition. The war band moved slow enough for those on foot but fast enough to justify a canter for the horses.

The rain never ceased. The line frequently stopped as it had become nearly impossible to make out the road along the coast. Deep mud and water hid pathways and edge markings. Scouts had to be continually sent out to make sure they were staying close to the coast and not straying inland to the east. This would have slowed things considerably, but King Thorn would have none of it. His desire to reach Adriel deepened as much as the men's desire to get out of the rain. They did not sleep at all that night, but continued on, passing Nearlyn and pressing south along the coast. Casterness was getting much closer, they could all feel it. But they could also feel the overwhelming fatigue that set in as the rising sun turned their atmosphere from a deep black to the drab and suffocating gray they had marched with these past four days. The ground was fighting against them, too. Now every footstep required twice as much effort to pull it out of the mire. Horses were even more annoyed by this, draining their strength twice as fast with two more feet to pull up. By mid afternoon progress had slowed, but Thorn would not give up nor allow any of his men one moment to wallow or grow faint of heart.

"Keep moving!" he would cry out. "Casterness lies just beyond and Adriel awaits you!" The message was passed back through the line as always, but now it fell on tired and weary ears. Luik glanced behind to see men hunched over from the wet and cold, dragging their legs with each stride. Morgui's plan was taking its toll.

"And all this from some water and some cold," Jrio said to Luik, riding just beside him.

"Aye. Is it not amazing what water will do when coming down on you instead of flowing below you?"

"Hey'a! But it is below me, too!" Jrio pointed to the mess. "I'll take mine in a waterfall, thank you very much! You can have this to yourself!"

"A warm bed, a hot meal, and a fire will do me just fine right about now," Luik said with a lilt to his voice.

"And a song might be nice."

"Aye, a song or two." Luik tried not to dwell on the thought. "So, the rest of the Dibor, how do they fare?"

"Well, Luik, they are spread throughout the line, lending their horses when a man is too weak to walk further. A few have been scouting for the king up ahead."

"Aye, I have seen Cage and Quoin busy up there, coming and going with rhythm."

"Gorn rides further back with Li-Saide for company."

"They make odd friends."

"True, though they talk without ceasing."

"Really?"

"Seems they have known one another for quite some time."

"Interesting," Luik said, pondering the two men.

"And you, Dibor?" Jrio punched his shoulder.

"Could be better, I suppose, but until that bed shows up I have nothing else to ask for. It's been a delight to see my old friend Fane again."

"How many summers did you say it was?"

"Five since I saw him last, at the Gvindollion."

"Ah, so he was that boy in the cloak behind the dwarf when we first saw Gorn."

"The one."

"And he is a student of Li-Saide, I imagine?"

"*Was*—now he has been released from his mentorship, but I do not know his title or to which king or region he is employed."

"Well, no matter, a fine man he seems."

"That he is."

"And what of this Gyinan, the king's house steward?"

"He is much more than an errand boy, Jrio, I assure you that."

"You think?"

"I know."

"Aye, I did see you speaking to him the day before. Was it not something trivial?"

"Nay, he is a fine warrior, it would appear, and an exquisite teacher at that."

"Teacher?"

"Of the king's daughter, no less."

"You speak the truth?"

"Aye, Jrio, and he is as wise as a fox and as swift as a hawk. I have not seen him move, but something in his words betrays his agility and stealth."

"Then you approve of him?"

"Let's hope he approves of me, my friend. You will see me fighting by his side, given the option."

Jrio nodded his head in understanding and held new admiration for the man that rode next to the king.

The rain slowly lessened and within hours turned to a light drizzle as they crossed into Casterness. A shout went back through the ranks with the good news and a second wind lit their legs afresh. No man was disappointed when the sun broke through a patch of clouds briefly. The rays had familiar warmth to them and hurt their eyes gladly.

"We must be getting close to Adriel," one man shouted out.

"How's that?" said another.

"Why, the sky is clearing! The Light of the Most High always shines on Adriel!"

And as sure as the sun rises, he was right.

It was not long before the war band came to a halt high atop an overlook just west of the palace. This was a familiar place to Luik. In fact, he had not stopped long enough to fully realize that they had journeyed through Bensotha, not half a day's walk from his home, *from his family*. A waterfall spewed forth a deluge of brown floodwaters from beneath their feet that fell five tree lengths to a mangled basin below. Luik had been here many times before. In fact, this was his favorite place from which to view the castle. But today, as if in a bad dream, the broad sweeping valley did not look as he remembered it: the looming willow trees had lost their leaves and splendor; the streams and pools had flooded and overtaken the stone houses and washed-out bridges. The land was a bitter brown and gray, cheered only by rays of sunlight that bathed the crown of Dionia in glimmering light: Adriel Palace.

The Faladrial Ocean raged in the distance, and the castle was lit against it like a white fire. For all the grieving of creation, for all the rain and the cold, and though the once green and shimmering Ison Peninsula lay barren and wrecked, the beauty of Adriel remained and rose high into the air as it always had.

Luik sat on his horse in dismay at the countryside, watching the trails of chimney smoke curl into the heights above. Five summers before he had stood on this hill with Fane, Anorra, and Hadrian, nearly late for the Princess' birth celebration. Today he sat with two thousand men, nearly late again, this time attempting to save that same Princess' home, *and inevitably her life.*

Chapter Twenty-eight

THE DREAM

How long I *had been standing there, I do not know. The smell of grass filled my head as the breeze licked it up along the valley floor. Running out from all around me, the ground surged a great distance toward the majestically silhouetted mountains beyond; past that a blackened sky, bold and immense, soaring high above me and filled with stars. It was a strange thing how both I and the long, gently swirling grass of the valley seemed to glow as if at mid-day.*

I stood, hands at my sides, marveling at the beauty of such a simple landscape. Everything was silent save the rustle of the warm wind through the grass around me. I turned slowly, admiring the stars and the distant mountain peaks. They awaited something, bound with anticipation. I turned quickly and caught the image of a large dark rock sitting in the middle of this field. It had not been there moments before.

As I walked toward the rock I realized it was three times my height and wrapped in a black so deep it seemed to originate from within. As I closed in I noticed the texture; rough and craggy with deep cracks. Withered vines laced certain areas, dead and sinewy. As I looked around the bulging mass of stone, an eerie feeling touched my spine, one I had never felt before. I was soon but five lengths away when an acute pressure pricked in my head. With every passing step the pressure grew, squeezing tighter and tighter. By the time I was near enough to touch the rock the level of pain was agonizing.

I gazed upward looking for an adequate ledge to grab, driven to climb it. My left hand found a wide outcropping while my right, a small three-fingered hole. My legs pressed up, and I pulled with my arms, looking for the next hand position. The pain inside my head grew, but my curiosity drove me on, further up toward the summit.

At last reaching the top, I turned to survey the ground below me but it was a feeble attempt. My temples throbbed with pain, and I grabbed my head in anguish. Then my squinting eyes met with another object far away in the distance: a large marble obelisk. It towered even higher than where I stood, thin and dominant, narrowing from its base to its pointed peak. The obelisk's presence and symbolism pronounced itself as a monument, hewn from a single piece of distinguished marble. It was reddish amber with a deeply etched inscription around the base, though it was too far away for me to make out; that or my increasing discomfort distracted me.

The now paralyzing pain started down my neck, into my shoulders, and wrapped my waist. I struggled for breath, straining to suck air. I couldn't even manage to keep my eyes open and felt my knees go limp. I was worried my dizzying state would send me slipping down the side of the great black stone, but it was inevitable. Within moments the unknown power that assailed me sent me tumbling to the grassy floor below.

I'm not sure if I actually passed out, but I am certain that when I opened my eyes, kissed by the green blades of grass, the pain had completely vanished. Relieved for the release I stood swiftly and backed away from the heap of black, staring at it with concern and unanswered bewilderment.

I walked steadily backwards, all the while keeping my eyes fixed on the stone is if half expecting it to leap and attack me. I made quick distance from it and was surprisingly comforted by the sight of the amber obelisk coming into view beyond the stone. The valor of the distant pinnacle soared, both in form and in nature, far above that of its weaker companion. The thought of the obelisk seemed to ease any remaining discomfort.

Still walking backwards, my shoulder blades intercepted a hard greeting from behind. I stumbled and swung around to meet my next encounter head on: a great white and shining wall. I jumped back, earnestly trying to assess the object. It appeared to be a large white pearl like that found in the sea, yet this one, at least ten times as tall as a man. Not even I could see to the top from where I stood. It was enormous and white, but more so glowing in a state of light and wonder.

I moved back toward it and closely examined the great pearl's surface. Color and light seemed to shimmer and dance beneath its glassy outer shell, as if moved by music and song. It was alive, a being in itself, full of emotion and movement—brilliant!

I reached out with my hand to touch it but hesitated, not even sure why. I saw my hand in stark contrast to this perfect form, the epitome of beauty and serenity. A moment come and gone, I held my breath and then stretched my hand out. I don't even remember touching the surface with my fingertips but the next thing I knew I was instantly standing on the very summit of the pearl. I looked down and saw glassy white firm beneath my feet. I dared not move on the smooth surface. I looked over my shoulder far below to see the small black stone and the mighty obelisk beyond, both dwarfed and small compared to the pearl.

The wind picked up and played with my hair. I lifted my arms just to keep my balance against the strong wind around me. Then up in the sky I saw a small white light. It differed from the stars, as it was much more piercing and it was moving. It started slowly at first sinking toward the top of the mountain range beyond, but soon it picked up speed and grew larger. It was coming toward me.

It passed in front of the mountains and sank low to the distant valley floor. The sound of a rushing wind like the beating of a drum filled the air. The rhythm broke into groupings, but fast and vibrating through the ground and right up into my chest. The light grew larger and larger, flying across the ground.

Wondering if my eyes deceived me, I watched in awe as the growing light finally took shape. First, I could make out the feet, giant paws digging into the ground, flinging heaps of earth and shredded grass high into the air, a cloak of dust remaining in its wake; next, the body, a rolling and lunging mass of white fur and muscles rippling and flexing in sequence; finally the head, the face of a lion adorned with a majestic white mane; then there were the eyes: they were fixed and intent on me, radiating blue with yellow bursts surrounding their black centers. I realized that this beast was not one of normal stature, but larger than even the great pearl I stood on. It bounded across the plains in immense strides. Within moments it was upon me, stopping a short way out.

I could hear the wind rushing through its nostrils and feel its hot breath come down on me like a blanket. Such a sense of disbelief filled me, I scarcely knew what to do or even think. Never had I been in the presence of anything that I felt so helpless against, naked and exposed. I stood, completely still, just watching, waiting.

My heart pounded in my chest. All at once the wind went still. In fact, nothing moved. The rhythm of life that flowed in the mountains, the stars, and the valley floor ceased. All bowed in awe and reverence. There was total silence save the breath of the lion. It stared down at me, intent and captivating. I didn't move.

Crashing the silence in a fury, it rose up on its hind legs and raised its head high into the air. A great roar loosed from its mouth, and I could see its teeth ablaze in the starlight. It shook everything, me most notably.

It was then I watched an outstretched paw, suspended high in the air, unleash the hidden claws from beneath. I marveled at this gesture. Then I noted it was still intent on me.

With one deft gesture the great lion lowered its arm, swiping clean across my chest. I flew backward, landing on the pearl surface. I lay there, looking up into the stars. I could not see the beast or feel his breath. But I could feel life draining out from me, the heat of the wound ravaging my chest. The taste of blood filled my mouth, and my lungs failed. My heartbeat slowed, resounding louder in my ears with every slowing pulse; and all it once, it stopped.

Luik lay in his bed staring at the ceiling, catching his breath. Once each summer the same dream haunted his sleep, and each summer he'd hoped it would not come. The rest of the men in Adriel's barracks slept soundly that night, but Luik lay waiting for the lion in his dream.

Chapter Twenty-nine

THE ARRIVAL

For the first time King Ragnar could ever remember, the sun did not rise on Adriel that next morning, at least not in the way he was accustomed to. Even with the notable rains to the east and increasingly cloudy skies over the ocean, beams of light had never failed to kiss the castle walls at dawn. That is, until this day. He stood to the west stroking his chin in thought, pondering the unsettling omen from atop one of the many palace spires. He wasn't even distracted by the two sets of distinctly different footsteps he heard come up the stairs from below.

"What do you make of it, my lord?" Gorn said with a deep, raspy voice.

The king did not reply but merely turned to look at his two friends and then faced back to the east. There the sky was darkest. Whatever light seeped through the clouds to the west, providing the faintest glow above, failed in the slightest to the east. The air over Bensotha was shrouded, choked by ominous clouds, layer upon layer, and weight upon weight. They undulated slowly, folding over one another in a sick tumult of churning dread and foreboding.

"I sense it is indeed a harbinger of what rises to the south," the king finally said. "And I sense their urgency to strike with haste and swiftness."

"And what of the reports, O King?" Li-Saide's boxy voice asked from below.

"Three of my four scouts returned in the night. All said it was as the prophecy indicated: Morgui assembles a war host to the south enveloping the southern edge of Grandath to the Sea of Lens in Bensotha."

"How many?" Gorn asked.

"Ten and two thousand," the king replied with no emotion. Gorn raised his brow.

"And what of the citizens?" asked Li-Saide.

"In his message, King Thorn offered Narin as a refuge for any that would wish to make the journey. As per my instructions five days ago, the women and children of Casterness and Bensotha have fled north in a slow trek accompanied by a host of warriors." The king turned to face them. "Tell me, is what those face who migrate north a difficult road?" Li-Saide was surprised to hear Gorn answer first.

"Aye, my liege, it is that."

"Then I pray the Most High protect you," the king spoke, arms outstretched toward the valley. "I pray He covers you and keeps you in the shadow of His Wing, O beauty and heart of Dionia! Whatever harm may befall you will be hunted down to the ends of the world! Peace be with you!" The king's voice echoed off the walls below and he slowly lowered his hands.

After a few moments Gorn spoke up again.

"Sire, what word do you have from the other kings?"

"All have sent word of their imminent arrival," he said. "King Lair has already arrived with four thousand fighting men. They sleep outside the palace gate in the city. Thorn has now come with his two thousand, and Purgos must be on your heels with the men of the mountains. The kings of the east have sent word that they bring ten thousand through the woods of Grandath, six thousand of whom are on horseback and the rest on foot."

"That's ten and six thousand fighting men, my lord," Li-Saide counted.

The king nodded.

"Then we have them outnumbered even without the known number from Tontha," Gorn said with a glimmer of hope.

"It would seem so," said Ragnar. "But of course those men need to be here in order to count," he paused, "and then the scouts fear the Dairne-Reih number is growing."

"Growing?" Gorn said slightly exasperated.

"And from where do they come?" asked Li-Saide.

"No one knows," Ragnar said.

"Then we must count on the other kings to arrive soon," Gorn stated.

"Aye, my friend, that and the Gracious Hand of the Lord of lords."

The three leaders descended the spire and walked through the hallways of Adriel in silence, finally entering a small room connected to the kitchen. A high, narrow table lay through the center and King Thorn sat on a stool eating a bowl of fruit with his sleeves pulled up.

"Hail, my king!" Thorn said placing his orange piece back down.

"Hail, king of Ligeon!" The two embraced.

"Forgive me, Ragnar, but we have not eaten in four days. Your house servants brought my men food this morning and then beckoned me to the kitchen here to await you."

"Not in four days?"

"The rains and the cold destroyed all the fruit along our route. We never thought to bring any with us. Times are changing, it would appear."

"Then you have eaten your fill here?"

"Aye, quite! C'symia!"

"You would do the same for me, Thorn. May we sit?"

"But Ragnar, it is your own table!"

"Not when my cooks have bade someone else to sit! They control this part of Adriel, Thorn, not I."

"Ha!" Thorn beat his chest. "Truly, you are a wise king! Come!" Thorn beamed with pride. Ragnar, Li-Saide, and Gorn all took up stools around the board, and Thorn passed the bowl. Immediately four mugs of hot-spiced mead were brought from the next room, fresh from the cooking fires.

"Speaking of your men," Ragnar said between sips, "how have they fared? I have not yet seen them this morning."

"They are most well and grateful for your generous accommodations. When we entered the city we made to make camp but your elders would have nothing of it. They bid us all to sleep within the fires of your walls.

Our men easily fit within the levels of the palace barracks. Our clothes have dried during the night and the mead in the evening, as well as this breakfast, have done us much good."

"Very good," Ragnar said, pleased with the hospitality of his house. "Tell me, Thorn, have you had any word from Purgos?"

"Nay, but I must assume he and the Mountain Men are not long behind us."

"Let us hope this is true, as I fear the enemy longs to make war sooner rather than later."

The door swung open and King Lair walked in. "So we have moved from the council chambers to the kitchen, I see?" he said in whimsical shock, hand still on the iron handle.

"Lair!" Thorn yelled rising off his stool.

"It is a blessing to see you once again, King of the Northerners," Lair said with a smile and a warm embrace.

"Come sit by my table!" Thorn said, beaming wide. Lair looked at Ragnar to confirm this boasting implication. Ragnar simply nodded with a smile. "Bring another draft!" he yelled into the kitchen. Lair sat on a stool beside Thorn.

"Tell me," he asked, "is it true my son, Luik, has ridden with you from Ligeon?"

"'Tis true, Lair. He wakes below us in the barracks hall."

"Then I must make to see him. It is now five years since I have beheld his face." Lair said standing from his stool.

"As it is for the rest of us," Ragnar said. "I bid you leave."

But his intention was short-lived. All five men froze as the sound of blasting horns echoed through the hallways of Adriel. Ragnar was first out the door, followed by Lair, Thorn, Gorn, and Li-Saide all bounding toward one of the high-lofted courtyard verandas. They stopped at the railing and looked past the King's Gate, down over the city, past the outer wall and into the valley that met the Ison Peninsula. A long line of men stretching out to the distant waterfall marched to the city wall and through the lower gate.

"Purgos has arrived!" Ragnar yelled. "Open the King's Gate!" He shouted to a watchman in the courtyard below. The order was distantly hollered many times over and passed up through to the gatekeeper's tower. With a deep groan, the massive doors lurched forward and the giant iron grate was hoisted by winches into its housing above. Ragnar and the rest rushed down through the castle and into the courtyard. The long line of their countrymen slowly made their way up to Adriel until Purgos himself emerged above the ramp and passed under the great gate of the west.

"Purgos!" Ragnar cried out. They all ran to greet him and the first of his men. But immediately everyone could see there was something wrong. Purgos's mantle was torn as was his maille shirt. Blood stained the rings of the metal armor, and his face was weary and dark with grime. The others that followed behind him nursed wounds also, some gravely worse and limping terribly.

"Bring my attendants!" Ragnar roared over his shoulder. "Make room!"

Thorn ran to the aid of one of Purgos's chiefs and caught him just before he stumbled to the ground in exhaustion. "Up you be! Battle Chiefs need not lay prostrate in this house!"

Li-Saide ran to another, as did Gorn and Lair. Ragnar put an arm around Tontha's king and helped him walk up the palace steps.

"In the name of the Creator God! What happened to you?"

Purgos spoke softly, "An ambush in the Border Mountains."

"Dairne-Reih?"

"Aye," he whispered.

Ragnar could tell it was tiring for him even to talk. "Say no more, my brother. The fires of Adriel await you."

Over the next hours the men of Ligeon filed out of the palace and made room for their northern brothers. Ragnar's elders attended to the wounds of the men, as did Fane, Li-Saide, and the Dibor. Faith stirred brightly, fanned into flame among those who ministered healing. They laid their hands on each man that suffered and spoke over them by the name of the Most High, the Mighty One of Athera. The power of the Great Spirit manifested freely; organs were healed and fresh skin sealed up over lacerations. Soaked, soiled garments were whisked away to be cleaned and then mended, and food was served around the roar of each blazing hearth. Soon the host of warriors, about nine hundred in all, was fast asleep. The great barracks hall was still, save for the flickering of flames and the moving about of various attendants. Only after everything had settled and the last of the men was laid down did Luik make out the figure of his father across the room.

His heart leapt inside and he wiped his blood-stained hands on his breecs. He weaved a course between the spindly beds and walked up behind Lair who stood gazing into a fire pit.

"It seems as though we have saved all who could be saved," Luik said with a calm voice though everything in him wanted to yell for joy.

"Aye, it would seem so," Lair said as he turned to face the voice behind him. "Luik!" The two men embraced tightly for several moments. "Let me look at you!" Lair pulled his son's face away with his hands and looked for the face of the boy he once knew. "Ah, my son, how we have missed you!"

"As have I, Father."

"My, you have filled out," Lair said looking down his strong body.

"Only as the seasons demand," he replied. "And you look the same as I remember you." They hugged once more. "How are Na na and Rourke?"

"Fine, fine, both fine. Come, to the Elder's Hall. We have much to speak of and I fear we would rouse all these mighty men should we continue here."

"Aye, Father."

With that they parted from the barracks arm-in-arm, a longing hope in both of their hearts now satisfied.

• • •

The main courtyard was a bustle of activity. Men were coming and going, running errands within the city, and moving supplies from the royal storehouses to their appropriate places. Swords, shields, axes, and spears were being dispensed and set up in easily reachable caches; skins of water and armor were set in rows for the taking; arrows were piled high in bundles along the walls and bows were strung and counted. As evening fell, guards were posted and rotated on every wall and rampart. The high towers were set ablaze with their beacon lights, and countless torches were lit throughout the city. Barriers were constructed on the sides of the road down the main artery of the city. These closed off all access to the side roads and homes, denying the enemy any flanking position if they breached the city. After the men from Tontha had been let in, the City

Gate was closed and the King's Gate was staffed with sentries. Adriel was being fortified and secured with each passing moment.

Even the grounds without the city were prepared by a host of workers and builders. Enormous spiked trestle walls were erected designed to direct a rushing army to the center track or face being driven through by their own momentum. The walls were tiered in rows on either side of the main road, forcing the advancing enemy into a single lane that approached the City Gate. Should the men in the field be overtaken and pressed back into Adriel, this was a powerful defense in funneling the enemy into an easily attackable formation.

By nightfall Adriel was transformed into a battle stronghold that glowed under the overcast night sky. She lay impenetrable to any that looked on, truly a refuge of kings.

Luik sat around a large fire along with the rest of the Dibor and a mixture of men from both Bensotha and the northern lands. Voices were raised high in singing throughout Adriel as drafts of mead and bread passed to every fire within her walls. Wherever men could gather and sing praise to the Most High and enjoy one another's fellowship, they did, and that without restraint. They sang loudly and shared many a story with one another, singing songs of victory and valor and of noble deeds done.

The fire that Luik happened to sit by was right in the middle of the main courtyard, the palace steps just to his left. Despite her warlike dress now, the palace and surrounding city still flowed with beauty and grace. The men's singing faded from his ears and he looked over past a fountain to the set of gravel trees. He remembered climbing them to get a better view of King Ragnar and the Princess. Over there, the two sculpted lions perched on the sides of the staircase leading to the palace doors. Even the hanging bell was in place. Did he still remember its clarion tone? It seemed like a lifetime ago for him, and a far more innocent time than now. A time before he knew about people being *taken* and words like *evil, sin* and *death*. It was a time before he knew about fighting, training, and endurance. And it was certainly a time before he knew about the disobedience of fallen lythlae and the pride of one, *Morgui*. How had everything changed so quickly? One minute he remembered playing with his friends and running to the Sea Cave, and the next he was driving a sword through the body of demon. He drank deeply from his mug and stared into the flames.

"They emerged from the fray victorious! Victorious! Victorious!" came the familiar tune from the host gathered around him. He watched the flames lick up from the embers beneath. They pulsed intensely. He could feel the warmth soak up into his skin. It felt good. He wondered about Anorra and Hadrian. Where were they now? What were they doing beneath this same dark sky? Were they safe? He missed them.

"And the enemy fell with their heads beneath heels! Victorious! Victorious! Triumphant all the day!"

Looking up Luik tried to make out stars, but the low cloud cover was thick and oppressing. It seemed like a long time since he had seen any stars. Then he caught something moving in the darkness toward the palace. He glanced quickly to the gravel trees and then toward the main door of the castle. A dark figure moved up the steps between the two lions and reached for the door without stopping to ring the bell. Something inside Luik pricked him, and he immediately felt uneasy about the silhouette. He excused himself from his company and moved quickly in the shadows to the steps.

"Who goes there?" he asked boldly up the stairs. The figure turned abruptly.

"'Tis I, Valdenil of Bensotha."

"Valdenil?" He searched out the name. "Do I know you?" Luik asked, mounting up to meet him.

"Well, what might your name be, sir?" the man asked covered in a cloak, his face shrouded by the shadow of his hood.

"Luik of the Dibor, Son of Lair."

"No, I do believe we have not yet met, but I consider it a privilege and an honor. Your reputation as a member of the Dibor precedes you."

"Thank you, Valdenil. I wish I could say the same of you; alas I have never heard your name before. Please enlighten me."

"Hey'a, Luik! What are you doing over there?" Rab shouted from the fire. "You don't need any saving yet, do you?"

"No, Rab, but I'll be sure to let you be the first to know!" Luik called over his shoulder. "Just one of my friends," he said to Valdenil, gesturing back toward the group but never taking his eyes from the stranger. "Would you mind removing your hood?" Luik tensed.

"Forgive me, sir. I am indeed rude to keep concealed in the night light." He reached up and removed his hood. Shadows covered most of his face but his blue eyes and light hair stood out the most. Luik was somehow quite relieved. "Well, I must attend to a few of the men from Tontha; a pity what happened. I should be on my way. It was a pleasure to meet you, Luik of the Dibor. Perhaps we can spend more time together soon."

"Uh, aye, have a good night, Valdenil."

They bade each other good night and Valdenil replaced his hood. He pressed through the great doors, and Luik turned reluctantly, feeling he had missed something. It was not often he met someone he did not know, especially from his own realm.

"Valdenil," he whispered to himself as he stepped down, the name lingering on his lips. "Valdenil, from where do you come?" His mind was a fury of activity, searching deep into the furthest recesses, hunting for a thread within the darkness. "I have heard your name before, but where?" Nearing the last step he froze. "*Valdenil! Son of the Dead!*" Luik drew his sword and roared in the darkness with a warrior's rage.

"*Intruder!*"

The men by the fire stood and looked on in shock. Luik ran back up the steps and flung wide the doors. Standing there in the emptiness of the mysterious palace entry room was a figure far removed from the fair-haired man Luik had seen moments before. The grotesque being stood in the blackness plain as the light of day, revealed for what he truly was: one of the *taken*. It reeled looking back at Luik, eyes sunken and dark, cheek bones protruding, and its flesh matted and pale. The creature screamed and flailed its arms wildly, then quickly turned away. A door appeared in the distance; clearly it knew how to use the power of the entry room.

"He's going to the Throne Room!" Luik yelled over his shoulder as the Dibor raced up the steps with swords drawn. The figure opened the door and shut it behind him. Luik ran and then lunged for the handle, but when he yanked it open there was simply mute blackness. The door was gone. The Dibor filed into the entry room.

"I need an attendant!" Luik hollered.

"No need, I'm here," Fane said running to the front.

"Get us a door to the Throne Room!" Fane waved his hand and suddenly the door reappeared. Luik yanked it open.

• • •

Two of the palace guards rested against the stone wall high above on the ramparts of the city gate. Torch flames flickered around them and the air was still, save for the distant songs and laughter around the campfires below. A slight mist fell around them, slowly soaking the wall and their garments.

"A drink, Drennel?" the lanky one said handing over his canteen skin. Drennel took it appreciatively and swallowed a gulp of water, wiping his mouth with his forearm. It had been a long day, but much had been accomplished. They looked out and surveyed the work in the field; tall trestle walls staggered across the valley, their spikes protruding into the air. Along the ramparts, row upon row of bundled arrows lay neatly stacked as far as they could see.

"What a peaceful night."

"Aye, a shame there are no stars to keep us company," Drennel said, mildly forlorn, handing back the canteen. He was husky and stout, his bravery being tested by this night. Word had spread all day about the sizeable foe that waited to attack. With only the men of Bensotha, Ligeon and the battered of Tontha to fight, the guards sought company and strength wherever it could be found.

"Well, no matter, we are almost done with our watch and soon our pillows will keep us company."

Just then a third guard mounted the stairs beside and greeted them.

"Hail Drennel and Tilly, guards of Adriel!"

"Isn't he the perky one," Drennel whispered to Tilly with a poke.

"Greetings, Fonish," Tilly replied. "You've come to relieve us?"

"Aye, your tents await you."

"True, and a draft of mead. Where is your second man?"

"He will be along shortly, I trust."

"Then I will wait with you until he arrives," Drennel said.

"Nay, commander, bid this night farewell and make for your camp."

Drennel was normally intolerant of suggestions from his men, but tonight he was too tired to argue. "You are gracious, Fonish," Drennel said.

"It is the least that I—" Fonish stopped. His gazed was suddenly fixed on something far beyond. Drennel was perplexed at his behavior and turned to match his stunned curiosity, as did Tilly.

"What is it?" Tilly asked, leaning between two large crenellations in the wall.

There, above the highest horizon point to the east, at the waterfall of Casterness, a strange glow warmed the low-lying clouds.

"Fire glow."

"Someone is approaching the ridge," Fonish murmured.

"Dairne-Reih?" Tilly inclined his head.

"Perhaps, but there appear to be many. Listen there!" Drennel said.

A strange stirring filled the air, beatings from within the ground.

"Horse hooves," Fonish uttered.

"Possibly," Drennel said.

"The men of Jerovah! They have arrived!" Fonish was clearly elated.

"Peace, Fonish," Drennel cautioned with hushed tone. "We do not know for sure. Let us wait to see if the purple banner of the equestrian order flies high. We will wait here." He looked squarely at Fonish. "Go and give word along the wall and to the watch towers to look for the banners. Say no more as we are not certain until we note what colors they herald."

"But it must be the kings of the east!"

"Nay, man," Drennel scolded him. "We must not be hasty in this, but do so in passing on my message! Off with you!" He turned to the lanky one. "Tilly, send four men to bring word from the outlying scout posts. I will set two men outside the gate should any scout return by a different way."

Tilly nodded and Fonish reluctantly pressed off. He was upset that his enthusiasm for the imminent arrival of the eastern kings was not shared by his commanding officer.

"He just wants to be right," Fonish said under his breath as he moved away. Jealousy and pride had taken root as one. He ran down the left flank to the first patrol stand. Two guards stood high on the wooden platform.

"Eyes to the east!" Fonish yelled up. "Keep watch for the colors." His heart was being consumed. "Surely they will be that of our eastern kings! They have arrived to join us!"

"Hey'a!" the two guards above gave up a shout and turned to the east. Their hearts soared with hope and expectation. Fonish ran on down to the next station, this one a watchtower. He raced through the arched doorway and bounded up the spiraled stairs.

"Guards of Adriel, the kings of the east arrive, there, to the horizon!" He pointed to the ridge where the fire glow grew. The watchmen beamed widely with anticipation.

And so it went on like this to every stand, post, and watchtower. Hope was passed through a vessel of corruption like flames licking up dry wood. Every man at every post watched on as the firelight grew stronger and more distinct. *Their rescuers had arrived.* Men from within the city were stirred by the news and mounted along the wall to see. Before long the ramparts were full of onlookers all cheering and embracing.

Tilly returned from his errand a short time later and mounted to the City Gatehouse to report.

"What is this that my eyes behold?" Drennel said as Tilly walked in. They both surveyed the growing masses along the wall.

"Why, I do not know, sir."

Suddenly they heard a yell from below as well as from a few guards along the wall.

"*Open the gate!*"

"Open the gate?" Drennel was completely taken aback. "Who has given this order?" He demanded in a state of fury.

"I don't know, sir." Tilly was petrified.

"I am Keeper of the City Wall! Is it not King Ragnar and he alone that bids my action?" He slammed a fist against the wall. "*Fonish*," he uttered seething through clenched teeth.

The call came again.

"*Open the City Gate! The Kings of the East arrive forthwith!*"

"No, they don't!" Drennel cried unheard. The situation was clearly mounting out of control. The despair of being outnumbered and underpowered had enflamed a raging fire of frenzied hope within the fighting men of the city. Soon two guards ran to the gatehouse where Tilly and Drennel stood.

"Hail Drennel, Keeper of the City Gate. Why has the way not been opened?"

"Because the King has not given the order!" Drennel shouted, completely enraged.

The two men were taken aback.

Drennel spat, "Where did you hear that those coming over the ridge were men from Jerovah, Trennesol, and Somahguard?" The watchmen hesitated. By now the walls were filled with cheering men both above and below. Those in the gatehouse had to shout just to be heard. "We no more know if they are countrymen than we do if they are Dairne-Reih! If we confirm they are indeed our brothers, then we will open the gate and receive them; but if they be our enemy, we have lost valuable time in deploying our men into the valley! We will enter the battle defending our city without ever gaining a chance to attack in the field! *Fools!*"

Soon guards and fighting men entered the gatehouse from both directions in a wild attempt to open the way. False hope had consumed them. Drennel yelled and stepped toward the wheel and winch gears. Men continued to press in, all thinking his cries were like that of their own. He reached down and drew out his sword. This caught their attention.

"Anyone who takes another step, I will not spare from wrath!" Drennel's chest heaved as his face reddened. Everyone within the room went silent.

"But the king has given orders, Drennel," came a voice from within the throng.

"What?"

"King Ragnar has wished it so," said another whom Drennel could not see.

"It is not true! He would not do such a foolish and misguided thing!" Drennel yelled back. His heart beat fast.

"Open the gate!" someone cried out.

"*Open the gate!*" they all joined in with crazed rebellion. They pressed toward Drennel. He squeezed the handle of his sword with both hands and lofted his blade high above his head.

"O Most High, *forgive me.*"

• • •

"Stop!" Luik cried out violently. But the being paid him no attention. Ragnar, Thorn, Lair, Gorn, and Li-Saide sat around a table to one side of the Throne Room. They all turned to the sudden outburst. The creature was halfway to the table. Ragnar rose first followed by the others, chairs sliding back or falling over. The Dibor rushed in behind Luik and fanned out. The possessed beast shrieked and swung its arm in a wide arch loosing a spray of shiny objects through the air. They pelted the group of leaders who ducked in an attempt to avoid the attack. Gorn had drawn his sword and rushed headlong at the enemy; but a moment before the collision the being leapt high into the air, bounded off the massive table, and perched on the side of a pillar above their heads. Everyone looked on in astonishment. The man-like beast purred, clucking its throat, and turned its head to survey the men below. It moved with a sickening stealth, half man—half demon. Benigan raised a spear and heaved it up but the monster leapt to another pillar and then crawled up an arch to the domed ceiling above. Taking one last glance as if to further study the men below, it jumped into the air and broke through a window to the outside.

"Outside! Don't let it get away!"

"Wait, Luik!" Gorn cried out. The Dibor stopped and looked to their friend. He knelt at the head of the table. Everyone gathered around Ragnar, lying on his back with his eyes closed, his head in the arms of Li-Saide.

"Great Spirit of the Living, what happened?" Fane inquired.

"A tipped dart," Gorn replied solemnly.

"Li-Saide, remove it quickly!" Fane pleaded.

"Nay, we must make war for him," the dwarf inclined his head for Fane to draw near. "The dart is deep in his neck and keeps blood within his body. Should we remove it, I fear that his body will not heal quickly enough to stop the bleeding."

"Will not heal?"

"The dart is poisoned. An evil even now courses through his veins, suffering hope and diluting faith. We must move against it, and quickly."

"What can we do, Li-Saide?" Luik asked.

"Rise up, O Warriors of Dionia! Let your faith implore the hand of the Creator for His sustaining Life and healing power. But, I pray you, do not linger here."

"Aye," Gorn said. "Surely this creature was not alone."

"To the valley!" Thorn said.

"To the Valley of Casterness!" Lair roared.

"We shall leave you with our king as such?" Luik grieved.

"Aye. Fane and I will suffice. You must go and attend to the city! I sense a great evil marches against us as we speak!"

"Gorn! Your arm!" Rab called out. Everyone looked at his maille-sleeved bicep. A silver metal spike lay wedged between rings of the armor on his right arm. Gorn glanced at the object and pulled it out with a grunt. The tip was black and a light coating of blood slid slowly down the dart.

"Are you well?" Quoin asked.

"Fine," Gorn barked sternly. "Let us make haste!" He rose and drew his sword. They all made the sign of blessing over their king and ran back through the entryway, down the stairs, and into the main courtyard beyond. It was completely empty, the campfire burning alone. That did not startle them nearly as much as what they heard.

"Cheering!" Benigan said in bewilderment.

"The city does not make for war," Gorn added.

"Perhaps the Kings of the East arrive this night?"

"Not if my spirit confirms what the dwarf has implied," said Gorn.

"As does mine," said Luik.

They all ran across the square past the storehouses and mounted the secluded stairs to the top of the palace wall. Mounting the ramparts they looked out over the city.

"Why is the City Gate open?" Jrio asked, standing next to Luik and Gorn, his heart sinking low. "The king has not given such a command!"

"No, he has not," Gorn replied softly, searching the horizon.

"There, the fire-glow atop the ridge!" Luik pointed.

Gorn's eyes narrowed. "That is not a lane of cavalry; *it is the breadth and span of a battle line.*" He suddenly raised his voice in a command. "Rally the foot soldiers to the field! Fyfler, sound the battle horn in the King's Gatehouse! Get those fools off the wall! The enemy draws near! We will meet our assailants in the valley!"

The Dibor rushed from the wall and mounted their horses housed in the stables. Fyfler released the ballast weights in the gatehouse and sent the giant doors slowly outward. The Dibor sheathed their swords and grabbed spears and pikes. A few took up round shields. They raced down the main track toward the wide open city gate, horse hooves clacking on the stone road. Luik rode beside Gorn when the King's battle horn sounded from above. It severed the night air like a razor and pierced every ear that heard it. The crazed chaos brought on by the lying spirit, infecting the souls of Dionia's men, was instantly vanquished, leaving the warriors idle where they stood. The sound of the battle horn echoed off the walls and resonated throughout the city. The men looked to one another, dazed as if being woken from a deep slumber. Suddenly it dawned on them that it was not the war host of the eastern lands; *it was their enemy*. The King's horn had clarified all.

They watched from the wall as a small group of men rode down the main street with swords drawn, hollering war cries with every stride.

"*To the valley!*" Gorn yelled.

"*Make war!*" called the others.

The entire mass of the city, that had just moments before been expecting to welcome their kinsmen, was now caught on their heels bearing the gravity of their grievous mistake.

"*Men, arm yourselves!*" a few began to cry out.

"*Archers to the walls!*" others yelled.

The men of the city had lost valuable time, but in the most unnoticed of tragedies, they had also done the unthinkable. Tilly climbed back up the stairs to the gatehouse, weaving between the on-rush of descending men. He nursed his shoulder from the fall, having been shoved off by the swell earlier. He turned in through the doorway and froze in complete horror; the body of Drennel had been trampled to a mangled pulp as well as two other men who had been pressed against the gears. Drennel had died defending his city and the gate he was sworn to protect. His sword was tossed to the side of the room, and Tilly wept bitterly as he picked it up. The blade was covered in blood. He was suddenly overwhelmed by the irony and helplessness of his commanding officer, of his friend, of his brother in arms.

The Dibor passed beneath the threshold of the City Gate and rode hard out into the thoroughfare, passing row upon row of trestle walls on either side. Finally they emerged into the valley and spread out in a line. Their horses whinnied and snorted. Luik turned in his seat to see a thick line of warriors pouring out through the gate behind them. They had followed the Dibor's lead. Gorn rode out a few steps and then turned his horse to address his men.

"The bulk of the enemy will advance down the left flank of the waterfall as it provides the widest avenue of passage. The right flank is steeper and narrower, perched with boulders, probably less of a threat. Jrio, I want you to take five ranks of archers to the base. Shoot anything that moves down the right side.

"Benigan, take your brothers back into the city and prepare a defense with five hundred men. Should we fall in the field, you must hold the city and ultimately the palace at all costs. You will, of course, have the majority of the archers. Keep Fyfler in the gatehouse at the palace.

"Dibor, we are outnumbered two to one. Even if the men of Tontha rise up from their stupor to meet the challenge, that only gives us another nine hundred on top of our six thousand. We must make wise use of our numbers.

"Luik, take the long spear foot soldiers to the front. Create schiltrons from the basin of the waterfall to the cliffs of the peninsula on the left. The first of their advancing line will be impaled. Fall back and draw swords. I am giving you the most prone position and full control of the entire leading assault on the left flank. Are you up to it?"

"Without question, sir." Luik beat his chest. "Benigan, give word to the archers on the wall to watch for my signal."

"What signal?" Benigan asked.

"I don't know, I'll think of something."

"You want them to shoot?"

"Probably. Be creative."

"Sons of Somahguard," Gorn continued, "take five ranks of swordsmen each. Fill in behind the long spears. Sons of Trennesol, take five ranks each and fill in behind them." Jrio, Benigan, Luik and the six other Dibor all nodded and then kicked their horses hard, riding off to meet the men behind them with their orders. Gorn addressed the remaining six Dibor.

"Sons of Ligeon and sons of Jerovah, you ride with me!"

"Hey'a!" They shouted back in one voice.

"Where do we ride to?" Cage asked.

"To the beach."

"We mean to run away?"

"Nay! We make to attack them from behind! He-yah!" Gorn kicked his horse and charged south to the coast along the strand of sand and waves. Cage, Daquin, Quoin, Thad, Thero, and Anondo filed in behind Gorn as he sprinted away from Adriel.

• • •

"Quickly now! A quillion starting here stretching to the northern cliffs!" Luik shouted from atop Fedowah. His horse was clearly growing restless with anticipation. With the late hour turning into the next day, the sun was far from rising and the darkness reached its peak. A thousand and five hundred men filed out in a long sweeping arch cupping the base of the northern hill below the ridge. Torches in one hand, long spears in the other, the line was soon formed, each man kneeling shoulder-to-shoulder with spear butts driven deep into the hard soil and raised a few feet off the ground in front of them. A second row lowered their spears just above and between the shoulders of those in front and a third row above and between the first two. The effect was a long menacing wall of spears, five hundred wide and three deep.

Once the quillion had been formed, Fallon, Naffe, Kinfen, Najrion, Naron, and Rab arrived, each leading a division of five hundred men. They lined up behind the spearmen and drew their swords with one hand, shields in the other. The sound of clanging metal and armor rustled through the night air. Luik rode out in front of them and slightly higher onto the rising base.

"Men of Dionia! I bid you courage and valor this night! Hold fast; and having done everything to remain fixed, hold fast!" Luik's personal feelings erupted as he spoke from the head of the army. *Morgui.* "Be strong and courageous! The enemy must not be allowed to pass through our ranks! We are not here to defend our city but to destroy our enemy!" *Defeat Morgui.* He waved his hand high above his head as the men let out a mighty roar that echoed off the ridge and back into the city. *Defeat Morgui. Crush his head beneath my heel,* Luik said within. "Listen for my voice, warriors! Listen to my commands! This night we make to end our world's suffering against the plight of evil, against Morgui himself!" They broke out in cheering once more. Luik turned Fedowah and ran back to the basin.

"Take one last drink of water, my friend, for tonight there will only be blood." Luik patted Fedowah's neck as he bent low to drink from the pool of the waterfall.

Chapter Thirty

DOWN THE WATERFALL

Fyfler replaced the horn in the gatehouse and looked down over the city. Most of the men had left the walled fortress and filled the distant valley while only a handful remained inside. The majority of men made for the north, the left of the valley floor, while a small group covered the steep slopes of the right flank to the south. It was easy to note placement from where Fyfler stood, as torches looked like little groupings of candles spaced all over the countryside. He was eager to join the war host but quickly saw the City Gate slowly closing.

"Hey'a!" he yelled out, mostly for himself. "Wait for me!"

He ran down the high rampart to the stairs and out through the small concealed side door of the palace wall. But no sooner had he entered out onto the main track then one of the twins met him.

"Back up you go!" Brax called out.

"What?"

"Gorn gave us all separate posts. Yours is in the King's Gatehouse."

"But I—"

"Fyfler, take the order."

"Aye," he conceded. There was no use arguing the wisdom of his elder or the instruction of his friend.

"And where are you going, Brax?"

"The brothers and I are making a defense within the city should the valley be taken. Benigan is taking the main road while Boran and I sweep the side streets and man the walls with archers. Benigan instructed me to come tell you—"

"I know, I know, I go to the King's Gatehouse."

"Right."

"Peace be with you, Dibor."

"And with you." They embraced and departed.

Fyfler retraced his steps through the concealed doorway to the inside of the King's Gate and mounted the steep stairs to the ramparts above. He decided on a prime vantage point in one of the high towers slightly to the left of the gate. He climbed the internal ladder up through the narrow turret and emerged on top with a breathtaking view of the entire peninsula. He wiped his brow of the damp mist that soaked him through, though he was too hot from his climb to be cold from it. The speed at which his fellow warriors had organized the fighting men of Dionia was staggering. Six thousand men had been routed from certain self-inflicted disaster and suddenly organized by divisions and ranks to take up strategic positions along an entire region; and that by only *ten and nine men. Of course these are not ordinary men*, he thought proudly. *These are Dibor.* Gorn was truly a master, one for whom he only gained more and more respect with each day.

Fyfler snapped from his reverie by a bright line of light that crested the far ridge. It was like watching a sunrise and the thin line that spreads across the ocean's edge. Only this light did not rise from the west, and there was nothing glorious about it; it was the entire force of the Dairne-Reih. There were thousands upon thousands of torches that approached the line; all packed tightly together like a single fire. He saw no heralds, no banners and no flags; the army was led by an unseen force that found no use for the trivial markers of man.

• • •

The men along the front line gazed up the long hill to the ridgeline above. The thunderous rhythm of marching came up through their bodies and only proved to get louder as the enemy neared. From their vantage point the clouds above grew brighter and brighter. The sheer magnitude and awe of the closing enemy had an intimidating effect on the spearmen. Luik could sense their hearts waning. The line of spears was quivering ever so slightly.

"Courage!" he yelled from the side. But his voice was being drowned out by the overwhelming tumult of marching above. He needed to do something.

"Let's give them something to shout about. What do ya' say, my friend?" Fedowah reared and took off along the front lines once more. Luik pressed his horse hard and then released his hands from their grip on the mane. Luik pulled his legs up beneath him, kneeling on Fedowah's back. The horse ran on, passing the first hundred men across. With highly skilled balance, Luik stretched out his arms, sword in hand, and pressed himself up on the undulating back below his feet. He was now standing fully erect on horseback and the men who saw him do so raised their weapons and their voices high in praise; about four thousand and five hundred men in all shouted words of courage and strength in loud voices. Luik crossed to the far side of the line and then returned in the same way, still balancing with sword held high. The shouting was all-encompassing and for a moment they forgot the sound of the marching above; they forgot about the imminent and indescribable terror that loomed over them; they forgot the fact that their wives and children had left only days before with no word if any of them had arrived in Ligeon safely; and they forgot about the fact that they may never see them again, or anyone else for that matter. Just as Luik and Fedowah passed back into the basin, the cheers stopped.

Two thousand Dairneags poured over the crest of the ridge above and plummeted down, firelight casting a wide glare along the slope. The spearmen gaped in terror. The demons came at them with no armor and no weapons; at least not in the sense they knew them to be. Their dark bodies stood twice as tall as a normal man and their arms extended revealing horns and claws wielded in the torchlight. They screamed and shrieked as they mounted over the side of the headwall. It was piercing beyond imagination. The men-at-arms instinctively took one step back but the Dibor on horseback pleaded with them to remain strong. The gap of space between the quillion and the first lines of the Dairne-Reih closed with each second, thousands more spilling over the ridge, filling in behind.

"O Great God of All," Luik said, stunned, "please protect us by Your Mighty Hand." Already the mass that raced down the hill was as large as the entire company of men gathered in Casterness. "The slaughter will be of countless ranks of men," Luik said under his breath. "You must save us."

The demons raced on, now a tidal wave of unstoppable momentum and insurmountable force. There was nowhere to retreat, nowhere to run. Those men in the front lines came to grips with this reality, and those in the rear were grateful they were not in the front. A second later there was no more room for thinking.

The din of the battle clash was deafening and resounded back to Adriel and beyond. Even King Ragnar in his crippled and unconscious state from within the castle groaned and twisted from the sound. The demons fell upon the long spears with such force, the entire line was mowed over and swallowed whole. Wood splintered and snapped like kindling in a fire. Shrapnel flew in every direction and screams and cries of men and demons filled the spaces between flesh and spirit. Demons flew through the air, driven through with spears, and landed on swordsmen further back. The quillion was mauled and disappeared under the flood, not a man ever to be seen again.

Dairneag plunged into the lines of men, swinging and gnashing at anything that moved. But soon the momentum from above pushed even their own number into an uncontrolled state. Men and demons were crushed together in the suffocating strangle of war. Piles of beast and man formed, and those descending climbed over them, leaping into the fray. A number of the demon war host was inadvertently pushed off the waterfall nearly five tree lengths above. They sailed through the air and crashed into the basin where Luik and Fedowah were. A few landed on the rocks nearby, bodies shattering and breaking apart in a spray of carnage. Any that emerged from the pool, dazed and daunted, Luik rode over to and drove them through with his spear. The water turned red with the churning of the falls, and the all too familiar stench of the fallen lythlae returned to Luik's nostrils.

To the right, Jrio contended with his own waterfall: demons spilling down the rocky steeps. His archers immediately retreated a short distance so as not to be crushed beneath one of the hapless creatures that tumbled to its doom. Regaining a better position further out, they commenced firing on any creature that walked from the heap. At first there were so many that leapt to their destruction, the deathblow had already been dealt and there was nothing to do save watch. As the mound increased, falls were broken and more Dairne-Reih were able to stand and walk away, but not very far. As more of the war host surged down the left side, the numbers coming down the right side thinned to a select few that skillfully weaved between boulders and dodged the arrows from below.

"Do not let them pass!" Jrio cried out.

The archers continued to fire but had difficulty estimating the lead-time necessary to catch the demons between boulders. A few Dairneag above watched at the success of those that descended and followed them down through the boulders in the same fashion. It wasn't long before a great number had amassed toward the valley floor. The small band rushed the archers. Most of them were driven through with hundreds of arrows, but a few managed to resist the assault and run into the line, taking out a swath before being thwarted by more arrows. A small portion of the enemy above found favor with the plan, seeing the less defended right flank more appealing than simply gouging through the mainline to the left.

Countless scores began dodging between the boulders and amassing at the bottom, only then to charge the archers. Each time they lost most of their number but a few would break through and kill before being overrun. A handful of men would be killed, and more and more arrows were used up. The enemy was relentless and saw the toll being taken on their foe.

"We are running out of arrows!" cried one of the rank commanders. The original number of five hundred archers was now down to about half that. They were killing less and being killed more. "What should we do, Dibor?"

Jrio was dismayed. The plan was not working.

"We hold the line, commander! We hold the line to the last man! Nothing gets through!"

"Aye, Dibor." The commander ordered his men to notch another round. "Fire at will!"

More Dairneags charged, increasing in strength and number with every volley. This time about ten rushed into the line and caught the lightly armed bowmen like a blade sifting wheat. They were eventually shot down but during the same time the archers should have been firing on the next advancement. Soon arrows ceased being fired at the boulders and the demons descended freely. The remaining one hundred archers focused on the advancing line, now a full-fledged battle horde. But the arrows were not enough to stop them.

"Fall back!" Jrio cried out in defeat. "Fall back to the center!"

Luik heard the hollering of his friend and watched as his men fled from the Dairne-Reih. The pace of the men, albeit heartfelt, was no match for the speed of the demons who soon overtook the bowmen, cutting them down from the back. Jrio escaped only because of his horse. He ran toward Luik in a mad rush of desperation. Luik turned to view the battle to the left.

The swordsmen at the forefront, a line that was ever moving back, tried as best they could to fend off the assault. Men swung at the giant monsters, swords severing arms and hands, and piercing deep between plates of hardened skin that repelled most other blows. But the mass of the demon numbers was undeniably the greatest advantage on the battlefield. The Men of Dionia were being beaten, not because of skill or heart, but because of size, and it was utterly degrading. All in all, Luik estimated that over two thousand men had already been lost in the opening span of the battle. It had been folly to try and defend the valley. The city was their only hope.

"To the city!" Luik shouted. The order was repeated throughout the lines, some being mowed over just after giving the order.

Just then Luik pulled a bow from a man beside him. "Quick, man! Hand me an arrow!" The warrior did so and Luik tore his sleeve and wrapped it around just below the tip. He nocked it deftly. "Your torch!" The soldier raised it up to Luik as he lit the fabric. "Let's hope they get the message," he murmured to himself. Luik leaned back and drew the bowstring to his cheek. He let fly the arrow, and it sailed ablaze straight overhead, arching ever so slightly and falling into the demon mass.

The fighting was getting fierce, and the movement down the right side of the waterfall was perpetual. Jrio was almost to Luik with the demons right behind.

"Jrio! Head for the city!"

Jrio bobbed his head and turned for the City Gate. His horse kicked up dirt and beat hard along the road. Luik waited a few seconds longer.

"Come on!" he pleaded with the archers along the wall.

The enemy was now closing in on the center from both sides. He would have to leave now to escape. The men were reeling on their heels, stumbling to make the city. Luik was nearly alone by the pool.

"Shoot!" he yelled out. "*Shoot! Shoot them back to Haides!*"

Coming not a moment soon enough for Luik, Adriel suddenly launched a thousand arrows skyward, all alight in flames.

"*Aye!*" Luik yelled, nearly leaping off Fedowah. But Fedowah was much more concerned with the enclosing foe than he was any flying arrows, so he took Luik's holler to mean he should run for the city in like manner. Luik almost fell off his horse's hindquarters but caught the mane just in time.

"Aye, my valiant steed! Run swiftly!" They ran fast underneath the blanket of arrows above, quickly followed by a second series of arrows on the same path. Luik watched the first set land just steps behind them, impaling the advancing demon lines with staggering effect. It would give the men on foot just enough advantage to make the city. A few demons nipped at Fedowah's heels but were suddenly beat down by the merciless bowmen's wrath.

"Run, men of Dionia! Run!"

Luik saw a man falter in his steps just ahead. The soldier fell forward in the air, hands extended, but before hitting the ground a hand grabbed his shirt and heaved him onto the back of a horse.

"How 'bout a ride? Walking seems a trifle inadequate these days, no?"

The man was speechless and simply nodded, having been saved from certain death. Luik kicked Fedowah harder, and they pressed on, now with extra weight.

The second round of arrows rained down on the Dairne-Reih, piercing shoulders, drilling skulls, and riveting limbs together in mid-stride. A third and a fourth set were unleashed, all bearing the same effect. A small gap opened and separated Luik and the last of the men from the advancing line of the demon war host. *Five! Six!* Luik counted the volleys that went up from the walls. Now they passed by the first of the trestle walls, the giant spikes whizzing by their heads reaching for anything to devour like bloodthirsty claws. Luik slowed to let all those run inside in front of him. He let the man off, who lost no time in running ahead quickly. The small gap that the archers created was closing.

"Move along! Move along!" Luik prodded in earnest.

The Dairne-Reih shrieked and batted helplessly at the assailing missiles that befouled them, *surely cursing in their native tongues*, Luik thought. Then one massive demon with three horns in each hand and three in its skull focused in on Luik and Fedowah. A few stray arrows drove into the beast's forearms and a leg, but it was not fazed. It knew power and authority when it saw it, drilling Luik with its yellow eyes.

This warrior would surely be a prize, it thought.

The last of the men were nearly squeezed through the threshold.

"Make way!" Luik yelled, unaware of the foe behind him. "Quickly now!"

The three-horned Dairneag leaned forward and broke into a full run, saliva flinging out of its mouth, and blood squirting past the arrows wedged in the veins of its flesh. It barked for air and clucked relentlessly, crazed for the kill.

Luik heard noise behind and spun Fedowah around. He watched in complete dismay as the demon ran straight for him at full speed, its narrow eyes consumed with lust and its teeth spread wide. Both arms were outreached to the sides ready to swing, and its black and blue flesh was rough and flowing with swill.

Fedowah reared in a helpless attempt to intimidate the monster, but it was of no effect. Luik braced for the impact, and Fedowah closed his eyes. The sound of metal chains clanged through the air and rumbled in Luik's ears. The massive spiked iron gate dropped from its lofted housing and pinned the beast to the ground in mid-stride, severing the head from the body. Then the ironbound wooden doors swung shut on the outside of the gate and sealed the city in tightly, the corpse of the demon between them, and the head rolling to a stop at Fedowah's hooves.

Chapter Thirty-one

BATTLE OF ADRIEL

"I do believe we are lost." Naronel's black hair was soaked and matted against his face. Lack of sleep, damp cold, and little food had taken their toll, coaxing black circles to form under his eyes. The horses, too, were exhausted and malnourished. Daunt forced a weak smile and slid easily off his horse to the muddy ground below.

"What makes you think that, my friend?" Daunt said brushing the rain from his brow with a forearm. He acted as if he didn't already know the answer. The muted light that managed to seep through the overcast sky above was little more than a dim wash by the time it reached the forest floor. Though most every tree in Dionia had lost its leaves by now, the great oaks and pines of Grandath managed to stay green. Perhaps the giant redwood trunks held on to life more deeply than other trees; or maybe the roots sipped of sustenance held within the ground far below. Even still, maybe there was something in the air here, some unseen power that even Morgui's strength could not dissuade.

"Well," Naronel replied with a question, "how many days does it normally take for you to make Bensotha from the Great Plains?" Daunt knew where this was going. He bent his head and watched the raindrops splatter in the muddy pools made by marching feet. His steed whinnied and bobbed its head.

"Easy, Sidbrynn. Peace to you." Daunt slipped his hand along the wet skin of his horse's neck and whispered gently. Then he looked up and returned Naronel's gaze. "It takes seven days on foot and four on horse. Because we are eight days along you assume we are lost?"

"Aye, I do."

Nenrick joined them after coming up from the back of the line. His horse slowed, pulling its feet strenuously from the mire.

"Lord of Somahguard, how do you fare this morning?" Naronel asked.

"Weary, my friends, and not ashamed to say so, as I am sure to be in the company of others who bode the same."

Daunt smiled a little more easily this time, encouraged by Nenrick's humility. "Of that you can be assured." Nenrick dismounted to join Daunt, as did Naronel. "How many is the count today?"

"We are nearly ten thousand, save for the scouts."

"And have they brought any reports?"

Nenrick was silent and lowered his head. His skin was deep black in the low light; only the whites of his eyes and teeth stood out when he spoke.

"In two days, no."

"Two days?" Naronel uttered wildly.

"Two days."

"Surely one of them has returned?" Daunt questioned.

"Of fifty I released, none have returned. Their orders were to return by sundown, the next morning at the latest."

"Then we must assume they are lost," Naronel said.

"Lost or—"

Daunt raised a hand to stop Nenrick. "Let us assume they are as directionless as we are."

"But they are the best trackers and readers in the east!" Naronel added, his voice losing hope.

"Then we admit there must be something veiling our way." Daunt looked upward and searched for any direction from the sun. "Something resists our progress and confuses our perception."

"And all the while a battle rages on without us," Naronel said staring into the woods.

"Athera be near them," Nenrick whispered and then no one else spoke.

They were tired and cold, and they had run out of things to talk about. They all stood holding the reins of their horses as the rain smothered them like a blanket, dripping heavily from the immense leaves above. Naronel shivered and clenched his hands. How could it be that the same formidable battle host that rallied together in the east just a few days prior was now a ten thousand-man line of weakness and misdirection? And all this before even swinging a sword or pulling back a bowstring.

Riding through Grandath and taking the enemy by surprise had seemed an easy enough endeavor. And everyone in the march savored the thought of sending the Dairne-Reih back to their pit. But the battle lust had been beaten out of them by the cold and lack of nourishment. The enemy had executed a cunning scheme void of confrontation and self-detriment afforded by its unseen and unattended nature; rather than physically strike a man only to be supported by one following behind, Morgui succeeded in belittling and stripping the men of their dignity at war, their desire even to press on against adversity. He knew they would be coming from the east and his control of the air and the elements had surely elevated. So, casting a haze of confusion and a storm to prey upon the ever-growing mortality of Dionia's warriors was a work done from a remote place and time, allowing all eyes to be fixed on destroying Adriel and leaving the Kings of the East to their own demise. *Maybe we should turn back,* each man thought to himself. *Maybe we are not supposed to go. What if our own land needs to be defended; who will save our families and our lands?*

The ranks of men stretched on through half the forest, it seemed. All were beginning to wonder why they had come. *Where is the battle?* they thought. Their pride was in shambles as they yearned for places to sit and rest their saddle-sore legs, finally resorting to the muck underfoot; it was disgraceful. All down the path men sought shelter by huddling close to tree trunks in order to escape the unrelenting drizzle, now days of it. Their clothes were caked with mud and they sat amongst the feces of horses, too tired to care. Talk among some men finally turned to the subject of turning back and heading home. No one mentioned that they didn't know which direction home was, but some course of action had to be taken as their leaders obviously were failing at it miserably. Days of slow trudging through a thick soup of a trail had rendered them hopeless and misdirected in more ways than one. Through it all one among them managed to sort out a thread of hope and was determined to follow its course no matter how dark it became.

"We must move on!" Daunt resolved suddenly. The other two kings snapped out of their lethargy. "We must make Adriel! We must not fail our brothers!" The Horse King leapt onto Sidbrynn's back and kicked hard against the auburn flanks.

"But how do you know which way to go?" Naronel yelled. Daunt spun his horse in a wash of mud and water, shouting from the back of his throat.

"Have we so quickly forgotten the direction and leading of the Great Spirit? Is His arm too short to rescue us? Is His voice too soft to break through the deafening of our enemy's call? No, my brothers! No, good kings of Dionia! There is still hope! As I breathe, there is still hope!" he yelled and turned his horse down the trail, Sidbrynn notably stirred with renewed vigor and zeal. Naronel and Nenrick looked at each other, but before they could speak a word, a warrior on horseback ripped through the mire beside them in hot pursuit of Daunt, kicking up a spray as he went. They watched in shock.

"Who—," but Naronel was shut up; another rider rushed by followed by two more. The two kings turned behind them to see all the men mounting their horses with a great pack of them already galloping toward them after Daunt. It was just what was needed. The fire of freedom had been rekindled even more quickly than it had been snuffed out, and the embers had been fanned once again into a blaze of determination.

"But where is he going?" Naronel asked loudly above the stampede.

"Have a little faith, my friend," Nenrick exhorted as he leapt upon his mount. "There remains at least one king in Dionia with more fortitude and persuasion than I, and for that I'm willing to follow him, even if he's wrong. He-yah!" With that Nenrick was caught up in the river of warhorses and their riders.

• • •

"Archers on the mark!" Benigan cried out from below, rallying their attention to the main track and the trestle walls. He yanked Luik from his horse and they ran up to the ramparts together. "How many have we lost?"

"I'd say at least two thousand!" Luik yelled above the frantic clamor. "That many?"

"Aye, maybe more. The spearmen were lost, all of them." But Benigan did not have a chance to reply with the grief he felt within. They had mounted the last step and were let through the rows of archers to survey the battlefield. The plan had worked as intended; the Dairne-Reih were pressed to form a single column leading straight up to the City Gate. The archers let out a constant stream of unrelenting torment from all along the wall. Any sense of accomplishment Luik and Benigan felt quickly dissipated as they surveyed further out into the darkness.

"If he could not seduce us, he will crush us." Benigan spoke without moving a muscle. Luik suddenly felt distraught at his noble friend's words, maybe because he was the biggest and most fearless of all his friends, or maybe also because he had once rescued Luik's life; what if Luik could not rescue his? The entire peninsula of Casterness had turned into a churning tide of torches and evil, moving forward with sadistic resolve. The land was so bloated with the demon hoard that even the shorelines and waters absorbed the overflow. Surely the most disheartening sight of all was the masses that still continued to pour from the waterfall's edges; Adriel hadn't yet seen all of Morgui's number.

"How can that be?" Benigan asked bewildered.

"I don't know my friend, but this will surely be the longest of nights."

Benigan simply shook his head.

"Take courage, Dibor!" Luik hit him on the back. "There is still a king in Adriel and there is yet a friend beside you!"

• • •

"Rest easy, my king," Li-Saide said softly. Fane pulled the heavy blanket up over the wounded royal and pressed down the sides to tuck him in. Two attendants stoked the fire in Ragnar's bedchamber and brought the supplies Li-Saide had requested. Torches had been moved in to properly light the area, and ample towels had been stacked beside vessels of fresh water. The attendants still did not understand the strange orders of boiling the water, but they had no desire to cross the dwarf in the midst of such dire circumstances; he clearly knew what he was doing.

"Even the water seeks to take our king's life," Li-Saide had told them when they first made to move the king to his room. "All is set against us."

Other strange items had been gathered for the dwarf including plant leaves from the royal reserves, herbal extracts from the kitchen, and even a knife that had been held in flames and then washed with launderer's soap, only to be heated once more before being wrapped in a clean towel.

"Leave us!" Li-Saide finally asked with great force.

The door swung shut and Fane took a deep breath.

"Do you think—"

"I do not know. Come," the dwarf answered," bring me a towel, water, and the knife."

• • •

The mangled heap of corpses piled high down the center lane leading to the City Gate like a drainage trough brimming over with floodwater. Luik walked along the southernmost rampart encouraging the archers in their deadly assault. He watched as the demons climbed over one another in a desperate attempt to reach the wall. He marveled at the Dairneag's complete and perfect absence of fear as they relentlessly surged forward. As expected, with the increasing number of slain victims cut down by the arrows the trestle walls finally gave out one at a time, shattering under the immense pressure; but not before their massive spikes claimed scores of attacking foe in mid stride.

"The lane widens now! Be on your guard!" Luik's words were spread rapidly down the walls. He had quickly become the commanding authority on the wall along with Benigan. Brax and Boran stood attentively on the ramparts to the far right and left while Jrio joined with Fyfler and the rest of the Dibor in the city below. They organized the remaining swordsmen for the brutal attack should the Dairne-Reih break through the outer gate. Things were still going according to plan, except for the considerably larger mass of the enemy than was expected.

"Where do they keep coming from?" Benigan asked as Luik returned from a jog down the right flank on the southern most part of the wall. They both looked out over the peninsula to the waterfall once more. There was no end to the onslaught.

"I am beginning to wonder," Luik said more quietly so as to let no one overhear.

"Go on," Benigan prodded.

"Are we really killing them?"

"Pardon?"

"Tell me, Benigan, what happens to a dead spirit when it is killed?"

Benigan thought for a moment. "I never thought about that."

"Aye, isn't it strange that none of us have?"

"So what are you saying?"

Luik stared off the side of the wall far below.

"I think they are merely playing with us. Watch the way they show no fear as they bound headlong into our archers." Luik pointed to one dark beast clambering over a pile of dead. Its beady eyes stared up in resilience as more than ten and twenty arrows gorged into its chest and shoulders, finally bidding it away to the fate of those before it.

"Either that is truly courage and tenacity of the most demonic sort—"

"Or they are assured of another attempt," Luik offered.

"They are immortal?"

"They are regenerating. How can you kill what has already been cast out of the presence of the Most High? My father once told me that in other worlds, the Dairne-Reih are invisible, just spirits without form, but here we see a physical body, a true representation of reality. If that body is as much a shell or case as ours is, where is their spirit released to?"

"Right back into another state of being. Another body, perhaps?"

"Perhaps," Luik said with his eyes examining the distant hill, "*or exactly*."

"So we are simply stopping them here only to replenish their numbers at the source."

"Aye."

Benigan was quiet for a moment.

"Do you have any ideas, Luik?"

"One," he said turning to Benigan.

"And?"

"Let us hope Gorn is still alive and that he figures out what we have. They are closer to that hilltop than we ever could be right now."

Benigan breathed deeply, realizing that Luik's answer had nothing to do with any means within his own ability.

"What about the Horse King and the warriors from the eastern lands?" Benigan asked.

"They should have been here days ago. I fear they are lost or have been ambushed just as Purgos was."

"But there remains some hope they may come."

"Aye, a thread of hope."

Suddenly cries were heard within the city.

"They're on the northern wall!" Benigan pointed to the ramparts. In the torchlight the two men could make out three Dairneags thrashing at a group of archers. A handful were knocked clear off the wall and tumbled into the houses far below.

"They're mounting the walls!" Luik yelled. He turned toward the palace above and hollered as loud as he could. "Rab!" He waved his arms in a panic. "*Rab!*" It was pointless. The distance to the King's Gatehouse was too great. Even on a quiet day a shout would only be an echo by the time it reached to the palace wall.

"You there!" Luik grabbed one of the archers closest to him. "Light an arrow." The archer was quick to the task. "Send it through the window there, on the King's Gatehouse." The archer regarded Luik oddly. "Do it, man!" The archer drew back and loosed the arrow. One shot was all he needed.

Rab had moved back down from his tower perch to the Gatehouse should anyone need him. He was busy watching the progress of the siege when he caught a bright speck out of the corner of his eye. It flashed wide in size, and his reflexes twisted his head out of the way. The incoming arrow whizzed by and smacked hard against the far wall behind him, the vibration simmering away as the flames gently ate up the shaft. He pulled the arrow from the wall and trampled the flames out, then looked down to where it came from. He saw a distant figure waving his arms frantically in the air. He looked harder and realized it was Luik.

"Hey'a!" Rab yelled with a wave out the window. Then Luik stopped waving and pointed across the great expanse of the city. Rab's eye followed the gesture across the housetops to the center lane. Hundreds of men stood ready with swords drawn.

"What?" Rab mouthed with little voice but with great expression from his hands. *What is he pointing to?*

Luik pumped his arm again signaling further away this time. Rab looked again, but this time commotion on the left wall caught his attention. It was a Dairneag. Nay, three of them! Rab spun around and grabbed the horn from a wall-mounted cradle. He held it to his lips and gave three long blasts followed by a fourth signaling the swordsmen to the ramparts. The city was a swirl of movement in an instant.

Luik turned to the young man, quickly thanking him. "What is your name?"

"Guyana, of Ligeon."

"One of Thorn's men?"

"Aye."

"You are good with that bow."

"Thank you, but I had the best teacher."

It was no time for talking but somehow Luik's interest was stirred.

"Let me guess, he stands on the wall there to the north. Gyinan of Ligeon?"

"No, one of his students; and Gyinan is not from Ligeon." The last words stung Luik's memory with a residue of disdained trivia.

"His students?" Luik asked?

"Aye, the Princess of Ligeon."

"O? Which of them?"

"Anorra."

Luik's soul quivered. He saw her face whisper through his mind's eye. His heart raced. He was instantly caught up in thinking what she must look like now, so many summers later. Then his thoughts turned to her well-being. *Is she all right?* But more importantly, *where is she?* All at once a new emotion surged through Luik's heart, one he had never felt before. A new sense of survival penetrated his thoughts and deposited a resolute fortitude far greater than preserving just his own life for his own life's sake; it was preserving his own life for *her* sake. He was no longer fighting for just himself or all of Dionia even; *I am fighting for Anorra. I must live to see her one more time*, he thought.

"Sir," Guyana said a third time, "are you all right?" Luik snapped from his thoughts.

"Aye, Anorra, just fine."

The young man was baffled.

"You just called me Anorra, sir."

Luik winced. "Aye, sorry for that, I meant, what is your name again?"

"Guyana."

"Right, so sorry, Guyana. Maybe we will meet again one day. Fight for the King!" With that Luik ran toward the Gatehouse and drew his sword, shaking off his thoughts, but not her face.

• • •

By the time the kings of the east finally emerged from their wanderings in the Great Forest, the battle fires illuminated the distant sky above Casterness like an orange ember suspended in the low lying clouds. For all the rain that soaked the ground, there still arose a haze of dust and debris that smothered the battle lines like fog. Through it all, the sounds of battle, of men pitted against demons in a fight to the death, screeched through the air as if sent on the wings of a wounded falcon pleading for aid.

"We are not too late!" Naronel said defiantly, pausing on the edge of the forest.

"Let us go quickly so as not to prolong an ill-fated appointment!" Nenrick said as he drew his sword. Daunt turned in his seat and called loudly over his shoulder.

"We make for Adriel! And we bind to death whatever comes between us!"

The three kings rode hard toward the glowing light as a surge of mounted warriors followed quickly behind. Like a mighty headwater, the Great Forest gave birth to a river of horse and rider, spewing them out as if it could no longer bear the pressure pent up within. Bushes tore as horses leapt over them, tearing the foliage with their hooves; low limbs of trees shattered, pummeled by shields and severed by swords. There seemed to be no end to the great line that ripped out of the shrouded forest and into the eastern most meadows of Bensotha. Though covered by a dark twilight, the horses, free at last from days in the shadowed forest, yearned for every stride and dug hard into the grassy expanses; the animals of the plains were not used to the smothering blanket of Grandath and gulped the open air about them. The men, too, were finally grateful for the summons into wide stretching plains and rolling hills once more. Hooves thundered forward and shook every blade of grass within reach. What they had come for was finally within reach. One more day of riding and their swords were certain to taste blood.

• • •

Li-Saide had removed the dart and lanced the now swollen wound, releasing a caustic flow of dark fluid that saturated the towels. The king remained unconscious, something that worried Li-Saide, but he was glad for the lack of pain this would surely be causing. After a brief moment of pressing out any remaining puss with his fingers, he bent near and sucked at the laceration, spitting whatever was in his mouth into a pitcher in Fane's hands. He continued this for another few moments before splashing the neck with water and a medicinal wash. Fane quickly dried the wound and handed Li-Saide the prescribed herbal pack. The dwarf swiped up some of the mashed leaves and ground-up roots and pushed them into the hole with his finger. Fane winced in proxy for the king. Then Li-Saide pressed the pack against the king's neck and bound it with a bandage.

"What now?"

"We intercede," Li-Saide answered, "—and wait."

They both bent low over the bed and began to speak blessings over the king, audibly praising the Great God for Ragnar's life, his rule and reign, and the blessing the Creator had been in bestowing such a marvelous man to lead them. They blessed the Name of the Most High for His gracious act of rendering unto men leaders who were not ashamed of their Maker and who had no other ambition or agenda than to remain in His Presence and ensure all people of the same. The atmosphere in the room was changing, but Fane never sensed it, at least not with his intellect. They were establishing the Great King's rule and authority in the room. Soon the words of their hearts shifted, combating and resisting whatever unseen forces were attacking the king's well-being. They came against powers and principalities of unseen realms, dominions of darkness, and authorities that had changed the dynamics of their world to such a state that the wound of a king might go unhealed.

Fane became so adamant that he forgot about where he was. He forgot about the room he was kneeling in and the people around him, even the king of Dionia. He took on such a weight of responsibility that he even failed to recognize his own words. The burden of life and death had become his. He had yielded so much of his will to the Mighty Father that he simply lost himself and found *Him*. Suddenly the asking and telling of his lips was not his own anymore, but another's. Li-Saide stopped for a brief moment and looked up. Fane was no longer speaking Dionian, but the ancient tongues of the Mosfar. He was speaking in the purest of words, removed from understanding and flesh; he was speaking in the Spirit. Li-Saide smiled wide and began uttering fully in the Spirit with him. They were lost now, lost in the realm of Athera, touching the very presence of God once more, even in the midst of a world so consumed with evil. It was in this place that promise became louder than reality; no matter how lost Dionia may become, the presence of the Most High would always be attainable for those who would choose to die to themselves for it.

But would there always be one willing enough?

• • •

The first rays of dawn touched the tops of the clouds like a gentle breeze caressing cotton blossoms. This high the air was clean and the space about it was vast and pure. The sun washed away the night as effortlessly as a wave sliding over sand. But far below in what seemed a world away, shrouded beneath the overcast sky in war, Luik lifted his head toward the dim sky and pulled in a morbid breath of rot and rancid decay. Flames licked the flesh of man and beast alike, sending up a foul, thick smoke skyward. It was a haze that smothered Adriel like a plague.

The continually advancing Dairne-Reih had slowed during the pre-dawn hours. Fewer and fewer demons attempted to climb the walls only to be hewn away by the awaiting swordsmen Rab had summoned to the ramparts with his horn around midnight. The line of Dairneags pressing down the central lane also receded. By early afternoon nothing approached closer than five tree lengths in front of the City Gate. The battle had reached an apparent lull.

Trampled corpses mashed in the rush were all that stood between the city wall and a line of waiting demons who stood a short distance off, stretching all the way back over the distant hill. Clearly every home, every residence, every track of land, and every tree had been destroyed beneath their feet. In the face of such destruction there sat a heavy stillness over the entire scene. It was the most awkward moment of the battle for Luik and the rest of the Dibor in the city. *Why had they stopped? Clearly the Sons of Ad were outnumbered! Why didn't they mount the walls and crush them?*

This was also the first time most of the men of Dionia had had an opportunity to carefully examine their foe with any great detail. The Dairne-Reih stood shoulder-to-shoulder, their chests heaving for breath and muscles still tensed, awaiting some unheard signal to arms. Each one was as ugly as the next, all forged from the same vessel of evil it seemed. But oddly, each creature was unique; some had eyes as wide as fists while others were small, narrow slits that didn't blink; some mouths were large, gaping wide with rows of pristine teeth, others were closed but mangled teeth protruded nonetheless; horns of all sizes pierced out of their bodies in the strangest of places. Some Dairneags had skin of deepest black while others showed hues of red, purple, and blue. Most stood still, intently looking toward the city as they dripped with fluid of the most horrific sort. A few groups worked to collect the bodies of the fallen and heap them up in burning piles of the dead. This smell was far more disconcerting than the sight of them, and Luik began to think they knew it, too.

King Lair and King Thorn, having both been kicked from Ragnar's bedchamber by the small but very demonstrative dwarf, finally made their way through the city and down to meet Luik in the gatehouse. The demons must have sensed the presence of royalty because they let out a multitude of weird screeches when the kings looked through the crenellations to observe the throng without.

"What is going on, Luik?" Lair asked his son.

"The attack has subsided." Luik was very pleased to see his father.

"But only momentarily, I would think," added Thorn. Both kings donned new metal battle armor provided by Ragnar, swords hanging from their sides. They wore long capes from their shoulders and had recently been given ornate but functional head coverings, told they would protect against blows to the head. The strange golden *helmets*, as they had been called, were forged out of the same type of steel as their swords were, strong, resilient and nearly unbreakable. They remained open in the front with a wide metal strip coming down from the forehead to cover the nose, and a leather chinstrap to secure the helmet tightly in place.

"What's this?" Luik asked pointing to their new gear.

"A gift from the king's armorer," his father replied with a tap on his head. "It is said to be nearly impenetrable."

"Who needs it?" Thorn scoffed. "But they wouldn't let us leave without them, and they made us promise to not take them off." Luik smiled at Thorn's obvious discontent.

"How many men do we have left, Son?"

Luik led the way to a set of stairs and climbed up to the roof of the gatehouse with the kings for a better view. He pointed as he spoke.

"On the northern wall Brax commands nearly two hundred archers, as does Boran to the south. Six of the other Dibor have command over about twenty-three ranks of swordsmen in the city below, there and there, some of which you also see along the ramparts." He gestured to them accordingly. "Dairne-Reih were climbing the bare walls earlier, and Rab, the Dibor in the tower, summoned a defense to the walls."

"Well done," Thorn said loudly. "And the spearmen?"

Luik hesitated. He knew most of them had come from Ligeon. "Perished," he said solemnly, "to the man." Thorn's expression was one of stupefied disbelief. Luik thought the king would challenge his remark, but then he noticed the king's cheeks flush red and the veins bulge along his neck.

"By the Great God in Athera, I swear that I will avenge their deaths by nightfall a hundredfold!" He raised a fist out over the valley floor and spit in the air. No one questioned his resolve.

"And you will have your chance, my friend," Lair laid a hand on Thorn's armored shoulder. "T'will soon be upon us. Luik, what of the rest of the archers?"

"Most were slain there, to the right side of the waterfall. Jrio and a few others made it back before the gate closed."

Luik surveyed the eerily quiet host of Dairneags below. Thousands upon thousands of them stretched out and back up the hill. They wrapped around the sides of the city down to the waterline, many standing up to their waists in the surf, all simply standing by. *Waiting for orders*, Luik thought. *But what is this all about? Why are they waiting? Is Morgui afraid of something? Is there something confusing him or his minions? Maybe it is all part of his plan; maybe Morgui is simply letting his victims writhe in unknown terror before dealing the deathblow.*

"Our assets include the swordsmen within the city, the walls with their height and vantage, and the archers," Luik said as he listed them on his fingers.

"What of Gorn and the other Dibor, have they fallen, too?" Thorn asked.

"Nay, I hope not. They left at the beginning of the fight riding south along the coast and then presumably up and behind the bulk of the enemy."

"With so few men?" asked Lair.

"I have learned not to question the man I have so fully come to trust," Luik said persuasively.

"Well spoken," his father said. "I will adhere to such a statement in like mind. Any sign of the western kings?"

"Nothing. I fear they may be lost."

Lair and Thorn both lowered their heads, thinking the same.

Speaking of kings—"How are Purgos and his men?" Luik asked.

"Not yet ready for the fight, I'm afraid," his father continued.

"No?"

"Their trek south was far more troubling than their appearances let on."

"*Worse?*" Luik asked surprised.

"Aye, imagine that? Seems now they are plagued by dreams of the worst kind, a slew of memories combined with subjects of terror and an unimaginable woe."

"In their sleep?"

Lair nodded his head. "They are so weary from the lack of rest the dreams produce that they can only manage to stay awake for a brief time before falling back. Even now they struggle to wake, and many to tears, crying after wives, children, and kin."

"I, too, had a dream in the barracks," Luik said.

"Have you now?" Both Lair and Thorn looked at Luik.

"But I have had it many times before." Luik's voice grew quieter.

"What of, my son?" Lair drew close. Luik hesitated.

"My death, Ta na," Luik whispered. Lair raised his eyebrows, but Luik could not see them under Lair's helmet.

Sensing the awkward moment, Thorn jumped in. "Well, we may have another asset that we did not count on, lads."

Luik and Lair turned to regard the grand king. "And what is that?"

"The Knights of the Lion."

There was an awkward silence.

"You mean, *the Lion Vrie?*" Luik sputtered.

"The same," Thorn said with a nod.

"But they are just a story of men who fought long ago!" Luik was beside himself.

"Perhaps, but if they are indeed real, then they would be here in Adriel for such a time as this."

"True, King Thorn," said Lair.

"Ta na, you are serious?" Luik was quite surprised. Truly there must have been such an order of warrior during the First Battle as told and retold for generations, but to actually think that such a rank existed now was unimaginable. Every piece of land in Dionia was accounted for, every name of every man, every task of every laborer.

"There is no such person who bears that title!" Luik said adamantly. "And if there was, why have they not yet come?"

"Calm yourself, Son," Lair placed a hand on Luik's shoulder.

"Why would they allow hundreds of men to perish without bothering to raise a sword with them?" Luik demanded. "Then they are not as noble as we would have believed. Cursed be their endeavors for having the means but failing to preserve and protect Life!"

"Luik!" Lair said. "Do not utter such words!"

"But Father, what can be said of such men who allow death to be executed on such a level, condoning it with their absence and abdicating their responsibility?"

"Luik of the Dibor, you do not know what is done in secret," Thorn said as he rested his hand on Luik's back.

"Then tell me now so that I may be comforted in the deaths of so many!" Luik shrugged away from the king's hand. He neared the edge of the roof and tried to compose himself. A tear seeped from his eye and ran warmly beside his nose. For the first time during the siege his emotions flourished, and he was instantly overwhelmed by the great loss of life he had just witnessed. He had managed to hide everything very well, even finding humor in the strangest of places; but there was a limit and it had been reached. Though he was surely one of the greatest students of war that mankind had ever seen, no amount of training could have ever prepared him for such a day as this. He had learned how to steward his emotions and govern his thoughts, but he had no idea how to cope with seeing grown men dashed to pieces and torn from limb to limb before his very eyes. War is romantic only to those who have never lived it. Blood stained his cheeks and was caked on his hands and arms. Even his beloved sword, gifted weapon of the Dibor, was bruised and forever tainted by the shades of battle. Tears began to flow more freely.

"My son," his father said softly. Luik turned into his father's arms and gently wept on his shoulder. Thorn lowered his head. There is no weakness in weeping, only weakness in those who are not honest to their own hearts. Luik was as genuine about his heart as any man could have ever hoped to be. It was a priceless moment. Soon Lair spoke up as he hugged his son.

"Luik, Thorn is right. There are many things done in secret that we do not know about, and we may never understand why they are done just so. At the time they seem foolish or wrong, but there are always those with greater foresight than our own, greater wisdom for what yet awaits."

In the demon ranks below there was a soft murmuring; the death hunger was growing stronger.

Lair looked at the masses and then turned to his son, speaking softly. "When this battle is over, there remains one such thing I must share with you."

Luik pulled away. "What? What is it?" he asked, curious.

"There is some truth that has been spared you," his father said. "I'd tell you now only for the sake that if I do not survive this battle you would be forever ignorant. But should I fall, you must seek out the dwarf, Li-Saide."

"What are you talking about, Ta na?" Luik was frustrated.

The strange murmuring among the Dairne-Reih was increasing.

"Peace, my son! Listen to me now! Seek out the dwarf, he was there. He remembers all, and he will not lie. The tribes of Ot cannot lie. Remember, Luik, promise me!"

"I promise!" Luik was notably shaken. He could not fathom that his father had a secret to tell, and more, why not tell him himself? Why such precaution given to seek out the dwarf? His father had no reason to be afraid. He was a king after all! Kings were rarely called home to the Great Throne Room; but within moments Luik's spirit reminded him of the dark times in which he lived, and he came to grips with his father's wisdom.

"I promise to seek out Li-Saide," Luik said as he raised a bloodstained hand and smeared his tears across his dirty face.

"Kinsmen, I regret to interrupt once more, but if you have anything more to say it should be put so quickly. Something stirs from among the enemy host."

Luik and Lair turned to look out over the masses. The Dairne-Reih were growing restless, bobbing and swaying with growls, and clucks chattered up from throughout their host. Arms began swinging and many of them jumped with anticipation. Even more waded into the flanking ocean waters and pressed the sides of the peninsula.

"They make to charge!" Thorn yelled, realizing the inevitable was upon them.

"Hold fast along the walls!" Luik yelled down the line. "Jrio!" The tan-faced warrior looked up from the main city road below.

"Luik!" Jrio replied.

"More swordsmen to the ramparts! Reinforce the lines! They make to pile over our flanks!"

"Right!" Jrio began shouting orders to his fellow Dibor and then on to the foot soldiers. Hundreds of men rushed up and filled out evenly along the entire wall all the way to where it met the base of the inner Palace Wall further back on the peninsula. The remaining men began dismantling the structures intended to confine the demons to the center lane should they have broken through the City Gate. But it was clear now the gate posed no real deterrent; the Dairne-Reih would simply climb the walls and overwhelm them with sheer mass.

"Where would you like us, Son?" Lair asked.

"Why, you are kings! Go where you wish." Luik was astounded.

"But we are asking you, battle chief. Where can we serve you best?" Thorn said, agreeing with Lair. Such humility was truly the mark of the greatest kings.

"The fighting will be the fiercest here at the center. So I think—"

"Then that's where we'll be," Thorn said.

"No! I mean to—"

"Are we not kings?" Lair protested.

Luik was dumbfounded.

"Then do not argue with us!" They pushed Luik out of the way and drew their swords. They were crafty indeed.

"So we face them one last time together?" Thorn yelled loudly looking to Lair.

"Aye, that we do, King of Ligeon!" Lair removed his cape and discarded it on the roof with a grand arch of his arm. Thorn followed in like manner, his cape flourishing off the side of the roof.

"For the Glory of the King of all kings and the Lord of all lords!" Thorn boomed.

"For the Glory of the Most High!" Lair yelled aloud.

"For the Glory of the Warrior King!" Luik shouted, standing next to his father, sword lofted high. The two kings looked over at him and gave a grin.

It wasn't a moment later that the end had begun. Tearing through the atmosphere like a thunderclap, the likes of which had never been heard, the entire enemy war host was a frenzy of horrific noise, derived from some deeply demonic source of energy and bitter hatred. But the warrior men of Dionia were not to be so quickly drowned out. Their volleyed replies were the cries of those fighting valiantly for their survival, and more, for that which they knew was right: for Truth that spat in the face of every wicked lie; for Life that surpassed the strongest chains of death; and for a Love so deep that any man among them would have bravely taken on the whole lot of them if faced with the choice of denying its existence or fighting.

Luik watched in a marveled terror as the enemy surged forward like a massive lunging wave, scaling the wall like spiders, claws gouging deeply into the stone. But it was Rab who saw everything most clearly from high up above the city; his mouth gaped wide, hands clinging to the stone window, as the Dairne-Reih spilled over the outer wall, poured into the city like water cascading over the rim of a goblet, and filled the basin within.

• • •

"Look, there!" Nenrick hollered above the thunder of horse hooves, pointing with his sword to a thin line on the horizon.

"Their easternmost flank!" Naronel quickly surmised.

"Aye!" Nenrick grunted.

"Battle line!" Daunt yelled, waving his sword in circles above his head. They were not too late. The multitude of horsemen behind them suddenly started to merge up the sides in a slow change of formation, each following the lead of the next. Over the next few moments the mounted warriors spread out to form a wide, concave arch nearly a thousand wide and ten rows deep. It was a highly practiced maneuver, but normally at a fraction of the size. The only difference was the added time needed for the furthermost riders to reach the edges while still keeping up with the advancing center. The three kings slowed slightly to give the outermost riders an easier time. When the formation was squared up, the line advanced again at a full gallop.

A front line of lunging necks and prodding hooves ate up the ground with tremendous speed. Warhorses of every color flew forward, muscles flexing and heads bobbing in rhythm, with adorning manes swishing in the air. Spears protruded between their heads and swords were held high. Though every man and horse was nearly exhausted from the days of hardship and sleepless nights, they ran on as if it were a new day, knowing it may be their last. From here on out it was not their endurance that prompted them onward, but a power unseen that gave them strength beyond their own resources. The enemy line closed with every stride, growing clearer all the while. *It won't be long now*, they all thought, *just a little further*.

Each man encouraged his horse with shouts and whoops. They responded in like measure by not lessening the pace despite their obvious discomfort and fatigue. Sweat turned to foam on every flank and thigh. Breathing became labored and more rapid, but still the horses galloped on. They sensed the weight of this day as much as their riders did, and would not fail on their part as long as it was within their power to perform it. Extra breaths were taken off rhythm just to make up for the lack of air in their lungs. They blew out with snorts and grunted against the pain; *almost there*.

The mighty roar of the closing cavalry was not a secret for long. Soon a Dairneag on the fringe of the line, a dark horn sprouting from its bluish forehead, felt the earth quake and turned to find its source. Its eyes met the awesome sight of nearly ten thousand mounted warriors surging toward them with unrelenting power. For the first time in ages, the demon felt a righteous fear wash over its dark soul and permeate its being. It let out a screech that drew the attention of many more which all spun around in kind. It even caught the attention of another who was surprised to see that his plans to delay the eastern Kings, if not kill them, had failed. A deep growl emanated from beneath his black hood. Bony fingers with long nails closed together and squeezed in rage as he watched the advancing warriors. Suddenly the cloaked figure raised his arms and opened his hands wide. A distorted power wave shot out from his palms and expanded through the atmosphere, rippling the air.

Daunt pressed his horse harder. He could see the demons turning now to address the confrontation. The Dairne-Reih formed a line, and thousands filled in behind the first. Another few moments and they would meet head on. Then a shock wave met Daunt, smacking him and all the other riders in the face. He winced in discomfort but urged Sidbrynn forward. Daunt's head swirled and he felt dizzy, holding tightly to his horse's mane for balance. All at once he realized it was no longer the air that sent him reeling, but the ground shaking beneath his horse. The valley shook so violently, a few horses were knocked clear off their feet, sending many others around them and their riders to a trampled end. Daunt and Sidbrynn managed to regain their sense of balance despite the movement beneath them, but up ahead they both saw clearly what was causing all the mayhem. A giant crack had appeared across the width of the valley floor. It started as a thin line and rapidly widened to a span and then two. It shot sideways covering the entire width of the advancing warriors and then some. Rocks shattered and heaved broken stone debris into the air. The separation grew wider by the second, the sub-level walls violently tearing away from each other all the way to the edges.

There was no going around it, and there was not time to slow down. Whatever distance was being forged by the evil below would have to be embraced without a second guess. The closer Daunt rode, the wider the crack grew. What he thought only moments before would be a manageable jump suddenly turned into a leap of blind faith. The crack was now a chasm, a gorge spiraling down into an abyss without end. He had not come this far to stop or be redirected. He would not bow to such a threat!

Out of the corner of his eye he watched in horror as a few brave warriors surged ahead of the line in a desperate attempt to jump the expanse before it widened any further. They rushed forward, their valiant steeds leaping high into the air. Daunt realized as they hung suspended in midair that the power was not enough for many of them. Only five or six managed to land safely on the other side. The rest slammed into the far wall, some with front legs straining at the top of the other side only to lose the struggle and tumble to a dark fate. The Horse King could not allow the emotion to deter his concentration, or that of his mount. He yelled loudly and kicked Sidbrynn's flanks for all he was worth. The noble horse did not fail to respond in the least.

Ten more strides and they were there, and it came in an instant. Daunt squeezed with his legs and held his breath as Sidbrynn's back arched before the violent jerk forward, a motion that would have sent a less experienced rider right off the back. Daunt looked down over his horse's right shoulder into the sea of unending black below them. It was in that weightless and silent moment that Daunt knew he would never see Jerovah again.

• • •

Ragnar's mouth gaped wide and he let out a deep, gut-wrenching groan that nearly startled Fane right out of the room. Li-Saide stood up and drew near.

"My king!" he said forcefully. "Can you hear me?"

Ragnar let out another groan and winced at the pain coming from his neck. His eyes shot wide-open with the excruciating discomfort. He looked frantically around the room but everything was out of focus.

"Who's-ere?" His first words were a mumbled, raspy whisper.

"This is Li-Saide, my lord, and Fane is with me as well." Fane just nodded, too afraid to speak.

The king yelped again against the pain. It was apparently much worse than Li-Saide had deduced. Ragnar tried moving his right arm up to his head.

"I cuh move muhrm." He squeezed his eyes and pursed his lips. A tear escaped the corner of his eye.

"Rest, my king. Do not try and move. We are here for you. Fane, the goblet!" Fane turned and produced a small drinking vessel of plant and juice extracts, handing it to Li-Saide. The dwarf noticed the shaking in Fane's hands.

"Try to drink this, Ragnar, it will soothe the pain." He ever so gently lifted the king's head and pressed the rim to his lips. A little of the drink found its way down Ragnar's swollen throat but, with a cough, the rest poured out the corners of his mouth and down his neck. Li-Saide refused any indecency and swiftly dried up his skin and neck. "Easy, easy there," Li-Saide prodded.

"Hu—," the king coughed deeply, "hu is Drie–el?"

"The warriors make a defense of the city as we—," Li-Saide tried to answer but Ragnar went into a convulsion and began coughing again. The dwarf grabbed a towel and held it near his mouth as blood flew into it. The king did the best he could to spit up the rest.

Fane looked back and forth incessantly between Li-Saide and the king, searching desperately for a sign of hope. Li-Saide felt his shifting eyes and regarded him solemnly. *What?* Fane asked. Then he heard Li-Saide's voice in his spirit. *We are losing him.*

"No!" Fane yelled out loud.

"Hush, my friend. Take the quill and the parchment there, on the table. Quickly!"

• • •

The first Dairneag that rose above the crest of the gatehouse had been fully driven through with arrows. By the time it weakly looked into Luik's eyes, it was all over. The Dibor yelled and lowered his Vinfae straight on top of its head, splitting it like a melon. The next two demons were also in a weakened state from the archer's assault, but their bloodlust drove them on in a wild state only to meet similar fates. The fourth had managed to scale the wall unscathed, and his power was full. He leapt in front of Luik and swung swiftly from right to left. Luik ducked and jabbed his blade deeply into the demon's stomach. It screamed and then brought its arm back across to the right. Luik let go of his sword and leapt, twisting high into the air as the giant horned limb passed beneath him. In midair he reached below and took the handle, withdrawing the weapon cleanly, only to swing it around with the momentum of his spinning body, connecting with a knee at the last moment. The damaging blow severed the leg in two and sent the beast tumbling back off the roof to the sea of demons below.

"Hey'a!" Lair yelled. "Marvelous deed!"

"C'symia!" Luik smiled. "Watch it!" Lair turned to see a black beast summit the roof and leap at him. Lair knelt and leaned forward with his sword pommel against his shoulder. The demon's arms shot past Lair's head, and the sword point sank deeply into the demon's left shoulder. Its forward momentum knocked Lair onto his back, sending the Dairneag flipping over him, flying wildly off the roof to the swordsmen below.

"My sword!" Lair yelled. It went over the side still impaled in the demon's shoulder. He rolled over and pushed himself up to his feet.

"Here!" Thorn yelled. "Take mine!" Before Lair could protest, the king tossed his long sword to him handle first.

"But what about you?" Lair asked.

"What good are my hands if I can't use them?" Thorn grinned wildly.

"What?" Lair was bewildered and yet amused.

The next mounting beast had quite a surprise in store as Thorn jumped at it delivering a mighty blow to its face. His right fist knocked the demon sideways while his left hand caught the monster around the neck and squeezed with a force of a lion. The thing shrieked, batting its arms against the human on its chest, finally stumbling to a knee, hitting Thorn violently. Lair was quick to cut at its side and rescue his friend. The demon fell sideways onto its bleeding side but not before three more new arrivals rushed at Lair. They were too much. Luik finished off a flanking attacker that had bounded up the staircase from the ramparts below before running to aid his father. Lair swung heavily, catching the arm of the far right Dairneag. But the middle one seized advantage of Lair's wide swing and jabbed the small horns on its knuckles deep into his stomach.

"No!" Luik screamed out in terror. The three demons looked up at Luik, but he was already leaping high into the air with his sword cocked back ready to fly. When it did, the blade whistled through the air and decapitated the middle demon and slashed clear across the mouth of the far left one. Lair fell backwards into Luik's arms, looking skyward. Thorn shoved the two injured demons right off the ledge and then turned to Luik and Lair.

"Ta na! Speak to me!" Luik cried out. Lair issued a deep grunt, wrapping his one arm around the wound and using the other to push himself up.

"Ah! I'm all right! Let me up!" He shoved his son sideways, not realizing who he was. His body was in shock. Luik rolled and stood up, catching a glimpse over to the lower ramparts. The archers along the wall were quickly falling, unable to keep up with the sheer mass of Dairneags who rushed over the wall to the city below. The city was being overrun. Thorn reached down and pulled Lair to his feet.

"We must get off the roof!" Luik yelled. "There are too many now!" He glanced over at the two kings, at Thorn who was now shouldering Luik's father in an attempt to get him to the far stairs; but they never made it. To Luik's dismay, four Dairneags had summited the roof with ease and dove headlong at the two kings. Luik didn't hear his own scream as the unstoppable force of the giant beasts plowed Thorn and Lair over. Luik watched in agonizing terror as the group of them careened off the side. He reached after them in slow motion, helplessly, but not in time to save them from hurtling to the main lane far below, crushed beneath the four demons. Luik cried out in sorrow, but nothing changed. It was a waking nightmare far worse than anything his mind could comprehend. His world was forever changed.

Suddenly a voice echoed distantly in his head. It was buried beneath a watery ocean of emotion only to slowly emerge as reality came rushing back at full speed.

"Luik! Jump!"

His sense of survival took over and he leapt out into the air over the lane, leaving the roof far behind.

• • •

Daunt let out a deep breath when Sidbrynn finally landed on the other side. The impact was violent, both almost falling sideways; but Sidbrynn managed to stabilize them both, and Daunt pulled himself up by the mane. Naronel and Nenrick fared about the same. But it was a terrifying sight as the three of them glanced over their shoulders to their men behind.

Only a little more than half of the first row landed on the other side, many still falling off or being run over even if they did land. The second row fared much poorer as many of the horses were frightened, hesitating at the last second only to be run into by the third row and shoved over without ever attempting a leap. Many that jumped collided with previous horses still perched perilously on the far edge knocking both pairs off into the abyss. Men, who had fallen to the ground, thankful for the other side, were trampled seconds later beneath landing hooves, their cries heard all around. Daunt wished to look away, but he had to know how many still rode with him.

By the time the last row was presented an opportunity, the riders halted their horses. So much carnage lay before them, they couldn't stomach the thought of attempting the crossing only to risk landing on many of the crippled who still lay screaming on the other side. That, and the gap was now so wide they felt plunging to certain death was more likely than not. They conceded defeat and resorted to running sideways to where the crack thinned. By Daunt's highest estimate more than half the men were lost, many horses running alongside him without riders. The demonic plot was absolutely devastating. To come so far only to lose thousands of men in an instant was greater than any personal death Daunt could conceive of. His spirit was wounded deeply. He patted his stallion's neck one last time and encouraged him close to his perky ears.

"Just a few more strides, my friend." Daunt looked on at the battle line ahead.

Sidbrynn, for as much as a horse could understand, knew his ride was almost over. He was so tired, the thought of an end felt good. His legs were so close to giving out, it had taken everything in him to stop from falling on that last landing. But he was not giving up yet; not while there was still open land before him!

"Into the fray!" Daunt hollered with his sword held high. The men who heard him shouted loudly, knowing it would probably be their last. The enemy lowered their heads and unsheathed the horns on their bodies, poised to receive the rushing charge.

So the word spoken by Fane of the Mosfar came to pass that day, as it was said, as it was fulfilled. *Kings will fall standing side by side and riding to their end.*

• • •

"Do you have it all down?" Li-Saide asked quickly.

"Aye," Fane answered as sweat poured from his face. He feverishly dipped the quill in the ink reservoir and scratched across the pages of parchment. The king was nearly finished answering everything the dwarf had to ask, as was the ancient custom. Only one thing remained but Li-Saide was uncertain that the king would be coherent enough to reply with any definition. His voice was faint, nearly a distant whisper. The poison had stricken his body completely paralyzed, and the ointments Li-Saide had applied every few minutes, along with the sips of drink, did little to improve Ragnar's condition, but rather purchased only a few additional moments of priceless time. Li-Saide bent low and whispered softly in his ear.

"And to whom do you prefer the crown to go?" the dwarf asked.

Though kings were always appointed by the Most High, the word of Dionia's highest authority had much influence as it commonly was in alignment with the Maker's will. In such times when the Word of the Lord was rare, a clarion call from His appointed ruler was the next most assuring thing. Ragnar struggled at first, straining his neck against the effect of the poison for the last time. Fane even thought he might not answer. All of his affairs were recorded and ready to be put in order, passing first to Li-Saide's ear, and then Li-Saide had dictated them more loudly to Fane. But the greatest of them was always left until the end. This was the first time Li-Saide had ever had to rush through the Sacre Fina[29]. Normally a king talked at length with a dwarf from the Tribes of Ot as well as with his family and closest confidants over a meal and drinks. A home going was a joyous affair and celebrated with great enthusiasm among Dionians, but not this day. Not only had Li-Saide raced through the ancient tradition for the first time, but he also feared he might not receive an answer. With his very last breath, King Ragnar answered the question as loud and strong as he ever had answered any question.

[29] **Sacre Fina** (*SAH-cray FEE-nuh*): *noun; Ancient Dionian for Last Rights or Sacred Rights, the final wishes of a Dionian King before being called to the Great Throne Room.*

"My son." His eyes closed and his body fully relaxed. Ragnar was gone. His fight was over. Li-Saide began to cry for the first time Fane knew of; he couldn't write.

"But he has no son," Fane said softly, still unable to write with the quill.

"Aye," Li-Saide said with his head bowed, "he does."

Fane was still motionless.

"Write it!" Li-Saide commanded. Fane jumped and wrote it down and then finished the parchment. Li-Saide made the sign of blessing over Ragnar, kissed him gently on the forehead, and then raised a blanket over his face. Any sign of emotion or remorse was doused, and Li-Saide was back to his normal manner.

"We must move quickly," he said. "We don't have much time. The city is falling and we will not survive the night here."

"How do you know?" Fane asked.

Li-Saide shot back a deadly glare. "Because I do."

Fane nodded, "Of course." He tried to compose himself under the stress of it all.

"Call the two attendants back in. We must prepare his body to be moved."

"Where are we going?"

"To the Sea Cave."

Fane stared for a moment as his mind tried to put everything together. Memories flashed through his head of years gone by, of hours spent there with his friends, of adventures long faded, and conversations that surely still echoed in its walls. He suddenly remembered Li-Saide's odd departure that night when he himself left for the Border Mountains.

"It's a way out!" Fane blurted.

"No, my friend. It's a way *in*." Li-Saide allowed a small smile to grace his mouth, but then it was gone. "Go on!" the dwarf chirped.

Fane ran across the room and unlatched the oak door. He called after the two attendants who appeared a moment later further down the corridor. They had been up in one of the towers watching the progress and shared what they had seen before Fane thought to ask.

"They have breached the City Wall!" the shorter one offered the news while still far down the hallway.

Li-Saide heard it clearly. Fane turned to pass it on to him from the doorway but the dwarf interrupted him.

"I know, my friend," said Li-Saide. "Come here, I need you." Fane ran back to the bed. "Pull this under from the other side," Li-Saide had uncovered the body and pushed a dense blanket under it partway. Fane pulled the rest through and folded it back over toward Li-Saide. The attendants entered to see the burial cloth being tucked in. They both froze in the doorway.

"The king is dead," Li-Saide said flatly. "Come quickly." It was a stunned moment later that their legs finally engaged and they managed to near the dwarf. "We must finish the bonds and then carry him to the cellar." One of the attendants made to ask why, but Li-Saide shut him up. "There is no time for further questions. Do as I say. There is no other option." They both nodded emphatically, neither being of the skin to quarrel with a mysterious dwarf.

The four of them went to work securing the cocoon around the body and binding it with leather bands for easy carrying. Within moments the body was lifted from the bed and out the door.

• • •

Through the night, Thad, Thero, Anondo, Cage, Daquin, and Quoin had ridden south with Gorn along the beach and then banked left up into the southern portion of Bensotha by dawn. While they had no idea that Adriel's City Gate had been breached by late morning, Gorn was fairly certain that such a loss was imminent, though he did not speak of it. His hope was to strike at the apex of power, to cut down as many of the dark leaders as possible, even Morgui himself.

The sky remained a wash of gray as the seven horsemen proceeded over the rolling hills. All the land they surveyed bore similar scars of an advancing army bent on destruction. Trees were hewn to stumps while homes were decimated, dashed to little more than piles of rubble. The grass of the fields was trampled, pulverized into lumps of sod and beaten with the footprints of the masses of Dairne-Reih. An army had been here.

"Look there," Thad said aloud, pointing to a peculiar structure atop a nearby hill. Gorn and the others looked to see what the only structure still erect among the ruins was.

"That's not right," Anondo said. "Why would they leave something intact?"

Gorn spoke deep and low. "Because *we* didn't build it." They all looked at him. "Let's go," he said and pressed his horse toward the object.

The group mounted up the hill and circled around a giant stone arch, but with a flat top rather than a sweeping arch. It was assembled out of large stone blocks, presumably taken from the many homes around. But the stones had been altered, each with strange markings inscribed on their surface, and then the blocks themselves were somehow fused together. A strange feeling pricked the Dibor's spirits.

"By the Maker of Dionia, what is it?" Cage asked bewildered.

"It is a sif gate[30]," Gorn answered. "It's used to call up the Dairne-Reih from Haides. It is a portal."

"Like a doorway?" Cage asked.

"Aye, a doorway to the home of Morgui," Gorn said, eyes squinting as he studied its surface.

"Well then, let's tear it down!" rallied Thad.

"Aye!" the others yelled.

"You will be hard pressed to pull down that structure with so few men and horses," Gorn said, dampening their spirits with the reality of the matter. "The stones have been forged together somehow." He pointed to the strange bead of dark material that formed a horizontal line between every block. "Plus, this one is not the least of our worries."

"How so?" asked Anondo.

"Well," Gorn said, "for one, there is probably a first gate along the southern most point of Bensotha, near Grandath. That's where the scouts first saw them gathering, this probably to keep their arrival a surprise as long as possible. Then, as the Dairneags advanced, they constructed a second gate here, further up the interior so time was not wasted with marching their numbers along the same long path."

"So we ought to find the first gate?" Quoin asked.

"No. We must find the third one," Gorn said.

"There is a third?" Cage said with raised eyebrows.

"Aye, and that at least." Gorn was looking off toward Adriel. "I must believe that it's just above and behind the waterfall of Casterness."

"So these are obsolete?" Anondo surmised.

_____

[30] **Sif Gate** (*SIPH - gate*): *noun; a portal for the translation of Dairne-Reih from one realm or location to another.*

"For now, but to be found useful in the future when Morgui plans to take dominion over Dionia." Gorn was more somber than any of them had ever seen him. The six Dibor shuddered at the thought of Morgui's power and his plans.

"He is a worthy adversary," Thad stated with strength.

"And one that needs to be conquered," Gorn finished with resolve. "On we go! Varos!" A kick of the heels and the team was off again, distancing them from the second Sif gate as fast as possible.

By early afternoon the seven horsemen had made significant progress and ridden to within a short distance of the enemy war host. It was Gorn who had bid them all to slow as they crested a high rising hill at midday. Just as he had guessed, the Dairne-Reih were amassed in the distance and paid little attention to their southern rear guard, sure that no threat would follow behind them. There along the trailing edge was the third Sif gate just as Gorn had said. Only this one was enormous, able to let five or six Dairneags pass at a time.

The Dibor had left their horses and crawled on their stomachs through the warpath, now gazing down from their superior vantage point on the hill. They watched in awe as the space of air within the Sif gate suddenly produced four beasts, walking out from a translucent wall to the ranks that slowly surged forward.

"How is that possible?" Cage whispered to Gorn who lay just beside him.

"Because it's possible," Gorn said.

"O, I see," said Cage, so in awe of the manifestation that he didn't catch Gorn's wit in the slightest and just looked on with his mouth agape.

"Look there," Daquin said softly with a sudden lilt to his voice. He pointed along the easternmost edge of the war host to the gigantic chasm in the ground. Littered between the gaping crack and the Dairne-Reih were piles of mangled corpses mashed into the turf.

"The Kings of the East," Cage said, grieving for riders and horses he was sure were from Jerovah by the tattered flags strewn about. Limbs of horses and men could be picked out among the carnage, and not a soul among the slaughter moved in the slightest. It was a gruesome sight, and the three brothers from Jerovah wept bitterly, sure that their father, Daunt, was among them.

"But you don't know for sure, Sons of Jerovah," Anondo interjected encouragingly. "They may have stayed behind!"

Cage looked up and spoke on behalf of his brothers, tears streaming from his eyes. "Is not your own father fighting with his very life for Dionia? Did he not show up to defend Adriel? Then it is shameful to say that our father would not do the same, *and even more*."

"But I just meant—" Anondo tried to explain his statement, but Gorn touched his back and bid him to silence as the brothers cried. It was a dark moment for them all. The seven of them lay there, sickened in heart as the death plot unfolded before their eyes.

The demon host plodded forward in a droning pace as the relentless advancing of those far in front of them surged over the distant horizon, down the waterfall, and into Adriel. Gorn was convinced that most of the Dairneags that emerged from the gate now would never even see battle. The Sons of Dionia were so far outnumbered, there was no hope of victory unless by chance of a miracle. Gorn knew well that he would be one added to the casualties should he enter into the fray at any point. But he was trained for this. From the days of his youth long ago he had been trained to fight, to give everything he had, and to even sacrifice himself should it be needed. He counted his life as expendable, and the thought of losing it stirred no emotion; it had been trained out of him. Even during the First Battle when he had come so close to dying, he had neither fainted nor wavered. There was no turning back after committal; retreat was never an option once engaged.

It was then that Gorn spotted what he had been looking for. There, surrounded by the masses and set deep in the middle, was a dark figure standing on top of a wide stone pillar. The being wore a cloak from head to toe with arms outstretched toward the distant battle.

"You see there, Dibor?" he asked. They all looked up, even the brothers from Jerovah, wiping the tears from their eyes.

"It is Morgui?" Thero asked.

"Nay," Gorn said. "I think not. The great fallen angel seems not to be present this day. Instead he places faith in his prince; *too much faith*, I might add."

"Prince?" Cage spoke up, choking back the tears. "You mean, Velon?"

"*The Son of the Dead*, none other," Gorn said, never taking his eyes off of the stone pillar and its perched leader.

"So what do we do?" Thad asked. He paused to sum up the facts. "I know that no one has said it yet, but Adriel is probably far from being safe any longer. That means that the City Gate has surely been taken by now, and a remnant of Dibor and warriors has fallen back to defend the palace. Who knows how many fighting men have been killed and if any of the kings have survived. The horsemen of the east have been routed and slain," Thad paused to acknowledge the loss of the brothers, who in turn told him to continue, "and we sit here seven strong against a indestructible sif gate and untold numbers of Dairne-Reih surrounding the Prince of Morgui."

"When you say it like that, it doesn't seem so bad," Cage said with the last bit of humor he could muster. Everyone smiled, albeit slightly.

"I can have them take care of the Sif gate," Quoin said bravely.

"*Them?*" his brother Cage asked.

"Sure," Quoin said with a grin. "I'm the most slender of all so I have the best chance of sneaking down unnoticed. Surely that long upper section can't support too much more weight. So I figure if those mongrels get up on it, or at least grab hold of it, their own weight would easily pull it down. The supporting pillars are not nearly as close together as that other gate we saw. It's bound to collapse."

"And how do you intend to get them up on it, ask them to dance?" Daquin said.

"Well, basically." Quoin looked down at the wide spanning gate. "Running along that beam is about as easy as beating you in a race." Daquin glared at him; the others laughed. "I figure a little footwork up there and I'm bound to have a few takers join in, wouldn't you say so?"

"But they'd kill you!" Daquin said, fearful for the first time of his little brother's well-being.

"Aye, it's a chance," said the youngest of the three, "but what's the use of living when there's no one else to share it with? Plus, it's the only thing I can think of that I'd be better at doing than you, Daquin." The courage and resolve of the littlest brother was astounding, heroic at the very least.

"Well we can't let him do all the work on his own!" Thad added wildly. "As far as I see it, there's a traitor down there whom I've wanted to have some words with for quite some time." He pointed to Velon.

"As have I," Gorn said rubbing the chain maille over an itching scar on his chest. He liked how his students were thinking.

"And if we can't take them all, we might as well take their pride and joy!" Thero added with a fist in the ground.

"I'd like to settle the score with the easternmost flank if you don't mind," Daquin said, pointing to the remains of his kinsmen.

"I'm with you on that," Cage said to Daquin. "You have a plan in mind, brother?"

"Aye," he said.

"A crazy one?"

"Aye." Daquin smiled maliciously.

"Lots of dead Dairne-Reih?"

"Aye."

"Poor odds?"

"Aye."

"Certain death?"

"Aye."

"Wonderful," Cage said with a gleam in his eye. "Why do we tarry?" He turned to Gorn. "I shan't think you and the brothers from Ligeon will be needing us?"

"Nay, Cage. Go with your brother. We'll manage well enough without you, and make sure to get Quoin safely to the gate." Gorn couldn't have been more proud. Then he turned to Anondo, the youngest of Ligeon. "And what's *our* plan, Son of Thorn?"

Anondo had been watching the throng the whole time. "We *push* them," he said without diverting his gaze.

"Push them?" Thero asked, thinking his brother had gone mad.

"Aye, push them." Anondo pointed his finger down at the group. "See how tightly they are packed? Their blood lust is so great that they press one another in the hopes of getting to the front lines more quickly. Obviously a futile effort, proving how dumb the demons really are."

"And this is to our advantage?" Thero asked.

"Of a certainty, it is," Gorn said. "It's a brilliant idea."

"I'm missing it," Thero said.

"If we can manage to push just a few of those Dairneags over, the ones just coming out of the gate perhaps, then they'll fall into the next, and the next, and so on making a wave through the entire mass. They'll fall over like wind on blades of grass."

"It's that easy?" Thero questioned.

"Well, maybe with a lot of effort," Thad said, "but it's plausible. The demons are so close to each other that they don't have room to maneuver. Plus, the weight of one falling hits two, and the two falling hit four. They'll get up eventually, but that should give us enough time."

"Time to get to the Prince," Thero said, finally understanding.

"Aye!" Anondo put in with a wide smile.

"And then what?" Gorn asked. No one responded. "It's a death wish, Dibor," Gorn said. "Are you certain of this course of action?"

"We have to do something," Anondo said solemnly. "We're bound for Athera one way or another. We might as well get there doing something noble in the face of evil."

"Might as well," Thad said.

"Might as well," said Cage, echoed then by Daquin and Quoin.

"Hey'a, why not," Thero said at the end.

There was a brief moment there on that hillside when all seven of them felt like they were totally alone; they felt like they were the last persons living in Dionia pitted against an insurmountable foe. No one would know about their deeds; there would be no one to sing about their heroic acts or tell tales laced with the grandeur of their names. *They were it*. And their small and seemingly futile contribution to protecting the sanctity of life would be swallowed whole by an evil so great that not even all the living of their world could prevent it.

Within that moment there emerged a glimmer of the smallest proportion. It was a warmth kindled by the assurance of great promise and hope that there was an Advocate that had not lost sight of them there on the hillside. *He* was watching them and going with them into battle. They suddenly realized that *they were not alone after all*. Even at this moment, there were unseen forces being put into play that fought even for the very thoughts they were thinking, driving out the wicked and protecting the virtuous. *They were not alone—He* would always remember their names and sing about them for all eternity. *They were not alone*—they had one another. It was seven against a multitude, but somehow they knew their courage was of the noblest kind; their resolve was with greater purpose than that of their enemy; and their sacrifice would not be lost in a proud fit of rage and a self-serving gluttony of destruction, but marked as a selfless offering afforded by their own integrity for the lives of those worth fighting for, past, present, *and* future. *They were not alone.*

"So," Thad finally asked, "who goes first?"

• • •

Luik's body accelerated through the air at an exponential rate of speed. He had never fallen so far before and, had it not been for the adrenaline pumping through his veins, he would have been quite concerned as to his landing. It seemed like an eternity that he sailed down, legs kicking and arms flailing just to maintain stability. The momentum that he had asserted eventually sent him pitching forward and he reached out with his hands to brace his impact. He was instantly aware of the stone lane coming up toward his face, and bodies of men and demons alike scattered everywhere. He smacked down with a sickening sound.

Luik lay still for a moment before opening his eyes to see his father's face staring up at him, eyes wide and mouth open. Luik made to scream, but nothing came out. The wind had been knocked out of him on impact. He was lying atop one of the four Dairneags that had assailed Thorn and Lair, Lair's face visible just between the demon's arm and torso. Luik felt paralyzed, not able to properly respond to the carnage he lay amongst and the pool of blood on the stone beneath his father's head. He was also acutely aware of severe pain that gripped his left leg; while the rest of his body landed on the demon corpse, his leg hadn't and the kneecap had shattered on the stone lane.

"*Luik, move!*" said a voice above him. He felt a hand hook around his waist and another under his arm. A sudden jerk heaved him from the pile of bodies and onto his feet. Another person joined the rescue and supported him from the opposite side as Luik was half propelled up the lane toward the King's Gate. He was a bit dazed from the fall and the sight of his father, but his mind was clearing. He heard the battle clash just behind him. Soon he was able to support more of his own weight, until finally he turned to the person on his left and noticed it was Jrio.

"Hey'a, my brother," Luik said, still not all together.

"Run, Dibor!" Jrio yelled, in no mood for talking and strained with risking his own life for Luik's. Brax was on his other side.

"Can you make it?" Brax asked with his deep voice. Luik suddenly realized the Dairne-Reih had breached the City Wall and were probably right behind them.

"They are on our heels?" Luik asked.

"Aye, quite so," Brax said. Luik swung his arms down from off his friends' shoulders and looked back down the lane. A mob of possessed demons was eating up the ground between them, fended off by a few lingering foot soldiers who were valiantly trampled in the process.

"I see," Luik said and picked up his own pace, limping heavily with his broken leg. The three of them ran on until they joined the slow-moving crush of men pressing through the King's Gate. Any surviving men from the walls had retreated with those among the lower city dwellings and run for the sanctuary of the palace walls. Luik suddenly remembered the last time he was amongst such a thick crowd at this very spot; it was the day the princess had been dedicated. Amazing how it felt like only yesterday, and yet that place and time seemed a world away from where he was now. The pain of his left leg snapped him back to reality. He looked down to see blood covering his shin and smothering his left foot. Then Brax jostled him.

"Draw your sword, Luik! We must fight this through!" Brax helped Luik grip his sword.

"I can do it, Dibor," Luik insisted, "I'm all right now."

The men all turned in their retreat to see the war host plummeting toward them, and Luik, Jrio, and Brax were in the worst possible place. All the men started yelling and there was a fury of commotion. The Dairne-Reih raced on with uncanny speed, now almost to the top of the hill.

"This is really going to hurt," Jrio said flatly.

"Aye, that it is, brother," Brax agreed, "but what fun to give them a taste of my blade!" he roared at the last with his Vinfae lofted high.

When the front line of demons was about to meet them, a huge mass of the monsters fell to the ground in mid-stride, shot through with a barrage of arrows. The few remaining archers had found their way to the King's Gate ramparts, and not a moment too late. Luik was grateful for the quarter given, but knew the rest would be short-lived. Those beasts behind the slain bounded over the corpses and drove on toward Luik and the other men, horns high and teeth wide. Brax was the first to strike, followed by Jrio and Luik, both in guard positions. Brax swung and intercepted a swinging arm, cutting it straight through the bone and then dodging the massive body, which fell to the blades of the foot soldiers behind him, finishing off the monster. Jrio crouched low with his sword tip on the ground; a hulk of a beast took this as weakness and charged him with arms raised high. Jrio's timing was deadly as he raised the sword tip quickly into the demon's throat and then jumped up, pushing the weapon through the back of its neck. The Dairneag reeled backwards with a scream, Jrio withdrawing his blade. The flailing body was caught by two other Dairne-Reih behind it who violently spun the corpse away. These two aimed for the bleeding and seemingly crippled Luik, but he was ready. He drew his weapon back behind him out of sight. When they closed for the kill he unleashed a powerful arch of fury that cut both Dairneags clear across the face in a spray of blood and fluid. They grabbed their faces and fell to one side and the other. Brax was busy finishing off another set of monsters when Luik realized the flood of Dairne-Reih racing up the lane was pressing the enemy much too close. Almost unable to swing a sword, it was getting cramped and soon they would be smothered.

"How close are we getting to that gate?" Luik yelled.

"You're still a good two tree lengths from it, as are we all!" a foot soldier behind him cried.

"That's," Luik paused to thrust at a Dairneag who was much too close, "not good." He grunted as the wounded demon fell into him, pressed by its cohorts from behind. The noxious film on the creature's skin smeared across Luik's face and he spit wildly when the fluid filled his mouth. "Pass the word back, tell the men to clear the gate and make room to the sides!" He shoved the beast off him and to the side; another was right behind it to greet him.

"Aye, Luik," the man yelled and started to pass the order on to the men behind him, and so on to the front of the pack. Luik ducked as a lethal swing just missed his head. To his horror he heard it connect with the skull of the man behind him that he had just been talking with. The foot soldier fell sideways, his head bashed in. Luik screamed and drove his sword up into the jaw of the monster before him. It sickened his heart to know his parry had meant the death of one behind him. The creature flailed its arms and grabbed Luik's sword.

"Back off!" he yelled at the Dairneag and kicked it away with a foot in its torso.

The crush was getting worse and the pressure that the back line was experiencing was all but too much. Brax and Jrio could barely move, but fortunately neither could the attacking Dairne-Reih. The mighty swings and blows were now reduced to small prods with horns or jabs with sword points. A few Dairneags even bent low to try and chomp with their razor teeth and powerful jaws. Jrio leaned back to avoid a wild attempt at his head. A slop of drool met his face and burned his eyes. He retaliated with a push of his sword into the Dairneag's gut and then repeated the motion numerous times until the creature froze; though still standing dead, it was caught between him and the monsters behind it. Luik was focused on a meddling monster that was intent on stabbing at his eyes. He held off one claw with his left hand and poked feverishly at the creature's other claw with the sword in his right. But a third claw, from the Dairneag further behind, reached around and drove its fingers into Luik's side. He let out a desperate groan which Brax heard and lowered his blade on the wrist of the perpetrating monster. Suddenly two arrows, one after the other, sunk into the top of the nearest beast. Luik reminded himself to treat those archers to a draft of mead when this was all over. Then he noticed a trace of red rings near the feathers of the two arrows; they were the signature of a marksman. But he was distracted from further thought by the extreme pain in his abdomen. Luik looked down to the new wound and saw the hand of the Dairneag still dangling from his side. He yanked it out with a whimper and held his hand against the wound, half against the pain and half to stop the bleeding. The pain was nearly unbearable and he could feel himself getting weak after a whole day of fighting.

I am afraid, Luik thought. It was the reason for the pain. *I must trust the Most High.* Suddenly his dream came to mind; *the claw of the slayer.* It was a claw that slew him in the dream. *Is this how I am to die?* he thought, *but it was a lion, not some foul demon! Today will not be my day!*

"Today will not be my day!" Luik cried out to the shock of Jrio and Brax beside him.

"Aye!" Brax yelled back. "I think not!"

"Today will not be my day!" Luik hollered again and fought against the corpse wedged in between him and the bloodthirsty monsters beyond. He yelled the phrase again and again until he had wrestled another Dairneag into a hold and pierced him with his blade. *"Today will not be my day!"* The blood continued to flow from his side and his left leg was looking badly mangled but he never stopped speaking the phrase. *"Today will not be my day!"* The rhythm of the words spread to those within earshot. Each man could feel a new confidence rising within his spirit. Suddenly the atmosphere was vibrant and strong, the fighting men bold once more. Those behind Brax and Jrio suddenly reached over their shoulders to lend a blade to the closest demon. One soldier even passed Brax his sword, knowing Brax could do twice as much with two as he could with one. Every beast they slew was one more precious moment that brought them closer to the Gate.

Then, as if a dam had broken, the remaining men in the lane surged toward the palace courtyard finding the empty space at last. Luik, Jrio and Brax, feeling the pressure receding, turned to run with them. The Dairne-Reih at first fell over one another, not braced for the let-up. But they quickly regained their feet and tore off after the fleeing men. Luik ran with his limp and a hand to his side. He ran as though his life depended on it, for it did indeed. He looked up as he heard the sound of the gate winches grinding; they were closing the massive doors.

"Faster!" Jrio cried out. "Run faster!"

"They better not close the doors on us!" Brax yelled.

"If they do," Luik added, "I'll kill them!" They all smiled as they ran.

Luik could literally feel the hot breath of the Dairne-Reih breathing down his neck. It mixed with the painful heat he felt burning in his side and in his leg. *Get through those doors*, he told himself. *Get yourself through those doors.*

"A little bit further!" Brax hollered. The winches going strong, there would be no stopping the weight of those doors. They crept closer and closer together, the gap soon turning to a narrow sliver. Luik sensed the men up ahead slowing as less and less of them could fit through at a time.

"This is going to be close!" Jrio said. "Brax, you go first! You're the heftiest of the three of us. Then you, Luik. I'll squeeze in last."

The last few men pressing through the narrowing gap in the giant doors thinned whatever distance had been put between the retreating men and the advancing war host. It was precious moments that separated the three Dibor from safety to being impaled on the Palace Wall doors. The winches continued to grind away, and the more men that slipped through left Luik and the others feeling totally helpless. All they could do was run and hope that the men ahead afforded them enough time.

They were very close now and slowed to a standstill. Four men pressed through one at a time and then it was Brax's turn. He sucked in his chest and slipped through the crack. Men on the other side pulled on his arm. Luik turned sideways and looked back at Jrio and the on-coming rush of Dairne-Reih. They were gruesome and screamed at the sight of the two last men slipping between the doors. The men pulled Luik through with no regard for his tender wounds. Jrio turned and waved to the wall of advancing demons in a grand taunting farewell and then squeezed through a forearm's span of space, just barely making it past. The remaining sliver of light between the doors was filled with claws and horns that tried desperately to wedge themselves in, but nothing could stop the enormous gates. They sealed shut with the sound of breaking bones, the crushing of limbs, and the shrieks of the demonic.

• • •

Gorn, the three brothers from Ligeon, and Quoin raced straight down the hill toward the Sif gate, while Cage and Daquin took advantage of the diversion to ride east toward the southern start of the enormous chasm. Cage stayed on the west side of the chasm and turned north to ride the edge closest to the Dairne-Reih, while Daquin passed below the start of the crack and then turned left heading north along the east side. They rode with a long rope between them spanning the widening canyon. The rope was courtesy of their youngest brother, Quoin, who had taken it upon himself to always ride prepared.

Quoin rode in the middle of the pack with Gorn and the others. They charged down the hill as fast as their mounts would carry them, racing swiftly with the stealth of falcons toward their target. They rode tightly together to make as dense an impact as possible. The Dairne-Reih's own ruckus of commotion drowned out the stampeding hoof beats behind them. It wasn't until Gorn and the Dibor were but two strides from the gate that the demons turned to wonder at the strange sound; by then it was much too late. The riders had braced themselves on horseback for the mighty blow that was to ensue. At the very moment they passed under the gate, five demons appeared. It couldn't have been planned more perfectly; the five unsuspecting Dairneags took the brunt of the blow, which catapulted them, hurtling their snapped and limp bodies into the wall of Dairne-Reih before them. The desired effect was even more detrimental than the team had imagined. Each demon from the gate collided with another three or four mongrels; their momentum slammed incredibly hard. The wave was devastating and spread much faster than anticipated, but Gorn and the others took little time to study their achievement. They recovered from the blow with minimal injury and took off, bounding through the heap, trampling bodies with every stride. Their horses, challenging as it was, made quick work of advancing toward the center of the war host.

Quoin had dismounted just before impact, leaping skillfully from the back of his horse and reaching for the cross section above his head. His feet swung out beyond his grip, almost pulling him from the gate, but with all his might he held fast and pulled himself up onto the stone beam. Sliding up on his stomach he looked out and watched his friends gallop through the Dairne-Reih toward the stone pillar beyond.

"Be with them, O Mighty One," Quoin whispered, pushing himself up to his feet.

Gorn and the brothers were getting close to the pillar now, but they had finally caught the attention of the cloaked figure atop. The Prince spun around when he saw his legions fall flat on their faces; to his dismay it had been wrought by just four riders and a fifth horse following behind.

"Who is this that challenges me?" the Prince questioned with a low grating voice. "Who is this that rides so swiftly to their doom?" He tilted his head slowly and examined the riders. They hurtled over the masses of demons, now struggling to regain their feet. With every demon the horses trod over, a hoof smashed a head and ripped into flesh, breaking bone and mangling limbs.

"We approach!" Gorn said as they neared the base of the spire. "Loose the horses!" Thad, Thero, and Anondo dismounted in mid-stride and let the horses continue on circling the pillar in an attempt to beat down as many of the Dairne-Reih nearest the Prince as possible. If they were to have any chance at engaging this foe, it need not be interrupted by unnecessary flanking attacks; after all, the Dibor were rushing in only to willfully be surrounded. It was not the wisest martial tactic, but they had not the time, nor the stamina, to take on Morgui's entire army.

The horses went straight to work bashing every foe that lifted a hand or a head. They whinnied and snorted, their heads filled with the smell of battle and the sounds of war. They had ridden long through the night for this moment, and they dared not let it slip by in vain. Within moments they had beat down quite a large circle and then proceeded to defend it by running after any challenger that posed a threat. Once the Dairneags nearest got on their feet again, the horses ran up to them bucking wildly, legs kicking into the fray. A few demons were caught beneath the chin and sent sailing up and into the crowd behind; others received strikes to the chest that crushed rib cages and shattered legs. A few of the horses even landed double blows, delivering devastating concussions with each hoof, two bystanders at a time. The Prince simply gazed down at the dark man who attempted to climb the pillar, intrigued at the courage and relishing his demise.

But the dark warlord was soon distracted by a few demons which crawled onto the arch in the distance. They heaved their overweight bodies onto the stone beam as a little figure leapt around them like a fly. The Prince's eyes widened as he realized the weight would be too great.

"You fools!" he screeched. "Let him be!" But it was much too late; by now six bloodthirsty mongrels had been lured after Quoin. Their weight was simply too much and the stone gate was cracking in the middle like dry wood. Moments later the structure collapsed around Quoin and all of them fell, tumbling to the ground.

That wasn't the only matter that concerned the Prince; off to the east a disturbance was brewing. The warlord gazed out toward the chasm he had issued open to see a single man jumping frantically in the air. He leapt wildly and waved his hands, screaming aloud all the while. The Prince turned his ear and heard the man taunting his minions.

"Come on, you dumb slugs!" Cage screamed. "You're a pack of flowers that don't even smell good! I'll take you all!" Cage definitely had some attention now; an entire line was gazing at him and advancing.

"You know what else?" Cage hollered. "You're ugly, too!" Cage wasn't sure if they understood a word he was saying, but whatever the case, it was working. Soon the entire eastern flank of Dairne-Reih was converging on Cage with great speed. It seemed they all wanted a piece of him. None of them had seen any action all day and he looked like the only chance they'd get. This time, the Prince didn't waste his energy.

"Let them perish," he whispered with a haunting sigh.

Soon ten ranks of the demon host were bent on devouring the little man and they ran across the flats, centered on his dancing body. Other Dairneags who hadn't seen him simply followed the lead of the others, figuring there must be a battle brewing to that side.

"Not yet!" Cage yelled over his shoulder to Daquin who crouched on the far side. The enemy raced on, intent on destroying Cage.

"Wait just a little more!" he said again. Daquin remained motionless, the rope tied around his waist and gripped tightly in his hands. The demons were worked into a frenzy and had no idea that their rage had sealed their own fate.

"Come on, you maggots!" Cage yelled. They were just a tree length away when he finally crouched down and leapt backwards high into the air. Daquin jumped up and ran away from the canyon as fast as he could. He picked up the slack, and the rope around Cage's waist went taut, yanking him in midair and folding him like a blanket. The enraged demons jumped out after him never realizing what they had been lured into. They strained in midair for his body but fell out of reach and plummeted into the darkness below. Shrieks and cries for help echoed off the walls and reverberated down into the depths. Cage flew backwards, pulled on by his brother. He spun around in the air midway through in order to brace himself for the impact on the opposite wall. Like the demons, Cage fell quickly, except he swung into the pendulum of the rope's support and extended his hands and legs in front of him. The impact was grueling, and he was quite sure that some bones had been split, although his heart was beating too fast to be concerned. The rope squeezed around his skin and he started walking up the side of the canyon with his legs as Daquin trudged on above, carrying his brother's entire weight.

The masses of Dairne-Reih were obviously not as lucky. They spilled over the edge by the handfuls, leaping out only to discover that their bloodlust had betrayed them. There would be no landing for them, at least not for a very long time. Cage looked out into the chasm as he walked the wall, smiling as tens after tens of the demonic creatures perished at the hands of two little men less than half their size. He grinned for the revenge that quickly turned to grief as he thought of his father who must have perished here just hours before. Tears ran down his face; his smile was now more out of pain than revenge. His heart was so broken he couldn't stop smiling. He yelled out as the thoughts of his kinsmen flooded his mind. He no longer saw Dairneags falling into the canyon, but horses and men from the eastern lands; he saw the flag of his homeland flapping down into the darkness; he heard the screams of men crying out for help with nothing to hold onto, not a line to save them. And he was still smiling, eyes full of horror, as he crawled up over the eastern edge, Daquin there to lift him up. He embraced him and held his head tightly.

"It's all right my brother," Daquin said softly. "It's over now, everything will be all right." Cage sobbed, chest heaving and body shaking. He would never be the same after this day was over; for this day for him would never be over.

• • •

Luik instantly sank to the ground after the gates closed behind him. The injuries he had sustained were lethal if not treated quickly, and the loss of blood had finally exhausted him more than he was able to bear. But the battle was not yet finished; the Dairne-Reih were sure to scale the Palace Wall within moments and Luik was too weak to shout orders.

"Jrio," he said, tugging on his friend's leg. "Jrio, come near."

Jrio looked around and then saw Luik on the ground by his feet. "Whoa there, my brother!" Jrio knelt down. "So sleepy already? I think you need a nap, my friend."

"Jrio, there is no time for this, they're coming! They'll be over the walls any moment!" Luik was gasping for air.

"Aye," Jrio agreed. "The archers are standing by as are the remaining swordsmen." Jrio tried to keep his voice calm despite his own personal feelings of woe. *Even if Luik survives for another day*, he thought, *it might not matter much as none of us will survive the next hour.*

"We must get the king out," Luik said, now struggling to remain conscious. Jrio could see him faltering and realized his wounds were severe. He pulled back Luik's leather armor to examine the chain maille beneath; it had been severed clean through and the links were stained a deep red.

"The king is being taken care of," Jrio comforted him. "You, on the other hand, need some attention." Luik barely heard those last words. Somewhere between them and the thundering battle clash that ensued next, Luik was lost into a sea of darkness. He suddenly saw his father's face, fresh and young as if he were back on the farm at home. He saw his mother standing inside the door of their house with a basket in her hands, and then an image of his baby brother whom he knew for but a few days before leaving home. He could feel himself crying, or at least wanting to cry. It was as if he was being taunted by the sweetest memories he had ever known, only to watch them slip out of his hands. Then there was Anorra's face before him.

"I think your cheering is helping," she said sweetly. "I like it." His heart ached to see her again. Then her face vanished away. He felt his body ebb and sway, twisting in a cacophony of muted noise that seemed to swirl about him. *This is it*, he surmised. *This is how it feels to die and to be carried up into Athera. When I arrive in the Grand Throne Room*, he said in his mind, *I'll ask to see how it all ended, how my brothers fought bravely to the end, how Adriel was overrun, and how the children escaped to the north.*

Then he thought about it again—and the children. *Nay, perhaps I won't. Perhaps it is too much for one man to bear for all eternity. Perhaps I am better off to be ignorant.*

But I must know...

• • •

"You are climbing to your doom," the Prince said, glaring down at Gorn from beneath his dark hood. Gorn made no reply and simply kept on climbing up the vertical pillar to the wide surface above. "You have a debt to repay now, don't you?" Gorn still said nothing. "What makes you think you can beat me, Gorn Son of Jyne?" Gorn continued to climb though the warlord scolded him relentlessly. "You are nothing to me now. My power is far beyond anything you can imagine! You climb to your death."

The three brothers stood below, finishing off any Dairneag that managed to break through the horses' rampage. They cast long glances up at Gorn as he climbed higher. Soon he crawled over the edge and stood face to face with the Son of the Dead.

"You are truly a remarkably stupid man, Gorn," said the Prince. "Why do you even try?"

"Silence!" Gorn commanded with great authority. The Prince was taken aback at his audacity.

"You insolent fool! How dare you—"

But Gorn knew his place. "Enough! You are the fool, traitor. You are the one that forfeited your place in paradise and traded it for power! You are the one who exchanged your position as a Son and Prince of the Most High for prestige among the dregs of Athera. And you are the one who carries the blood of innocent children on your hands, not I. May your neck be eternally burdened with the weight of a millstone and tortured by the grief of relentless sorrows. *I curse you in the Name of the Most High God.*"

"Curse? But I'm already cursed, you fool! Look at me!" the Prince laughed and threw his hood back. Gorn's eyes narrowed as he gazed upon a face so foul it made his stomach turn. Barely resembling a man, the yellowed eyes were bloodshot and deeply sunken. His skin was marred and wrinkled, a peaked pale hue. Swelling blisters turned into patches of bulbous growths along his neck. The lips and nose appeared to be in constant degeneration as blood and fluid seeped from their deformed settings. The Prince was half man, half demon and knew his appearance disgusted Gorn more now than it had back in Ragnar's throne room. He smiled widely displaying rows of long, razor teeth and purred in the back of his throat. "You see, Gorn? You can't kill me; I'm already dead!"

"O but I can," Gorn said, "*and I will.*" Gorn reached back and drew his sword to middle guard, hands near his groin, the blade pointed up toward the monster's face. The two circled each other around the circumference of the pillar's broad summit. Gorn's sword suddenly swung around over his head and came down diagonally toward the Prince's left shoulder. The prince threw up his right arm and produced a one-handed sword from his sleeve, which he caught at the grip in time to parry the blow to his left. The blade was forged from a black metal with a dark hilt in the shape of a serpent. A strange gray script covered both sides of the weapon and the pommel was a white ball with metal vines that bound it to the end of the grip.

The Prince countered his parry with a sweeping horizontal cut at Gorn's left hip. Gorn turned his weapon upside down and fended off the blow to the left, countering with his own low cut to the Prince's legs. But the Prince saw it coming and thrust his blade to the ground intercepting the attack. Gorn's blade bounced off the parry and he brought it back to middle guard.

It had been a long time since he had faced Valdenil the first time, and it was apparent that Valdenil's skill had increased since then, too. While

Gorn's old enemy may have been demonic in many ways, he was still in the shell of a man and was limited to those laws, including the need to learn, something he had done with regard to the art of war. But there was also a supernatural element that Gorn sensed, powers that eluded Gorn's knowledge, that he felt his foe was hiding.

Gorn commenced a second wave, this time lofting his sword behind his head, then feinting back low only to return to middle guard and thrust directly at his opponent's face. The Prince leaned back as the point of Gorn's sword came within a finger's length of his forehead. Valdenil took advantage of Gorn's weight being forward, arms outstretched, and pushed the man's grip sideways exposing Gorn's side. The Prince brought his sword around and jabbed with its black point. But Gorn arched his back and watched to see the sword pass just behind him. Then he knocked Valdenil's blade away with his arm and sliced at the warlord's neck. It was the first successful cut in all their exchanges yet. Gorn's blade lightly grazed the Prince's left side below a deformed earlobe. The wound produced a trail of blood, and Valdenil screamed from somewhere deep within, placing a hand over the cut.

It was at this moment that the warlord's patience was tested and Gorn saw what power he had only surmised was available to the fallen traitor for his loyalty. Valdenil pulled his hand away from the wound and looked down at his blood. Enraged, he glared up at Gorn and growled. The Prince raised a hand and a wave shot through the air, smacking Gorn's body so hard it sent him flying off the pillar. Thad was astonished to see his teacher land just beside him, sunken into a heap of demon corpses.

"Gorn," he knelt down offering his hand, "are you all right?"

"Look out!" Gorn yelled as he pushed Thad away. Valdenil leapt from his towering position with his sword aimed at Gorn. Thad tumbled to one side, and Gorn rolled through the mess to the other side. He found his legs sure enough, though the footing left a lot to be desired. Suddenly all the Dairne-Reih were not so concerned with the horses and the Dibor as were with watching their champion fight the champion of men. Valdenil, overtly maddened, charged Gorn and swung at his head. Gorn merely ducked and sidestepped the angry warlord. The Prince turned around and raised his hand again, sending Gorn flying back toward a bystanding Dairneag. The demon was caught off guard and was knocked dead from the blow, snapping its neck. The surrounding monsters just watched as Gorn shook his head and stood up, but Valdenil was furious and already running after Gorn.

It was at this moment that the brothers from Ligeon saw Gorn use a tactic they had never seen before. He raised his sword beside his head with the point aiming directly at the Prince. Then, as the warlord neared, Gorn spoke out a strange word that seemed to echo and expand indefinitely. He then thrust the sword at Valdenil and, despite the Prince's efforts to displace the attack, the blade traveled deep into his chest with a percussive blow.

"Your reign of torment ends this day," Gorn said with a defiant tone.

Valdenil was stunned and looked down at Gorn's blade. He let out a hideous shriek and then walked backwards as Gorn's sword withdrew. The Dibor noticed the Prince was badly hurt. There was a murmuring from the strangely still throng of Dairne-Reih.

"Not even Morgui's power can sustain a crippled body forever, Velon," Gorn chided as the Prince made to recover. This time Valdenil made the first move. He raised his sword in a futile attempt to cut down Gorn near the shoulder, but Gorn easily parried the swing. The Prince came again, this time to Gorn's right leg, but this, too, was rebuffed. Gorn took advantage of the enemy's lowered sword, stepping on the blade and pinning the tip to the ground.

The Prince, hunched over with his grip, looked up at Gorn, "You should have never underestimated me, weakling!"

"I haven't," Gorn said. But Valdenil's response was not with words; before Gorn knew it, the warlord let go of his sword and clapped both hands and fingers against Gorn's neck, piercing his skin with his nails. Gorn cried out in agony. The wound had severed vital veins and nerves and all but paralyzed Gorn, if but for the moment. The Dibor gasped in disbelief and made to charge the Prince.

"Don't move, fools, or I end him now." The Prince turned his head slowly to address the brothers. Gorn remained frozen with mouth and eyes wide open in shock but it was Thad who first noticed that Gorn had still not released his sword; *a warrior who still holds his sword is still a warrior,* Gorn would always say to them. The Prince was still enjoying the response of the brothers when he noticed the grin on Thad's face. Quickly putting meaning to the expression, Valdenil turned back to look at Gorn. His sword was cocked back and Gorn eyed the traitor with deliberate violence.

"Never again will you haunt my people," Gorn said with finality. The next word Gorn uttered was not understandable to the brothers; like the one moments ago, the sound of his voice took on strange qualities as if booming from a mountaintop. At the same moment he unleashed his sword to do its work, which it did effortlessly, the powerful arch cutting clear across Valdenil's chest, slashing it wide open. The body burst like an over-ripened peach, and whatever air was left in its lungs didn't leave through the mouth, but out the front in a spray of fatality. Gorn then pulled the hands from his neck as Valdenil's eyes and gaping mouth looked up at him in terror. Gorn stumbled sideways and Thad was there to catch him.

"I really need to sit down," Gorn said, extremely dazed, nearly delirious from the demonic wound.

"I have a nice place for you right over here on a strong horse," Thad answered, trying to keep his voice calm despite his growing fear of the surrounding battle host.

"Brother," Anondo said to Thad as he came up underneath Gorn's other side, "I wouldn't recommend hanging around here any longer. The atmosphere just isn't my sort. And you?"

"I agree wholeheartedly. These good beasts have had enough trouble for the day," Thad said looking over at the Dairneags, trying not to make any sudden moves. "I recommend we leave them to tidy up the place. We can always come back tomorrow should they get lonely."

The Dairne-Reih watched in a sort of bewildered stare as the three brothers hoisted Gorn onto his horse. Then they looked at their leader who lay motionless, body split open in defeat.

"I don't think they quite get it yet," Thero added, "but something tells me they're not dumb enough to give up just yet."

"Aye," Thad said mounting his steed behind Gorn's enormous bulk. "So let's make this as quickly as possible." The other two mounted their rides as well. "Ready, my brothers?"

"Hey'a," they both said and drew their swords together. Thad kept one arm around Gorn who slumped into the horse's neck, and used his other hand to wield his sword. The two horses without riders sidled up close to the others, sensing an escape was imminent.

"If we make it to Quoin, someone grab him," Thad ordered, "And if we make it to the top of the hill, run for Grandath."

"Cage and Daquin?" Anondo asked.

"I think they are near the ruins of the Sif gate," Thad answered, "either *dead,* looking for Quoin, or *almost dead* looking for Quoin."

"Then they need some help," Anondo said, "and we are the best brothers to lend it."

"Indeed," Thero added.

"Indeed," agreed Thad. They had never been so proud to be brothers, to be Dibor, to be alive. Then they charged valiantly into the fray one more time knowing it would be their last.

• • •

The five-minute walk down to the rear-most cellar was disturbed only by a loud crash and a few screams heard a floor above.

"The Dairne-Reih erroneously assume that persons of great importance seek refuge in the heights of the palace," was the only thing Li-Saide paused to say. They moved quickly down stairwells and rushed with great haste through the remaining few corridors lit with large torches, finally reaching the vast chambers used for storage. Suddenly the dwarf motioned them to stop and lay the body down.

"Leave us," Li-Saide said turning to the two attendants. They didn't understand.

"But where should we go?"

"Hide yourselves. We must go alone."

"But you can't leave us here!"

"Well, we are, good man. May the Great God be with you and keep you safe from harm."

"But we will surely perish!" The one man was becoming hysterical.

"You will perish by my hand much sooner if you do not heed my instruction." Fane stared at Li-Saide in shock. He had never heard anyone speak like this before. Threaten to kill someone? He made to intervene but thought better of it. "Seek refuge in the barracks. Perhaps the men of Tontha will defend you. Off with you!" Li-Saide waved his hands in the air and made loud sounds with his mouth and tongue. The attendants yelped and ran back down the corridor, frightened out of their minds.

"A curse?" Fane asked in reference to his odd speech and hand movements.

"No, just scaring them."

"How could you do such a thing?"

"Quite easily, really; they already fear me slightly and—"

"No! I mean about threatening to kill them?"

"Because in their ignorance they will more than likely kill us and those we go to seek. We must not let the king's body fall into the hands of Morgui."

"I understand." He didn't really, but he took Li-Saide's word for it. Li-Saide doubled up on the front straps and Fane took up the rear, now doing the work of four men by themselves. The dwarf started down the main isle of the cellar and made his third right. They passed a series of identical rooms and took the fourth left. By the third turn Fane hoped he would not have to recount their trail on a later test as he was completely lost in the labyrinth. The torches were growing less frequent and the resulting blackness was making it much harder to tell where they were going. *As long as Li-Saide knows*, Fane thought, *I'm fine*. A few more turns and they were walking down a long passageway with a single torch lit far at the end.

"A dead end," Fane said in defeat. "We must have missed a turn back there somewhere." Li-Saide stopped to look at Fane.

"You really mistrust me so much?" A little of his old humor crept back into his voice.

"Am I missing something?" Fane smiled. Suddenly a screech echoed through the corridor, resonating throughout the entire cavern.

"Quickly!" Li-Saide prompted. They ran toward the last remaining torch, limping from the weight of the body. At the end of the hallway there was no door, only the torch.

"Now what?" Fane asked. The screech came again followed by a series of clucking sounds. Fane turned around. He could have been sure they were right behind him. Li-Saide reached up and pulled one of the iron supports that held the torch against the wall. Strangely it swung free, pivoting like a handle, and all at once a crack appeared in the wall to one side. A sliver of green light seeped through the darkness, and Fane squinted mildly as Li-Saide pressed hard against the wall.

"Here, let me help you," Fane offered and reached a hand forward against the stone door to lessen the dwarf's burden. The door swung wide and they walked through. Fane was stunned. They were in the Sea Cave. It was just the same as he remembered. And the strange aqua light still emanated from the pool in the middle of the room. He looked up and saw the strange markings again, only this time they weren't so strange.

"Hey'a, I can read those!" Fane exclaimed.

"Wonderful. Quickly now, we must close it! They are very close."

"The Dairne-Reih?"

"Aye. Come! Close the door!" Fane lowered the body and turned back, pressing the door closed within a few seconds.

"This thing is massive!" Fane said as the final seal was made and a click sounded from somewhere within.

"It is a stone wall, boralee."

"Hey'a, you said you wouldn't call me that anymore!"

"When such an obvious discovery is made, a teacher must resort to old ways." Fane laughed, but it was cut off. Something was scratching on the other side.

"We must be going!" Li-Saide whispered.

"But the words, what do they say? *Sacred stones*—"

"Fane! Lower the body into the pool!" Fane cast him an odd look.

"Are you crazy, my friend?"

"Did you ever go *into* the pool?"

"Well, we dangled our legs in and washed ourselves, but—"

"But you never actually went freely below the waters?"

The scratching came again but this time with a demonic scream.

"No." Fane looked at the wall. "I never knew there was a door there."

Li-Saide was beside himself. "You discover one of the Mosfar's most wonderful, hidden secrets and you fail to use it. Opportunity is wasted on the young. Had you slipped beneath those waters we could have met years before!"

"Joy," Fane said sarcastically. He grabbed the leather straps and heaved the body into the pool with a splash. Air bubbled up from garments and then the corpse slowly sank out of sight.

"Hey'a, such tone is not becoming the Mosfar."

"Sorry," Fane added. Suddenly there came a loud battle clash from above them. Men's voices shouted, as did the screams of demons mixed with the colliding of steel and bone.

"The palace has been overrun," Li-Saide said solemnly. "Adriel is lost."

"How do you know?" Fane finally spoke up.

"Because any remaining fighting men, hoping to escape, have exited secretly through the back of the Palace Wall only to walk into the arms of the enemy waiting on the ocean's edge." The dwarf pointed through the solid rock ceiling to the grounds above.

"So that is the last of our men?" Fane surmised.

"Well, at least *those* men," the dwarf said.

Fane was not sure how to deal with the suffering he heard above. "We must help them."

"You help them by escaping from this place alive," Li-Saide said.

"But—"

"But nothing, were you to venture above, which I'd kill you before you did, you wouldn't stand a chance."

Fane looked down at the pool and accepted his inability to help the dying men above. Then he remembered the king's corpse and decided to change the subject.

"I do hope you know the king's body has been sinking for some time," Fane said.

"Aye, I know it's sinking! You think I am so shallow so as to not see the obvious when it reveals itself, unlike some who didn't even know what treasure they had at their disposal?" The dwarf was indignant as he waved his arms around the room.

"Hey'a, we were bright children, all right? But it doesn't mean we knew *everything*. Honestly, would you have known there was a door there at our age or that this pool was a, well, whatever it is?"

The dwarf inched close to the waters and regarded Fane intently. Another muted scream came from the other side of the door and more violence shook the air above.

"In a word?"

Fane took a step closer. "Aye, *one word.*"

"Absolutely." And with that, the indignant dwarf hopped into the water holding his hat and sank like a rock out of view.

There was another long scratch at the door. Fane was alone in the Sea Cave once again. The last time he was here seemed like an eternity ago. He looked over to the corner where he used to sit upside down with his legs against the wall and talk to his friends for countless hours. They had been waiting for Luik that last time, Hadrian, Anorra, and himself. It seemed like the beginning of this all, long before he knew anything besides his family, friends, his little home in Bensotha, and everything was at peace and good. He never imagined he would be standing here under such circumstances, not in a thousand lifetimes. He wished he could go back and let this all be but a distant memory. Something deep inside him was saddened beyond description. The rope in the craggy opening above was gone. Somehow he didn't think Luik would be coming down this time. Fane took a deep breath and dove headfirst into the pool unsure of where it would take him, but hoping beyond hope that it would wash away all his pain.

AFTERWORD

Chapter Thirty-two

HAUNTED

The heavy sound of horse hooves plodded through the twilight of Luik's groggy head. Their muffled rhythm seemed distant, covered by a thick blanket of darkness. Murmurings of conversations weaved into his dismal world, though he did not have the strength to give them his full attention; that was reserved for something more demanding. A crippling pain gripped his entire body, arms and legs paralyzed in anguish. His chest felt as if a giant rock lay bearing its full weight on his ribcage. He struggled to take a breath but could only exhale repeatedly until his lungs were empty and dry. He panicked, and his broken body convulsed into a mild seizure. When his eyes finally rolled forward beneath closed eyelids they met with a brilliant white glare, the pain searing into his skull and burning his head. His mouth gaped wide, and his lungs desperately drew in breath. What came out was a miserable groan that would have brought any hearer to the conclusion that this man was far from being whole.

"He wakes!" said a tall man walking along the right side of the horse-pulled stretcher. The horse was quickly pulled to the side of the path and halted. Two other men joined the first as they knelt by Luik's side. The men pulled back the layers of furs and blankets to examine their patient. The freezing cold air bit hard at Luik's face. His eyes flew wide open with shock.

"Easy there," came a voice from above. "Try not to move."

"Rest easy," said a deeper voice. Luik struggled in his cot but his limbs would not comply; whether bound or immobile, he did not know. His eyes raced across the bright light about him yet managed only to gather shapes and shadows that left him without any answers as to where he was. The pain in his body flooded his emotions with a wave of agony and summoned up another wallowing cry for relief.

"Whoa, there," a voice pleaded. Luik sensed pressure on his forehead. It was someone's hand, cool and the first sensation of pleasure yet. "He is very warm," said the voice again. But Luik could not make out any of the words that followed after. He squinted intensely, now in desperate need to know where he was and who was around him. But still a bright white consumed his vision. Horse hooves passed close by. More murmurings permeated the fragile atmosphere within his head. Then everything began to swirl in his mind. Luik suddenly felt as if he was spinning out of control and struggled to grab anything within reach. But still his arms would not respond. He let out another scream, this time more forceful and definite.

"We must get him there quickly," said the deep voice.

"Aye, death makes for him with haste," said the third.

"Peace, be still," said the first voice, "in the Name of the Most High." Slowly Luik's head stopped spinning and he came to his right mind. He blinked and looked up into the three faces above him. Two of them he did not recognize, but the large ruddy face of Brax was unmistakable.

"Brrah," Luik tried to muster the strength to speak but fell short.

"Don't speak, my friend," Brax said lowly. "It is too much for you. Save your strength for we have far to go." Luik looked into the weary eyes of his fellow Dibor and noticed his bloodstained cheeks and damaged skin.

Then something fell into Luik's eye, cold and irritating. Within moments it had dissipated, and a tear flushed it away. A second and third entity lighted in the other eye and more on his cheeks and forehead. They were cold and pleasantly refreshing. He noticed the shimmering flakes fluttering down from an overcast sky above. Luik strained to look to the sides of his cot. White was everywhere. The rock wall to his right was covered in white, and the convoy of men and horses that passed by his left were adorned with the flakes like piles of dirt, only white and soft.

The men themselves were wearing the strangest of clothes, animal skins around their shoulders, others draped in blankets and wrapped in cloaks.

"Hhs coe," Luik attempted to speak through cracked lips.

"Aye, it's mighty cold, Luik," Brax said, "and bound to get colder still. Hold on my friend, you're almost home." Luik struggled to put it all together, his head still dim and pointless.

"Whrsee goin?" Luik said with a little more effort.

"Where are we going?" Brax repeated the question. "Why, the only place left to go. Mount Dakka, of course, in Tontha." Luik didn't understand. They were so far north. *Why?* Luik mustered the last of his strength, feeling his stamina waning thin.

"Ahtreel?" he said with a slur.

"Adriel?" Brax asked back, looking down at his friend. Brax's eyes filled with tears, and he choked on his words. "She has fallen," his voice cracked, "and so have the Kings of Dionia."

Luik didn't know how to respond and closed his eyes. His emotions burst with such force that neither his heart nor his head could contain them. The jolt caused him to wince in anguish, and he let out a soft whimper from the deepest part of his soul. *It can't be*, he thought, *not Adriel. How did we lose her?* But his mind was not long for the task of sorting it all out. He wanted to ask about the Dibor, but fatigue slowly crept over him and before long he had no choice but to retreat into a heavy slumber. Brax replaced the furs and blankets over his friend, tucking a certain blanket against his face, its corner embroidered with the initials *R.M.C.* Then Brax stood, bidding the horse to move on and rejoin the convoy.

Great lettings of snow had all but consumed the northern lands. The weather had grown most inhospitable, and creation was doing everything within her power to help maintain the fledgling remnant of life that still survived within her care. Adriel had been crushed by the legions of Morgui; her mighty walls had eventually succumbed to the sheer numbers of intruders. It was everything the defenders could do to escape alive, most fleeing north along the coast at night. Some swam to their deaths while others fought their way up the beaches. Eventually the retreating army amassed along Bensotha's northern coast and summoned the remaining horses to their aid. The wounded were bound to the horses or tied to stretchers and dragged through the mire. Those who could walk were encouraged to, and the dead were left where they lay. The casualties were too numerous to count and too disheartening to want to. Most friends, brothers, sons, and fathers had been split up in battle or in the retreat. Even when most of the men amassed along the coast, no one was sure if they were all that remained or if others moved north behind them, or before them.

When the bulk of the convoy reached Narin, hoping for respite and reunion with their wives and kin, all they found was a deserted city. Though not yet touched by the surely-advancing war host of Dairne-Reih on their heels, Narin lay still like a lifeless widow, devoid of breath. Her looming network of seaside dwellings lay motionless, and her Great Hall was barren and empty. Boats were left to their moorings, and tools were tossed in the grass. It was if the entire city, intended to be the refuge for the women and children, had simply vanished. The men convinced themselves that their wives and children had gone further north into Tontha and hoped Mt. Dakka would bid them a friendly welcome and much relief.

The capital of Tontha, the great city of Mt. Dakka, was the men's only option. A trek through Grandath would be far too long, and they assumed that Morgui would beat them to any of the easterly cities; the small number of fighting men was simply too low to even think about splitting up and holding any of the remaining cities. If their families had indeed fled to Mt. Dakka, why journey elsewhere? The mountains would give them safe refuge until a plan could be devised, and until they knew who was still living.

The defeat at Adriel was a crippling blow for Dionia and it was all the men could do to keep their spirits light. A great sense of depression, new to all of them, picked away at their hearts, gouging a common wound that made their journey northward a silent, bitter one. The men didn't speak to each other unless concerning direction or pace. Each man wrestled inwardly with the terror they had just witnessed. The tormenting memories of their brothers perishing plagued every step they took. The insecurity that blossomed from not knowing where or how many of their kinsmen remained alive left all the men feeling lost and directionless.

As Luik was dragged along the mountain path that followed the Hefkiln River, he dreamed deeply, unconscious of the cold, or of the war-torn army that escorted him. Though his body was in a perilous condition, his spirit was strong and lingered in what remaining presence of the Most High there was in Dionia. He walked back to his father's field and his mother preparing dinner in the little house. The groves of trees speckled the landscape and his favorite stream meandering to the west. His newborn baby brother lay sleeping in a cradle. His father tilled the field with a hand tool, and Luik longed to go and help him, to embrace him. The image faded and soon there was a rokla match where Luik leapt and ran with the other children, scoring one gita after the next. It was as easy as breathing for him. He saw Hadrian and Fane there, both waving their arms for a pass.

Anorra was also there, her face soft and young. She ran alongside him to one end of the field. But Luik kept running with her long after the field faded away, until suddenly they were alone together. She appeared much older than before, stronger and more beautiful than ever. They slowed and then stood overlooking the sea as the sun knelt low. His heart felt a deep ache as she reached a hand up and touched his face. Her palm was warm and inviting. *Is this real?* he thought. He looked into her blue eyes and wished to kiss her. The longing he felt in his heart was unbearable. *I have to be with her.*

But Anorra vanished, and Luik was in a great forest surrounded by trees on every side. They reached high and covered the sky, letting through only a dim light from above.

"Luik," said a voice behind him, "are you coming? They're waiting for you." Luik spun around and saw Fane standing in the midst of a tree whose trunk was split wide like a doorway.

"Fane?" Luik asked in surprise. He smiled at his freckle-faced friend, now older. Luik made to walk toward him but his feet would not move, and Fane was walking back through the tree. "Fane! Wait for me!" Luik cried, struggling to get his legs moving. "Who's waiting for me? Where are you going?"

The image faded to black and soon Luik was utterly alone. The stillness wrapped around him like a blanket. He felt a breeze on the back of his neck, then it was gone. A moment later it was back, this time more forceful and warm, then it was gone. Again the breeze blew onto his back, but hot and strong this time. Once more it dissipated. He could not see anything. The blast of air came again, nearly knocking him over and hot against his skin. Then, as before, it withdrew. Luik was puzzled, but was suddenly aware of a majestic presence in his company. As if thunder permeating the air all around him, a low and steady growl issued from a deep voice and shook the atmosphere. He knew that sound; it was the lion from his dreams.

THE
WHITE LION
CHRONICLES

THE STORY CONTINUES

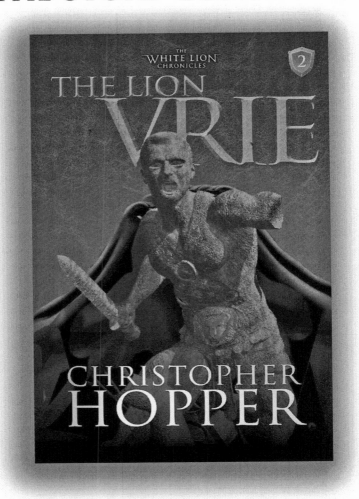

FROM THE AUTHOR

I don't think I ever read a single book in elementary school. My teachers never knew that, of course. Unless they liked giving me "A's" for bluffing, which at my private Christian school in upstate New York, I'm sure they wouldn't have. No, the passing grades came because I was creative. And made up for my slow reading ability with in-class perceptiveness. Book reports were all about me reading the back matter of the covers, and gathering enough conceptual understanding of the story in-class to fashion a fancy cardboard robot, write and record an epic song, or build a themed board game, all proving I was enthusiastic about the stories but nonetheless hadn't read the books. And it would be one of the only secrets I would ever be able to keep from my parents, too.

The truth was, I didn't *not* like reading, I simply couldn't figure out how all my other classmates could read as fast as they did. And sit still long enough to do so. The trees called my name, summoning me to build forts, as did the four-wheeler and snowmobile to roam the hills above our house.

By the time I hit 5th grade, I knew three things about myself: I was bad at math, I was bad at spelling, and I was a slow reader. But in time, that would all change, either exemplifying psychologists' examples of "late bloomers," or becoming a walking example of God using foolish things to confound the wise. Probably a little of both.

I first discovered that I liked to write stories in Mrs. Sandquist's 8th grade English class. It was also her sincere encouragement, upon completion of an alternate-history short story about the Alamo (where Davy Crockett won), that made a lasting impression on me. "This is amazing, Christopher."

While I couldn't read or digest stories through reading, I could actually create them through writing. This singular discovery has stayed with me to this day.

I attempted to read some of the more interesting stories my high school teachers pitched us, but found most of them too obscure or annoyingly progressive to merit the long hours I knew they'd take me. More creatively deceptive book reports would keep me in the top 10% of my class. *Lord of the Flies*, *1984*, and *Brave New World* are the only three I remember actually reading. And liking. Though still peculiar and dark.

Another of my teachers, Ms. Grace, English 101, took note of my creative writing abilities and made extra time to encourage the merits of my stories. Of course she also went to town on grammar and diagramming, elements that I'm only just now starting to grasp with any certainty. But her stern demeanor during class made her support of my work all the more meaningful when it came. And she would be one of the first people that I hand-delivered *Rise of the Dibor* to when the first edition came out.

Today I can say I have a true love for reading. It still takes me longer than most to finish a book. But I might add that my appreciation of actually finishing one is far greater than my friends who are legitimate speed-readers with high retention rates. It wasn't until the summer I graduated high school, when my best friend, Jordan, handed me Stephen R. Lawhead's *Song of Albion Trilogy,* that I discovered the magnificent world of books. "Just read the first chapter," he said. "I promise, you'll like it."

He pleaded with me so much I eventually gave in and read the first chapter. Then I read the second chapter. And the third. And the fourth. Whenever I wasn't selling mobile phones or teaching sailing, I had my nose in those books. And by the end of July, I had read an entire trilogy. I considered it my greatest academic achievement to date. And I wasn't even in school.

Somewhere in the process of following Mr. Lawhead into an alternate universe, I had a thought that sneaked up on me: *If I ever write a novel, I want to write one like this*. I can only say it was the impetus of God and His creative gift in me that would ever inspire such a thought. Today I have done more reading, re-reading, editing, studying, plotting, writing, and reviewing than any English teacher could have ever rightfully assigned. To the tune of *millions* of words.

Why the back-story? Because I'm an author, of course. But more importantly, what is the value of anything without context? The book you hold in your hands, or on your e-reader, as the case may now be, is a defiance of all the odds. Not only did my storycraft come hard fought, but the story itself was almost never written.

In 1996 my mother told us she'd had a remarkable dream: one in which she was placed on another planet in a different universe and left to wander. Knowing my outspoken mother, you'd understand why her first thought upon entering the simple home of one of the planet's inhabitants was to ask them if they knew Jesus. (She's where I get my outgoing genes).

The candid reply of these beautiful people surprised her. "Of course we know the Son," they said. "Everyone does." But while they knew him as Creator and part of the Triune nature of God, they didn't know him as Savior. And as such they did not share her common knowledge of the Gospel. Because their Adam and Eve had never sinned.

This singular premise consumed me as I dwelt on what such a world would look like and what the people and their culture must be like. Each thought haunted my notebooks and sketchpads well into the following summer when I graduated...and became the fuel that my "Lawhead match" caught on fire.

And that's when I decided to start writing. I had no idea what I was getting into, of course. Does anyone, attempting something beyond them? Ignorance is more often the blessing that keeps logic from messing with God-dreams.

Between one bogus floppy disc and two rogue hard drive failures, I wrote and re-wrote numerous chapters of my story three different times. Each time I sat down to begin again, discouragement from the previous data losses plagued me. Maybe it was a sign from the Lord? Maybe I was wasting my time to think I could write a book?

During one gap where I actually printed out three of the chapters (papers that would later become destroyed by a small flood in my bedroom), I presented them to retired professor and novelist David Bellin. Like Mrs. Sandquist and Ms. Grace before him, his encouragement of my gift sent me back to the computer. I can honestly say that there are few more influential positions in life than those of teachers.

But with the eventual loss of the manuscript for the third time, I put the entire thought of ever writing a novel on hold. Indefinitely. What a mistake that would have been. Discouragement should never endorse the opportunity to dismiss dreams of the heart, but perhaps cause us to reassess some intangibles, one of which is timing. The fact is I simply didn't know enough in the late 1990's, both spiritually and as a writer, to create the book God wanted me to. Of the original manuscript, Chapter 28, *The Dream*, is the only surviving composition (and the first chapter I ever penned).

It wouldn't be until 2004 – nearly seven years after I started writing – that I would feel the call to return to the manuscript that I simply termed *The White Lion*. It was the first year of my marriage with my bride, Jennifer, and I had just left a position with a national youth conference. Aside from traveling on the weekends to perform and speak, I had an unusual amount of free time during the weekdays. And that's when I felt a strong, urgent prompting in my spirit: *Write. And finish it.*

I threw out (literally, out of our second story window) my last disease-infested Windows PC, and happily bought my first iMac at my wife's prompting. (She didn't have to give me much encouragement; *permission* would be a better word). And then I set in, waking up at 6am every day and working until lunch. Those were happy creative days for me. The story was flowing, and half the time I couldn't even remember what I'd just written. The sense that the Holy Spirit was composing through me was palpable at times. Any poor form in story or grammar I own completely; I simply mean to say that inspiration was imparted rather than summoned. Jennifer was a constant encouragement to me, as she's remained every day since through all of my projects. And four months later, I held a completed 135,000-word manuscript in my hands.

I'd done it. If for no one else, I had proved to myself that I could indeed write a novel. Whether it was any good or not remained to be seen. But by the end of the 2004 summer, I had written my first book.

Just as sure as I'd heard *Write. And finish it,* I'd also felt that completing this manuscript wasn't just for me. That may have been more of my parents' strong missionary influence in my life, but either way I shared their *it's never just for or about you* mentality. So I was certain that I would get this story into at least a few people's hands, hopefully to encourage and inspire them just as Mr. Lawhead had done for me.

I'm fond of saying that I'm firmly convinced there are better writers out there than me, each with better stories than mine, but with one difference: I *wrote* my manuscript. God cannot promote what you have not initiated. This is one of the fundamental principles of the creative process that I've learned over the years. I often think God keeps giving me open doors with my endeavors – though they may be inferior in many ways – simply because I have the audacity to keep making art that genuinely seeks to glorify Him.

That fall I started spending time on a forum for publishing executives in the hopes of learning more about self-publishing my new book. After scouring the archives for weeks, I introduced myself as a "lurker" and hoped to build some insightful and hopefully meaningful publishing relationships. Within hours my inbox hosted an extraordinary email from the CEO of a mid-sized press in California, wanting to know more about the manuscript I'd written. Not one to let opportunity pass by, I called the publisher right away.

CEO of Tsaba House Inc., Pam Schwagerl would grow to be a good friend, if for no other reason than she took a chance on my book. And on me. After consulting my wife's aunt and uncle — both higher-ups in the greater publishing world – I sent Pam my manuscript and hoped for the best. Within seven days I got a call back. It was Pam. "I read it all, and I love your story. I want to publish your book, and the next two that you write."

Was this really happening? Did I just land a three-book deal on my first attempt? It was supposed to be harder than this, right?

But it wasn't over yet.

It seems to me that the closer we get to real breakthrough, the harder the enemy fights. Soon verbal agreement and the promised forthcoming contract distanced themselves by days, then weeks. Then a month passed, and no contact from the publisher. All at once the discouragements of my past crept in, and brought the tormenting spirits of suggestion with them. *You're really not that good of a writer. Someone else advised them to pass on your story. Plus, you don't have time to write more; you'll be stealing time from your wife and future children in a vain pursuit that won't affect anyone. Who would read you? And are you sure you can write two more books of this length? Where are you going to get more ideas? You're still a terrible speller. How many books have you actually read through completely? And you think you can be a professional author?*

By the fifth week I had become so tormented I was in depression. Not only had I failed to get my book published, I'd just wasted four months of my time, *and* quite possibly eight years of dreaming about a pointless idea.

On Thursday of that fateful week I'd given up on the idea of ever being published, and on ever writing again. I wanted to hit the delete key on my files, and do what had been done so many times before: erase my manuscript. I was to the point that I thought I'd actually missed God. That I was following some crazed fantasy of becoming a novelist. So I gave myself an ultimatum: if the publisher didn't contact me by Friday night, I'd delete my manuscript and forget about the whole thing.

Looking back now, I'm a little embarrassed at how easily put off I was. But remembering those moments still provokes a tremendous sense of frustration and fear, proving that things are always spiritual before they're natural. I was under attack. And God knew my finger was floating over that delete key on Friday when Pam called our home. "I'm so unbelievably sorry, Christopher. We haven't forgotten about you, but all of our staff have been working non-stop with multiple releases this month. I've overnighted your contract to you."

It arrived Monday morning via FedEx.

The first edition of *Rise of the Dibor* was published June of 2006, and quickly became the number one seller in Tsaba House's history. A month later I attended the gargantuan CRS (now ICRS – International Christian Retail Show) convention, hosted that year in Denver, Colorado, where another fateful meeting would transpire: my divine appointment with Wayne Thomas Batson.

Tsaba House would go on to publish *The Lion Vrie* the following year. But my late delivery of *Athera's Dawn,* combined with the economic crash of 2008's fourth quarter, meant that the publisher would never have the chance to bring thousands of fans the finish of our epic adventure together.

I can never repay Pam and her staff, including the patience of Jodie Nazaroff, for their incredible kindness to me. I can honestly say I would not be writing books for you to read today had she not been faithful to the Lord's call on her life to publish God-glorifying stories. I will always remember her as the woman who took a leap of faith to make me a success.

Since 2006 the publishing industry has changed immensely. A year ago the term "self-publishing" was another way of saying, "You're really not good enough to land a deal with a major publisher." As of my writing this, it's the only avenue of publishing I plan to pursue. I have fulfilled my formal contracts with traditional publishers and hope to bring you stories myself from here on out, and with other likeminded authors. I can reach more people more easily, produce less expensive products for you to purchase, retain 100% creative control over my work, and all this while keeping the majority of the sales to support my family and allow me to continue writing great stories for those who wish to keep reading.

With the release of these second editions, I intend to preserve the original style of the first editions of *Rise of the Dibor* and *The Lion Vrie,* while cleaning up a lot of what the first printings left in. Although I have improved in my storycraft since first penning these works, I had no desire to re-write them. My father taught me long ago in the recording studio that publishing anything artistic should be an act of faithfully documenting where you were in life at the time, not where you hoped to be. I find great rest in that. As such, I've kept the story as original as possible. Sue Kenney has done a masterful job cleaning up the original manuscript and asking all the right questions to provoke needed changes; any errors are solely my own, left in by choice or mistake. A big thanks also goes to all my friends and Proofies who've lent their watchful eyes to the process: Nathan Reimer, Lou Rathbun, Brian Fetzner, Leah Stockholm, Sarah Pennington, Glade, Noah Arsenault, Heather Ciferri, Emma McPhee, Laura Friemel, Daniela Arreola, Dannal Newman, and Ryan Paige Howard.

Rise of the Dibor will always serve me as a reminder that we never know what plans God has in store for us. I could never have conceived that I'd go on to run a school for five years, named after the book, dedicated to discipling young people after the ways of Jesus for ten months at a time. Even as I write this I'm preparing to land in Portland, Oregon, to perform the marriage of two of my staff, both graduates of Dibor in previous years, and both brought to the school where their lives were changed, in large part, because some slow-reading, bad-spelling teen decided to write a story about his mom's dream.

Biea Varos,

Christopher Hopper
Thursday, June 23rd 2011
35,000-feet, ORD to PDX

ABOUT THE AUTHOR

Christopher Hopper is a true modern-day renaissance man. A published author and co-author of numerous novels, he is also a recording artist, pastor, visual designer, and restaurateur. His prolific writings in both book and blog form have captured the imaginations of loyal readers around the world. He is a founding member of Spearhead Books, and lives with his wife, Jennifer, and their four children in the 1,000 Islands Region of northern New York.

CONNECT ONLINE

Christopher always enjoys hearing from his readers. You may contact him via e-mail at: ch@christopherhopper.com

Visit his website at: www.christopherhopper.com

On Facebook at: facebook.com/christopherhopper

And follow him on Twitter for daily musings: @find_ch

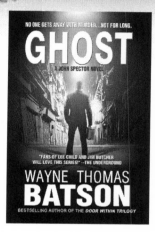

Made in the USA
Charleston, SC
27 November 2011